The rela... sometimes too close for comfort.

STAND BY ME

Three bestselling authors write about
what happens when bodyguards cross the line.

DALLAS SCHULZE

has written more than forty romance novels, both contemporary and historical. *Romantic Times* named her Storyteller of the Year, and her titles appear regularly on the *USA Today* bestseller list. She describes herself as a sucker for a happy ending and hopes that her readers have as much fun with her books as she does. Dallas and her husband live in Southern California.

ROBERTA LEIGH

is a workaholic, but loves every minute of it. How else could she have produced 150 romance novels, been a columnist on a national newspaper, written twenty-seven children's books and created and produced 247 films for children? But romance fiction has a special place in her life, and she was one of the first writers to introduce strong, career-minded heroines who wouldn't be bossed around by the hero. She lives in London, England, loves children, dogs and cats and, since the death of her husband, finds her romance in the books she loves writing.

LINDA RANDALL WISDOM

was a hard-working woman even before she sold her first two books and started writing full-time. She managed a personnel agency, and also held positions in advertising, marketing, public relations and medical manufacturing. Her last boss fired her because of all the attention she received from her book sales! She and her husband, Bob, live with a menagerie of animals, including five parrots, two dogs and a tortoise. When she's writing, Linda says she enjoys letting her imagination carry her along—it knows better than she what will happen to her characters. Her hobbies include fabric painting, jewelry making and finding T-shirts that have what she calls "personality."

Dallas
SCHULZE
Roberta
LEIGH
Linda Randall
WISDOM

STAND
BY ME

HARLEQUIN®

TORONTO • NEW YORK • LONDON
AMSTERDAM • PARIS • SYDNEY • HAMBURG
STOCKHOLM • ATHENS • TOKYO • MILAN • MADRID
PRAGUE • WARSAW • BUDAPEST • AUCKLAND

HARLEQUIN BOOKS

by Request—STAND BY ME

Copyright © 1998 by Harlequin Books S.A.

ISBN 0-373-20151-6

The publisher acknowledges the copyright holders of the individual works as follows:

STRONG ARMS OF THE LAW
Copyright © 1993 by Dallas Schulze

NOT WITHOUT LOVE
Copyright © 1989 by Roberta Leigh

SOMETIMES A LADY
Copyright © 1992 by Linda Randall Wisdom

This edition published by arrangement with Harlequin Books S.A.

CONTENTS

She was a voluntary hostage
to a stranger who was armed...
and dangerously sexy.

Lavery offered no words of sympathy. They had known each other long enough for the words to be unnecessary. He returned his attention to the file. The edge of a photo showed beneath the official reports and he pulled the picture out to lay it on top of the paperwork.

"An attractive woman," he commented, studying the photo.

Drew said nothing, and Lavery leaned back in his chair, steepling his fingers beneath his chin as he studied the younger man. "You've done this kind of work before. What's the problem this time?"

"I don't need any more rest. I've been sitting behind a desk for the past three months. I need something to sink my teeth into."

"Like Lester Davis?" Lavery asked softly.

A muscle twitched in Drew's jaw, confirming the accuracy of his superior's guess. Lavery looked back down at the report, tapping one long finger on the photograph.

"Kate Sloane stuck her neck out in coming to us. We're asking her to stick it out a lot farther by testifying. I don't think she knows just how far out. We've been trying to get a solid case on Davis for almost five years. For the first time, we've got enough on him to take it to court. I'd think you'd want to be in on this."

Drew stirred restlessly. Of course he wanted to see Davis fall. He had more reason than most to want the man brought to his knees. But this assignment... He glanced at the photo and then looked away, unable to explain his reluctance, either to himself or to Lavery.

"All she needs is someone to keep an eye on her. You could give this job to any one of half a dozen cops."

"But I'm giving it to you."

A muscle twitched in Drew's jaw—the only sign that he heard the iron in Lavery's soft voice. Whether he wanted it or not, he had the assignment. He knew just how far he could push, and when it no longer made sense to keep pushing. Lifting one shoulder in a half shrug of acknowledgment, he leaned back in his chair.

"Tell me about her."

If Lavery was pleased by his acquiescence, he didn't show it by so much as a glance. He shrugged.

"Most of it is in the report. She's Davis's personal secretary. Has been for about three years. He apparently got careless and she found some things that made her suspicious. She went snooping and came up with a tidy fistful of information, which she brought to us. Enough to get us into court. Now all we have to do is keep her alive to testify."

He closed the folder and tossed it across the desk. Drew picked it up but didn't open it. He'd already committed most of it to memory while he was deciding that he didn't want the assignment.

"Great. I'm going to be baby-sitting Nancy Drew."

Lavery fixed him with a cool look. "Ms. Sloane took quite a chance in coming to us. You, of all people, know what Davis is."

Drew's fingers tightened over the file, bending the edge of it. Yes, he knew what Davis was. He was a crime boss, to use an old term. Known but unprovable. On the surface, he was a respected member of the Los Angeles business community, but most of his money came from the drugs he smuggled into the country. The DEA knew it, but they hadn't been able to prove it. And he didn't limit himself to drugs. Prostitution, money laundering, outright theft—there wasn't a profitable crime in the city that Lester Davis didn't have his fingers most profitably dipped in.

He wanted Davis taken down. What he didn't want was to be sidelined, out of the action, baby-sitting a witness—no matter how important that witness.

Lavery watched him in silence. They'd worked together a long time and he could read Drew's thoughts better than most, which wasn't saying much. Drew Hunter walked very much alone. He revealed little of what he was thinking or feeling. He was closed in, controlled, and one of the best cops Lavery had. He was also on the ragged edge of burnout, whether he realized it or not. Keeping an eye on Kate Sloane was important, and it was almost equally important to get Drew away from the center of action for a few weeks. Besides, there were other reasons he wanted Drew on this assignment.

"We've got a leak in the department, Hunter." He drew the words out slowly, tasting their bitterness before letting them sour the air. Drew's eyes met his and there was no surprise in their cool depths.

"There had to be, considering what happened to Martinez and me. Martinez hadn't even talked to his wife about what we were doing. The only people who knew about it were cops. When it went bad…" He let the words trail off, his voice simmering with quiet, deadly rage.

"Martinez was a good cop. So are you, Hunter. You can't afford to go head-hunting. I want you out of town for a while," he said bluntly. "And I need someone I can trust to keep an eye on the Sloane woman. No one but you and I and a contact officer are going to know where you are. I don't want you calling in unless it's an emergency."

"If I take her to a known safe house, it won't be that hard to find us," Drew commented, knowing Lavery must have thought of the obvious.

"True." Lavery opened a desk drawer, pulled out a set of keys and tossed them across the desk. Drew caught them automatically, raising one dark brow in question.

"There's a small town in northern California. A distant cousin of my wife's just died and left the house empty. The heirs are in no hurry to do anything with the place, and they were happy to have tenants. A married couple who would take care of the place for a few weeks while they sort things out."

"Married?" Drew's brows rose. "Did Ms. Sloane agree to that?"

"We haven't even told her that she's leaving town. So far, Davis doesn't know who our witness is. We want to keep it that way, so we've tried to minimize our contact with the woman. You'll explain the situation to her."

"Great," Drew said, his tone sour. "I introduce myself to the woman, explain that her life is now in danger because she's done her civic duty, tell her she's going to have to go into hiding if she wants to stay alive long enough to testify and, 'oh by the way, I'm now your husband.'"

"That's a succinct summation," Lavery agreed. An almost imperceptible lightening of his dark eyes revealed an uncharacteristic humor. "I think you're just the man for the job."

"Thanks," Drew said without gratitude. Clutching the folder, he stood, ignoring the pain in his left leg when he refused to favor it.

"Hunter?" Drew turned at the doorway, raising a brow in question. "Be careful."

"I always am." He stepped through the door into the hustle of the outer offices.

"DAMN." THE CURSE was soft, carrying more frustration than heat. Drew adjusted his leg to a more comfortable angle on the pillow, trying to find a position where the ache wasn't quite so sharp. The doctors had warned him to give his leg time to heal, that he had to have patience. He had endless patience when it came to his job, but that left little to spare for things like injuries that were frustratingly slow to heal.

It was late—well after midnight—and the apartment was quiet, with that special kind of stillness that goes with the very early morning hours. He savored the stillness in the same way that he savored the fresh ground coffee he was drinking. He was a man who liked being alone, who appreciated solitude and the freedom that went with it.

Which was one of the things he disliked about this assignment—living with someone was not conducive to solitude. Drew lifted the Sloane folder off the back of the sofa, but he didn't immediately open it. He ran his thumb over the name stamped on the beige surface. There was something else that bothered him, but he couldn't quite put a finger on what it was.

Reluctantly he opened the folder. Kate Sloane's photograph lay on top and his eyes met the picture's. She was a pretty woman. Delicate features that were saved from being chocolate-box pretty by a strong chin that spoke of stubbornness. It was a black-and-white photo, but he knew from the paperwork that her eyes were green. They were thickly lashed and almost too big for her small features. In the photo, her hair was pulled back and it was impossible to do more than guess at its length. The description said it was brown, so why was he so sure that sunlight would find red highlights in it?

She was a pretty woman, but no prettier than half a dozen other women he could name off the top of his head. Why, then, did he feel such a surge of hunger when he looked at her picture? What was it about her that brought out this gut-level response, that made his fingers tense with the urge to see if her hair was as soft as it looked in the photo?

There was something there, something he couldn't define. His thumb brushed over her mouth and he could almost feel the softness of her lips, the moist warmth of her breath. He bit off a curse and shut his eyes, willing his body to relax. He was acting like a sex-starved teenager, getting aroused just looking at a photograph of a woman. Only this wasn't some stapled-in-the-stomach model, and he was a long way from being a teenager.

The folder hit the coffee table with a splat, the sound loud in the quiet room. Drew reached for his coffee cup and forced his mind away from the disturbing photograph and the strange effect it had on him. Time enough to think about the assignment tomorrow when he had to meet the Sloane woman.

He leaned his head back on the couch, cradling the mug against his chest, letting its warmth seep through the fabric of his shirt. The sound of the rain made him feel cut off from the rest of the world. Alone. Lonely.

He frowned. Now where had that thought come from? Loneliness implied a need for company other than his own.

A glance at the blank surface of the manila folder and he muttered a curse before getting to his feet. Damn, he must be getting old. Thirty-six seemed a bit early for mid-life crisis, but something was sure as hell wrong with him. Maybe it was all the painkillers they'd pumped into him when he was in the hospital. He'd stopped taking them as soon as he was conscious enough to argue with the nurses, but maybe the effects were still lingering. There had to be some excuse for the odd mood that seemed to have taken hold of him lately. He was damned if he was going to attribute it to Kate Sloane's photograph.

Drew limped into the kitchen and rinsed his cup out before setting it to drain. He moved over to the window that sat in the middle of one wall. Habit kept him to the side of the glass. It had been a long time since he'd been comfortable standing directly in front of a window.

The street was quiet, but an occasional car passed by, tires swishing on the wet pavement. Watching them, he suddenly wanted to know where they were going and what the passengers' lives were like. Did they have homes and families to go to on this damp night?

Now where the hell had that come from? His dark brows hooked together. What did he care whether they had homes or families? Since when did he stare out a window and wonder anything at all about the people passing by?

Annoyed by the uncharacteristically whimsical turn of his thoughts, Drew spun away from the window. The move was too quick for his injured leg and pain lanced through his hip as his knee buckled. He grabbed for the edge of the table, spitting out a curse that would have made a sailor blush. That, too, was uncharacteristic. He rarely cussed, rarely lost his temper.

But then he seemed to be doing a great many things he usually didn't do, he thought. Starting with getting shot three months ago.

He was limping heavily as he made his way back into the living room. Maybe Lavery was right to send him off on this baby-sitting job. Maybe he did need a rest, time for his leg to finish healing, time for him to get himself back on balance.

He hesitated by the sofa for a moment and then reached down to pick up the folder. Carrying it into the bedroom, Drew set it on the nightstand while he got ready for bed. It caught his eye as he slid beneath the covers. His hand on the light switch, he hesitated.

Annoyed at the compulsion he felt, he flipped it open and stared at the photo inside. Even on paper there was so much life in those features. Perhaps that was what made her linger in his mind. Was she as vibrant in person as she was on paper, or had the camera simply caught her at an unusual angle?

He realized he was running one finger caressingly over the photograph and he jerked his hand away as if stung, snapping the folder shut. A second later he clicked off the light.

He lay back against the pillows, letting the cool comfort of the sheets draw the ache from his leg. He was tired. Bone tired. That's all it was. Tomorrow, when he met Kate Sloane, he'd see that she was a very ordinary young woman. These strange feelings would disappear and he'd wonder why he'd ever thought it was any more than a flattering camera angle that made her seem so appealing.

BUT THE WOMAN who slipped into his dreams owed nothing to the flattery of camera angles. She was warm and alive, and Drew found himself reaching out to her, wanting to warm himself against her. She turned to smile at him, holding out her hands, taking his fingers in hers. At her touch, peace flooded through him, filling a void inside that he hadn't even realized existed.

He stirred in his sleep, disturbed by the intensity of his emotions, but she smiled again, pulling him closer, wrapping him in gentle warmth, and he relaxed back against the bed, sliding deeper into sleep.

KATE SLOANE LEANED against the wall beside the window and looked out at the wet street below. A car went by, tires kicking up sprays of water. In the light of a street lamp, she could see that there were two people in it. And then it was gone, leaving her to wonder where they were going, who they were, whether they were a couple in love.

She sighed and let her forehead rest against the cold glass. She didn't often have trouble sleeping, but tonight she'd tossed and turned until the sheets were a tangled mess. It was after midnight when she finally gave up trying to force sleep and got out of bed. She'd sipped a cup of cocoa, read a boring magazine and still sleep eluded her.

Well, maybe that was to be expected. She'd quit her job last week and had no particular prospects of finding another. Money wasn't a problem, at least not for a few more months. But she found that not having to go to work left her with a lot of time for thinking. And it seemed that a lot of her thinking centered around wondering where her life was going.

She was twenty-five years old, and she had no job, no

family and no one in her life but a few friends. She wasn't wrapped up in her career, such as it was. She liked being an executive secretary, but she suspected that there were any number of other jobs she would have liked just as much.

Once she'd found out what Lester Davis was up to and had taken the information to the police, she'd had no choice but to quit. She couldn't work for a man who was involved in the kinds of things Davis was. She'd felt not the slightest pang of regret about leaving her job. There'd even been a twinge of relief, as if now she might be forced to make some changes in her life.

The problem was, she didn't know how to go about making those changes. She wasn't even sure what they should be. She just knew that, at twenty-five, she was alone and there didn't seem to be any reason to think that would change.

Kate sighed. In a city of eight million people, you'd think she could have managed to stumble across one man who made her pulse beat faster, a man who wanted a home and a family and someone to share them with. But if he existed, he was keeping himself well hidden.

A flicker of light in the street below drew her attention from her melancholy thoughts. There was a black car parked across the street, almost directly in front of her window, and there was someone sitting in it. She wouldn't have been able to see them if they hadn't lit a cigarette. Match light flickered over their features for a moment and then disappeared as it was extinguished. The car was dark and still again.

Not quite sure why, Kate shivered and drew back from the window. She hadn't turned on the bedroom light, so whoever it was couldn't have seen her. Just as she wouldn't have seen them if they hadn't lit that match. Suddenly uneasy, she lowered the blinds and turned away from the window.

Cupping her hands around her elbows, she told herself not to be an idiot. There was nothing sinister about someone smoking a cigarette in a parked car at two in the morning. Okay, so it was a little odd, but that didn't make it ominous. There was no reason for Lester Davis's small eyes to come to mind, no reason for her to think that that car had anything at all to do with her. If the police had thought she was in danger, they'd have provided her with some sort of protection.

But all the talk in the world wouldn't make it any easier to fall asleep. And when she did finally drift off, her sleep was filled with dreams in which she was running from something terrible but could never quite escape.

Chapter Two

"Feldercarp!" Kate muttered the word under her breath.

With two bags of groceries and a leaky umbrella already balanced precariously in her arms, she was trying to maneuver her key into the mailbox. At least the mailboxes were sheltered by the archway that led to the inner courtyard, so she didn't have to get any wetter than she already was.

She gave a pleased murmur as the key finally hit the narrow slot and turned. A moment's concentrated effort and she'd managed to clutch the handful of bills and circulars and pull them out of the box. After that, it was a simple matter to drop them in one of the bags. Not so simple was getting up the stairs with all her burdens.

"The logical thing to do would be to put everything down and make two trips," she muttered. Talking to herself was safe enough since only her eyes managed to top the grocery sacks.

"But logic has never been one of your strong suits." She hefted the bags a little higher and tightened her grip on the umbrella. There was only one flight of stairs. Surely she could make it that far, even if her arms did feel as if they were being stretched by the weight of the bags.

She started up the stairs, shivering as a chill damp breeze worked its way under her collar. Every winter she swore she was going to move to a new apartment, one where the stairs weren't exposed to the elements, leaving the tenants at the mercy of rain, wind and dark of night. Or was that mail carriers who faced those hazards?

Giving a mental shrug, Kate continued to trudge up the stairs. The rain, which had been hardly more than a light mist for the past hour, increased to a drizzle. Water immediately found its way under her collar. Shivering, she doubled her pace up the stairs. Whoever said it never rained in California had obviously never spent the winter months in L.A.

She gave a small sigh as her foot finally hit the smooth surface of the walkway that circled above the courtyard. Ducking beneath the overhang, she restrained the urge to stick her tongue out at the increasingly heavy rain.

There was another juggling act when she reached her apartment door and tried to fit the key in the lock. But then it slid into place, the lock clicked open and she was able to step out of the cold wet afternoon into the warmth of her living room.

Kate released her hold on the umbrella, letting it drop to the carpet as she carried the groceries into the kitchen. She set the sacks on the counter and then bent to pull off the short black boots she wore, sighing with pleasure as she wiggled her stocking-clad feet.

She hummed softly to herself as she began unloading the groceries, sorting them as she went. She'd bought a few things for the elderly woman who lived downstairs, but there was nothing that couldn't wait until the rain eased up, as the weather report claimed it was sure to do anytime.

Before she ventured out again, she wanted a cup of hot tea and a few minutes to rest her feet. Maybe she'd get the classifieds out and see if there were any job possibilities.

She slid open a drawer and pulled out a knife to cut the tops off the carrots. Then again, maybe she wouldn't do anything productive at all. There was a new science fiction novel lying on the coffee table. Maybe she'd curl up with a cup of tea and—

"Ms. Sloane."

Without her volition, the knife continued its motion through the crisp carrot tops, hitting the cutting board with a soft thunk that sounded loud in the sudden silence. Kate stared at the board, thinking that she must have imagined it. She couldn't have heard a man say her name. That would mean—

"Kate Sloane?"

—that there was someone in the apartment with her.

"Ms. Sloane?" The voice was starting to sound impatient, but all Kate registered was that it was there—that it meant there was a man in her apartment with her.

When she didn't turn, she heard him move closer. She felt him reach for her, half saw a shadow of movement to her left and behind her, then reacted with a primitive instinct to survive. Spinning around, she swung out with the knife, hardly conscious that she still held it.

"Holy—" He jerked back, sucking in his stomach as the blade skimmed uncomfortably close. Kate had a vague impression of dark hair and a neat gray suit, but those things registered only subliminally. Her only conscious thoughts were that he was much bigger than she was and that she had to get away from him.

She jabbed at him again with the knife, less interested in causing injury than she was in clearing a path to the door. This time, though, he was ready for her. His hand closed over her wrist, halting the thrust. When she didn't immediately drop the knife, his long fingers tightened with brutal strength and pain shot up her arm. Gasping, her fingers numb, the knife clattered to the floor.

"Wait."

Kate wasn't interested in waiting. A man didn't break into a woman's apartment just to have a cozy chat. For a split second, they stood frozen, the knife gleaming dully at their feet. She hadn't bothered to turn on the overhead light, and she could make out few details in the dim light. But she didn't need to know the color of his eyes to know that she had to get away from him.

He still held her wrist in that implacable grasp. He made a movement with his other hand, but she didn't wait to see what he intended to do. She swung at him with her free arm, knowing it was a foolish effort. He fended the blow off easily, but he didn't have time to block her kick. She was aiming for his groin, but he twisted in automatic male response to that threat, and her bare toes caught him solidly on the thigh.

The results were more than she'd hoped for. His hand dropped from her wrist, his breath hissing out on a pained groan. His left leg—the one she'd kicked—seemed to give way and he dropped to one knee. Kate didn't wait for more. Darting by him, she raced for the front door. If she could just get outside, out where people could see them. Surely he wouldn't dare follow her, wouldn't try to drag her back inside.

But he was too quick. She'd barely reached the living room when his hand closed around her upper arm, leaving bruises as he dragged her to a halt. She turned, hands raised, her fingers crooked like claws, but he was ready for her this time.

His foot caught her behind the knees, and Kate gasped as she felt herself falling. But the fall was broken sooner than she'd expected as she felt the softness of the sofa come up under her. Before she had a chance to draw a breath, he was following her down, pinning her to the sofa with his body.

Feeling the contrast between the cushions beneath her and the unyielding length of male flesh and bone above, Kate froze, her mind going blank as pure panic washed over her.

He was going to rape her, and there wasn't a thing she could do to prevent it. He had her pinned down so solidly that every breath she drew pressed her breasts more firmly against his chest, every move she made only seemed to twist her closer to him.

Mindless with fear, she tried to arch upward, desperate to throw him off. She might as well have been trying to move a mountain. She tried to bring her hands up, but he caught them easily, holding her wrists in one hand as he drew her arms over her head and pinned them to the arm of the sofa, leaving her completely helpless. She drew breath to scream, even though she knew that there was no one to hear her. But he anticipated that, too, and his hand clamped across her mouth, leaving the scream to reverberate only in her mind.

Kate twisted frantically, but there was no escaping the lean body above her, no easing of the hold on her wrists. A buzzing in her ears warned her that she was about to black out and she forced herself to go still. Struggling was getting her nowhere. If she fainted, she'd be completely helpless and he'd be free to do as he pleased with her.

If she'd hoped that her sudden quiescence might catch him off guard and cause him to loosen his hold, she was disappointed. There was no give, either in the fingers clamped around her wrists or in the hard, masculine frame that crushed her into the soft cushions.

She stared up at him, her eyes wide and frightened. Maybe she could reason with him. At least, maybe she could, if he ever took his hand from her mouth.

"I'm not going to hurt you." His voice was low and slightly husky, the kind of voice that would have been reassuring under other circumstances. But when she could feel every inch of him pressed against her, it was a little hard to be reassured.

"I'm going to move my hand. If you try to scream, I'll knock you out." There was no threat in the words, only a matter-of-fact statement. He wasn't trying to scare her, he was simply telling her what would happen. And Kate believed him. Perhaps he read as much in her eyes.

He lifted his hand slowly, pale eyes watching her. Kate might have tried to scream, despite his warning, if she'd thought that there was any possibility of being heard.

"Please." The word came out in a breathless rush. She couldn't have said just what she was asking for. For him to let her go, that he not hurt her, that he vanish in a puff of smoke. Any of the above would do.

"I'm not going to hurt you. I just want to talk."

"People who want to talk usually don't break into my apartment to do it!" *No, no. That wasn't what she'd meant to say.* She wanted to soothe him, not antagonize him. "But that's all right," she added quickly. "I don't mind. Just let me go and we can talk all you want."

She thought she saw his mouth quirk at one corner with something that might have been amusement, but the expression came and went so quickly it was impossible to be sure.

"I'm a police officer, Ms. Sloane."

Kate stared at him, torn between relief and doubt. If he really *was* a police officer, then she had nothing to fear. But anyone could say they were with the police. Wouldn't a real officer have knocked on the door and identified himself? Why would he have broken into her apartment?

"I do have identification," he said, reading her thoughts.

"Oh, that's all right, then." Her voice was too cheerful, too bright. She sounded downright perky. But she wanted him to think she believed him. She wanted him to let her go. "If you're a policeman, then there's no problem. You can let me go now," she added hopefully.

She'd been told that she had a lousy poker face and it was apparently true. One lifted brow expressed his distrust of her suddenly cooperative attitude. There was no slackening of the hold on her wrists, no easing in the pressure of his weight on her body. Kate gasped, trying to shrink deeper into the cushions as his free hand slid between their bodies, the back of his hand pressed against her breasts. There was nothing in the least sexual in the gesture, but she could have done very well without the intimacy.

He pulled his hand out from between them and flipped open the wallet he'd taken from his coat pocket. The badge glinted in the dim light, looking very official and reassuring. Of course, it could still be a trick, she thought, but he hadn't offered her any harm so far. Aside from a few bruises, that was, and she couldn't entirely blame him for those. Considering she'd tried to stab the man, he'd been relatively restrained. And the police *had* said they'd be in touch.

The shackling hold of his fingers on her wrists eased. A moment later, he lifted his weight from her, and Kate was able to scramble into a sitting position. She scooted as far away from him as the sofa allowed. What she really wanted to do was run out the door, but she didn't need him to tell her that he wasn't going to allow that to happen.

She reached for the wallet and he gave it to her without argument. He even stretched out one arm and turned on a lamp so that she could see it better.

Kate stared at the badge, wishing it could speak and tell her something about the man who carried it. "It looks very official," she admitted cautiously.

"It is official."

"Badges can be faked."

"Cynical, aren't you?" But there was more approval than resentment in his voice.

"You're Andrew Hunter?" she asked, looking at the ID.

"Drew Hunter."

Kate lifted her eyes to his face and felt her breath catch in her throat. The eyes that had seemed pale in the dim light proved to be a vivid ice blue, the pupils ringed in dark gray. Penetrating and beautiful. The rest of his features were even, his chin a determined thrust. Medium brown hair was cut short in a plain style. He was handsome in an all-American way, but it was those brilliant eyes that made his face memorable. She blinked and forced her gaze away from his face.

"How do I know you're really a cop?" Beautiful eyes or not, he'd still broken into her apartment and scared the wits out of her.

"Would you like me to tell you what you were wearing when you came to the station? Or tell you exactly what you know about Lester Davis? Where you went to school? How many jobs you've held since graduation? The name of your favorite restaurant?"

Kate was flipping through his wallet as he spoke, feeling not even a twinge of guilt for her nosiness. God knows, he'd intruded on her privacy more than a little. Turnabout was fair play. There wasn't much there. A couple of credit cards, a card that listed his blood type and that he was allergic to penicillin. Odd that it should seem necessary to carry that sort of information around with him. Unless he was expecting a medical emergency, one that might require a blood transfusion and antibiotics. She shivered and flipped to his driver's license.

The information it gave was succinct. Andrew Hunter. Age: thirty-six. Height: six feet, one inch. Hair: brown. Eyes: blue. That definitely did not do justice to his eyes. Blue did not even begin to describe them. She looked from the photograph to the man himself, studying his face and finding it no more revealing than the picture. Still, there was something there...

Making up her mind with characteristic abruptness, she tossed the wallet back to him. "Why didn't you just knock on the door?"

Drew slid his wallet back into his pocket and wondered why he didn't feel more relieved that she'd decided to accept him. Had he been hoping that her refusal to believe him would be the key to getting him out of this assignment?

"The building is being watched," he said, answering her question. "There was a chance they would recognize me. It wouldn't be in your best interest for them to know you had a cop as a guest."

"Uninvited guest," Kate pointed out crisply.

"Uninvited guest." Drew accepted the correction. "Invited or not, it wouldn't be wise for Davis to know you've spoken to the police about his activities."

"You think Mr. Davis is having me watched?"

"There's a car out front with two men in it. I don't think they're admiring the view."

"Is it a black four door with a dent in the front left fender?"

"It's gray and there's no dent." Drew looked at her, his eyes intent. "Have you noticed another car?"

"Sometimes. I thought I was being paranoid, seeing the same car everywhere." She shrugged. "I figured it was my imagination."

"No. I recognized one of the men in the car out front. He's worked for Davis for several years now. He's a small-time thug, not too bright, but very good at breaking arms and legs to order."

Kate shivered and drew her legs onto the sofa, wrapping her arms around her knees. Drew tried not to notice how small and vulnerable she looked. Nor did he want to see the fear that darkened her eyes to smoky green. Noticing things like that made it harder to think of her as a package he had to take care of until it could be safely delivered. They made her too human, too appealing. His job was to protect her. And he didn't have to be concerned with what she was feeling to do that.

"How would Mr. Davis find out that I'd talked to the police?"

"Lester Davis has connections everywhere, including the police department, unfortunately." The admission was bitter.

"So he knows what I saw, what I told the police?" Kate shivered again and her arms tightened around her knees as if she could hug the inner chill away.

"If he knew anything for certain, you'd be dead already." Kate recoiled as if the words had an actual, physical impact. Seeing the color drain from her cheeks, Drew regretted his bluntness. It had been too long since he'd dealt with the real world, a world where violence was shocking rather than just a part of life.

He felt a sudden, unwelcome urge to reach out and touch her, to reassure her, to tell her that everything was going to be all right.

Damn Lavery for giving him this assignment.

"Davis knows that there's been a leak, that we have new information," he continued. "You can't keep an investigation like this quiet. The fact that you quit your job is bound to make him look in your direction."

"But I couldn't continue to work for him," Kate protested, as if Drew had suggested she should have. "Not after I found out what he was doing."

Not with a face like that, Drew thought. Those eyes revealed every emotion, every thought. Davis would have known immediately that something was up. And she would have been dead hours later. Davis was nothing if not efficient.

"It still made you an obvious suspect," he said shrugging.

"So what are you doing here? I assume you're here to make sure I stay alive long enough to testify." Her eyes were steady on his, making it clear that she understood exactly what her value was to the police. And she was right. He was here to keep her alive so her testimony could nail Lester Davis. So why did he feel guilty that he was only here because she was valuable to the case?

"That's exactly why I'm here," he said, without trying to soften the agreement.

There was a brief pause while Kate digested what he'd told her so far. Drew felt a reluctant twinge of admiration. He had to give her credit for keeping a cool head. No tears, no protests that she should have been told about the danger inherent in agreeing to testify. Actually, if he remembered the report, she *had* been told and she'd agreed, anyway. *A cool lady,* he thought.

"So what happens now?" Kate asked, only the slight unsteadiness in her voice betraying any stress.

"Now we make sure you're safe." He wanted to approach the topic of moving her obliquely, selling her on it before he actually suggested it.

"You want to move me to a safe house?" she asked.

Drew's eyes jerked to her face in surprise. The last thing he'd expected was for her to anticipate all his careful arguments.

"Yes, we do," he admitted, half-resentful that she'd skipped a few of his planned steps.

"I've seen this plot on television," she said. "The police always move the witness to a safe house. And the witness usually ends up killed because there's always a bad cop who reveals the location of the house. Which always made me wonder why they call them *safe* houses," she finished thoughtfully.

"Life is a little different from television."

"But you already said that Mr. Davis has connections in the police department," she pointed out. "So what's to stop him from using those connections to find out where I am?"

She was quick, he had to give her that. It shouldn't have surprised him. She'd been quick to recognize what she'd stumbled on to in Davis's office and quick to act on it. And she'd been quick to react when she'd thought he meant her harm. Too quick for comfort, he admitted, remembering the gleam of the knife in her hand.

"The place we have in mind isn't an official safe house.

And only myself and Lieutenant Lavery would know where you were.''

Kate took a moment to digest that. Then, "What if I refuse to go?''

"Then we'll do our best to protect you here," Drew said grimly.

"You don't think I'd make it to the hearing, do you?''

"No.''

He didn't add anything to the blunt denial. This was not the time to be softening his words. He wanted—had to have—her agreement. And if he could only get it by scaring her, then so be it. It wasn't as if he were telling her anything but the truth.

"So you break into my apartment, scare the wits out of me, physically attack me—''

"You were the one who did the attacking.''

"—and then expect me to trust you enough to ride off into the sunset with you," she finished, ignoring his interruption. "How do I know you don't work for Mr. Davis? How do I know you're not a bad cop?''

"Because if I were, you'd already be dead.''

And he could do it, Kate thought, looking into those ice blue eyes. If he had to, he could kill. He was right about who had attacked whom, though he could hardly blame her for reacting the way she had. When a man broke into a woman's apartment, she couldn't be blamed for not stopping to ask if he was with the police.

She looked away from him, rubbing her fingers absently over one bruised wrist. On the other hand, he hadn't hurt her, at least not deliberately. And what he was saying made sense. Hadn't there been a part of her that had known from the beginning that her life was never going to be the same once she went to the police with what she knew?

"Is this legal? Taking me to an 'unofficial' safe house, I mean? With just the two of you knowing where I am?''

"There's nothing illegal about it," Drew said carefully.

"But it's not officially sanctioned?"

"If it were, there'd be a lot more people who'd know where you were. The idea behind doing it this way is that no one would know. Is there anyone who'd worry if you weren't around for a few weeks?"

Kate didn't answer immediately, not because she didn't know the answer, but because she was suddenly reluctant to tell him what she suspected he already knew. If she'd been investigated as thoroughly as he said, then he had to know that there was no one who'd worry about her, hardly anyone who'd even notice her absence.

"No. No one would worry," she said at last, resenting him for making her say it.

"Good. That makes things easier."

Kate wasn't sure she'd have phrased it quite that way. Lonelier maybe, but rarely easier. But from his point of view it did make things simpler. She didn't have to be a cop to know that the fewer explanations that had to be made, the less chance of Lester Davis finding out what was going on.

Kate stood, suddenly restless beneath that cool blue gaze. She was aware of Drew Hunter's eyes following her, but she ignored him, at least for the moment. Picking up a soft pillow, she hugged it to her chest, feeling cold inside.

It had taken her three years to turn this apartment into a home, the first real home she'd ever had. The first place she'd lived for more than a few months. And now this stranger had burst into her life and was telling her that she was going to have to leave it and go with him to God knows where for an unspecified length of time, that she was going to have to leave behind everything she'd worked so hard to create.

"I wish I'd never seen those damn files," she said quietly.

Drew said nothing. He didn't need to. They both knew she was agreeing to go with him. She really had no choice.

RELUCTANTLY DREW ALLOWED Kate to take the groceries she'd bought for Mrs. Burnet down to her. Not that she seemed to think there was any question about her going.

"She's expecting me," she said, when he questioned the wisdom of her leaving the apartment.

"I'd rather you stayed inside."

"I can hardly ask an eighty-five-year-old woman to come out in the rain and climb an exposed flight of stairs and then carry a sack of groceries back down to her apartment," she said, as if pointing out the obvious.

"I don't like you going out."

"You can watch me the whole way." She sounded as if she was offering a consolation prize, Drew thought, gritting his teeth.

"What if Davis's men see you?"

"They've seen me any number of times today." Kate finished pulling on her boots and straightened, forcing herself to shrug as if the idea that hired killers might be watching her every move didn't chill her to the core.

"I don't like it."

"Mrs. Burnet needs her groceries. Her son usually looks after her but he's out of town this week and I said I'd keep an eye on her. I'll only be a few minutes."

And that seemed to be that, he thought, knowing he'd lost the argument.

Since the whole idea was to keep his presence hidden he didn't come with her, but Kate was vividly aware of him watching her as she crossed the courtyard. The feeling was at once reassuring and disconcerting—certainly it was nice to know that she had protection, but she wasn't accustomed to having her every move watched, especially not when the watcher happened to be one of the most attractive men she'd ever seen.

Not that that was relevant, she told herself as she tapped on Mrs. Burnet's door. It didn't matter to her whether Drew

Hunter looked like Frankenstein's monster or Mel Gibson. The fact that he was much closer to the latter than the former was of no interest to her. None at all.

FROM HIS POSITION beside the window, Drew watched as Kate stepped into the apartment across the courtyard. He should have told her not to go out of sight, he thought. But then she couldn't really have thrust the sack of groceries into the spindly arms of the old woman who'd opened the door, and then dashed away. The idea was *not* to arouse suspicion.

When the door closed behind her, he turned and glanced restlessly around the apartment. He'd had plenty of time to study the layout while he'd been waiting for her to come home this afternoon. Time to fall asleep, too, he admitted, angry with himself for that lapse. He'd sat on the sofa to await her arrival, and the next thing he was aware of was the sound of her umbrella hitting the floor.

He still couldn't believe that he'd slept through her opening the door, or that he'd been thrown off balance enough that it had taken him several minutes to make his presence known. Things like that could get a man killed. Damned near *had* gotten him killed, he thought, remembering the gleam of light on the knife as it had slashed toward him. Wouldn't that have been a laugh, to survive all these years only to end up killed by a witness he was supposed to be protecting?

Kate came out of the old woman's apartment, saying something before she closed the door behind her. Her smile lingered for a moment, and Drew felt that same odd little jolt of recognition that he'd felt when he saw her photograph, as if he'd known her somewhere before.

She glanced up at the window, her smile fading, though he knew she couldn't possibly see him. Apparently just the thought of him was enough to ruin her mood. Not that he could blame her, Drew thought, wondering why it mattered. She'd done what was right; she had come to the police with what she'd learned, and as a reward her life was in danger. But at least she had a life, he thought bleakly. Martinez hadn't been given that option.

He stepped back from the window as Kate opened the door, watching her, trying not to notice how the damp, misty air had darkened her hair, making it curl around her face. The last thing he wanted was to notice how attractive this "assignment" was.

"I told her I'd be going on vacation for a few weeks, just driving around the country." Kate pushed the door shut behind her and reached up to run her fingers through her hair, shaking the water droplets from it.

"Good." Drew curled his fingers into his palms against the urge to feel the dampness of her hair for himself.

Kate's eyes met his for a moment, and he read uncertainty and a touch of fear. He restrained the urge to reassure her. She was better off—they were both better off—if she remained just a little bit frightened. Fear could make a person more careful.

"I guess I'll finish putting the groceries away," she said, breaking eye contact. Drew said nothing, letting her walk by him while he struggled with the absurd urge to put his arms around her and hold her until the fear went away.

It had to be lack of sleep, he told himself. He hadn't been sleeping well since the shooting. Nightmares woke him more nights than not. It must be catching up with him.

Marginally satisfied with that explanation, he turned and followed his reluctant hostess into the kitchen, stopping in the doorway when he saw her bending to pick up the knife he'd forced her to drop earlier. She straightened but didn't look at him. She set the knife on the counter and then brought the fingers of her left hand up to rub the bruises that were beginning to show on her right wrist. Bruises he'd put there, Drew thought, surprised that the realization disturbed him.

"Let me see."

Kate glanced up, her eyes startled as he eliminated the few feet between them and took her hand in his. She would have drawn back, but she was suddenly aware of a strange current that seemed to flow from where his hand held hers. Her gaze lifted to his face, but if he felt it, too, she couldn't read it in his expression.

Drew looped his fingers around her wrist, laying them over the faint blue bruises, bruises that would undoubtedly grow much darker by morning. Seeing the mark of his fingers on her pale skin, he felt a wave of self-anger that made no sense. She'd been trying to kill him, for God's sake. He could have hurt her a lot worse than he had and still considered himself justified.

"I'm sorry," he said gruffly.

"It's okay. I'd get pretty hostile if someone came at me with a knife." Kate managed a smile and told herself that she didn't really like the feel of his hand on hers. "I suspect you could have done a lot more damage than you did."

"Yes." Drew looked at her, his eyes as flat as his answer. She repressed a shiver and forced another smile. "I hope I didn't do too much damage when I kicked you. I noticed you were limping a minute ago."

"An old injury." Drew dropped her wrist and moved back a step, careful to balance his weight evenly on both legs, resenting that she'd noticed the slight limp.

"Well, it obviously didn't do it much good to have me kick you. I'm sorry."

"Forget it." The cool response and the fact that he didn't bother to look at her gave Kate a sudden urge to kick him again, harder this time. "It doesn't bother me."

"Good," she said brightly. "Then why don't you fix dinner while I start packing."

"Dinner?" Drew looked at her blankly, caught off balance by the sudden shift of topic.

"You know, the meal that most people eat in the evening. There's no sense in you sitting around like a bump on a log. The taxpayers are paying your salary. I'm a taxpayer and I don't see why I shouldn't get my money's worth out of you."

"I'm a cop, not a short-order cook."

"I'm sure you can manage," Kate said, giving him a cheerful smile that made him want to shake her. "If you need help finding anything, let me know."

"One suitcase," he ordered, turning as she walked out of the kitchen.

She didn't bother to respond, but at least he had the satisfaction of having had the last word.

Chapter Three

Kate rolled over and stared up at the darkened ceiling. She didn't need to look at the clock to know that she should have been asleep hours ago. Drew wanted to leave as soon as the sun came up.

Drew. Funny, how easily his name came to her, as if she'd known him a long time, as if they'd been introduced at a party, rather than having met over the flash of a knife.

Was he sleeping? Probably. This must be just part of the routine for him. Was there someone lying awake somewhere wondering if he was safe? A wife? Girlfriend? Somehow the image wouldn't come into focus. There was something about Drew Hunter that made her think of the Rudyard Kipling poem about the cat who walked alone.

She turned on her side and stared at the curtained window, wondering if the dark sedan was still out there. Her fingers plucked restlessly at the quilt that covered her. How was she supposed to sleep when her entire life had been turned upside down? Tomorrow she was to leave this apartment—her home—and go off with a man she didn't know to a place she didn't know, to wait for an unknown length of time before coming back to testify against the man she'd worked for. And after that, maybe a trial. And after that? Kate's mind shied away from thinking that far into the future. The near future was unnerving enough all on its own.

Was she a fool to trust Drew Hunter? What if it was all lies, all part of some plot to prevent her from testifying? But then, if that were the case, he could have killed her here and been done with it. She didn't doubt that Lester Davis was ruthless enough to do just that if he thought it necessary. She'd learned that much about the man during the three years she'd worked for him. Even if she—

Kate sat up abruptly, her train of thought scattered as she heard a sound from the living room. She sat there, her heart pounding, her ears straining for a repeat of the sound that had startled her. A low cry, perhaps a word too mumbled to understand. Drew? It didn't seem possible that he could sound so vulnerable.

But when the sound came again, she swung her feet out of bed and went to the door. Opening it just wide enough to slip through, she tiptoed into the living room. He'd fallen asleep with the light on, probably while reading, she thought, noting the book that lay on the floor next to the sofa.

The quilt she'd given him for cover was twisted around his hips, baring a somewhat daunting expanse of muscled chest dusted with jet black hair. One hand was flung over his head, the fingers trailing on the table at the end of the sofa. The other hand was twisted in the sheet beneath him, knotting the fabric as if clinging to a lifeline.

As she watched, he jerked in his sleep, the movement so abrupt that Kate jumped. His head twisted, his features going tight, as if he were in pain. He muttered under his breath and then cried out again. This time she thought she distinguished the word "no" but she couldn't be sure.

Obviously he was having a nightmare. She hovered uncertainly, curling her bare toes into the carpet as she debated whether or not to wake him. Certainly he wouldn't thank her for seeing him with his guard down. On the other hand, she couldn't just go off and leave him in such obvious distress. She edged toward him, coming to a stop beside the sofa.

She hesitated, not sure what to do next. Was there some special way to wake someone in the midst of a nightmare? Kate nibbled on her bottom lip, wishing she weren't so vividly aware of the way the lamplight gleamed on the muscles in his shoulders and the way his hair fell in a thick black wave onto his forehead.

He shifted and the quilt slid down another half an inch. She caught her breath, her eyes followed the line of silky black hair that arrowed down his flat stomach and disappeared beneath the edge of the quilt. Surely he wasn't naked. Was he? Ashamed of the unwelcome tug of curiosity, she bent and set her hand on his shoulder, shaking lightly.

"Drew?"

He moved with blurring speed. One moment, she was standing over him, looking into his flushed face. The next, she was flattened on his chest, her hands trapped under her, her breath stolen from her.

Frozen, she stared into the pale blue eyes only inches from hers, eyes that looked more than capable of murder. One of his hands was flattened across her back, holding her to him. The other was cupped around her chin, the grip anything but tender. Something told her that, if he chose, he could break her neck in less than a heartbeat.

She held her breath, not moving, though every instinct screamed for her to struggle. Something more powerful held her still. Drew stared up at her, the murderous rage in his eyes gradually fading as he recognized her, sorting her out from whatever nightmare images had followed him into wakefulness.

"Kate."

It was the first time he'd used her name and Kate felt it shiver over her in a featherlight stroke. The fingers cupped around her chin gentled, their touch becoming almost a caress.

"You were having a nightmare," she whispered. She was

vividly aware that her breasts were pressed intimately close to the hard planes of his chest.

"Yes." His voice was low and husky, roughened by sleep.

"I...was trying to wake you," she said after a moment. "Thanks."

His eyes searched her face, an intensity in them that made her tinglingly aware of the lateness of the hour, her own state of dishabille, and the fact that, as far as she could tell, he wore nothing but a slipping quilt for cover.

She should pull away. And so she would. Just as soon as she was sure that he was fully awake. The odd shivery feeling that was working its way up her spine was because the room was cool. It had nothing to do with the fact that her palms were flattened against the muscled width of his chest, allowing her to feel his every heartbeat. And she hardly noticed the way the dark stubble along his jaw made his eyes seem even bluer. Her knees only felt weak because he'd startled her.

And she certainly hadn't wondered, even for an instant, what it would be like if he were to pull her onto the sofa with him, wrapping the quilt around the two of them and—

"I couldn't remember whether or not you were supposed to wake someone who was having a nightmare," she said, bursting into speech and hoping he'd attribute her breathlessness to the awkwardness of her position.

With an effort, she looked away from his face and pressed upward against the hand still flattened along her spine. Was there an almost imperceptible hesitation before he released her, or was her imagination working overtime?

"I thought I remembered reading somewhere that if you woke a person having a nightmare, you could damage their psyche, but then it seemed to me that it couldn't be all that good for a psyche to just let you continue a bad dream."

She eased away from Drew as she spoke, first sliding to her knees on the carpet and then standing. Smoothing her hands over the sides of her nightgown, Kate tried to ignore the small voice that wished she were wearing black silk and lace rather than plain white cotton. It was a ridiculous thought, brought on by the lateness of the hour and lack of sleep, she told herself briskly.

Drew Hunter probably wouldn't notice her if she were wearing a mesh bikini, which suited her just fine.

DREW WONDERED WHY it had never occurred to him that white cotton could be so sensual. There was nothing in the least provocative about Kate's sleeping attire, unless you considered long sleeves and a knee-length ruffle sexy. He never had before, but there was something about it... Maybe it was the very innocence of the garment that made him want to strip it away and find out what lay beneath its prim facade.

Not that he didn't already have a pretty good idea of exactly what it concealed. Between the struggle earlier in the afternoon and having her crushed to his chest moments ago, there wasn't much about Kate Sloane's shape that he didn't know. But it wasn't the same as sliding his hands over bare skin, as molding the softness of her breast with his palm.

Drew shut his eyes and curled the fingers of one hand into a fist. What the hell was wrong with him? First, he'd spent time mooning over her photograph, and now he was lying here wanting her so much that he was grateful that the heavy quilt was still draped over his lap. Otherwise, his thoroughly unprofessional thoughts might have become more than a little apparent.

"Are you all right?"

Drew opened his eyes and looked up at Kate's anxious expression. Her hair was tousled from contact with the pillow and it fell around her face in shining, light brown waves. It had felt like the finest silk against his chest.

"I'm fine." He had to clear his throat to get the words out. Even then, his voice remained husky.

"Do you want to talk about it?"

"About what?"

"About your nightmare. I read somewhere that it helps to talk about it."

"I don't think that would help."

"How do you know? Talking about it might help you understand it."

"I understand it just fine," he said shortly.

"Are you sure?" She frowned down at him, unconvinced. "I read somewhere that a person sometimes thinks a dream is about one thing when it's really about something else entirely."

"I know exactly what this was about," Drew snapped. He swung his legs off the side of the couch, hardly noticing Kate's indrawn breath and then relieved exhalation when she saw the striped pajama bottoms.

He thrust his fingers through his hair, feeling a nagging ache behind his eyes. He wished he hadn't quit smoking. He wished he'd never heard of Lester Davis and never met Kate Sloane. He wished she'd take her virginal white gown and her concern and get out of his sight.

And more than anything, he wished he could reach out and put his hands on her hips and draw her closer. He wanted to pull her down onto the sofa with him and see if he could lose himself in her.

"I'm really very easy to talk to," she said, her voice full of soft concern.

Looking up at her, Drew noticed that the cool air had had a predictable effect and that the dusky peaks of her nipples were pressed against the thin white cotton of her gown. The sight had an equally predictable effect on his body and he bit back a groan as he dragged more of the quilt across his lap.

"Why don't you go back to bed?"

"Are you sure—"

"I'm sure." He softened the quick answer with a half smile. "I'm fine."

She continued to hover there, her eyes all smoky green with concern, so close he could smell the clean tang of the soap she'd used earlier.

"Go to bed, Kate. Please." Perhaps she heard something in his voice or read something in his eyes. Whatever it was, the message seemed to finally get through to her. She flushed lightly.

"Good night, then."

"Good night."

Drew watched her disappear into the bedroom and heard the soft snick of the latch clicking home. Elbows braced on knees, he dropped his head into the cradle of his hands.

This assignment was going to be the death of him, he thought, not sure he was kidding. Where Davis had failed, Kate Sloane just might succeed. And she wasn't going to have to lift a finger to do it. All she had to do was stand around and wait for him to make a fool of himself.

What was it about her that got under his skin? He was no green kid to fall to pieces over a pair of pretty eyes. There was just something about her...

Shaking his head, he lay back against the pillows and pulled the heavy warmth of the quilt up to his shoulders, his fingers unconsciously tracing the textured surface. It was handmade. The second foster home he'd been in, the woman had made quilts. He'd stayed with them more than a year, and when he left, she'd given him a quilt—blue-and-white stars—and she'd cried when he left.

That quilt had been one of the few stable things in his life. He'd slept under it in each succeeding foster home until he was finally old enough to leave the system. He wasn't quite sure what had happened to it after that. There'd been times while he was putting himself through college when he'd slept in his car and the quilt had served as a cover. But somewhere in the years between then and now, it had disappeared.

He hadn't thought of that quilt in years. Not until Kate had spread this one over the sofa. The moment he'd crawled under it, felt the weight of it settle around him, it had brought back a flood of memories.

She could have bought it, of course, but she hadn't. He knew, as surely as if he'd seen her working on it, that Kate had set each stitch herself. What had she been thinking of while she worked on it? Certainly not that it would one day be used to cover a slightly burned-out, more-than-a-little-battered cop.

Drew's mouth curved in a half smile, his eyes drifting shut. It was ridiculous, of course, but it seemed to him as if the weight of the hand-stitched cover was somehow more warming than any purchased blanket could have been.

"CAREFUL. IT'S A GUITAR, not an old board, you know." Kate frowned down at him from her perch on the block wall.

"Feels more like an anvil," Drew muttered. Nevertheless he handed the case up to her as gently as if it were a Stradivarius.

She set it on the wall next to her and reached down to take the first of two large tote bags from him. They joined the suitcase and an enormous purse on top of the wall.

Staring up at the array of items, including the witness he was supposed to be protecting, Drew tried to figure out how his strict orders for her to pack one suitcase had been bypassed. Certainly he'd protested when he'd seen everything she'd packed. He distinctly remembered telling her that one suitcase meant just that and nothing more.

"I'm not leaving my guitar behind," she said flatly.

He looked at the set of her jaw and nodded reluctantly. "Okay." He'd never been musically inclined himself, but he understood that people could become very attached to their chosen instruments. "The guitar I'll allow, but what about all the rest of this stuff."

"There's not that much," she protested.

"I've seen entire circus troupes move with less baggage," he said acidly, eyeing the pile of canvas totes at her feet.

"This is my purse," she said, lifting an object that was almost big enough to qualify as a duffel bag. "You're not going to tell me I can't take my purse, are you?"

"Okay. The purse can go." He drew the sentence out slowly, loath to give more ground.

"And you told me to pack one suitcase," she pointed out, looking mildly injured.

He nodded again, even more reluctantly. He hadn't realized they made Pullman suitcases as big as that, but it *was* a suitcase and he *had* said she could bring one suitcase.

"That doesn't explain those things." He gestured to the two brightly colored bags that remained.

"That's some of my quilting." She looked surprised that he should need it explained to him.

"You're not taking them." He'd make his stand here.

"Of course I am. They don't weigh all that much. Besides, we're not flying anywhere, so it isn't like there's a weight limit, is there?"

"The idea was to travel light," he snapped. "We're going into hiding. You don't normally take your every earthly possession into hiding with you."

"Why not?"

"Why not?" Drew jammed his fingers through his hair and tried to think of a way to explain why not.

"If I'm going to be stuck with you, God knows where, for God knows how long, I'm going to need something to do, aren't I?" She asked it in the tone of someone dealing with a slow-witted child. "My quilting will give me something to do."

He looked at the stubborn set of her mouth, but he also

saw the vulnerability in her eyes. He'd seen the way she'd looked at everything in the apartment, as if she might be leaving forever and wanted to be sure to remember it. And he couldn't guarantee that she *would* be back.

"All right, dammit! Bring the stupid things. Bring the whole damned apartment, if you want to. What's a little furniture when you're running from killers? Maybe we can hide behind the sofa when the shooting starts."

"Thank you." Wisely, she chose to ignore his sarcasm. She gave him a sweet smile and went to get her jacket.

Which was how he'd ended up shoving two totes, a suitcase, a guitar and a fifty-pound purse up onto the block wall behind Kate's apartment building. Not to mention getting Kate herself up there.

"I feel like a kid running away from home," Kate said as Drew heaved himself up onto the wall and straddled it.

"The Incredible Hulk couldn't manage to run with all this stuff," Drew muttered.

"Don't sound so cranky," she admonished him cheerfully.

"Cranky?" Drew stared at her, trying to remember the last time someone had called him cranky. Not since he was an infant, surely.

"Obviously you're not a morning person."

"Morning person?" He was starting to sound like a parrot, he thought irritably. "Not particularly."

"I should warn you that I am."

"Thanks. I'll keep that in mind."

"I'll try not to be too cheerful," she told him soothingly.

"I'd appreciate that."

Despite himself, Drew felt a smile tug at one corner of his mouth. Never in his life would he have imagined himself perched on top of a wall at six-thirty in the morning, having a conversation about whether or not he was a morning person with the witness he was supposed to be protecting. And he'd thought this job had just about run out of surprises.

THEY MADE IT ALMOST to Malibu before Kate gave in to the urge to look over her shoulder. She tried to make the gesture casual, as if she just wanted to see the Pacific Coast Highway from a new direction. But she discovered there really is no casual way to crane your head around to stare out the rear window of a car.

Of course, there was nothing to see. No ominous black sedan lurking just behind their rear bumper. No cars with personalized plates that read Goons or I Killer. Nothing but a perfectly normal assortment of cars. Any one of which could be carrying someone who wanted her silenced.

She caught Drew's sideways glance and shrugged self-consciously. "I suppose if someone is following us, they're not likely to put a sign on their front bumper."

"No. But there's no one following us." He accelerated around a delivery truck.

"How do you know?"

"It's my job." He could have left it at that. With most people he *would* have left it at that. But most people didn't have soft hazel eyes that tried to look unconcerned and failed.

"No one saw me enter your building last night. And no one saw us leave this morning. They don't even know you're gone." Which was a miracle considering the way they'd been loaded down like pack mules, he thought, but he didn't say it.

"I hope you're right." But she glanced over her shoulder again before facing forward.

On their left, the Pacific Ocean spread endlessly to the horizon. To the right, the Santa Monica Mountains pressed down, their quest for the sea blocked by the thin black ribbon of highway. The rains were gone, leaving the sky a pale blue and the mountainsides washed in bright spring green.

Drew was relieved to find that Kate didn't feel it necessary to fill every second with conversation. They'd been barely a block away from her apartment building when she pulled some scraps of fabric out of the tote at her feet and began sewing. Her fingers had been shaking so badly that it was a miracle she could even get the needle into the fabric.

He'd been shocked by the urge to reach out and close his fingers over hers, to still their trembling, to comfort her. Instead, he'd curled his fingers more tightly around the steering wheel and kept his gaze focused out the windshield. Offering comfort wasn't part of his job description. He was only concerned with keeping her safe, not with keeping her happy. He was surprised that it was necessary to remind himself of that.

Still, despite a few snags, like the amount of luggage she'd brought and his own tendency toward unwanted softness when it came to her, he was starting to think these next few weeks might not be completely unbearable. She knew how to maintain a silence and she didn't insist on changing the radio station every five minutes. That boded well for the remainder of the trip, anyway.

"THERE'S A GAS STATION up ahead. We'll stop there." Kate looked up from her sewing and glanced at her companion.

Two whole sentences. And only an hour and a half since he'd last spoken. If he wasn't careful, he'd become downright chatty. "Good. I could use a chance to stretch my legs." She folded her quilt block and slipped it back into the tote bag as Drew flipped on the turn signal and guided the car toward the exit.

He didn't speak again until he'd pulled up next to the gas pumps. "Don't go too far," he cautioned her as she reached for the door handle.

"I thought you said they hadn't followed us." Kate turned to look at him, feeling her stomach go tight at the warning.

"Nothing's guaranteed," he told her, his ice blue gaze unemotional. "Don't go far."

He got out of the car. Kate hesitated before following him. *Nothing's guaranteed.* The flat words—neither promise nor threat—sent a chill up her spine. *Nothing's guaranteed.* Including her own survival? she hazarded.

Setting her jaw, she pushed the door open and stepped out onto the pavement. If someone wanted to kill her, cowering in the car wasn't going to offer much protection. If Drew hadn't thought it was safe, he wouldn't have stopped. She hadn't yet made up her mind as to whether or not she liked Drew Hunter, but she trusted him. Keeping her alive was his job and there was something about him that made her believe that he was very good at his job. She certainly hoped her faith wasn't misplaced, she thought with slightly grim humor.

After getting the key from the gas station attendant, Kate went around the side of the building to use the bathroom. The ladies' room was stark but clean and she lingered, splashing water onto her face in an attempt to wash away the torpid feeling that came from sitting in the car all morning.

Staring at her reflection in the mirror, she was suddenly struck by a feeling of total unreality. It didn't seem possible that she was actually on the run. Running for her life. No matter how she tried, she couldn't make it seem real. It just wasn't possible that her life had changed so completely.

No amount of pretending could change the reality of what had happened. If she hadn't seen those documents... If she hadn't gone to the police with what she'd learned... Shaking her head, Kate smoothed the hem of her moss green camp shirt over her jeans. There was no sense in thinking about what if. She *had* seen the documents and she *had* gone to the police. She had no one to blame for the situation she was in except her own conscience.

Pulling open the door, she stepped out into the sunshine, wishing it could do more to warm the chill that seemed to have settled inside her. But it was going to take more than a sunny day to melt that chill.

She turned toward the front of the building where Drew was probably waiting impatiently. It would be nice if the man were a little more open and friendly. They were apparently going to be spending quite a bit of time together. Was he planning on spending all of it in dead silence?

Kate had gone only a few steps when she heard the sound of laughter coming from the back of the station. There was a moment's silence and then a sharp yip, followed by another burst of laughter. Without hesitation, she turned and moved toward the sound.

She circled the Dumpster that sat at the corner of the building and stopped abruptly. There were four boys standing in a semicircle. In front of them was a large dog of indeterminate parentage. He was braced on three legs, the fourth hung at an awkward angle, obviously broken. From the prominence of the ribs that showed through his shaggy coat, it was obvious that a broken leg was only part of his problems.

Kate's heart immediately went out to the injured animal and tears welled up in her eyes. Rage burned them away when one of the boys reached out and poked the dog in the side with a stick, hard enough to draw a yelp from him. It was immediately followed by a low growl, but they had the animal backed against a fence, unable to run away and obviously too weak to fight.

Kate was upon them before she was even aware of moving.

"What do you think you're doing?" she demanded, pushing her way between two of them and snatching the stick away from the youth who held it. She stopped in front of the dog and spun to face them, her eyes flashing angrily. "You ought to be ashamed of yourselves."

Surprise held them silent for a moment. A couple of them

glanced over their shoulders as if assuming that she had re-inforcements on the way. Seeing nothing but the blank wall of the garage, they turned back to look at the woman who stood like an avenging angel between them and their victim.

They were older than she'd thought and, for the first time, she registered that they were wearing gang colors. Kate swallowed but she didn't allow her eyes to flicker from theirs for even a moment.

"What did you think you were doing?" she demanded, deciding that maintaining the offensive was the best strategy.

"Who wants to know?" It was a tall, fair-haired boy who asked, the sort of boy who should be in a Norman Rockwell painting, not standing on the cracked asphalt behind a gas station, tormenting injured animals.

"It looked as if you were tormenting this dog."

"And what if we were?" one of the others asked, sneering.

"I won't let you do it anymore." She wished the words would have come out more forcefully, but it was becoming obvious that the dog might not be the only one in need of rescuing. She tightened her hold on the stick and tried to look completely calm and confident.

"What if we said it was our dog?"

"I still won't let you torment him."

"You gonna stop us?" the blonde demanded incredulously.

"If I have to." Kate lifted her chin, hoping the sweat breaking out on her forehead would be attributed to the warmth of the sun and not to the cold fear creeping through her.

DREW CAME AROUND the side of the building in search of his missing witness and stopped abruptly. It took only an instant to interpret the scene before him. The young toughs, the injured dog and Kate standing between them, a stick clutched in her hands as if it was the only oar in a sinking rowboat. She looked like an avenging angel, but the stick was hardly an adequate weapon, angel or no.

One of the youths started toward Kate. Their attention was focused so completely on her that none of them noticed that there was a new player in the game. The tall blond kid reached for Kate. She edged back until she stood next to the dog, who growled warningly, whether at Kate or the boys facing them was anyone's guess.

In the few seconds it took him to reach the group, Drew debated his options. He could try to reason with the boys, try to make them see the error of their ways. Or he could simply give them a graphic demonstration of just how in error they were. The decision was really quite simple.

There was a startled cry from the two boys who had the misfortune to be first in Drew's path. He wrapped his fingers around the back of each neck and rapped their heads together with an audible thud. They staggered back and fell to their knees, clutching their hands over their skulls as if trying to hold them together.

The other two spun to face him, their eyes widening when they saw their companions' quick and painful fate.

"Hey, man!" The startled protest came from the blonde.

"Back off," Drew told him, his eyes like chips of ice.

"This ain't none of your business," the boy protested, looking both nervous and angry.

"She's my business." Drew jerked his head toward Kate. "Now back off."

The boy looked from his companion who remained standing to the two who were attempting to stagger to their feet. From there, he looked at the cold threat in Drew's eyes.

"We don't want no trouble, man," he mumbled sullenly.

"Wise choice."

Drew watched as they gathered up their dazed companions and disappeared through a break in the wooden fence that separated the gas station from the next lot. Satisfied that they were gone, he turned back to Kate. The blistering words he'd intended to utter died unspoken.

She'd tossed the stick aside and dropped to her knees next to the dog, reaching toward him.

"Don't!" Drew snapped out the command and took a quick step toward her, knowing there was no way he could pull her back before the dog reacted as any injured animal would and probably tear her throat out.

Before Drew could get to her, she'd put her hand on the dog's shaggy head, stroking gently and murmuring to him. The animal trembled, but to Drew's surprise he didn't so much as bare his teeth in her direction.

"They were tormenting him," she said. "He's hurt and they were tormenting him." She looked up at him, her eyes swimming with tears, hurt and anger tangled in her expression. "I'm glad you bashed their heads together," she said fiercely. "I wish you'd bashed the other two."

Drew opened his mouth, intending to make some comment about the stupidity of her actions, about how badly she could have been hurt, about fools rushing in and the fact that the dog was no concern of theirs. He looked from her to the dog, who looked as if it took every bit of strength he had just to remain upright on three good legs. He sighed.

"I wish I had, too."

"We need to take him to a vet," Kate said, stroking her hand gently over the dog's back.

He could have pointed out that they were, more or less, on the run; that if, by chance, someone managed to pick up their trail, lingering in this tiny town was hardly the smartest thing they could do. He could have made some comment about not drawing attention to themselves, or the need to keep moving. But he didn't say any of those things. Instead, he sighed again and pulled the car keys out of his pocket.

"I'll wait with him in case our friends come back. You

go bring the car around and we'll try to coax him into the back of it. Maybe the guy out front knows where there's a vet.''

He was rewarded by Kate's brilliant smile as she stood up and took the keys from him. She bent to pat the dog reassuringly.

''You'll be fine with Drew,'' she told him reassuringly. ''He'll take good care of you.''

Throwing another smile in Drew's direction, she sprinted off toward the front of the station. Drew watched her out of sight and then turned to look at the dog, who eyed him suspiciously.

''Why do I have the feeling that this is *not* going to be an isolated incident?''

Chapter Four

"We'll stop here for tonight."

At Drew's announcement, Kate blinked the tired fog from her eyes and sat up straighter. She glanced at the clock on the dashboard and saw that it was only seven. It felt much later. After almost no sleep the night before and their early start this morning, it seemed as if it should be past midnight.

Flipping on the right turn signal, Drew guided the car off the highway and onto a gravel parking lot. There was a quivery neon sign beside the road that announced the name of the motel. Kozy Korner, it said in mottled pink letters. If she hadn't been too tired to care about anything but a hot shower and a bed, the cute spelling would have made Kate flinch.

"I was beginning to think you were going to drive all night," she commented as Drew shut the engine off.

"I'd planned on being a lot farther along by now," Drew said. "If we hadn't been delayed..."

"By 'delay,' I assume you're talking about the time it took to see the dog settled."

"It *did* cost us a good portion of the afternoon," he pointed out.

"You could no more have left him there than I could have. You were just as relieved as I was when the vet said he could patch him up. And I saw the money you gave him to pay for his care until he could find a home for him."

"I didn't say I wasn't glad the dog was going to recover." Drew heard the edge that temper gave his voice and stopped to draw a slow breath. "All I said was that we lost a lot of time," he finished in a carefully controlled tone.

"It was worth it," Kate said firmly.

Drew lifted one shoulder in a half shrug, unable to argue and unwilling to agree. "I'll go check us in. You wait here. The fewer people who see you, the better," he added, forestalling any possible argument about his autocratic order.

The reminder of just why the two of them were here, at this dumpy little motel, on an obscure highway in the middle of California, sent a chill through Kate. She'd almost managed to put Lester Davis and the possibility that he wanted her dead out of her mind entirely.

"I thought you were sure they hadn't followed us."

"They didn't follow us this morning, but by now they've probably figured out that you ditched them. The chances of them getting this far are slim. But the less visible you are, the safer you'll be. You haven't exactly been invisible so far."

"I suppose you're talking about the dog again," Kate said. Even in the marginal light that illuminated the car's interior, Drew could see the way her chin firmed.

"Well, it's a sure bet that the owner of that gas station would remember you. And the vet. Not to mention those four young punks you tangled with. If anyone was looking for you and they got that far, they'd know they were following the right woman. They'd know you weren't traveling alone. And they'd know what kind of car we're driving." He sighed tiredly and thrust his fingers through his hair. "And the way my luck has been lately, one of those people had a photographic memory and they'd remember the license plate number."

Hearing him lay the facts out like that made Kate swallow hard, but her chin didn't come down even a fraction of an inch. "I'm sorry if it's going to cause trouble, but I'd do it again. The dog was hurt. I couldn't just walk away from him."

Drew's eyes skimmed her face, unreadable in the dim light. "No, I don't suppose you could have."

And she supposed she could interpret that any way she pleased, Kate thought as he pushed open the car door and got out. She watched him until he reached the door marked Office and pulled it open.

Leaning her head back against the seat, she closed her eyes, letting exhaustion wash over her. Forty-eight hours ago, she'd had nothing more pressing to worry about than finding a job before her savings ran out. Now she was wondering whether she was going to live long enough to see that.

No, that wasn't entirely true. She opened her eyes and frowned at the architecturally uninspired building in front of her. Despite everything, she wasn't as worried about her survival as she might have been—as she should have been. Something about Drew Hunter made her feel safe. He'd keep her alive, at the cost of his own life, if it came to that.

She shuddered, feeling a chill that went all the way to her bones. God, what a mess she'd gotten herself into when she stumbled across those files. For a moment, she wished that she was the sort of person who could have turned a comfortably blind eye to her employer's illicit activities. It had been a decent job. Lester Davis had been tolerable to work for. If she hadn't been so damned efficient, she wouldn't have found those files and she could have continued with her life, blissfully ignorant.

She was so absorbed in her thoughts that she didn't notice Drew leaving the office and walking to the car. She jumped when the door beside her was suddenly pulled open. Her head jerked around so quickly that she actually felt dizzy for a moment.

"Don't do that!" she snapped, her voice sharp with the quick rush of adrenaline.

"Sorry. I assumed you'd seen me." Tiredness put an edge to Drew's husky tone as he stepped back from the open door.

"No. I'm sorry for snapping." Kate passed her hand over her face, her fingers shaky with fatigue and nerves. "I'm a little uptight," she said, offering a thin smile by way of apology.

"You've got reason." Drew opened the back door and reached for his duffel bag. "Which bag do you want?"

Kate gestured to one of the totes, too tired to even make a token offer to carry it. She swung her legs out of the car and stood, arching her back to ease the stiffness of too many hours in the same position. Wearily she followed Drew, watching as he set down her tote bag and slid the key into the lock. He pushed the door open with his shoulder, reaching in to flip on the light before stepping into the room.

She saw him give the room a quick, searching glance before turning to gesture her inside. She could have pointed out that the likelihood of finding someone lurking in a room at the Kozy Korner Motel seemed slim, but she knew his caution was more habit than expectation. What must it feel like to have to check out every room you entered for potential danger? she wondered. And then it occurred to her that she was going to learn exactly what it was like.

She heard Drew set her tote bag down and turned to thank him, her hand already going out for the room key. The polite good-night died unspoken as she saw him shut the door—with him on the inside. Her eyes swiveled from his lean figure to the twin beds set neatly against the wall and then back to him.

"You only got one room?"

"Just one." His eyes were ice blue and ready for an argument.

"Do I get any say in the matter?"

"No." There was no attempt to soften the blunt answer. "Protecting you is my job and you're not getting out of my sight until Davis goes to trial."

Kate closed her eyes for a moment, feeling incredibly tired. She opened them again and looked at him, reading the determination in his gaze and knowing that she could protest till she was blue in the face and she wouldn't get anywhere. With a sigh, she reached up and pulled the elastic band from the ponytail that had held her hair since before sunrise. Running the fingers of one hand through her loosened hair, she bent to pick up the brightly colored tote. Straightening, she looked at her companion.

"Do you want to check and see if there are any assassins lurking in the bathroom before I take a shower?" She gained some satisfaction from the quick look of surprise that flared in his eyes at her easy acceptance of the situation.

"I think the bathroom should be safe enough," he said slowly, watching her as if waiting for the objection he knew had to be coming.

Kate took considerable pleasure in giving him nothing more than a pleasant smile before disappearing into the bathroom and closing the door.

THOUGH SHE WOULD HAVE liked to stand under the shower for at least twenty-four hours, Kate forced herself to remember that she wasn't the only one who'd spent the day traveling and limited herself to only ten minutes. She toweled herself dry and pulled on a fresh pair of jeans and a loose T-shirt, but left her hair to fall in damp waves on her shoulders.

"Shower's all yours," she announced cheerfully as she stepped into the room. Drew turned from the bed where he'd tossed his duffel and nodded.

"Thanks." And a moment later, the bathroom door shut behind him.

"Well, at least I don't have to worry about him talking my ear off," Kate muttered under her breath. "A chatterbox, he ain't."

Shrugging off Drew's taciturn behavior, she tossed her tote bag on the other bed and began rummaging through it. She pulled out a small brass alarm clock and set it on the night table. The clock had been one of the first things she'd bought for herself when she got her own apartment and she hadn't wanted to leave it behind. Next came a small tan teddy bear, barely five inches high, wearing a red ribbon around his neck. He was settled carefully on the pillow.

She heard the shower go on and wondered if lots of nice, hot water would improve her companion's mood. She was sure there was a human under the impenetrable surface. She'd caught glimpses of him once or twice. Last night, certainly, when he'd had that nightmare. And the way he'd handled the injured dog today had shown a definite humanity. Despite his remarks about lost time, she'd seen the absolute patience he'd shown when he was coaxing the big animal to get into the car, as well as the anger in his eyes when he'd seen the animal's abused condition.

Yes, there was definitely a human inside Drew Hunter somewhere. It might take a little time to coax him out, but it didn't look as if she was going to have much else to do over the next couple of weeks.

A knock on the door interrupted both her unpacking and her thoughts. Going over to the door, she peered through the peephole. The boy standing on the other side of the panel could have posed for an advertisement for an average American teenager. From the shaggy layer of dark hair, to the T-shirt displaying a logo for a rock band whose name Kate didn't recognize, to the faded jeans, he could have been any kid from any high school anywhere in the country. The pizza box balanced on his hand made the reason for his presence immediately obvious. Which was why Kate didn't hesitate to open the door.

"You ordered a pizza?" The words hovered somewhere between statement and question.

"Probably." Drew must have remembered that they hadn't stopped for dinner, she thought. "Just set it down over there. What do I owe you?"

He named an amount and Kate turned to get her purse. "That your guitar?" he asked, his eyes lighting on the case propped up in the corner.

Kate turned to look at it, surprised. Obviously dinner wasn't the only thing Drew had thought of.

"Yes, it is. Do you play?"

"Yeah. Electric, mostly, but I got an old acoustic, too. You like Clapton?"

"Of course." Vaguely Kate was aware of the cessation of sound as the shower was turned off.

"You know 'Layla'? I'm learning that now."

"It's a great song."

"The greatest." His eyes shining with enthusiasm, he crooked his hands to hold an invisible guitar. His vocal rendition of the appropriate chords left something to be desired musically, but he made up for it with enthusiasm.

Biting her lip to hold back a smile, Kate wondered if he provided impromptu concerts with every pizza delivery, and just how she could politely cut this one short so that she could open the box to discover the source of the wonderful smells that were permeating the room.

As it happened, she didn't have to worry about cutting the concert short. Drew did that for her.

The moment he shut off the shower, he'd heard the pained sounds coming from the next room. Thinking that Kate was either desperately ill or under attack, he jerked a towel from the rack and wrapped it around his waist. Drawing his gun from the shoulder holster he'd hung over the hook on the back of the door, Drew yanked open the door, thinking to gain the element of surprise.

He definitely accomplished that.

Startled by the sound of the door banging back against the sink, Kate and the Clapton wannabe jerked their heads toward Drew, their eyes widening at the sight of him standing in the doorway, soaking wet and naked but for a towel and a .38.

The concert ended abruptly. A particularly complex vocal riff concluded on a high squeaky note that no guitar could ever have duplicated. The three of them stared at one another in stunned silence.

"You ordered a pizza," Kate said, after a moment when it seemed as if the room's other occupants had turned to marble.

"A pizza." He'd forgotten the damned pizza, Drew realized. Forgotten to tell Kate he'd ordered it; forgotten it was going to be delivered. The kid with Kate must be the delivery boy. Why was he holding his hands in such a strange position?

"I heard noises," he said, his tone accusing.

"I was just playin' a riff, man." The boy's voice broke, skidding into a falsetto.

"A riff?" Drew had lowered the gun as soon as he realized that Kate was in no danger. But the gesture didn't seem to offer much reassurance, judging by the glazed look in the kid's eyes.

"On the guitar," Kate explained when the boy seemed incapable of speaking. She bit her lip when Drew's brows rose, nearly meeting the wave of dripping wet hair that fell onto his forehead.

"Here." She held out a twenty-dollar bill to pay for the pizza, but there was no response from the delivery boy, unless you counted the bobbing of his Adam's apple. Kate finally stepped forward and pushed the bill into the hand that was still crooked around the neck of his air guitar.

He jerked as if her touch were electrically charged, his fingers closing convulsively over the bill. He didn't take his eyes from Drew as he started edging toward the door.

"I didn't mean to startle you," Drew offered. "I thought there was a problem."

"That's okay, man. No problem. Really. No problem." His mouth twitched toward a smile, but couldn't quite make it. He bobbed his head. "No problem." He groped behind him for the doorknob, unwilling to take his eyes from Drew's dripping figure.

"Keep the change," Kate said kindly, though she doubted that he heard her. She doubted he even remembered her existence.

"No problem," he said again as he got the door open.

"Nice talking to you," Kate offered, her voice choked.

"No problem." He pulled the door open, shot one last terrified glance in Drew's direction and then darted outside, slamming the door shut behind him. A few seconds later, they heard tires spinning on gravel and the grinding of gears as he completed his escape.

Kate promptly collapsed on one of the beds, her contained laughter spilling out. Drew glared at her, feeling like a fool and yet unable to see how he could have reacted any other way.

"Why did you answer the door?" he demanded angrily.

"Because he knocked." She didn't even have the decency to stop laughing long enough to answer him. Drew stepped back into the bathroom to pick up his holster and shove the gun into it.

"I suppose if Lester Davis had knocked, you would have opened the door?" he inquired.

"If he was carrying a pizza." She put her hand over her mouth, but it was not enough to stifle her giggles. "His face when you came out..." The sentence trailed off in renewed laughter.

"How the hell was I to know that wailing was supposed to be a guitar?" he snapped. "It sounded like someone was killing a cat."

That set her off on another fit of laughter. "His face when you came bursting out of the bathroom like the Lone Ranger... Only without the mask. Or much else."

"You shouldn't have answered the damned door," Drew said accusingly, trying not to notice the way her nose wrinkled when she laughed.

"Sorry." She didn't sound in the least sorry. "I guess I'm just not used to seeing assassins lurking behind every piece of pepperoni."

"You'd better get used to it."

"I'll try." Her humble look might have been more effective if she hadn't spoiled it by giggling again. "Maybe I'd better stick to plain cheese from now on. It'll give them less to hide behind."

Drew glared at her. The truth was, he was angry at himself more than at her. He should have remembered to tell her about ordering dinner. And if he'd forgotten that, he should at least have remembered it when he heard the kid doing his bad imitation of a guitar.

He rammed his fingers through his hair and glared at Kate again. The only effect it had was to make her giggle harder. Dammit all. Did she have to be so appealing?

Looking over her shoulder, he caught sight of his reflection in the mirror on the dresser. His hair stood up in dark waves, reminding him of a cartoon of an electrocution victim. Water beaded his bare torso. The white towel clung crookedly on his hips. And clutched in one hand was the shoulder holster, complete with gun.

He looked like an idiot. And he must have looked even more ridiculous bursting out of the bathroom like a madman, gun at the ready. No wonder that kid's eyes had bulged out so far they could have been scraped off with a stick.

"I suppose we can count on the delivery boy remembering us, if anyone comes looking," Kate said through her giggles. "Especially you. I think he'll remember you the rest of his life."

"He'll probably never play guitar again," Drew said, his mouth twisting in a reluctant smile.

"For a while there, I thought his fingers might be permanently frozen on an F chord. Which would severely limit his repertoire."

"Well, if he sounds as bad on a real guitar as he does on a fake one, I don't think the world has suffered a real blow."

The reluctant smile became a full-blown grin as he remembered the boy's stammering departure. "His voice may not drop until he's thirty," he said on a chuckle.

Kate felt her breath catch, her eyes widening at the way the smile transformed his features. She'd thought him handsome before, but when he smiled...

She swallowed hard and dragged her eyes away, suddenly wondering if she wouldn't have been safer staying in L.A. There were more kinds of danger than the overt one offered by Lester Davis. And she had the distinct feeling that Drew Hunter was a prime example of one of them.

THE LAUGHTER SERVED to ease some of the tension. It made them a little less strangers and a little more companions. They were a long way from being friends. Actually Kate couldn't quite imagine ever being friends with Drew Hunter, but if they were going to be stuck with each other for an undetermined length of time, it would be nice to be on friendly terms, at least.

After they shared the pizza, Drew turned on the television to watch the news. Kate wasn't sure at what point the tension of the past couple of days and their early-morning start caught up with her. She was aware of the newscaster's voice droning on, but the words were starting to slur together. As soon as the news was over she'd go to bed. At least, she would once she figured out how to go about doing that while sharing a room with a man she'd known barely thirty-six hours. She'd have to give that some thought. Just as soon as the news ended....

She wasn't aware of Drew getting up to switch off the television. Nor of him coming to stand beside her bed, his expression unreadable as he looked down at her. She stirred slightly when he bent to lift her up, tugging the covers down before easing her back against the pillows.

He hesitated a moment, frowning at the snug jeans. He finally reached down and loosened the button at the top, trying to ignore the silky feel of her skin against the backs of his fingers. He pulled the covers up over her, but didn't move away immediately.

He glanced at the clock, at the little teddy bear and then back down at the woman who'd set them in place. The motel room already felt like more of a home than his apartment did after he'd lived there for five years. He stared down at her, his pale eyes brooding, and wondered whether he wasn't in more danger now than he'd ever been in his life.

BY MORNING, HE'D BEEN able to put the odd sense of danger from him, chalking it up to proximity and too little sleep. Kate was his job, nothing more, nothing less.

They drove throughout the day, stopping only for lunch and to fill the gas tank. Kate questioned the route he was taking—zigzagging up the state, adding miles to their journey.

"It's harder to trace a circuitous route," he said. He looked at the speedometer and eased his foot off the gas. He didn't want an encounter with the highway patrol any more than he wanted one with Davis's men. "If anyone manages to follow us part way, it will be harder to figure out where we're going," he added.

He glanced across the car at her, feeling his jaw tighten when he saw the animation momentarily drain from her face, the way it did whenever she was reminded of the reason for the journey. It left her looking altogether too fragile for his peace of mind.

"Why did you come to us?" he asked abruptly.

"The police? Why did I go to the police?" The question seemed to surprise her.

"Most people would have looked the other way. A few would have demanded a piece of the action."

"I think they'd have ended up wearing concrete shoes," she said slowly, looking out the window at the passing scenery. "I don't think Mr. Davis would have taken kindly to anyone making demands like that."

"No, he wouldn't. But that doesn't explain why you didn't just look the other way."

"I couldn't," she said, sounding almost surprised that he could ask. "What he's doing is wrong. If I ignored it, then I'd be just as guilty as he is."

"Or smart enough to look out for yourself," Drew commented dryly.

"That, too," she admitted with a smile. The smile faded almost immediately. "He'll kill me if he finds out that I'm your witness, won't he?"

"He's probably already figured it out by now. Your disappearance is as good as an admission of guilt." He paused, giving her the chance to point out that it hadn't been her idea to run. She met his look, saying nothing, and he realized that she must have known that from the start. His reluctant admiration for her went up another notch.

"As for killing you, that's why we're moving you to someplace he can't find you."

"What if he does find me? What if he sends someone to kill me?"

"Then I'll just have to get them first." The words were spoken coolly, without a hint of doubt that he could do just that, without a moment's hesitation for what he might have to do to protect her.

Kate shivered. There was something frightening and yet oddly reassuring about Drew Hunter's ruthless determination. She was suddenly very glad they were on the same side. She wouldn't want to have him as an enemy.

Drew sensed her uneasiness, but kept his eyes resolutely on the road in front of him. It was his job to keep her alive so that she could testify, not to shield her from the realities of the situation.

SINCE HE WANTED to arrive at their destination early in the day so that he could take a look at the town, Drew had already decided that they'd be spending one more night on the road. They stopped at a motel on the edge of a small town less than a hundred miles from their destination.

This time there was no question about their sharing a room. In fact, it felt so natural that Kate might have worried about herself if she hadn't been too tired to worry about anything but hot water and a soft bed.

It was after ten when they stopped. Kate pulled her nightgown on after she showered. She stared at her reflection in the steam-fogged mirror. It was the same gown she'd worn two nights before when she'd awakened Drew from his nightmare. It was a perfectly modest nightgown, knee length, long sleeved, with a shallow scoop neck. It even had a ruffle at the hem. No one could possibly accuse it of any overt allure. So why was she hesitating about walking out of the bathroom?

She nibbled on her lower lip. Was it that she didn't know Drew? Or was it that she knew him too well? Not that she could say she knew him at all. She suspected there weren't very many people who did know him. But spending two days and nights together did tend to force a certain intimacy. She thought they were developing a sort of tentative companionship. He'd actually talked to her today.

Which should have made it easier to contemplate sharing a motel room with him, right? He wasn't quite as much of a stranger as he had been the night before.

Which was exactly why it was harder to open the door and walk out into the room. Kate sighed at the illogic of it and turned away from her reflection to open the door.

Drew had turned on the television and was watching a situation comedy that hadn't been particularly funny even before it went to reruns. He'd been trying not to think about how little distance lay between the room's two beds and was annoyed with himself for even noticing such a thing.

When he heard the bathroom door open, he looked up, relieved to have his thoughts interrupted.

The relief disappeared the moment he saw her. She was wearing that same damned virginal nightgown she'd worn two nights ago. White cotton with just a hint of lace at the neck, it exposed less flesh than the T-shirt she'd worn all day. There was nothing in the least alluring about it. So why did the sight of her in it make him feel a hot rush of arousal?

"The shower's all yours," she said, her voice a shade brighter than necessary.

"Thanks." Drew's jaw hardened in self-directed annoyance. He stood as she moved farther into the room. He caught a whiff of her scent, a mixture of soap and toothpaste. Nice, homey smells that had no business making him think of cool sheets and warm skin.

"Better get some sleep," he growled as he brushed by her. The bathroom door snapped shut with more force than was strictly necessary.

By the time he'd finished his shower, he'd managed to

convince himself that he was overreacting. There was nothing wrong with noticing that Kate was an attractive woman. And that's all that was happening. He was just a normal man reacting to an attractive woman. And if the response seemed more gut level than that, then it was strictly his imagination.

Which didn't mean he wasn't just as glad to find that she was already asleep when he stepped into the room. If it occurred to him that pretending to be Kate's husband until the time came for her to testify was not going to be as easy as he'd anticipated, he put the thought from him as he slid between the covers.

Tomorrow they'd reach the town of Hayfield, where they were going to be staying. It would be easier to ignore her undeniable attraction then. They'd be sharing a roof but not a bedroom, and he refused to admit to even the slightest twinge of regret at that thought.

Reaching out to snap off the light, Drew let his eyes linger on the soft curve of Kate's cheek, the tangle of pale brown hair that spilled over the pristine white pillow. Why couldn't it have been a nice little old lady who'd brought in the evidence against Davis?

There was a click as the lamp flicked off. Drew sank back against the slightly lumpy pillow and closed his eyes. A good night's sleep was all he needed.

HE DIDN'T KNOW how long he'd slept when the nightmare began. Nor could he have said how long he lay tangled in it, watching events unfold, knowing what was going to happen, yet also a participant, unable to stop what was to come.

There was Martinez turning toward him, his teeth gleaming against his swarthy skin as he started to say something about how long it had taken Drew to get back with the coffee. And then his eyes widened in surprise as a neat round hole appeared in the middle of his forehead.

Drew felt the sting of hot coffee spilling over his hands, heard as if from a great distance the pop of gunshots as he reached for his weapon. And then he felt his leg go out from under him, felt the night-cooled sidewalk come up beneath him. There was no pain, though he knew he'd been shot. Martinez was dead. His partner was dead. Martinez was dead.

The words repeated themselves over and over again as he lay there, bleeding, waiting for whoever had fired the shots to come and finish the job, knowing he couldn't lift a finger to stop it from happening.

He woke abruptly, coming upright in the bed, his breathing fast and hard, his body damp with sweat. Martinez was dead. Though it had been months since the shooting, each time the nightmare came, it was as if it had just happened and the pain was still raw and new, churning in his gut.

It was over. There was nothing he could do. Just as there'd been nothing he could do at the time. As if it had been preordained that Martinez would die that night. And that he would survive. Only there hadn't been anything mystical about the shooting. It had been a hit, plain and simple. A hit that had been only half-successful. Because he'd survived. And he was going to continue to survive, if only for the sheer pleasure of bringing down the man responsible for his partner's murder.

"Sometimes it helps to talk about it." Kate's voice came out of the darkness, soft as a whisper.

Drew jerked toward her, his pulse too fast, dream-induced adrenaline still pumping through him.

"I thought you were asleep." There was a snap to the words that made them an accusation.

"I was, but you were muttering in your sleep."

"Sorry." In the darkness he could make out no more than the shape of her beneath the covers.

"Sometimes it helps to talk about it."

For a moment, he was caught by a shocking urge to do just that. He hadn't talked about the nightmares with anyone, not even the department shrink who'd carefully explained all the phases he was going to go through in dealing with the natural grief and guilt that came with being a survivor.

"There's nothing to talk about. Just a bad dream. Sorry I woke you." His tone was dismissing, but he couldn't quite bring himself to lie back down. He'd learned that if he went back to sleep too quickly, the dream sometimes returned.

"Who's Martinez? You said the name in your sleep."

"He was my partner. My friend," he added, almost under his breath.

"Was?" Kate was quick to pick up on the implications of that.

"Go back to sleep, Kate." Drew's voice was taut.

"Sometimes things aren't so bad if you talk about them." Her voice was husky with sleep, coming out of the darkness, running over his bare skin in the lightest of caresses.

"This isn't a nightmare full of boogeymen, Kate. It's a memory. And no amount of talking about it is going to make it better."

"What happened to Martinez?" she asked, as if he hadn't spoken.

Drew closed his eyes, knowing she wasn't going to give up, knowing that a part of him wanted—needed—to tell her. Needed for her to understand what was at stake.

"We were on a stakeout," he said slowly, his voice rough. "We'd gotten a tip about one of Davis's warehouses."

He heard her quick indrawn breath as he said the name, but he didn't stop. She'd asked for the truth and she was going to get it.

"There was a coffee shop on the corner. We flipped a coin to see who'd go get coffee. I won. When I got back to the car, Martinez turned to say something to me. And then he was dead. The bullet that should have killed me went wide—maybe the shooter sneezed,'' he said, without humor. "It caught me in the leg instead of in the head.''

"That's why you limp sometimes,'' she said, talking as much to herself as to him.

"That's why.''

The motel room was silent while she absorbed his words. Drew could hear her breathing, a little too quick, as if his words had upset her. Good, he thought harshly. Let her be upset if it made her realize just what was at stake here.

"You're counting on me to destroy him, aren't you?'' she said into the silence.

"Yes.'' He didn't add anything to soften the flat agreement. She was the best weapon he had, short of going after Davis with a shotgun himself. And this would be better in the end. Better to see Davis behind bars—the social position he'd so carefully cultivated stripped from him—than to see him dead.

Neither of them spoke again. Drew lay back against the pillows, his mind churning with old memories and new regrets. He shouldn't have said anything to her about the shooting. If it came out in court, he could be accused of tampering with the witness. Not that it mattered to him except that it could affect her testimony. Nothing mattered except bringing Davis down.

Kate lay staring into the darkness, digesting what Drew had told her. She'd known he wanted to see Lester Davis stopped, but she hadn't known that he had quite such a personal stake in it. His partner's murder, his own injury. He hungered for vengeance as much as justice.

And she was the key to both. She had to remember that. She was useful to him, and she'd be a fool to forget it.

Chapter Five

"This is where we'll be staying." Drew pulled the car up next to the curb in front of a small yellow house with a neatly fenced yard.

Kate looked from Drew to the house, her brows lifting in surprise. She wasn't sure what she'd been expecting, but this slice of small town suburbia wasn't it. The setting was much too...normal.

"Here?" she questioned, her disbelief obvious.

"Here. The neighbors should have the keys." He turned off the engine and then sat scowling at the little house. "They're expecting us."

"They are?" It was starting to occur to Kate that she'd been remiss in not asking for more details about the arrangements that had been made to protect her. She'd simply accepted Drew's assurance that she'd be safe. "Do they know what the situation is?"

"No." Drew seemed to hesitate and then slanted her an unreadable glance. "No one is to know why we're here."

"That makes sense." Kate unsnapped her seat belt and turned slightly in her seat to face him. "So what's our story?"

Drew didn't answer immediately. At least, not verbally. Reaching into his shirt pocket, he drew out a plain gold wedding band. Kate stared at it for a moment, her eyes wide and uncertain. It was the obvious cover, of course. They could have been brother and sister, but it wasn't as obvious a choice as being husband and wife.

She should have seen it coming when he'd insisted that they share a motel room. She *would* have seen it coming if she'd taken the trouble to look. But she'd been thinking about other things—like whether or not she'd ever get her life back again and the possibility that someone might be looking for her, wanting her dead. And the way Drew's rare smile made her stomach jump. She hadn't given nearly enough thought to the near future.

Held between Drew's thumb and forefinger, the ring gleamed dull gold in the sunlight. It was the most practical arrangement. That's all it was—pure practicality. It wasn't as if they were actually going to have to get married. The ring didn't mean a thing, really.

Which didn't explain the faint trembling of Kate's hand as she held it out. Drew hesitated and it occurred to her that she should have taken the ring from him and put it on herself, but it was already too late. He'd already taken her hand, his fingers strong and hard around hers as he slid the ring into place.

Their eyes met for an instant and it seemed—almost—as if something passed between them, something that sent an odd little shiver up Kate's spine. His fingers tightened over hers. Did he lean toward her or was it her imagination? And then he released her hand and reached for the door handle.

"Let me do most of the talking."

"All right." But she was talking to thin air. He was already out of the car.

Kate was aware of a slight unsteadiness of her hand as she pushed open her door. It was just the situation, she told herself. There was nothing to her reaction to Drew except the fact that she was dependent on him. It had been a long time since she'd been dependent on anyone else and it was bringing out a strange reaction in her. That's all it was.

IF SHE THOUGHT she'd gotten to know her companion during the past few days, Kate soon discovered how wrong she was. Standing on the concrete porch of the house next door to the one they'd be sharing, he seemed to change in some subtle way. His features relaxed, the taut lines easing from beside his mouth. His eyes softened, losing the hard edge that made her think of pale blue diamonds.

By the time the door opened in answer to the bell, the tough cop had disappeared and in his place was someone younger, more...ordinary. It could have been a different man entirely.

"Mrs. Dumont?" he asked the woman who pulled open the door and looked at them through the screen. "I'm Drew Ralston. This is my wife, Kate. We're renting the house next door. The Marsdens said we should get the key from you."

"Mr. Marsden called and said you'd be getting here today." The faint wariness in her eyes was replaced by friendly welcome. "Wait just a second and I'll get the key and take you over."

She was back in little more than the second she'd promised, pushing open the screen to join Kate and Drew on the porch. "You must be exhausted, driving all that way. I'm Jane, by the way. It's Janine, really, but everybody calls me Jane. I don't know why. Janine's a prettier name, don't you think?"

She didn't wait for an answer but swept by them and down the steps, her dark hair bouncing on the shoulders of her pale blue shirt.

"I think you'll like the neighborhood. It's pretty quiet, but everybody's friendly, too. We've been here almost fifteen years and we can't imagine living anywhere else. Did you drive straight through? I hope not. We drove all the way up the coast when Kenny—that's our son—was just a baby. Bill had to get back to work so we really didn't have a choice, but it was tiring. Do you plan on staying long?"

"We're not sure." It was Kate who responded when Drew didn't answer immediately. He'd been letting the words roll over him, paying little attention to them as they followed her down a sidewalk buckled by the roots of the elms that lined the street. Kate could hardly blame him for his inattention since, for a moment, it had seemed as if Jane Dumont could happily carry the conversation without any outside assistance.

"It all depends on how things go with my book," Drew added.

"Oh, you're a writer." Jane threw him a quick, speculative look over her shoulder as she led the way up the walk. "Should I know your name?"

"Not yet. I'm taking a year off from teaching to write a novel." His smile managed to be both hopeful and a little self-deprecating. Kate didn't doubt that he could have called up a blush, if necessary.

"Well, you've picked a good place if you need peace and quiet." Jane started to slide the key into the lock, but Drew reached out to take it from her.

"This is our first real place together," he said, in answer to Jane's startled look. "We'd sort of like to explore it alone, if you don't mind."

Kate wondered if Jane heard the iron under the request or if she simply accepted his explanation at face value. Whichever it was, her startled look faded into an indulgent smile.

"Newlyweds. I'm not surprised. There's still a little of that starry-eyed look about the two of you."

More like an exhausted daze, Kate thought. But she did her best to look shy and bridal.

"I'll leave you two alone, then, but don't forget that I'm right next door if you need anything."

"Thank you, Jane." Drew gave her another of those wide open smiles that made Kate feel as if he was someone else entirely. She murmured her farewells as Jane's plump figure brushed past her and down the two steps to the cement walkway. She turned to watch the other woman, who paused at the sidewalk to smile back at them.

Behind her, she heard Drew mutter something uncomplimentary about friendly neighbors and then she gasped, barely swallowing a startled shriek as she felt herself being swept off her feet and lifted against his chest. Her arms came up automatically to circle his neck, her wide eyes meeting his.

"Newlyweds," he muttered by way of explanation and pushed open the door with his foot before carrying her over the threshold.

He set her down the moment the door shut behind them, stepping back so quickly that Kate might have been offended. At least, she might have been if she hadn't been occupied with controlling the odd flutter in the pit of her stomach.

"She was expecting me to carry you over the threshold," Drew said, as if she'd demanded an explanation.

"Of course." Kate looked at her hands and was annoyed to find them less than steady. She lifted her chin and forced herself to look at him. "Why newlyweds?"

"It helps explain any conflict in our stories. We can always pass it off as not having been married long enough to get the details straight."

"Of course." She cleared her throat, wishing she could think of a more intelligent response than just those two words. The truth was that it was starting to sink in on her that she was going to be sharing this house for an unknown length of time with a man she barely knew. A man who made her knees tremble and set butterflies in her stomach.

It was ironic, she thought. She'd left L.A. to escape one dangerous man...and ended up in the hands of another.

"I NEED THE CAR KEYS."

Drew lifted his eyes from the newspaper and gave Kate a questioning glance. "What for?"

"I need to get some things. I won't be gone long." She held out her hand and smiled.

"Give me a minute," Drew said. He snapped the paper shut. It was their first day in the house and he hadn't planned on doing anything more energetic than reading the paper, at least not before noon.

"You don't have to come with me," she protested as he stood. "I'm not going far."

"You don't go anywhere without me."

"You don't think Davis has killers lurking in town, do you?" Her tone was disbelieving.

"Probably not." He picked up his coffee cup and drained the last of its contents before rinsing the cup and setting it in the dishwasher. He'd been looking forward to a second cup, as well as a chance to read the paper at his leisure.

Kate had been right that first morning—he was *not* a morning person, not if he had a choice. It seemed like a real injustice that he had to protect a woman who woke up as chipper as a damned bird.

"I didn't want to drag you out," Kate was saying apologetically. "I really could go alone."

"No." He turned to look at her. "You don't go anywhere without me. Don't even walk next door without letting me know where you're going."

"But..."

"Nowhere, Kate." He interrupted her without apology. "I can't protect you if I don't know where you are."

"You don't think he'll find us here, do you?" Kate wrapped her arms around herself, unconsciously trying to hug away the chill his words had created.

"No, I don't. That's why Lavery sent us here." He buried the urge to put his arms around her and tell her not to worry, that there was nothing to worry about. But there was a lot to worry about, not least of which was his completely unprofessional and unwanted reaction to her.

"So you're just being extra cautious?" she suggested, looking a little less haunted.

"It's my job to be extra cautious. That's why I'm here. That's what's going to keep you alive."

"I know." She gave him a quick smile. "I appreciate it. I don't know if I've said that, but I really do appreciate what you're doing for me."

Drew's fingers curled into his palms. He wanted to taste that smile. He wanted to see if her mouth could possibly be as soft as it looked.

"I'm doing my job," he said shortly, making it clear that only a fool would read anything personal into his actions.

"I know." Kate flushed lightly, her eyes dropping away from his, and Drew felt as if he'd just slapped a friendly puppy for no reason.

"I'll get the keys," he said gruffly.

WHEN SHE'D SAID she needed to go shopping, he'd assumed she was talking about buying food, though they'd stopped at a grocery store on their way to the house the day before. Besides, if last night's dinner was any indication, cooking was hardly one of Kate's great loves and it certainly wasn't one of her talents.

He'd never realized that it was possible to cook hamburger to the actual consistency of concrete. But she'd proven it could be done and last night's meatballs could have been registered as weapons. He'd politely downed two of them and then waited until she went to bed to sneak back out to the kitchen to raid the refrigerator.

He felt a definite twinge of uneasiness at the thought that she planned to buy more food. If she could do that to hamburger, there was no telling what she could do to chicken. And he didn't really want to find out.

To his relief, Kate directed him to the discount store they'd passed on their way into town. At least she wasn't buying food. He parked the car and followed her into the store.

"I suppose you like blue," Kate said as she headed for the section marked Home Decor.

"I like it well enough," he admitted cautiously. What did his color preferences have to do with anything?

"Men always seem to like blue. Must be something genetic." She stopped in front of a display of throw pillows. "Here. These are perfect. They're bright and they're cheap."

"For what?"

"For the living room." She pulled two pillows out of the middle and Drew held his breath, waiting to see the loosely piled mound tumble to the floor. By some miracle, it stayed in place. "Hold these, please."

He automatically took the pillows from her. She circled the pile like a boxer looking for an opening in an opponent's guard. She disappeared behind it and he saw the pillows tremble as she yanked some more free. When she came around the other side, she was carrying four more pillows.

"Aren't these great?" she asked.

"I guess." He took two of the pillows from her. He could only hope that he didn't have a sudden need to draw his gun. Burdened as he was, if a bad guy showed up, he'd probably have to bombard him with pillows, rather than bullets. "Why are you buying pillows for the living room?"

"Because it needs them." She seemed surprised that he had to ask. "It's practically crying out for a little color. Oh, look, they've got some vases on sale."

"Oh." Drew didn't pursue the question. The living room hadn't said anything to him about needing color. In fact, none of the rooms had spoken to him at all.

WITHIN A WEEK, Kate had transformed the empty house into a home. The heavy curtains had been drawn back from the multipaned windows. There were vases filled with flowers in every room. The pillows had been tossed on the sofa, lightening the rather gloomy tweed fabric. Kate's quilting had taken up permanent residence in one corner of the small living room, adding bright colors and soft textures. The atmosphere was warm, cozy and welcoming.

Though he'd watched the transformation, even gone with Kate when she'd bought the pillows, Drew still found it hard to believe the change. Just as she'd done in the motels where they'd stayed, she'd somehow managed to turn a house into a home. It wasn't just the pillows or opening the curtains or rearranging the furniture. It was a subtle difference in the atmosphere, as though a gentle wind had blown through, sweeping away the staleness of the empty house and leaving something warm and vibrant in its place.

The change made him uncomfortable. Or maybe it was that it made him *too* comfortable. He found himself wanting to sink down on the sofa, pile the pillows behind his back, stretch his legs out and drowse the afternoon away. He had to remind himself that this was a job, not a vacation. The fact that he needed such a reminder annoyed him.

And the fact that Kate Sloane was creeping into his thoughts in a way that had nothing to do with her being a part of his job annoyed him even more.

"WHAT ARE YOU DOING?"

Kate looked over her shoulder, careful not to move suddenly lest she lose her precarious balance on the chair.

"I'm measuring for curtains."

"What for?" Drew frowned at the window over the sink, seeing nothing wrong with the blinds that were there.

"Because the window needs something to soften it. The

blinds are too hard by themselves.'' She turned back to the window, leaning forward to reach the window.

Drew's frown deepened as the movement tightened her jeans over her derriere. He curled his fingers into his palms, trying to ignore the urge to set his hands on those soft curves.

Kate was vividly aware of Drew standing behind her, watching her. The knowledge made her fingers tremble and her knees feel slightly rubbery. A ridiculous reaction, she scolded herself. Other than her value to him as a witness, Drew Hunter probably didn't even know she was alive.

Exasperated with herself, Kate leaned toward the window, her movements quick as she sought to distract herself from her thoughts. She gasped as the chair shifted beneath her, edging backward slightly. It couldn't have moved more than an inch, but it was enough to make her grab for the edge of the counter, her heart bumping with sudden fright.

An instant later, her heart bumped again, not exactly with fright as she felt Drew's hands close over her hips. The firm grip steadied her balance even as it unraveled her nerves.

''You're going to get yourself killed if you don't look out.''

''Wouldn't it be funny if you brought me all this way to keep me safe, only to have me break my neck measuring a window?'' Since Drew showed no signs of releasing her as long as she was perched on the chair and the feel of his hands was too disturbing to ignore, Kate stepped down and turned to look at him.

''I don't know why you're doing all this work, anyway. This isn't your home. It's just a place you're staying for a little while.''

''I spent most of my childhood in places where I was just 'staying for a little while.''' Her full mouth curved in a smile of slightly sad remembrance. ''It sometimes seemed like my mother and I moved on a daily basis. I learned to make homes wherever we stopped, even if it was only for a few days. To put down a few roots.''

''Why put down roots if you know they're going to be yanked up?'' Drew asked, thinking of his own unsettled childhood and how he'd learned never to allow roots to grow, never to give in to the urge to think of any place as home.

''You can't survive without roots,'' Kate said softly, her eyes searching.

''Better to keep them inside yourself, then,'' he said, his voice harsher than he'd intended.

''Is that what you do? Try to keep them all inside?'' Kate's expression was thoughtful as she considered the idea. She shook her head slowly. ''It sounds very lonely, I think.''

''It's a lot more comfortable,'' Drew snapped, aware that she'd touched a nerve. ''Here, if you're determined to put up new curtains, let me do the measuring.''

Kate wrote down the measurements he gave her, but her thoughts weren't on the curtains anymore. She was wondering what had happened in his life to make him guard himself so carefully, holding everything inside.

''Let me know when you want to go get the curtains,'' he said as he stepped down from the chair. ''Remember, you're not to go out alone.''

''I remember.'' Though she thought the precaution unnecessary since she couldn't see how Lester Davis could have tracked her this far, Kate didn't argue. It was Drew's job to protect her. She'd accept his judgment on how to go about it.

When the measurements were complete, Drew set down the measuring tape and started to leave. He hesitated in the doorway and turned back to her, looking at her with an unreadable expression. Warning? Concern? Impatience?

''This isn't real, Kate. Don't lose sight of that.''

''I won't.''

She hoped Drew accepted her reassurance. She wasn't sure she believed it herself. The past few days, it had been incredibly easy to forget the reason she was here. Los Angeles and Lester Davis and the possibility of testifying seemed a very long way away.

Kate turned and leaned her arms on the counter as she looked out the window at the backyard. How many times had she fantasized about having a house like this in a peaceful little town, with a window over the kitchen sink that looked out on a view of flower beds and sweet, green grass?

During all the many moves she and her mother had made, they'd lived in houses only a time or two. Mostly Belinda had preferred apartments. Less upkeep, less to leave behind, she'd say when the question of a house came up. Kate had accepted her decision, just as she'd accepted all her mother's decisions. But in her heart, she'd dreamed of a time when she'd stay in one place for more than a few months, a place where she'd put down strong, solid roots that wouldn't be torn loose by someone else's restless urge to travel.

A house that looked something like this one. There was even the white picket fence of her childish fantasies, she thought ruefully. How could she help but fall just a little in love with the place?

And the man who shared it with her?

She winced away from that question, afraid to look at it too directly. As Drew had pointed out, this was all pretend. It wouldn't do to forget that. It was one thing to play at keeping house, but she couldn't afford to lose sight of reality. And the reality was that Drew was here to protect her and he was only doing that because it was his job, because he had a personal stake in seeing that she lived to testify.

This isn't real, Kate.

She closed her eyes as she heard the echo of his warning. No, it wasn't real, but she was very much afraid that she was starting to wish it were.

BY THE END of a week and a half, Drew was starting to feel like a tiger in a ruffle-trimmed cage.

There'd been no word from Lavery. No word about how long it might be before Drew could return Kate Sloane to L.A. and get out of her life. And the disturbing thing was that, deep down, he was afraid that he wasn't in as much of a hurry to do that as he should have been.

A month ago, if someone had suggested that he could spend more than an hour in a town with only one main street, sharing a house with a woman he didn't know, living like a typical, suburban husband and that he wouldn't be climbing the walls with boredom, Drew would have told them that they were crazy.

But here he was, and it wasn't boredom that had him climbing the walls. He only wished it were.

He stood near the window of the room that had been set aside as his office. Since he was supposed to be writing a book, a computer sat squarely in the middle of the desk. He turned it on when he came into the room, but the only time he touched the keyboard was to play solitaire or blackjack. Most of the hours he was in the room were spent reading.

Or simply avoiding Kate.

And that was a hell of a thing to admit. He was a grown man, an experienced police officer, and he was all but barricading himself in a ten-by-ten room to avoid spending time with the witness he was protecting. And it wasn't even because he disliked her company. If that had been the reason, he would have shrugged it off as a part of the job. The problem was that he found himself wanting to seek out her company, looking for reasons to talk to her, to see her. And that scared the hell out of him.

He stared out the window at the slender figure kneeling next to one of the neglected rosebushes. What was it about her? He'd known women more beautiful, more sophisticated.

None of them had lingered in his thoughts past the moment he left their company.

Kate braced one hand in the dirt and stretched forward, reaching for a weed that was trying to hide behind the rose. The movement made her T-shirt ride up, baring a palm's width of pale skin between waistband and hem. If he were really her husband, he'd have every right to go out there and put his hand on that innocently exposed skin. He could slide his fingers beneath her shirt, exploring the length of her spine. She'd arch into his touch like a sleek little cat, turning her head to look at him, her eyes all green and hungry. They'd come into the house and...

Aware that his jeans were suddenly much too tight, Drew cursed and spun away from the window. What the hell was the matter with him? Standing here, fantasizing about the woman he was supposed to be protecting. She should be nothing more than a package to him, no different than if he were protecting a valuable statue.

So what if her eyes crinkled at the corners when she smiled. What difference did it make that she created a home wherever she went. If he'd wanted a home, he'd have stayed married, right? He'd have been willing to give up his job if that's what it took to make Diane happy. If there was one thing he'd learned from his childhood, it was that there were few things more ephemeral, more easily taken away, than a home.

Drawn against his will, Drew turned back to the window. Kate was sitting back on her heels, holding out her hand to the scruffy gray cat who lived next door. At least, he lived next door now. Kate had found the cat when they went out to buy some food one day. He'd been scrounging through a trash can and her heart had immediately gone out to him.

Remembering the incident with the dog, Drew hadn't wasted his breath arguing with her when she'd said that the cat was coming home with them—she'd find him a home.

And she had. Since Jane Dumont and her family had two large dogs, Kate had introduced herself to the elderly man who lived on the other side of them and suggested that he might like to adopt a cat.

Remembering the old man's surprised expression, Drew felt his mouth curve.

"I've never had a pet," he'd told her in the tone of someone who was quite content to continue that way.

"Oh, how sad." Kate's eyes filled with quick tears. "Then you'll be so glad to have Sammy." She thrust the huge gray cat into his arms. "He'll be such a wonderful companion."

Drew, who'd been standing on the sidelines, waited to see the big tom prove his companionable nature by clawing his new owner. To his surprise, Sammy, who must have been smarter than he looked, immediately rubbed his scarred head against the old man's hand and began purring loudly.

"He knows he's going to be happy with you," Kate said happily.

"But, I..." Mr. Waterman looked down at the cat as if he wasn't sure how he'd come to be holding it. "I don't know what to do with a cat," he said plaintively.

"Oh, cats practically take care of themselves. We bought a litter pan and some litter and a bag of food and a cat dish for him."

Drew set the bag containing those items on the porch and gave Mr. Waterman a sympathetic look. The man was doomed. There was no way he wasn't taking the cat. Between them, Kate and Sammy had him beat.

"I don't know, Mrs. Ralston. I've never had a pet." Sammy butted his chin against the old man's hand, who automatically began scratching behind one torn ear.

"Sammy will let you know what he needs," Kate said. She reached out to give Sammy a pat on the head. Sammy turned his big yellow eyes on her and blinked indifferently. He obviously understood which side his future bread was buttered on. He began to knead his paws against Mr. Waterman's arm. "See, he loves you already."

"Well, I suppose a cat… They're not a great deal of trouble, after all." He was going down for the third time, still floundering but sinking rapidly. "It's not as if it were a dog."

Drew didn't doubt that Kate could have persuaded him to take in a full-grown Great Dane if she'd decided that they were made for each other.

"Maybe he would make a nice companion," he said weakly, giving up the battle.

"He'll be a wonderful companion, Mr. Waterman. I thought of you as soon as I saw him."

Drew wondered what it was in the battle-scarred gray tom that had reminded her of the neat-as-a-pin retired bank clerk, but he decided it was better not to ask.

"Yes, well, thank you, Mrs. Ralston." He still looked faintly surprised by his agreement.

He didn't seem to regret the decision. Several times since then, Drew had seen him sitting on the front porch, the gray cat settled on his lap, looking quite content.

Kate's fingers stroked over the gray fur, less tattered looking than it had been a week ago. The cat leaned into her hand, and Drew found himself envying the animal his freedom to enjoy Kate's touch.

He realized the direction his thoughts were heading and spun away from the window, his dark brows hooking together in a frown. "You're losing it, Hunter. You're jealous of a cat, for God's sake! And you're talking to yourself."

He thrust his fingers through his hair and glared at the silent telephone. "When are you going to call, Lavery?"

But there was a part of him that didn't want Lavery to call because it would mean an end to the pretend world in which they were living. The thought was enough to send him out of the den and then out of the house.

It was a beautiful day, full of sunshine and singing birds. Drew paused on the edge of the front porch, glaring at the blue sky and the bright splash of poppies that grew near the corner of the house. If Norman Rockwell had been a Californian, he probably would have painted Hayfield. All pretty houses and neat lawns and flower beds.

Where was concrete and smog when you needed it? Drew wondered sourly. Still frowning, he strode down the walkway and turned onto the sidewalk. He needed to get away for a while, even if it was only for a few minutes. He was spending too much time sitting in his "office" with nothing to do but think. Too much thinking could be hazardous.

"Hi, Mr. Ralston."

Drew slowed his stride and smiled at the teenager, slipping instantly into the skin of history teacher-budding writer-friendly neighbor. Kenny Dumont was almost fifteen and at a stage in his growth where he seemed to be all arms and legs.

"Hi, Kenny. No school today?"

"Nah. Some kinda teachers' conference." As he spoke, he continued to absently bounce the basketball he held, the thunk of leather hitting the concrete drive punctuating his speech.

"Great weather for a day off," Drew commented, preparing to move on.

"Yeah. 'Cept Mom won't let me have anybody over cause I ditched a test last week. One dumb old math test and I'm grounded for a week." It was obvious that he thought the punishment much too harsh for the crime. He slanted Drew a look of blended defiance and guilt. "I guess you think that kind of thing is important, huh? Bein' a teacher and all."

"Actually, math was my worst subject," Drew admitted. "I ditched a test or two myself."

"Yeah?" Kenny brightened. "And you graduated, right?"

"Yes. But I spent a couple of years in summer school to

do it. And it's a lot tougher to get into college these days than it was twenty years ago. You need to keep your grades up.''

"That's what Mom and Dad keep telling me," Kenny said, his tone glum. Clearly he was disappointed to have their point of view corroborated.

"I hate to say it, but they're right." Drew tried to sound properly regretful, forcing the amusement from his voice.

"You play basketball?" Kenny apparently decided to abandon the unsatisfactory topic of school.

"In high school."

"You want to play a little one-on-one?" The boy's voice was both uncertain and hopeful.

Drew opened his mouth to refuse politely. "Won't your mom object? You're grounded, right?"

"She won't mind. She just doesn't want me seeing my friends."

And since he wasn't a friend, it had to be all right, Drew thought, amused. Not that he was going to play basketball with the kid, of course. He was in no mood for company. Especially not fourteen-year-old-kid company. He just wanted to take a brisk walk and get his thoughts in order.

"I haven't played in a long time," he said.

"That's okay. I'll go easy on you." There was brash challenge in Kenny's grin, his dark eyes sparkling with anticipation.

Of course, he wasn't going to accept that challenge. He'd smile and refuse. Playing basketball with the neighbor's kid was hardly essential to maintaining his cover. Which didn't explain how he came to be walking up the driveway. Or the rush of pure competition he felt when Kenny thrust the ball into his hands.

"Since you're an old dude, I'll give you first shot."

"You may live to regret that," Drew said, grinning recklessly.

ALMOST AN HOUR LATER, Drew pushed open the front door and stepped into the cool interior of the house. He was hot, sweaty and exhausted. And for the first time in weeks, completely relaxed. He rolled his shoulders, enjoying the pull of overworked muscles.

He'd forgotten how much energy it took to play basketball. And what Kenny lacked in experience was more than compensated for by his youth. Had *he* ever had that much energy, Drew wondered, his mouth curving in a half smile. The kid had run him ragged. It had taken every bit of half-forgotten skill he'd ever had to manage to hold his own. He'd done it, but he had a feeling that his muscles were going to punish him for it tomorrow. At least he no longer felt as if he were going to explode.

He started away from the door and stopped abruptly, his eyes meeting Kate's. Coming in from the bright sunlight, he hadn't seen her standing in the hallway just a few feet away, a glass of ice tea in her hand.

KATE HAD STOPPED, startled by his abrupt entrance. Out the window, she'd seen him playing basketball with Kenny. She'd stood there, mesmerized by the quick movements of his body, watching the play of muscles under his thin T-shirt. It had taken a considerable exercise of will to force herself to turn away from the window and go back to her gardening.

It had taken even more willpower to stay away from that same window when she came in again. Now she wished she'd given in to temptation. At least then she wouldn't have been so completely unprepared to come face-to-face with him.

Their eyes met and then Kate's dropped to his bare chest. He must have taken his T-shirt off partway through the game and now it dangled from his hand. It wasn't the first time she'd seen his chest. Certainly when he'd burst out of the motel bathroom to save her from the pizza boy, he'd been wearing less. It wasn't as if she hadn't seen him before, she reminded herself.

But that didn't prevent her mouth from going dry or the sudden increase of her pulse. Her fingers tightened around the icy glass. She wanted to cross the few feet that separated them and lay her palms against that mat of black hair and feel the muscles beneath. The strength of the urge was almost frightening and she jerked her eyes upward, staring at Drew's face.

Drew read the hunger in her gaze and felt his whole body tighten in reaction. All the tension he'd thought worked off by the basketball game was suddenly back, increased tenfold. It was one thing to know he wanted Kate. He was accustomed to suppressing his own needs and desires. But to see his own hunger reflected in her eyes...

His hand tightened over the T-shirt as sexual tension became an almost living, breathing presence between them. He had only to cover the short distance that separated them and pull her into his arms and she wouldn't offer even a whisper of protest.

He knew it.

She knew it.

What was worse, she wanted him to do just that. He could read it in her eyes. And God knew, she couldn't want it any more than he did.

So why not do it? The small, sly voice whispered in his mind, nudging him toward what could only be disaster.

With a mutter that could have been either curse or greeting, Drew moved away from the door. Kate caught her breath and braced herself for his touch, knowing she should push him away.

Knowing she'd pull him closer.

But he brushed past her, striding down the hall and disappearing into his bedroom, the door shutting with a decisive click behind him.

For a moment, she stood exactly where she was, feeling her knees tremble. She closed her eyes, wanting to believe that what she felt was relief.

And knowing it was disappointment.

Chapter Six

Neither Drew nor Kate mentioned the incident in the hallway. After all, there was really nothing to talk about, right? They hadn't spoken, hadn't touched, hadn't done anything out of the ordinary. So they'd exchanged a glance. And it had seemed, for a moment, as if that glance contained enough heat to melt paint off the walls.

But it had probably been her imagination, Kate told herself.

He was spending too much time thinking, Drew thought. He was starting to imagine things.

They were scrupulously polite. And each was careful to spend as little time as possible with the other.

Drew spent an hour or so most afternoons playing basketball with Kenny, telling himself that he was doing it because he wanted to keep in shape, because it strengthened his injured leg. It had nothing to do with the need to work off tension.

Kate spent a lot of time in the garden and she was extremely careful to avoid the entryway when there was any chance that Drew might be coming in after playing ball, his shirt off, his torso sun warmed and damp with sweat. Not that she cared what his torso looked like, she told herself. She'd barely even noticed it.

If there was any attraction between them at all, it was just a case of propinquity or familiarity breeding lust. That's all it could possibly be. That's all she'd *let* it be.

IT WAS TWO DAYS after the nonincident in the hallway that Kate didn't get up for breakfast. Since she hadn't been kidding when she'd told him she was a morning person, Drew was surprised to find the kitchen empty when he wandered out for a cup of coffee.

He added water and coffee to the coffeemaker, sure that Kate would come stumbling out any minute, surprised that the coffee wasn't already made since she usually made it. It was about the only thing he could safely let her do in the kitchen. She might be a whiz at sewing and gardening, but she was the worst cook he'd ever seen.

As much out of self-defense as out of desire for a fair division of labor, the cooking had become his job. In a way, she'd chosen him for it that first night, when she'd told him to cook dinner in her apartment. The memory made Drew smile, remembering his annoyance at her peremptory order.

Kate still hadn't appeared by the time the coffee was ready. Drew poured himself a cup and sipped it, savoring the silence. It was so peaceful without Kate's usual morning chatter. Nothing to hear but the birds perched in the old maple outside the back door.

Drew took another sip of coffee and frowned out the window at the early-spring morning. It was nice to be up like this, alone. In the quiet. He could drink his coffee in peace for a change. It felt great. Really, really great.

He glanced over his shoulder, his ears tuned for any sound from the direction of Kate's room. But there was nothing. Just the silence. That wonderful silence. The silence that was beginning to feel downright oppressive, he admitted.

Setting his cup on the counter, Drew left the kitchen. The fact was, he'd gotten used to her talking his ear off every morning. It didn't matter what she said. It didn't even really matter if he listened. He was just used to the sound of her voice. Later, he'd think about what a bad sign *that* was. At the moment, he wanted to make sure she was all right.

He stood outside her bedroom door for a moment, listening. If she was sleeping in, he was going to look like an idiot if he woke her. On the other hand, if something had happened to her...

Like what, Hunter?

Like she could have fallen and hurt herself.

So badly that she couldn't even call for help?

It was possible.

God, now he was starting to carry on arguments with himself! Next thing he knew, he'd start *losing* the argument.

This assignment was going to be the death of him. Or at least the death of his sanity. Drew thrust his fingers through his hair and glared at the blank door. He'd just about talked himself into going back to his coffee when he heard Kate cough.

He tapped on the door. "Kate?"

"Go away."

She sounded...odd.

"Are you okay?"

"I'm fine." She didn't sound fine. Drew hesitated. He could just take her word for it and go away as she'd told him to. But she didn't sound right. She didn't sound like Kate. On the other hand, what could be wrong? He'd checked the house out and installed his own simple but effective security system. There was no way someone could have gotten in to hold her hostage in her bedroom.

Still frowning, he turned away from the door. Maybe she just felt like being alone. It was his job to protect her, not to interpret her moods.

He'd taken only a step or two when there was a solid crash from the room behind him, followed by a muffled string of words that didn't bear repeating. He turned back, setting one palm flat against the door, the fingers of the other circling the knob.

"Kate? What's wrong?"

"Nothing. Go away." The command was somewhat weakened by the fit of coughing that ended it.

"You sound like hell. I'm coming in." Without giving her time to argue any further, he pushed open the door and stepped inside.

It was the first time he'd been in the room since the day they'd arrived. It had been bad enough to know that she was sleeping just a few feet down the hallway without being able to picture exactly what the room looked like.

Like the rest of the house, Kate's bedroom had a feeling of having been lived in, of being a home. Maybe it was the glass eyes of the small teddy bear that stared at him from the dresser or the casual way she'd looped the curtains back, framing the sunny green vista of the backyard. Maybe it was the jeans draped over the foot of the bed or the tennis shoes that sat next to the closet, their toes at crazy angles to each other.

It was nothing and everything. It was Kate. It was what drew him to her even as his instincts said he should back away. But at the moment, he was less interested in the decor than he was in the room's occupant.

Kate sat in the middle of the bed, her pillows a rumpled mound behind her, her hair a tangled mass on her shoulders, her face flushed with annoyance. On the floor beside the bed was a plastic pitcher, a broken glass and a damp spot on the carpet that was, presumably, the contents of the glass.

"What happened?"

"I dropped a glass," she snapped. "Is that illegal?"

"No." Drew's brows lifted at her uncharacteristic grouchiness. "I'll clean up the glass before you step on it."

"I can do that." But he was already beside the bed, crouching down to pick up the pieces of broken glass.

Kate watched in silence, pulling the covers closer around her shoulders. He stood and tossed the glass into the trash.

"I'll get the vacuum."

"Don't worry about it."

"There are bound to be glass chips in the carpet."

"I doubt the carpet minds."

Drew didn't bother to comment but left, returning a moment later with the vacuum. Kate didn't speak again until he'd vacuumed the area to his satisfaction and reached down to turn off the machine. The silence it left behind seemed painfully loud.

Kate sniffled discreetly into a tissue, hoping Drew was too busy winding the cord into place to notice.

"Thank you," she said when he straightened and looked at her. She tried to look dignified, which wasn't easy when she was sitting in bed, her hair uncombed, and wearing a red football jersey with a white number one emblazoned across the chest.

"I appreciate the help." She hoped he'd take the words as dismissal and go away, leaving her to suffer in private. The last thing she wanted was to have him standing there, looking at her with those pale blue eyes that seemed capable of seeing right through her.

The silence stretched and she shifted uneasily, wishing she could get up and stalk into the bathroom, dignity intact. Unfortunately the football jersey barely covered her thighs and she wasn't entirely sure her knees could be depended on to support her for a casual stroll, let alone a proper walk. She settled for lifting her chin an inch and doing her best to look impatient.

"You look like hell," Drew said bluntly, destroying her faint hope that the light was dim enough to conceal her red nose.

"Thank you." The intended sarcasm was somewhat muffled by the sneeze that forced her to bury her nose in a tissue.

The first sneeze was followed by two more in quick succession, and by the time the fit had ended Kate was incapable of offering more than a weak glare in his direction as she leaned back against the pillows.

"How long have you been sick?" Drew asked, looking less than sympathetic.

"I started feeling it yesterday afternoon. But I'm not really sick." She proved the statement by coughing.

"You should have gone to bed as soon as you started feeling bad."

"I wanted to finish planting the flowers Jane gave us," she muttered.

"Why? We're probably not even going to be here to see the damn things bloom." His tone was sharper than he'd intended, edged by concern.

"I couldn't leave them in those pots. They were suffocating."

"Fine. And you're sick."

"I'm not sick because of the plants," she snapped, feeling her eyes sting with the threat of tears. She blinked rapidly, annoyed by her own weakness.

"I didn't mean to snarl," Drew said, his tone gentling. Illogically Kate felt even more like crying.

"I'm sorry I snapped," she offered in return, hoping he'd attribute her watery eyes to the cold.

"You're flushed." He reached out to put his hand on her forehead and the feel of his cool touch on her hot skin made Kate want to cry again. "You feel warm."

"I feel like hell," she said, finding a certain relief in admitting it.

"Maybe you should see a doctor." He let his hand fall to his side and frowned down at her.

"It's just a cold." He continued to frown and Kate drew the covers higher over her shoulders, huddling under them.

"Don't worry, Drew. I'm not going to die before you get me to court."

"That wasn't what I was thinking of," he said stiffly and Kate was immediately ashamed of her peevishness.

"I know. I'm sorry." She reached out and caught his hand when he started to step away. "Colds always make me crabby."

He hesitated a moment and then his hand relaxed in hers, his mouth curving in a faint smile. "Like mornings make me?"

A stuffy head and a fever were not enough to completely muffle the effect of that smile. Kate felt her heart bump against her breastbone and hoped he'd attribute her sudden flush to her cold.

THERE WAS, DREW SOON discovered, no way to nurse someone through a cold and still maintain your distance from them. If Kate had simply developed a sniffle, he could have offered his sympathy and stayed out of her way. But she quickly developed enough symptoms to qualify for a cold-tablet commercial.

It wasn't that she asked for help. Far from it. But it would have taken a harder heart than his own to simply ignore her misery. And if the thought strayed in that he couldn't ignore Kate, with or without a cold, Drew pushed it aside. He was just doing his job. Okay, so his job description didn't exactly say anything about making chicken soup and squeezing oranges, but he *was* supposed to take care of her.

For Kate's part, she was just grateful for the hot soup, cold juice and unending supply of tissues. Who would have thought that Drew Hunter—Mr. Taciturn himself—would turn out to make such a mean bowl of soup? When she commented on it, he shrugged.

"Your taste buds aren't at their best," he pointed out. "I

don't think you'd qualify as a discerning critic, at the moment.''

But she thought he looked pleased and she found that small touch of vanity oddly endearing, evidence that he was human, no matter how much he tried to conceal the fact. Not that she'd had any real doubts about his humanity. It was just that her illness was providing more proof of it. In fact, it might almost be possible to enjoy being sick just for the pleasure of having Drew hover over her.

"BOARDWALK! OH, NO." Kenny's voice descended into something perilously close to a whine. "Come on, Kate. You could let me off the hook, just this one time, couldn't you? You don't need the money," he pointed out, looking at the stacks of colorful bills in front of her.

"It's the principle of the thing," Kate told him. "If I let you off this time, what about the next time? And what do I tell my other tenants?" She gave him a look that managed to contain both impossible virtue and out-and-out greed. "Pay up."

Kenny looked at Drew, but he could only offer a sympathetic shrug as he reached for the dice to take his own turn. He'd never have believed that sweet, sympathetic Kate would turn out to have the soul of a Wall Street banker when it came to Monopoly. The woman had a talent for buying property and hanging on to it, not to mention the luck of the devil.

He shook the dice absently in one hand as he watched her transact her business with Kenny. It was a good thing she'd nearly cleaned both him and Kenny out, he thought. This was her first full day out of bed and she was starting to look a little pale. It had taken a week to get her to this point. He didn't want her staying up much longer and risking a relapse.

It struck him suddenly that he was thinking very much like a husband. He frowned down at the meager stack of play money in front of him. It was his job, of course. He was supposed to take care of her, to make sure that she was safe and well. But there were moments lately when he suspected that his feelings for Kate weren't as strictly professional as he'd have liked.

"Are you trying to shake the spots off?" Kate's polite inquiry brought Drew's eyes up and made him realize that he was still shaking the dice.

"I'm thinking about my next move," he told her coolly before tossing the dice onto the board. Six spots stared up at him.

"Oooh, good move! Marvin Gardens with two hotels." Kate's voice dripped with gleeful avarice. "Let's see how much you owe me."

Drew exchanged a long-suffering look with Kenny. "She's been sick," Kenny said, shaking his head sadly. "That's why we gotta let her win."

"Let me win? Ha! You just can't admit that you've been beaten by superior skill." She stared down her nose at them, looking so adorably smug that Drew had the sudden urge to lean across the table and kiss her. But he supposed that would embarrass Kenny so he settled for reaching out to tug a lock of silky hair.

"Pride goes before a fall," he warned her.

"It's not pride. It's simply an unbiased assessment of my superior Monopoly-playing ability." Her expression was so exaggeratedly haughty that Drew couldn't repress a grin. Damn, she was cute.

It was only much later that it occurred to him that, for a few minutes, he'd completely forgotten that this was all a game of pretend, that he and Kate weren't really husband and wife.

The doorbell rang just as Kate announced the outrageous rental fee that Drew owed her.

"Probably my mom," Kenny said, glancing over his

shoulder with a hunted look. "I told her I'd take out the trash. Tell her I'll be home in a few minutes, would you?" He gave Drew a pleading look. "Kate's bound to land on one of my properties this time around."

"I'll tell her." Drew pushed back his chair and stood, choosing not to point out that Baltic Avenue with one house was hardly likely to make a dent in the fortune Kate had amassed. "Pay her for me, would you?" He shoved his small stack of bills in Kenny's direction and went to answer the door.

Behind him, he could hear Kenny arguing that her rent was excessive and asking had she ever heard of the term "slum lord." He shook his head. The kid was probably going to make a hell of a lawyer some day. He was still smiling as he pulled open the door, expecting to see Jane's exasperated face.

But it wasn't Jane. The man standing on the porch was about Drew's height but outweighed him by fifty pounds. His round features and the shock of curling red hair that was starting to inch its way back from his forehead gave him a look of friendly innocence. He looked as if he should be growing wheat somewhere in Kansas or running a café named Mom's. What he didn't look like was a cop, which was part of what made him a good one.

Drew's smile vanished as if it had never existed, the lingering warmth fading from his eyes, leaving them glacial blue.

"Murphy." There was no welcome in the greeting. Just flat acknowledgment.

"Ralston." The other man's round face split in a grin as he thrust out his hand. "Hope you don't mind me dropping by like this. I was in the area and remembered this was where you'd said you were going to be staying while you were writing your great American novel. Thought you might welcome a little news from your old stomping grounds."

Drew took his hand, forcing a smile that didn't even approach his eyes. If anyone happened to be watching, it would simply look like two old acquaintances greeting each other. In a way that's exactly what they were. He'd never worked directly with Dave Murphy, but he knew him by reputation. His reputation was that he was a good cop, one who couldn't be bought at any price.

He wasn't surprised that Lavery had chosen Murphy to act as contact. What did surprise him was the fierce wave of resentment he felt at the other man's presence. But now was not the time to analyze that resentment.

"Come in." He stepped back to let Murphy enter the hallway.

"Nice little place you got here," Murphy said.

"Yes." Drew's flat response was not encouraging. "We can talk in my office." But to get to the office, they had to pass the living room and it would look odd if he didn't stop.

"I don't think you've met my wife," he said as they stopped in the doorway. Later he'd consider how easily the words "my wife" had come to him. "And this is our neighbor's son, Kenny. This is Dave Murphy, Kate. An old colleague of mine."

Kenny acknowledged the introduction and returned his attention to the Monopoly board, his expression glum. Kate rose, her eyes fixed on Drew, holding both fear and questions. She didn't know Murphy, of course, but she knew, as Kenny didn't, that a "colleague" of Drew's was not a history teacher.

"You'll have to finish without me," Drew said with a tight smile.

"Of course." Kate's smile was tense around the edges, her eyes anxious as she watched them leave. Drew wanted to offer her reassurance, but he had none to give.

"Never thought I'd see Drew Hunter playing Monopoly," Murphy said as soon as the door of the den shut behind them.

"Why did Lavery send you?" Drew asked, ignoring the comment. Stopping in front of the desk, he turned to look at Murphy.

Murphy's brows rose slightly at Drew's abrupt tone, but he chose not to comment. Without waiting for an invitation—perhaps sensing that it wouldn't be forthcoming—he settled himself in the room's one chair.

"Since I was heading this way to go fishing at my brother's place in Oregon, Lavery figured there'd be no reason for anyone to question my going. He asked me to stop by and update you."

"And…" Drew saw no reason to conceal his impatience.

"And Davis is looking for her." He jerked his head in the direction of the living room.

Though it was no more than he'd been expecting, Drew felt the words strike him with the force of a physical blow. "How long?"

Murphy shrugged. "Since right after you left. He was suspicious, and when she disappeared he must have figured she had a reason."

"What does he know?"

"Not much. Just that she's gone. Since Lavery spirited you off like this, there isn't much Davis *can* know. Rumor is, the lieutenant has taken a lot of heat on this one."

"He can handle it." Drew wasn't worried about Lavery. He'd known what he was doing when he set this up, and even if it ended up costing him his job, he wouldn't cave in to pressure from above to reveal their whereabouts. The man was pure steel.

"There ain't much he can't handle," Murphy agreed. "He wants you to stay put. Says you're not to call in unless it's an emergency and that he'll be in touch when they're ready for you to bring the witness back to L.A."

Drew was surprised by the flash of annoyance he felt at

hearing Kate called "the witness." She was a person, dammit, not a chess piece.

"Never thought I'd see you playing Monopoly," Murphy said again. He studied Drew as if seeing him for the first time. "Domesticity seems to suit you, Hunter."

"It's all part of the cover," Drew said, his tone repressive. The fact was that playing Monopoly with the neighbors' son could hardly be labeled an essential part of maintaining their cover. They could simply have established themselves as a couple with little interest in neighborly relations.

Or they could have if Kate hadn't been the kind of person she was. Drew doubted that she could be reserved if her life depended on it. *And it very well might,* he thought grimly.

MURPHY DIDN'T STAY long. Having delivered the message that Lavery wanted Drew and Kate to continue as they were until he contacted them, he made his departure, continuing on his trip to Oregon. The side journey had cost him so little time that, even if someone were to be around to note his arrival at his brother's fishing shack, they'd have no reason to think he might have made a detour.

The house was quiet when the two men left the den. The Monopoly game had been returned to its box and Kenny had gone home, presumably to attend to the trash he'd neglected earlier. Kate was not in sight, but Drew knew she must be wondering what Murphy had said, wondering what his arrival might mean to her future.

Drew shut the door behind the other man, but didn't immediately go in search of her. He stood in the hallway for a minute, trying to sort out his own tangled thoughts.

He'd nearly managed to forget the reason he was here, he thought. He'd been sitting there, playing silly games and, for a little while, the pretend had seemed like reality. Before Murphy showed up, he hadn't been thinking like a cop. He'd been thinking like a history teacher, turned would-be writer, with nothing more to worry about than whether a throw of the dice was going to land a little metal shoe on Boardwalk.

And his first emotion on seeing Murphy hadn't been concern or even question. It had been a stab of bitter resentment at the sudden reminder that the cozy little domestic scene was all pretend.

What the hell was happening to him?

But there was no answer to that question. Or at least none he was willing to accept.

KATE HEARD DREW ENTER the kitchen behind her, but she didn't immediately turn. She wasn't sure she wanted to see his expression, was even less sure she wanted to hear what their visitor had had to say. She continued to stir the milk she was heating for cocoa, watching the swirl of motion as if it demanded every bit of her concentration.

They'd been doing just fine, she thought fiercely, aware that Drew was watching her. Sometimes she didn't even think about why they were here. There'd even been a few moments when it had almost been possible to believe that it was all real.

"Davis is looking for you."

It took a moment for the quiet words to reach her and then the spoon clattered onto the stove top. Kate didn't turn to look at him, staring instead at the droplets of milk, hardly visible against the white enamel. One sentence and her pretend life was suddenly full of cracks.

"Does he know where I am?" She was surprised by the evenness of her voice, surprised to see that her hand was steady as she reached out to pick up a dishcloth.

"No."

"That's good, isn't it?" She wiped the milk from the stove before finally turning to look at him, her features set in a look of calm acceptance.

"It's good." Drew was leaning against the counter, but

Kate could almost feel the tension in him, belying his casual stance.

"Good." She turned back to the stove, staring at the pan of milk without seeing it, trying not to think, trying not to feel.

"If he finds me, he's going to kill me, isn't he?" It was the first time she'd actually said the words out loud.

"He's not going to find you," Drew said roughly.

"But if he did, he'd kill me." It was no longer a question. It was a statement of fact and she heard confirmation in Drew's silence.

Kate reached for the pan of milk and then drew her hand back when she saw that it was no longer steady. Though she'd been living with it for weeks now, the idea that someone actually wanted her dead was nearly impossible to grasp.

"He'd have to go through me to get to you, Kate." Drew's words were intended to reassure, but instead, they conjured up an immediate image of him lying on the ground, life drained from him. And all because of her.

Kate crossed her arms at her waist, feeling a chill that had nothing to do with the temperature of the room. When they'd arrived here, she'd made up her mind to forget the reason she was here, to forget what waited for her in Los Angeles. She'd determined to play the role she'd been given and look neither forward nor back. She'd done such a good job of it that she'd almost managed to forget reality completely.

"I wish I'd never seen those damned files."

Drew said nothing. He couldn't bring himself to agree with her. He'd been trying to bring Davis down for too long. But there was a part of him that wished the same thing, that wished it had been someone else who'd brought them the information they needed. Anyone but Kate.

He was not even conscious that he'd moved until he saw his hands close over her shoulders, felt the softness of her through the cotton of her shirt. She was trembling, an almost imperceptible shiver running over her. Drew felt something hard and tight in his chest, something he couldn't— wouldn't—put a name to.

"You're going to be all right," he said, his voice rough with emotion. He turned her to face him. "You're going to be all right." As if repeating it could make it a fact.

Kate smiled, but he could see the shimmer of tears in her eyes. "It's stupid," she muttered, brushing impatiently at the moisture that threatened to overflow. "It's this dumb cold that's making me weepy. I know you'll take care of me."

She gave him a watery smile that seemed to go straight inside him, causing a funny little ache in his chest.

"Don't cry." Her cheek was petal soft beneath his fingers as he brushed away the last traces of dampness. At his touch, Kate's breathing developed an odd little catch to it.

And suddenly there was a new element in the atmosphere, a new tension that edged its way between them. She looked up at him, her eyes all golden green and full of questions.

Full of need.

Drew didn't know how to answer the questions, but he understood the need. The hunger. It was the same hunger that had been gnawing at him for days. Or was it weeks? Maybe it was all his life. It was a hunger he couldn't define. Or maybe he was afraid to define it. But he knew exactly what it would take to satisfy it.

Kate.

"Don't cry," he said again, hardly aware of speaking, hardly aware of drawing her closer.

Ignoring the small voice of reason that told him he was making a mistake, Drew lowered his head, moving slowly, giving her time to pull back. Time to stop the madness before it started.

But Kate didn't want to stop it. She'd been waiting for this, wanting it forever. It didn't matter that she'd only known Drew a few weeks. She'd been waiting all her life for this moment, this man.

His mouth was warm against hers. The first touch was light, undemanding. A gentle kiss, meant to offer nothing but comfort. It could have stopped there, could have ended with only that small touch. If Kate hadn't reached up to set her hands on his chest. If Drew hadn't drawn her just a fraction closer. If hunger long denied hadn't welled up in both of them.

It was impossible to know whether Drew's mouth hardened over hers, demanding a deeper surrender, or whether Kate's lips opened even before his tongue came out to trace the fullness of her lower lip.

There was nothing tentative in the embrace, no sense that they needed to ease into it, to discover each other's wants and needs. There was too much pent-up hunger for that, too many weeks of wanting and not having, of needing and pretending not to.

Kate's fingers curled against his chest, feeling the solid strength of muscle beneath his shirt. Drew's tongue slid into the welcoming cavern of her mouth, tasting the heat of her response as her tongue twined with his.

His fingers found the elastic band that secured her hair and pulled it loose. Her hair tumbled across his hand like pale brown satin and he buried his fingers in it, cupping the back of her skull, tilting her head so that he could deepen the kiss.

Kate felt as if everything in the world had disappeared but the two of them. The fact that they would never have met if her life hadn't been in danger didn't seem relevant. This was right. This was what she'd been longing for all her life.

She rose up on her toes, fitting her body more closely to the lean planes of his, needing to feel him with every inch of her being. Drew murmured something indistinguishable against her mouth and slid one hand the length of her spine, trailing fire in its wake. When his fingers splayed across her bottom, Kate arched her hips forward and heard him groan with approval as the movement brought her firmly against his rapidly hardening arousal.

His fingers left her hair, dropping to her waist before sliding up to rest against the side of her breast. Kate caught her breath, her body tensing in anticipation, in need. And then his palm was closing over her breast, burning through the fabric of bra and shirt.

She gasped, her head falling back against his shoulder as her knees weakened. Drew's mouth left hers, trailing a string of biting kisses the length of her throat before his tongue came out to taste the pulse that beat at the base.

His thumb stroked over her swollen nipple and Kate shuddered, feeling liquid heat pool in the pit of her stomach. When he reached for the buttons of her shirt, she offered no protest. She'd have unbuttoned it herself, but her fingers were shaking too badly.

The rise of passion had been so sudden, the heat so fierce, that they'd been deeply involved before rational thought had a chance to assert itself. Once past that first moment, neither was interested in rational thought, only in slaking a thirst long denied.

If the milk Kate had been warming hadn't reached the boiling point just as Drew's hand was sliding inside Kate's open shirt, there could be little doubt about where the scene would have ended. In Drew's bed. Or Kate's. Or, at the speed they were moving, maybe they wouldn't even have made it that far.

As it was, it took several seconds for the angry hissing of hot milk on the even hotter burner to penetrate. Drew dragged his mouth from the soft temptation of Kate's skin, resting his forehead on hers, his breathing ragged.

"The milk's boiling over," Kate said after a moment when he made no effort to move farther. To tell the truth, she didn't really care if the house was on fire.

But the moment had been broken and reality was already popping up between them. Drew's hand slid away from her and he absently tugged the edges of her shirt back together. Reaching over her shoulder, he twisted the burner off and the milk subsided back into the pan.

Kate stood in front of him, caught between his broad frame and the stove. She knew she should move away, but she more than half hoped that they might take up where they'd left off.

Drew slanted her a quick look from under his lashes, his expression unreadable. His eyes seemed to linger on her mouth, swollen from his kisses, and Kate held her breath, wanting him to take her in his arms, unable to move the few inches that would have put her there.

And then he was stepping back, putting distance between them. And the room seemed suddenly a great deal cooler. Her face still, she brought her hands up and began sliding buttons into buttonholes. She was pleased to see that her fingers were reasonably steady, though she couldn't imagine how it was possible considering her pulse was still racing.

"That shouldn't have happened." Drew's voice was husky. He looked at her, looked away.

"You were trying to comfort me," Kate said, willing to come to his rescue when he couldn't seem to think of anything else to say. "It's all right, Drew. Things just got a little out of hand for a minute."

"That's an understatement." He shook his head, his expression disbelieving, as if he still couldn't quite absorb what had just happened—what had almost happened.

"Well, no harm done," she said, trying to sound brusque. The truth was, if she hadn't been surreptitiously leaning against the counter, she wasn't at all sure that her knees would have supported her.

"No harm done," he repeated, not looking quite as relieved as she might have expected.

No harm done at all unless you counted the fact that she was very much afraid she was falling in love with him.

Chapter Seven

Since sleep proved elusive, Kate had plenty of time to think about what had happened—what had nearly happened—between her and Drew. In the dark hours just before dawn, she decided that it was an obvious case of propinquity. Nothing more profound than that.

Circumstances had thrown the two of them together and forced them to rely on each other. It was only natural that two young, healthy adults should be attracted to each other. Under normal circumstances, they might have crossed paths, been mildly attracted and gone their separate ways without giving it another thought. But circumstances were far from normal, and the time they'd been forced to spend together had simply blown the attraction all out of proportion.

And her bizarre idea that she might be falling in love with him could be chalked up to the same cause. She'd been frightened, abruptly reminded of her own mortality. Drew was, it seemed, all that stood between her and a rude introduction to that mortality. And for a moment, she'd fancied herself in love with him. Sort of a twist on the Stockholm Syndrome where people fell in love with their captors. Now that she understood it, she could watch that it didn't get out of hand.

Propinquity, plain and simple. Nothing to worry about.

Which was exactly what she'd tell Drew when she saw him.

He'd retreated to his den the night before and hadn't come out until nearly midnight. Kate knew exactly when he'd gone to his room because she'd still been awake and had heard his footsteps go down the hall. She'd also heard them pause outside her door and had held her breath, not sure whether to hope that he continued on his way, or pray that he opened the door and came in.

Now that she'd gotten a handle on the problem, she was glad that her door had stayed shut. Very glad, she told herself, refusing to acknowledge even the smallest pang of doubt.

When Drew stepped into the kitchen, it was their first meeting since their shattering embrace the night before. Kate looked up from the crossword puzzle she'd been staring at for the past thirty minutes, though she hadn't yet filled in a single clue. Their eyes crossed briefly and she felt her heart bump. Nerves, she told herself. It had nothing to do with the ice blue of his eyes or the chiseled line of his jaw.

"Good morning," she said, forcing her voice to sound normal.

"Morning." Drew reached for the coffee she'd made, nodding his thanks as he poured his first cup and sipped the steaming brew. He turned to face her, leaning one hip on the counter.

"I've been doing a lot of thinking," he began.

"So have I," Kate interrupted. "And I know exactly what happened last night."

"You do?" Drew raised one brow. He wasn't sure what he'd expected, but he hadn't been anticipating her cheerful smile. She looked as if nothing had happened. Considering the way he felt, he wasn't at all sure he liked seeing her look so calm.

"I do." She smiled and reached for her coffee, and Drew

found himself unreasonably pleased to see that her hand was not quite steady. So she wasn't as unmoved as she was trying to appear.

"Then maybe you can explain it to me." For some reason, seeing evidence that she was not as cool as she seemed made him feel better.

"Propinquity."

"What?" Drew's brows nearly disappeared in the thick wave of black hair that lay on his forehead.

"Propinquity," Kate said again, her smile determined. "It was almost inevitable, really."

"It was?"

"Well, yes." She shrugged, but he noticed that she was clinging to her coffee cup as if it were a life preserver.

"So you're not upset?" he probed.

"Of course not. There's nothing to be upset about. It was just that there I was. And there you were..."

"And there we were," he finished dryly when she seemed to run out of words.

"Yes. There we were." The memory of just where they'd been seemed to dry up her well of good humor momentarily. Her eyes dropped from his and she swallowed visibly, the color running up her cheeks. But she grabbed determinedly for the explanation she'd decided on.

"It was bound to happen."

"You think so?" Drew kept his tone carefully neutral.

Not that he didn't agree with her. It had been bound to happen. If there was one thing he'd decided during last night's sleeplessness, it was that. From the moment he'd seen her picture, there'd been something drawing him to her, something more than just the fact that she was a part of his job.

"Well, look at the situation. Here we are, the two of us stuck away from everything and everyone, pretending that we're married." Kate shrugged. "It seems obvious that, sooner or later, something like…last night was bound to happen.''

''Probably.'' Drew noticed that she stumbled over finding a description of what had happened between them. Not that he could have done any better. Wildfire? Conflagration? Detonation?

''Well, now that it's happened, we can forget about it.'' She didn't seem as relieved by his apparent agreement as he might have expected. Was there just the faintest trace of disappointment in her eyes?

''So you just want to forget it?'' he asked.

''It seems best, don't you think?'' She got up and went to the sink to rinse her cup. ''It happened and we got through it. Now we can forget about it.''

''Propinquity?'' He sidestepped the issue of forgetting.

''Propinquity,'' she said firmly. She smiled in his general direction, but Drew noticed that her eyes showed a tendency to sheer away from him.

''Hmm.'' She seemed to take the noncommittal murmur for agreement and her smile brightened another notch.

''I'm glad we could talk about it. It's always better to get things out in the open. I read once that almost any problem can be resolved if people just talk about it.''

''Probably true.''

''Yes.'' She hesitated, as if feeling that something more should be said. Drew offered no help, sipping at his cooling coffee and letting the silence stretch.

''Well, I'm going to go make my bed,'' she said at last, sounding as if the task might take all day.

''Thanks for the coffee,'' Drew said, lifting his cup.

''You're welcome.'' There was another brief pause and then she gave him a quick, meaningless smile and beat a hasty retreat.

Drew watched her go, wondering if he should feel guilty that he hadn't made the conversation any easier for her. He reached for the coffeepot and freshened his cup. He wrapped one hand around the warm porcelain, his eyes focused on nothing at all.

Propinquity? He could think of several words that described it better. Hunger. Lust. Need. Any one of them was a better match than propinquity. Only a woman could have come up with such a word, he thought, shaking his head in disgust. No man would dismiss a near explosion like last night's embrace with a namby-pamby word like propinquity.

Still, maybe she was partially right. Maybe what had happened last night was the result of the two of them being thrown together like this. God knew he couldn't think of another acceptable excuse. Not that there *was* an acceptable excuse.

Forgetting that he'd refilled the cup, Drew took a large swallow of coffee, wincing as it scalded the inside of his mouth. But a scalded tongue was the least of his problems. The biggest problem he had at the moment was coming to terms with his own thoroughly unprofessional behavior.

He frowned down into his coffee, his thoughts circling back over the same ground they'd covered repeatedly during the night. He was an officer of the law, assigned to protect a witness. A witness, moreover, who was testifying on a case he had a personal interest in seeing brought to a successful conclusion.

He was supposed to be protecting Kate, not kissing her. If the milk hadn't boiled over when it had, they wouldn't have stopped at kisses. He should have been grateful for the interruption, but he had to admit that gratitude was not what he felt. What he felt was frustration that things hadn't progressed to their natural conclusion.

And *that* was a very bad sign, indeed.

He downed the last of the coffee, hardly noticing the discomfort as it stung his already burned mouth. He was a cop. A good cop. He set the cup down with a thump. He'd been known to bend a rule or two, but only if it helped the system work the way it was meant to. From the day he'd pinned on his badge, he'd never forgotten who and what he was.

Until he met Kate Sloane.

Somehow, with Kate, it was easy to forget that he was a cop first and a man second. Even now, in the clear light of day, when he should have been consumed with guilt, all he could think about was how it had felt to kiss her, the soft, silky weight of her breast in his hand and the eager response she'd given him.

"Damn." He was getting aroused just thinking about it. "Damn, damn, damn."

He was obviously losing his mind. Last night he'd stepped over the line. If he wasn't careful, he was going to step over it again, and this time he might step so far there'd be no getting back. He was simply going to have to keep his distance.

Right. Like you did before.

The jeering mental comment made him wince. But he couldn't change what had already happened. All he could do was make sure it didn't happen again.

No matter how much he wanted it.

FOR THE NEXT few days, Kate and Drew played a game of "let's pretend." They pretended they'd never kissed. They pretended that the attraction wasn't still simmering between them. And most of all they pretended that the kiss and the conclusion it hadn't reached was not the main thing on both their minds.

It occurred to Kate that if Drew had been looking for a way to distract her from her worries about being found by Davis, he certainly couldn't have chosen a more effective method. The knowledge that her former boss was looking for her, most probably planning to kill her, just didn't seem as real and vivid as those few minutes in Drew's arms.

It was starting to sink in that her life wasn't ever going to be the same. No matter what happened at the trial, she wasn't going to be able to go back to her old life. Not just because of a possible threat from Davis, but because she was simply no longer the same person she had been.

It was a frightening thought, and one she wasn't quite ready to examine too closely, not any more than she could bring herself to look closely at her feelings for Drew Hunter. She wanted to—had to—accept her own explanation that she'd momentarily gotten gratitude confused with love. She could not—would not—fall in love with the man.

IF PROPINQUITY was the source of their problems, then the obvious solution would have been to put some distance between them. Unfortunately circumstances dictated otherwise. They were stuck with each other until word came that it was safe to go back to Los Angeles.

Which left only the option of pretending that nothing had changed when, in reality, everything had changed. It was not a comfortable solution. The house, not particularly large to start with, soon began to seem like little more than a hut.

Where before, it hadn't presented too much of a challenge to avoid each other, now it seemed as if every time Kate turned around, she bumped into Drew. And every time she bumped into him, she had to remind herself that the fact that her heart beat faster when he was near was just a result of the situation they were in.

It wasn't really Drew Hunter she was attracted to—it was the fact that he was helping to keep her alive. And the fact that he had eyes the pale blue of a winter sky and shoulders that seemed made for pillowing a woman's head and a mouth that... But those were the sorts of things she wasn't going to think about.

KATE SET TWO SQUARES of fabric together and slid the needle into the beginning of the seam. The late news mumbled from the television in the corner, but she didn't pay much attention to it. Any more than she was paying much attention to her sewing. The fact was, with Drew in the room it was difficult to concentrate on anything.

Since the KISS, which Kate had begun to think of in capital letters, the only time they'd spent together had been while watching the news before going to bed. It had occurred to her that, to anyone looking in the window, they must look like exactly what they were pretending to be—a married couple ending the day in front of the television.

Of course, if they were really married, she wouldn't have found Drew's presence so distracting. She might actually have been able to pay attention to what was on the screen rather than noticing—not for the first time—how good he looked in the faded jeans that hugged his legs. Or how well he filled out the black T-shirt that stretched across his chest.

"Damn!" The exclamation was startled from her as the point of the needle jabbed into her skin. She smiled and shook her head as she met Drew's eyes. Lifting the injured finger to her mouth, she licked away the droplet of blood.

DREW WATCHED AS Kate sucked lightly at the small wound. The television was droning in the background, but he no longer had any idea what the newscaster was saying. He couldn't pull his eyes from the sight of Kate's lips pressed against her finger.

His body tightened with the memory of how those lips had felt against his, with the fantasy of how they'd feel against his skin. He'd spent three days trying to pretend that one kiss had never happened. It seemed the memory only grew more vivid.

He dragged his eyes from her and stared unseeingly at the flickering screen. What the hell had happened to his self-control? He had to be losing his mind to be getting aroused just by the sight of a woman's finger in her mouth.

But the worst part of it was that it wasn't just any woman who made him feel this way. If what he'd experienced had been only generic lust, he would have felt nothing more than a vague annoyance with himself. But he didn't want any woman but Kate Sloane, and that scared the hell out of him.

If he stayed in this room another minute, he wasn't sure he could count on his self-control holding. And next time he kissed her, it was going to take something approaching a nuclear blast to remind him of reality.

He glanced at Kate, ready to offer some banal excuse about retiring early. But Kate's attention was riveted to the television, her hands frozen on the quilt block she'd been sewing.

"The body of Joseph Smithson was discovered in a hotel room in downtown San Francisco yesterday afternoon. Police are unwilling to speculate at this time, but they do admit that the execution-style murder could be the work of organized crime."

There was a picture of a man in the upper right corner of the screen. An ordinary-looking man, slightly balding, a little overweight. Nothing particularly heroic looking about him.

"Smithson was a key witness four years ago in the Gambini murder trial, which resulted in the conviction of two members of the Stephani family. Smithson was..."

Drew snapped off the television. But he knew it was too late. As if he could read her mind, he knew what was going through Kate's head. She didn't need to hear the rest of the story. She didn't need to see Joseph Smithson's picture. It was locked in her brain. An ordinary-looking man who'd done the right thing, testified at a trial and helped convict two murderers.

And now, four years later, he was dead.

There was something chilling about the fact that they

hadn't killed him right away. Somehow the delay seemed particularly cold, as if they'd simply been letting him live a little while, letting him hope that he wasn't going to pay the price for his testimony. Like a cat playing with a mouse.

Kate's face was pale and set, her eyes haunted. Drew let his fingers drop away from the switch, but he continued to stand there, wishing there was something he could say, some reassurance he could offer. He wanted to go to her, take her in his arms and tell her that he'd keep her safe, that he wasn't going to let anything happen to her.

Instead, he stayed where he was, saying nothing, doing nothing.

After a moment, Kate moved. She slid the needle very carefully into the fabric and then set the partially sewn block on the end table beside her chair, arranging the pieces very carefully. She set her thimble just so beside the block and shifted the box of pins a quarter of an inch to bring it into precise alignment with the thimble.

Drew watched her, trying not to notice the faint trembling of her hands, curling his fingers into his palms against the urge to pull her into his arms and hold her until the trembling went away.

"I'm tired now," she said, her voice flat and without expression. "I think I'll go to bed a little early."

She stood and offered him a quick, meaningless smile, her eyes sliding across his face without meeting his.

"Good night."

"Good night, Kate."

He watched her leave, feeling as if he should have said something, done something, offered her some reassurance. But what could he have said? That she wasn't putting herself at risk? That what happened to Joseph Smithson would never happen to her? She'd know the first for a lie, and the second for a promise he couldn't keep.

"Damn." Drew shoved his fingers through his dark hair, feeling frustration churn in the pit of his stomach.

He didn't like what was happening to him. He didn't like the fact that he couldn't seem to maintain any kind of professional distance on this case. He didn't like the fact that the woman who should have been only a witness he was to protect had become a great deal more. He didn't like finding that the control on which he'd always prided himself was not as impervious as he'd thought.

Most of all, he didn't like the ache in the pit of his stomach when he thought about the end of this assignment, when his responsibility for Kate would end and he'd have to walk away from her.

"Damn. Damn. Damn." Repeating it didn't help. He felt all knotted up inside, angry with everything and nothing. He wanted to slam out of the house and run and run until he was too exhausted to think. He wanted to walk down the hall and push open Kate's door and find her waiting for him, eager for his touch, as hungry for him as he was for her.

Drew closed his eyes, feeling his body respond to the mental image of her, her skin like silk under his hands, her hair spread out on the pillow, her body arching upward, her legs shifting restlessly, her eyes almost pure green with hunger. She'd whisper his name.

"Drew."

For a moment, the sound of his name seemed a part of the fantasy in his mind. It wasn't until she spoke again that he realized Kate's voice wasn't in his head.

"Drew."

He spun to face her, grateful that he was standing out of the lamplight, knowing that his arousal would have been obvious if he hadn't been. He felt like a fool, and there was a quick flare of anger that she could do this to him without even being in the room. But the anger vanished, replaced by a rush of hunger almost powerful enough to bring him to his knees.

She'd already changed for bed and was wearing the virginal white nightgown that had haunted more of his dreams than he was willing to admit. The rounded neckline bared her collarbone before the gown dropped softly to her knees. It looked like something out of a Victorian novel, not the kind of thing to fuel a man's fantasies. And he'd never seen anything more arousing in his life.

Until he saw her eyes.

He felt his mouth go dry at the look in them, at the need that reflected his own. She didn't have to say a word for him to know what she was thinking, what she was feeling.

"Go to bed, Kate." His voice was hardly more than a whisper but she heard him.

"Come with me."

It was a siren's call, the words stroking over him with an almost physical touch. Drew clenched his hands into fists, trying to remember all the reasons he couldn't do what she was asking, what he wanted more than anything.

"You're upset," he managed finally. "You're not thinking clearly."

"I'm thinking clearly for the first time in days." Her voice trembled, but her words didn't falter. "I'm tired of pretending, Drew. I'm tired of pretending I don't want you. That you don't want me."

If she'd had any doubts about the rightness of what she was doing, they'd disappeared the moment she'd seen him. She'd gone to her room to get ready for bed and the newscast had played in her mind on an endless loop, only it hadn't been Joseph Smithson's face they were showing. It had been hers.

It had come to her, more powerfully than ever before, that life was short, and that hers might be even shorter than she might have anticipated. She'd felt fear and then anger and then a quick rush of determination that she was going to live life to its fullest. No matter what happened later, she didn't want to look back with regret for the things she could have done.

Before she could change her mind, she'd left her room, hurrying down the hall, praying that Drew was still up. She wasn't quite sure her courage would extend to tracking him down in his bedroom. But she was in luck—or not, depending on how you looked at it. Drew was standing where she'd left him, one hand resting on top of the television.

She saw him stiffen when she spoke his name, read the wariness in his eyes when he turned to look at her. And she felt rather than saw the hunger in him. It was that hunger that gave her the courage to step into the room, to walk toward him.

"Go to bed, Kate." There was a ragged edge of desperation in the repeated command. She ignored the words, listening instead to the ache in his voice.

"Come with me," she said again. She stopped in front of him. Later she'd wonder at her own boldness. Later she'd be shocked at her actions. But here and now, all she could think of was that it shouldn't have taken so long to reach this point.

Drew stared down at her, telling himself that he was going to walk away, that this wasn't going to go any further. He drew in a deep breath, his head filling with the scent of her, soap and shampoo. He saw his hands come up to settle on her shoulders. To push her away, he told himself.

"This is wrong." He wasn't sure whether he was asking her or telling her.

"It feels right." She leaned into his touch and he let his elbows bend, let her weight carry her closer.

"I'm supposed to be protecting you."

"Then you shouldn't let me out of your sight." Her hands came up to rest against his chest and Drew felt their touch burn through the fabric of his T-shirt.

He lowered his head, brushing his mouth over her forehead. This couldn't go any further. He had to stop this now before it got out of hand, as if it wasn't already out of hand.

"This has to stop."

"Why?" She turned her face up to his, her mouth a whisper away.

"It's just not right." His eyes searched hers, seeing his own need reflected there.

"You want me."

As if to prove her point, Kate let one hand slide down his chest. Drew sucked in a harsh breath as her fingers slipped past his belt and settled on the hard bulge of his arousal.

"Kate." Her name was a protest. A plea. Aching need and weakening resistance.

One hand left her shoulder. He'd intended to draw her hand away, to set her from him, to walk—no run—from temptation. But somehow his fingers were cupping one of her breasts, feeling the sweet weight of it through the thin white cotton of her nightgown.

She drew in a quick breath and he watched as the color came up in her cheeks, a soft flush of pleasure. Without his volition, his thumb brushed over her taut nipple, his eyes on her face. He saw the flush deepen, saw her mouth part to allow her to draw a shaken breath.

And he was lost.

With a groan, he lowered his head, giving in to the hunger that boiled in him, the need that had been gnawing at his gut for weeks. Kate's mouth opened to his, her eager response fanning the heat building in him.

There was nothing tentative about their coming together. This might have been only the second kiss they'd shared and yet each seemed to know just what the other needed.

Drew shifted his hands on her, flattening one against her back, letting the other sweep down to cup her buttocks, crushing her up against him. Kate whimpered against his mouth, her legs instinctively shifting apart to cradle the hardness of his arousal against her feminine core.

Drew groaned and rocked his hips forward, torturing himself with the feel of her, so close and yet still out of reach. His mouth opened over hers, his tongue plunging deep to find and tangle with hers. God, she tasted like heaven. Her response was everything he'd dreamed, everything he'd remembered from that all-too-brief encounter in the kitchen.

Afterward, neither of them could have said just how they reached Drew's bedroom. It didn't matter. Nothing mattered beyond this long overdue coming together. Oddly enough, once in the dim intimacy of his room, Kate's earlier confidence seemed to disappear. The fingers that had so boldly cupped him a few moments ago now fumbled with the buckle of his belt. And when Drew's hands found their way beneath the hem of her nightgown, Kate's fingers could only cling to his belt as her knees began to tremble.

His hands stroked upward along her thighs, pausing to cup the rounded softness of her bottom. His mouth caught hers in a long, drugging kiss. His hands urged her forward until she felt the hard length of his arousal pressed to the supple skin of her stomach through the denim of his jeans. She shifted instinctively, wanting to get closer, needing to feel him against her. Drew groaned, rocking his hips forward, his tongue thrusting into her mouth in an unmistakable rhythm.

Kate whimpered, her head falling back, her surrender complete. She'd never have believed she could feel so completely, deliciously wanton. The past, the future—both were unimportant. All that mattered was this man and the fact that she'd waited all her life for him—for this moment.

Drew's hands swept upward, taking the soft cotton nightgown with them. Kate lifted her arms and the gown drifted from her, settling to the floor in a white pool. She felt a moment's shy uncertainty at standing in front of him completely nude. She had a woman's instant awareness of the ten extra pounds she'd never quite managed to lose. Her hands shifted, half lifting as if to cover herself, but the movement was never completed.

"My God, you're beautiful." Drew's voice was husky.

"No, I'm not." The protest was automatic.

"Yes, you are." His fingers against her mouth stilled her denial. "I've never in my life wanted anything the way I want you."

His eyes never left her as his fingers trailed down her throat, pausing to test the pulse that beat so frantically at its base. Kate felt as if his touch was stealing her voice, draining away every thought, leaving her capable only of feeling.

"Unbutton my shirt," he whispered, still holding her with that clear blue look.

Fingers trembling, she lifted her hands to his chest, sliding buttons through impossibly small buttonholes. She'd nearly completed the task when his hands drifted downward to cup her breasts. Kate gasped at the feel of him touching her.

How many nights had she lain awake imagining—trying not to imagine—what it would feel like to have him touch her? Her imagination had fallen far short of reality. He caught her nipples between thumb and forefinger of each hand, plucking gently. Kate's head fell back, her fingers clinging to the edges of his open shirt. She felt the touch at her breasts, felt it deeper still in the heavy, damp heat that pooled in the most private part of her.

When he bent his head and his mouth closed over one swollen nipple, she moaned low in her throat, hardly recognizing the sound as hers. Her fingers came up to clasp his head as his teeth abraded the tender bud before his tongue soothed the puckered flesh.

Kate's knees gave out completely. If it hadn't been for Drew's support, she would have sunk to the floor. His mouth lifted, catching hers again as he turned, lowering her onto the bed. Kate felt the bed dip beneath her weight and then felt him moving away. She reached up blindly, feeling something close to panic at the thought that he was leaving her, that she might not find the end of the journey they'd begun.

Drew's hands were shaking so badly, he had trouble unbuckling his belt. Seeing Kate lying beneath him, her slender body flushed with desire, her eyes almost pure green with need, he felt an almost savage hunger sweep over him. *This* was what he'd wanted from the moment he'd first seen her picture. He'd never felt this gut-level response to a woman before, never felt so close to the edge of control.

He finally wrenched open the belt, feeling as if he might explode if he didn't free himself, if he couldn't sheathe himself in her, feel the silken heat of her close around him. He reached for the zipper tab, but Kate's fingers were there first.

"Let me."

Drew's hands fell to his sides, his fingers curling into his palms as she inched the zipper down. It seemed to take forever. He could feel the backs of her fingers rubbing against his swollen flesh, a sweet torture through the denim of his jeans. She seemed to be having trouble with the task, her hand lingering until he was sure he would burst. And then he caught her eyes, saw the wicked gleam in them and realized she was deliberately lingering over it, enjoying the power she had over him.

"Witch." The word was a thick accusation as he caught her hand in his, crushing it to him for an instant before he quickly finished the job. He stripped off his jeans and shorts in one quick motion and set one knee on the edge of the bed, looming over her like a conquering warrior.

And then she opened her arms to him, her hips lifting in sweet invitation and he knew he was the one being conquered. The very force of his need made him hesitate for a moment. This was such madness. It was against all the rules.

"Drew." His name was a breath, a sigh. And he was lost.

"God, Kate."

He came to her in a rush, his hips sliding between her thighs, his hardness finding her softness. As in their kiss, there was no need for tentative exploration, for hesitation. He sheathed himself in her with one long, smooth thrust.

She cried out, her neck arching as she pressed her head back into the pillow, and she welcomed him into her. He felt that welcome in the way her hands clung to his hips, drawing him closer as her knees drew up on either side of his body, cradling him as she took him deep into herself.

It was completion. An emptiness filled. An emptiness that was only partly physical. Kate knew that in her entire life she'd never been whole. Not until this moment. Not until this man.

He shifted, withdrawing from her and then thrusting home again. She moaned low in her throat, her eyes tightly closed as he repeated the movement, each new thrust seeming to take him deeper than the last, each making him even more a part of her.

The world narrowed to that one room, to the bed on which they lay and finally to the sweet friction of his body on hers, within hers. Kate felt tension building in the pit of her stomach, like a spring being coiled tighter and tighter until the sensation became almost painful.

Her head twisted against the covers they'd been in too much of a hurry to pull down. She'd never known anything could feel so intense. She wanted him to stop, knew she'd surely fly apart if he didn't stop. And yet her hands clung to him, feeling the dampness of sweat on his back, feeling the tautness of his muscles as he fought to hold his own completion back long enough to allow her to reach hers.

And then she did fly apart, spinning outward into a million pieces as her body arched against his, her eyes jerking open to stare up into his face in astonished wonder as the tension exploded into fulfillment.

Drew held back, watching the color run up from her

breasts to her face, seeing her eyes go wide and startled and then seeing them grow heavy with pleasure. Only then did he let himself go, letting the soft contractions of her pleasure take him over the edge into his own satisfaction.

Kate felt the first shudder run through him, felt him swell inside her, saw his face go taut as his climax took him. Instinctively she arched her hips, taking him still deeper, letting her muscles contract around him. She felt him shudder in her arms, felt him throb inside her and knew that she'd never in her life felt complete.

Knew, too, that she'd never again feel complete except with this man. All her determination had failed. It wasn't propinquity at all.

It was love.

And God help her.

Chapter Eight

Drew felt as if he'd been drugged. Every muscle and bone felt heavy, relaxed in a way he'd never known. Even when he'd been in the hospital and they'd been pumping him full of pain medication, he hadn't felt so completely relaxed. Of course, then he'd been fighting the drugs, determined to recover without their help, resenting that he needed them, even for a short while.

He was through fighting his need for Kate Sloane. Through pretending it didn't exist. He didn't know why, didn't understand what it was between them, but for the moment, at least, he couldn't pretend anymore.

He'd just sent every rule of ethics up in flames, set himself up for dismissal—a dismissal he couldn't even argue he didn't deserve. The argument could be made that he'd compromised a witness, maybe even jeopardized a case that meant a lot to him, personally and professionally.

And the only thought in his head was to wonder how soon he could do it again.

It took every ounce of strength he could muster to lift himself off Kate's warm body and roll onto the bed. Even then, he swept one arm beneath her, pulling her up against his side. Without looking at it too closely, he knew he wanted her as close as it was possible to be without the two of them being physically joined. If it hadn't been for the fact that he was too heavy for her, he wouldn't have left her at all.

If he'd thought that making love to her would quench the hunger that had been gnawing at him for weeks, he knew already that he'd been dead wrong. His body felt heavy—sated. Yet he could already feel hunger stirring deep inside—a need he couldn't quite define and was afraid to examine too closely. The thought made him stir uneasily.

His arm tightened around Kate as she settled against him, pillowing her head on his shoulder and throwing one leg across his hips. She curled up to him as if it were the most natural thing in the world. As if they really were what they were pretending to be—husband and wife.

"This isn't real."

Though his voice was low and husky, the abrupt words sounded loud in the quiet room. He felt Kate stiffen slightly, her body tensing as if in defense against a potential blow.

"This isn't real," he said again, wondering just who he was trying to remind—Kate or himself.

"It feels real," Kate said, her tone deliberately light. Her hand stroked over his chest, her fingers threading through the mat of black hair that covered his muscles.

"But it's not. This is all just pretend."

She flinched as if the words had a physical impact. Drew cursed under his breath, wishing he could call them back and yet knowing they had to be said. One of them had to retain some grasp of reality, no matter how fragile that hold was.

"Kate…"

"Don't." She lifted her head from his shoulder and braced herself on her elbow so that she could look down at him. "Let's pretend."

"But…"

"Please, Drew." She set the tips of her fingers against his mouth, silencing him. "Just for a little while. What can it hurt?"

They both knew it could end up hurting a great deal. They weren't children, playing at house. They were adults, already playing a dangerous game. Adding a new element of pretend could be fatal, in more ways than one.

Drew reached up to stroke her tangled hair back from her face, knowing he should force her—force both of them—to look at what they'd done in a cold, hard light. But in her eyes, he saw traces of the fear that had driven her to him, the fear that her life might be over before it had really begun. And he saw a need that echoed his own, the same hunger he'd felt for weeks.

"God, I must be crazy."

Kate's smile was his reward. He slid his fingers deeper into her hair, drawing her face down to his, catching her mouth in a slow, drugging kiss. Kate didn't argue, either with his statement or with the kiss.

It was, Drew found, frighteningly easy to pretend. Easier than it had been when he was a child. Growing up in foster homes had left him with a cold appreciation for the truth. At first, he'd tried to convince himself that he was truly wanted by the families that took him in, not just for the extra money his presence brought them or even out of a genuine concern for those less fortunate, but that they really wanted *him*.

By the time he was eight he'd realized that there was no sense in pretending he was a part of any of the families he stayed with. No matter how nice they were, he was still an outsider, never really a part of the inner circle. He'd been lucky in some ways. He'd never been abused, always been clothed and fed. It hadn't been a physical hunger he'd felt but an emotional one. The human need to matter to someone, to love and be loved.

Long before he grew to adulthood, he'd learned to close off the part of him that craved affection. There had been no sense in pretending to be anything other than what he was—

a boarder, occasionally unwelcome. To pretend that he might really become a part of the family was to guarantee nothing but hurt when it came time to move again.

His marriage to Diane had proven, once and for all, that he was incapable of making the sort of emotional connections that were necessary to sustain a relationship. He'd accepted that with no real regrets. And if he'd occasionally felt an ache that might have been loneliness, he'd shrugged it off. He was what he was and nothing was going to change that.

So how was it that Kate Sloane had managed to make him doubt what he was? Made him think about things he'd put out of his life a long time ago—things like home and family?

When he was with her, it was easy to forget reality, forget the future.

And it was remarkably easy to pretend that they weren't living in a dream world.

"I THINK THE HOUSE would look better green." Kate frowned at the house, narrowing her eyes against the sunlight as if trying to picture the small house painted a different color.

Drew turned his head slowly, reluctant to disturb the pleasant lethargy that had taken hold of him. It had been Kate's idea to bring their take-out chicken dinner into the backyard and have a picnic. He couldn't remember the last time he'd been on a picnic. There must have been occasions when he was a child, but none came to mind.

Though he'd grumbled about the discomforts of sitting on the ground and said that it was ridiculous to eat in the backyard, only yards from a comfortable table where they wouldn't have to worry about ants, Drew had to admit that lying on a blanket spread on the soft green grass and looking up into the spreading branches of the big sycamore tree was not a bad way to spend an afternoon. He'd been on the verge of falling asleep until Kate had made her comment about the house.

"Houses should be white," he said after a moment.

"Houses should be all different colors," she disagreed. "Think how dull a neighborhood would look if every single house was white." She was spinning a dandelion between her fingers, the soft yellow flower almost matching the sleeveless top she wore with her white shorts.

"Organized," Drew corrected, turning his face back up to the dappled sunlight. "It would look organized. You wouldn't have disasters like that purple monstrosity down the street."

That silenced her momentarily. Half a block away was a house that had been painted what could only be described as brothel purple, with eye-searingly white trim. The owners had completed the picture by planting the flower beds in front with orange and red cosmos fronted by marigolds. The combination was arresting, to put it mildly.

"I didn't have in mind anything quite that...cheerful," she said after a moment.

"Cheerful?" Drew raised his brows without bothering to open his eyes. "If that color were any more 'cheerful,' it would be fatal."

Kate grinned but refused to be dissuaded from the topic at hand. "A nice pale green would be perfect, maybe with white trim."

"Houses should be white," Drew repeated. He didn't really care what color the house was, this one or any other. But there was something pleasant about the lazy argument.

"A house should reflect the inherent uniqueness of its occupants." Kate's voice took on the solemnity of a social critic. "Many of today's problems would be solved if people developed a deeper appreciation for the individuality of their neighbors."

"Many of today's problems would be solved if people didn't paint their houses purple."

"Maybe they felt the color deep in their souls." Drew felt her move and caught the faint scent of her shampoo, telling him that she'd shifted closer. Desire stirred in him, the way it always did when she was near. If he'd ever thought that once he'd had Kate the hunger would be slaked, this past week had shown him how wrong he'd been. The more he had of her, the more he wanted.

"The rest of the world feels it in their stomachs. No one could see that house without getting bilious."

"You just don't appreciate the artistic statement they've made."

From the sound of her voice, he guessed that she was lying on her stomach, propped on her elbows beside him. The still, warm air carried her scent—soap and shampoo, fresh, innocent smells. How was it that he'd never noticed how incredibly sensual those scents could be until he'd met Kate Sloane?

"If that house is an artistic statement, I'd hate to meet the artist." It was a nonsensical argument, one neither of them had any interest in winning. It was simply a way to pass a hot, summer afternoon.

He felt Kate shift again, but didn't bother to open his eyes to verify her new position. Then he felt her fingers on the buttons of his shirt. He felt the muscles in his stomach clench in anticipation as she slid first one button loose and then another.

She was a passionate and eager lover, but she didn't often initiate sex, unless he could count the fact that her presence alone was enough to keep him in a state of latent arousal. Kate slipped her hand inside his opened shirt and Drew knew she must be able to feel the accelerated beat of his heart.

For a moment, he felt a flash of anger. Anger at himself for having so little control, anger at Kate for showing him just how fragile that control was. But the anger was quickly drowned out by the rising tide of hunger and the need that never failed to surprise him. Not since he was a child had he allowed himself to need anyone.

"You're too stuck in the mud," she said softly. Her fingers combed through the soft black hair that covered his chest, and Drew's jeans were suddenly too tight. "What you need is something to shake you up."

"I can think of several things I need more," he told her huskily. He opened his eyes, one hand coming up to catch her arm. But the movement was never completed. He caught a glimpse of Kate's eyes, bright with mischief, and then the remains of a glass of ice water hit him full in the chest.

"What the...?" The words were cut off by the shock of icy water against hot skin. Drew gasped as if the water had hit him full in the face.

"Complacency is bad for you," Kate said, scrambling backward as she rose to her feet.

"So is being strangled." Drew stood, wiping one hand over his chest and then staring at it, hardly able to believe it was really wet.

"Now, Drew, I was just trying to give you a little surprise. Everyone likes surprises."

"You damn near drowned me, you little witch." He advanced toward her.

"It's so hot, I thought you'd enjoy a little cool water."

Drew didn't bother to respond but only continued to move toward her at a slow, deliberate pace that made her heart beat faster. She giggled and backed away.

"I was just trying to be helpful, Drew."

"If I were you, I'd quit while I was ahead," he suggested, his voice soft and menacing.

Kate glanced over her shoulder at the back door, gauging her chances of reaching it before he could catch her. Remembering his lightning-fast reflexes, she wouldn't have placed a bet on herself.

She looked back at Drew, feeling a delicious shiver of fear at the expression on his face. He looked like a jungle cat eyeing a particularly juicy bit of prey. She gave him an ingratiating smile and edged a little closer to the door.

"I read in a magazine once that a good sense of humor is a mark of a well-rounded individual."

"Revenge is one of the strongest human needs," he commented softly.

"Forgiveness is another great quality."

"No crime should go unpunished."

"Now, Drew..." She held out one hand, her nervous protest only half-feigned. She knew he'd never hurt her, but she had to admit to being just a little uncertain of his temper. Maybe the impulse to douse him with ice water had not been one of her better ideas.

"Now, Kate..." His voice was husky, his expression unreadable.

He took a quick step toward her and she shrieked. She still held the plastic cup that had held the water and she flung it at him. It bounced off his chest to land in the grass, but she didn't wait to see it fall. Spinning on her heel, Kate sprinted for the back door, flinging it open and dashing inside.

Drew caught her just inside the door. She had no doubt that he could have caught her sooner. He'd simply allowed her to prolong the chase. Kate's heart was pounding against her breastbone as his weight pinned her back against the wall.

His eyes gleamed down at her—ice blue and yet full of fire. She felt like a maiden caught in the arms of a ruthless pirate, knowing ravishment was only a heartbeat away and yet knowing it would be a sweet ravishment.

"Apologize," he whispered. He pressed closer, his chest dampening her T-shirt.

"I'm sorry you're such a stick-in-the-mud," she offered, finding it difficult to form a coherent sentence. Not that Drew was interested in her apology. She could feel him pressed against her lower stomach, already hard.

"You're asking for trouble." He tilted his head to let his mouth find the soft shell of her ear. Kate felt a shiver run through her as his teeth closed over her earlobe and nibbled gently.

"Did I find it?" She pushed his shirt the rest of the way off his shoulders before letting her fingers settle on his damp chest.

"In spades, sweetheart. In spades."

Her arms clung to his neck as he swept her off her feet and into his arms, carrying her through the kitchen and into the hallway that led to the bedrooms. He shouldered open the door to his room—their room for the past week—and let her slide to her feet beside the bed.

Looking up at him, Kate decided that if this was trouble, she never wanted to be without it again.

THERE WAS A PART of Kate that had recognized from the beginning the fact that she and Drew would be lovers. A deep feminine knowledge that made their coming together inevitable. So inevitable that she felt little surprise when it happened.

What did surprise her was discovering the depths of her own sexuality. Her experience with sex had generally led her to feel that sex was either highly overrated or simply not something for which she had much talent. With Drew, she discovered how completely wrong she'd been. If it hadn't been so clichéd, she'd have been inclined to think that the earth moved when he made love to her.

The other thing that surprised her was the playful side

Drew revealed. Once they'd become lovers, some of the mask disappeared, revealing a man who smiled more easily and laughed more often than she'd expected. And every smile, every laugh, served to work his image deeper into her heart.

It was no longer possible for Kate to pretend she didn't love him. Her imagination didn't stretch that far. Oh, she'd tried telling herself that what she felt was sexual fascination, that a lover like Drew made it easy to confuse love with lust.

That might have explained her eagerness to share his bed, but it couldn't explain the warm, melting feeling that came over her every time she looked at him. Nor did it explain away the sharp ache in her chest whenever she let herself remember that the game they were playing had to end soon.

She'd never been good at lying to herself and she didn't try now. She'd fallen in love with Drew Hunter and that was all there was to it. It might be one of the most foolish things she'd ever done, but she didn't compound her foolishness by thinking that Drew had to return her feelings. Despite the new closeness they shared, she couldn't judge his feelings for her. Becoming his lover hadn't made it any easier for her to read his thoughts.

That he desired her was obvious. That a part of him resented that desire was equally obvious. Beyond that, she wasn't sure of anything when it came to Drew Hunter. He was her protector, her lover...and still more than half a stranger. It didn't matter. She loved him. And whatever might await them in the real world, for this little space of time, he was hers and she was going to enjoy every moment of it.

She had the sense of time running out and she was determined to enjoy whatever time remained to them. No matter what happened later, she was going to have these few days or weeks to remember.

DEFT STROKES of the chef's knife cut the carrots into neat diagonal slices. Except for the soft thwack of the knife against the wooden cutting board, the kitchen was quiet. Drew whistled tunelessly under his breath, aware that he couldn't remember the last time he'd felt the sort of deep contentment he felt in that moment.

Kate was taking a shower, the low hum of water running through the old pipes clearly audible in the kitchen. He didn't have to close his eyes to picture her—silky brown hair caught up on top of her head, her wet skin flushed from the heat of the water.

''Damn.'' The soft exclamation was startled from him as the knife came down uncomfortably close to his thumb. Using the flat of the blade to lift the sliced carrots onto a plate ready for stir-frying later, Drew forced Kate's image from his mind.

He was tempted to join her, but the one time they'd showered together, they'd both nearly ended up with concussions. Wet ceramic tile was a slippery and unforgiving surface. They'd barely made it out of the bathroom and they hadn't made it all the way to the bed. He'd had rug burns on his knees for two days.

He grinned as he reached for a stalk of celery. It had been worth it. More than worth it.

Drawing a deep breath, he sent the knife through the celery with quick, chopping motions. Cooking was his only domestic skill, developed more in self-defense than anything else. Other than the brief years of his marriage, he'd had the choice of learning to cook or of relying on TV dinners and restaurants.

It had turned out to be a handy talent. Kate had a number of domestic talents but cooking was not among them. She cheerfully admitted to being a whiz with a microwave. Beyond that, it was safer not to turn her loose in a kitchen.

Domesticity suits you, Hunter. The half-mocking words

made Drew's fingers hesitate over a pile of mushrooms. He hadn't given much thought to Dave Murphy's visit lately, had given even less thought to the reason for it. These past few days had been like stolen time.

It had to come to an end. It couldn't be long now before Lavery called them back to L.A. But he wasn't going to think about that now. He had pretended this long. He could keep reality at bay a little while longer. His mouth curved in a rueful smile. One thing he'd found was that pretending got easier with practice.

With the plate of vegetables neatly sliced, ready to stir-fry with the chicken that was already marinating, Drew turned from the counter and started to clear the table. Kate had set her purse on it when they'd come back from the market earlier and he picked it up, along with two magazines and a paperback novel.

He started to carry the items into the living room, but the snap on Kate's purse was apparently not quite closed and he'd gone only a few feet when its contents started to shower out at his feet. Cursing, he twisted his wrist to bring it upright. But not before he heard something hit the floor with a very solid sound.

Glancing down, Drew froze for an instant. Moving slowly, he sank to his haunches, his left hand coming out. He brushed aside a checkbook, a package of gum, a packet of tissues and half a dozen hairpins. His fingers closed around the solid weight of a .32 automatic.

Dropping the magazines and the book, he checked the clip, finding it fully loaded. The safety was on, but that didn't do anything to ease the sudden grimness around his mouth. Just how long had Kate been carrying a gun?

KATE WAS HUMMING under her breath as she left the bedroom. Her hair was still damp, but it would dry soon enough in the warm evening air. Just before she'd gone in to take a shower, she'd heard Drew whistling in the kitchen, a tuneless sound that expressed the same contentment she felt.

Though she knew little of Drew's past, she didn't need his life history to realize that contentment was something of which he'd known very little. The thought that he'd found it in this little house with her was almost as good as hearing him say that he loved her. Since she didn't dare let herself hope for that, she savored what she did have.

She didn't hear him whistling now, but he was probably in the midst of stirring together whatever he was making for dinner. She stepped into the kitchen, expecting to find Drew standing in front of the stove.

But he wasn't at the stove and there were no savory smells to indicate that dinner was nearly done. Instead, he was standing next to the table, watching her with the same cool eyes she remembered from when they'd first met—the eyes of the cop, not the lover.

"You want to explain this?" Drew's voice matched the ice in his eyes. Kate looked from his face to the gun that lay on his palm to her purse, which sat open on the kitchen table.

"I don't recall giving you permission to go through my purse." She reached for the gun, but he closed his fingers over it, drawing it back out of her reach.

"Your purse was open and the gun fell out when I went to move it." There was nothing apologetic about his explanation. "The question is, what was it doing there in the first place?"

"It's mine." Kate wasn't sure what he'd wanted her to say, but the simple statement obviously wasn't it.

"I figured that out on my own," he said, his tone chilly and sarcastic.

When she didn't respond, Drew's jaw tightened momentarily before relaxing as if with a conscious effort. He set the gun on the table. Out of her reach, Kate noted, wondering if that had been deliberate.

"Have you been carrying this all along?"

"Yes." She lifted her chin and met his eyes. She hadn't done anything wrong and she was darned if she was going to feel guilty. That he was upset was obvious. The reasons weren't so obvious.

"When did you get it?"

"Two years ago. Shouldn't I have an attorney present when I'm being interrogated?" She arched her brows, coolly questioning.

"I'm not interrogating you," he snapped.

"Funny. It *feels* like you are."

"Dammit, Kate!" He stopped and drew a deep breath, releasing it slowly. When he continued, his voice was even. "Did it occur to you to tell me that you were carrying a gun?"

"At first." She shrugged in answer to the question in his eyes. "I didn't know you. I didn't feel obligated to tell you everything."

"What about now? Now that you *know* me, in every sense of the word?"

Kate flushed. She lifted her chin another notch, her eyes cool. "To tell the truth, I more or less forgot about it."

There was a moment of silence while Drew absorbed her words. "You *forgot* you were carrying a gun?"

"No. I forgot to tell you about it."

"You didn't think I'd be interested?" he suggested politely.

"I thought you'd make a production out of it," she corrected. "Obviously I was right."

"I'm not making a production out of it." He stopped and ran the fingers of one hand through his hair, trying to keep hold of his temper.

"I don't suppose I should even bother to ask whether or not you have a license to carry a concealed weapon."

"You know I don't. I don't usually carry it with me. I keep it in the drawer in my nightstand at home."

"But you've been carrying it since we met and you didn't bother to tell me. What are you doing with it in the first place?"

"I bought it a couple of years ago. Someone broke into a house a few blocks away from my apartment. The woman who lived there was raped. It seemed like a good idea for me to have some protection."

"Do you know how to use it?"

"I took a few lessons when I first got it." Kate lifted one shoulder in a half shrug, wishing, not for the first time, that she could read his thoughts.

When she'd entered the room and he'd thrust the gun at her, it had been simple enough. There'd been no mistaking the anger in those glacial blue eyes. But he'd gotten that under control almost immediately and now it was impossible to read anything behind that expressionless mask.

"Were you any good?"

"I hit the center of the target a couple of times," she admitted.

"Great. Now all we need is a law that requires bad guys to have a target painted on their chests. Then you'd be in great shape."

"I don't expect anybody to have a target on their chest," she said stiffly.

"There's a big difference between shooting holes in a paper target and shooting holes in a human being, Kate."

"I know that."

"Do you?" He ran his fingers through his hair again, suddenly more weary than angry. "Do you have any idea what it feels like to shoot someone?"

"Of course not. I've never shot anyone. And I don't have any plans to shoot anyone."

"Then what the hell are you doing with a gun?"

"Any criminal in his right mind is going to run when he sees the way my finger is shaking on the trigger." She tried a tentative smile, wanting to coax him out of his bleak mood.

"When you pick up a gun, you'd better be prepared to use it."

"If the time comes, I'll do what I have to do."

"Will you?" he asked, watching her with a brooding expression.

"If I didn't believe I could use it, I wouldn't have bought it."

He continued to watch her for a moment longer, those ice blue eyes expressionless. Kate met his look, wondering what he was thinking.

"Why are you upset?" she asked abruptly. "I would have thought you'd approve of my having a little extra protection."

A good question, Drew thought. Too bad he didn't know the answer. Or didn't want to admit it. He turned away from her and picked up the gun, weighing it in his hand, trying to think of words that would answer her question without revealing things he wasn't sure of himself.

"You don't need extra protection," he said finally. "That's my job."

"You don't think that I have that gun because I think you can't protect me, do you?" The distress in her voice was mirrored in her eyes. She closed the distance between them and put her hand on his arm. "Drew, I know nothing will happen to me while you're with me."

He said nothing. Let her think that it was wounded pride that had put the ice in his voice, in his eyes. It was a perfectly reasonable explanation. It was certainly more reasonable than the truth, which was that he'd been angry because the gun had been a reminder that she was in danger, that the past couple of weeks had been a charade.

They'd been playing at happily-ever-after and he'd gotten

so involved in the game that he'd almost managed to forget that it *was* a game.

He brought his hand up, his fingers skimming over her cheek. Kate's eyes searched his, asking questions he couldn't—wouldn't—answer. He couldn't tell her that he'd have given almost anything to be able to say that she had nothing to be afraid of, that the danger was a thing of the past.

"Just try not to shoot me," he said at last, his mouth quirking in a half smile.

"I'll try to keep that in mind," Kate promised, wishing for the thousandth time that she could read what he was thinking.

She closed her eyes as he lowered his mouth to hers. Though there was passion in the kiss, there was also a sense of urgency, a feeling that time was slipping away from them. The gun had served as a reminder that their time was finite and that its end was in the near future.

Dinner was forgotten. The gun was forgotten. Nothing mattered but the hunger they felt for each other. The past was unimportant. The future was uncertain. All they had was the present. It was enough. It had to be.

Chapter Nine

Neither of them mentioned the gun again. Drew watched Kate put it back into her purse, his expression deliberately blank. Kate wished she could read his thoughts. Did he think she didn't trust him to protect her? She'd trusted him with her life from the very beginning. It was her heart she was worried about.

But if she told him that, then he'd know that she'd fallen in love with him, and she wasn't quite ready for that. She wasn't sure she'd *ever* be ready. There were moments when she thought he must know how she felt. How could he *not* know? It had to be in her eyes when she looked at him. And every time they made love...surely he could feel it in her touch.

But if he'd guessed how she felt, Kate could never read it in his face. And as far as trying to guess what he felt about her... She'd have had better luck reading the expression on the great Sphinx.

Under ordinary circumstances, she might have made demands, insisted on defining their relationship, asked him to tell her how he felt. But the circumstances were far from ordinary. If they had been, she would probably never have met Drew Hunter. Never have fallen in love with him. Never have wanted so desperately to believe that he loved her.

And never have had to wonder whether or not she'd live long enough to feel the hurt if he *didn't* love her.

"JUST A LITTLE to the left. Now back a few inches. Up a little. There! Hold it and I'll push a little dirt underneath the root ball." Kate's voice bubbled with enthusiasm.

It was an enthusiasm Drew didn't particularly share. But then it was hard to be enthused when he was straddling a hole in the ground, supporting what felt like a thousand pounds of dirt and tree, and trying to hold the whole thing in the position Kate had decreed as correct.

Peering through the mass of leafy branches that were beating him in the face, Drew watched as Kate knelt on the ground and shoved dirt into the hole she'd dug the day before. She was wearing a pair of bright pink shorts and a lime green T-shirt—a traffic-stopping color combination. Her soft brown hair was caught up in a ponytail and decorated with a pink scrunchy thing.

She looked fresh and innocent and full of life, and Drew wanted nothing so much as to drop the stupid tree into the hole, tumble Kate to the soft green grass and make love to her under the fading afternoon sunlight. But then, when didn't he want to make love to her?

"Could you tilt the trunk a little to the right?"

Drew tilted obediently and tried not to think about tugging that bright T-shirt over Kate's head, seeing her eyes go all soft, smoky green and her mouth soften in anticipation of his kiss.

"Hang on just a few more seconds. I just want to make sure there's plenty of dirt underneath so it doesn't sink too low when we set it in." Kate was kneeling on the ground, using her hands to push dirt under the root ball.

As far as Drew was concerned, the tree could sink all the way to the top leaf and he wouldn't object. But Kate was determined that another tree was just what the backyard needed and he'd agreed to help her. He wondered what La-very would say if he could see him now. Would he comment, the way Murphy had, that domesticity seemed to suit him?

Drew frowned at the slender trunk he was holding. He'd certainly never thought of himself as a domestic animal. His marriage to Diane had seemed to confirm that he was a loner, unsuited to sharing his life with someone. When they'd divorced, he'd felt nothing more than annoyance that he'd made such a monumental mistake and regret that someone else had been hurt by that mistake. He was a loner, and the sooner he accepted it the better. And if, occasionally, lone-liness seemed to catch him by the throat, well, better that than trying to be something he wasn't.

Then he was assigned to protect Kate Sloane. In the weeks since they'd met he'd begun to lose sight of just what he was. He was a loner, yet he'd never known contentment until these past few weeks—sharing a house with Kate, feeling it become a home, something he'd never had and never expected to have. He was a cop, but he'd done things no cop had any business doing. And what was worse, he didn't even regret what he'd done.

There were moments when he felt as if he didn't know himself anymore. What the hell had happened to him?

"There. You can set it down now."

Drew was grateful for the interruption. He wasn't sure he liked the direction his thoughts had been taking, a direction they took all too often lately.

He allowed the tree to settle into the hole and then knelt down and began shoving dirt in around the root ball. Kate worked from the opposite side, frowning slightly with concentration as she pushed the soil into place. Drew found himself wanting to lean over and kiss her.

There was hardly a time when he didn't want to kiss her. If he had been sure that it was nothing more than an over-developed sex drive on his part, it wouldn't have bothered him as much as the knowledge that there were times when wanting to kiss her had no particular connection to wanting to make love to her. And that implied an emotional involvement, which scared the hell out of him.

"It looks perfect, doesn't it?" Kate sat back on her heels to admire the young tree. Sunlight caught in her hair, picking out the subtle red highlights in the brown.

"Perfect." Drew's eyes weren't on the tree.

"I think it's exactly what this corner of the yard needed."

"Exactly."

What a time to discover he was in love. The thought had him shooting to his feet, his pulse too quick, something akin to panic making his breathing a little ragged. He wasn't, of course. In love. Not with Kate. Not with anyone. He cared for her. It was safe to admit that much. He could even stretch a point and say that it was part of his job to care for her. Though he'd cared for her in ways that weren't in any training manuals on witness protection.

Drew jammed his fingers through his hair, unconcerned that they were still covered in dirt. He wasn't in love with Kate. He refused to be.

"Drew?" From Kate's tone, it was obvious that it wasn't the first time she'd said his name. He shoved his tangled thoughts aside and forced himself to focus on Kate's anxious expression.

"Are you all right?"

"Fine." He smiled, drawing on every bit of acting skill he'd picked up from years of undercover work. "My mind was wandering."

"Don't you think the tree looks just right?" she said again, accepting his explanation at face value. She slid her arm through his and looked at the young tree as if she were a proud parent admiring a clever child.

"It looks fine." Drew glanced at the old sycamore that

dominated the other corner of the yard and then looked back at the sapling. "It looks a little scrawny, doesn't it?"

"In a few years it will fill out. Even by next spring, you'll be able to see a lot of growth."

"We won't be here next spring."

He felt the impact of the bare statement in the way Kate's hand tightened on his arm, heard it in the odd little catch in her breathing. He wanted to take the words back, and at the same time he felt as if he should say them again, louder this time.

"It doesn't matter," she said after a moment, her voice quiet. "It doesn't matter whether I'm here to see it or not. I'll know it's here, growing. That's good enough."

Drew looked at the tree, suddenly seeing it through Kate's eyes, seeing the hope and promise of it. It was a gift to the future, one given freely, without expectations, without conditions.

"I'm never going to be able to go back, am I?" Kate asked suddenly. "To my old life, I mean. No matter what happens at the trial. Whether Davis goes to prison or not, I won't be safe, will I?" There was no fear in her voice, no anger, just a question and an acceptance of the answer to that question.

Drew's fingers curled into a fist at his side. He would have given his life to have been able to tell her that she was wrong, that everything could go back to the way it had once been. But he couldn't lie to her.

"Davis is a powerful man," he said slowly. "Going to prison won't destroy that power completely."

"I guess I'd better start thinking about new places to live," she said lightly. But her voice wavered slightly at the end, revealing the fear under the bravado.

"Don't." Drew put his fingers under her chin, tilting her face up to his, his eyes bright blue and fierce. "You don't have to testify, Kate."

Kate caught her breath, her eyes searching his face. She knew how he felt about seeing Davis brought to justice. And yet he was telling her that she didn't have to testify, knowing what that would mean to the case—the case against the man who'd had his partner murdered.

She felt something blossom in her chest, something so fragile she hardly dared to breathe for fear of damaging it. Maybe, just maybe, Drew Hunter cared for her. Since realizing her own feelings for him, the thought had been in the back of her mind, but she'd rarely allowed it to creep into her consciousness. But if Drew could say what he had, then surely she could dare to hope...

"Even if I didn't testify, he already knows I talked to the police. He'd want to make sure I didn't change my mind in the future."

She was only pointing out what he already knew. It had been crazy to suggest that she back out now. There could be no going back. Drew reached up to brush back a lock of hair that had escaped from her ponytail.

"It's going to be all right." He said it with such total assurance that Kate could almost believe that his saying it made it the truth.

"I'd do it again," she said, her eyes clear and steady, without regrets.

"Does it mean so much to you to see Davis punished?" There was an odd combination of pride and anger in the question.

It means that much to me to know you. But she didn't say the words out loud.

"I can't just forget what I know about him," she said, giving him part of the truth. "Somebody has to try and stop him."

Drew looked down at her, unable to argue, unwilling to agree. It wasn't that he didn't want to see Davis ground into the dirt. A few months ago, he'd have sworn that he'd use any weapon to destroy the man who'd killed his partner. But he hadn't known Kate then.

Half-afraid of what she might read in his eyes, he bent to kiss her. Her mouth was soft under his, warm and welcoming. Her arms circled his waist as she tilted her head back to deepen the kiss.

There was passion in the kiss, the hunger that always lay between them, never sated. But there was something more there—a tenderness, a need, something that might almost have been a promise. Unspoken. Undefined. It was enough to make Kate's heart beat just a little faster, to make the fragile hope she nurtured grow a little stronger.

"Hey, you two! None of that. Bill's about to throw the steaks on." Jane's cheery voice sailed over the waist-high fence that separated the two yards.

Drew and Kate ended their kiss without haste. For a moment, Kate looked into Drew's eyes, trying to read what he was feeling. But the combination of twilight and his natural tendency to conceal his thoughts defeated her. Whatever Drew felt for her—if anything—she could read nothing in his face.

"Come on, lovebirds. Dinner awaits." Jane's laughing order banished any lingering fragments of the tender moment between them.

Smiling, Kate turned to wave at her, wondering if Drew felt as she did that they'd been on the verge of discovering something about each other, about whatever it was that lay between them. And she wondered whether he was glad or sorry that the moment had been broken.

FAMILY BARBECUES were not something with which Drew had had much experience. He'd never considered himself the backyard barbecue type. But then, he'd been doing a lot of things lately that he'd never imagined himself doing. Things like making love to a witness he was supposed to be protecting.

At least enjoying the barbecue wasn't likely to get him kicked off the force, he thought, finding a kind of black humor in the thought. Later he'd wonder at how little it bothered him to think about the mess he'd be in if it came out that he'd taken his role as Kate's husband so much to heart. For now he intended to enjoy himself.

It wasn't difficult. Jane and Bill Dumont were pleasant company. After nearly twenty years of marriage, they were so closely attuned that, often, one would start a sentence and the other would finish it.

Kate found herself watching the two of them quarrel good-naturedly over who had to take the blame for the fact that the steaks had been cooked considerably past the stage where they could be labeled rare. Even in the midst of a disagreement, they were obviously two halves of the same whole, a tightly knit unit that required no outside input to sustain it.

But they were generous about bringing others into their circle, commenting on Kate's work in the yard, asking Drew about his novel. Kate wasn't surprised to hear Drew discuss the progress on his nonexistent book. She suspected he could probably quote a passage or two if someone demanded it. He was nothing if not thoroughly prepared for this role.

It was not an entirely comforting thought, she admitted, frowning down at her plate. No wonder it was so difficult to read anything of what he was thinking. He was so good at hiding who he really was that it had become habit.

"Actually, this is by way of a celebration," Bill announced, drawing Kate's attention away from pondering the difficulties of falling in love with a man who'd been trained to lie for a living.

"A celebration?" Drew lifted one brow questioningly, his mouth curved in a lazy smile. No one looking at him would ever think he was anything other than what he was pretending to be—a mild-mannered teacher on sabbatical. The thought of how far that was from the truth made Kate feel suddenly very uncertain.

"What are we celebrating?" she asked, forcing herself to put aside the thought that, while she might be in love with Drew, she wasn't at all sure she really knew him.

"Do you want to tell them?" Bill asked his wife.

"You can break the news. You're the one who's so all-fired smug about it." Jane's grin made it clear that she was feeling a trifle smug herself.

"Well, one of you tell us before curiosity does us in," Drew said, laughing.

"In approximately six and one-half months, we're going to be rediscovering the joys of 2:00 a.m. feedings, no sleep and dirty diapers," Bill announced, looking both excited and slightly embarrassed.

It took a few seconds for his meaning to sink in and then Kate and Drew both spoke at once, offering their congratulations and asking questions. Jane was flushed with pleasure, admitting that she'd never thought she'd want another child until it had suddenly occurred to her that time was running out on her option to try.

"How does Kenny feel about the prospect of having a baby brother or sister?" Drew asked. He grinned when Bill groaned and rolled his eyes in an obvious imitation of Kenny's response.

"He was horrified to think his parents were still capable of procreating," Jane said. She laughed. "He seemed to think it was going to cause him great embarrassment with his friends when they realized that we must have done something more than sleep together for me to get in this condition."

"He'll get over it," Kate said.

"Yeah, but wait until he finds out that he's expected to change diapers," Bill said.

"Can't say I blame him on that one," Drew said, shuddering theatrically.

"Just wait until the two of you start hearing the patter of little feet," Jane said. "Kate'll have you trained in no time."

Kate laughed, but she was careful not to look at Drew. The thought of having his child was suddenly an ache inside her.

"I think we're going to wait awhile," Drew said, and Kate wondered if it was only her imagination that made it seem as if his good humor was just a little forced.

"You've got plenty of time." Bill set his arm around his wife's shoulders and hugged her close. "Janey and I started early with Kenny and there were times we wished we'd had a few more years with just the two of us."

"Not that we ever regretted having Kenny," Jane added hastily.

"He's a great kid," Drew said.

"We think he's okay," Bill admitted with a grin. "But you two, you've only been married, what? A few months?"

"That's right." Drew glanced at Kate and smiled. "Just a few months."

Kate smiled back at him, wishing it weren't all lies. They did it so well, she thought, presented such a perfect image of a happy couple, their marriage still new and fresh. She'd have just about given her soul to make the image a reality. She was relieved when the conversation veered away from a discussion of babies and marriages. Neither topic was a particular favorite of hers at the moment.

Kate had brought her guitar, and she got it out after supper. They'd spent several evenings with the Dumonts and they almost always ended up the same way, with the four of them singing folk songs and laughing.

Drew had been surprised by Kate's skill on the guitar. She was no Segovia, but she had a good feel for the instrument. She tilted her head toward the neck of the guitar, her hair swinging forward to half conceal her face as she strummed the opening chords for "Tom Dooley." They all sang, mangling the verses occasionally, humming when they forgot the words.

He'd never in his life been part of such a gathering, never imagined himself a part of one. Which made it all the more amazing that he felt so completely at home. Amazing and just a little scary.

The small gathering broke up shortly before ten. The Dumonts walked to the edge of their property with Drew and Kate, commenting on the beauty of the summer night. The two couples parted at the sidewalk, exchanging quiet goodnights and more congratulations.

When they reached their own front porch, Kate glanced back and saw Bill and Jane entering their house. His arm was around her, his head bent over hers. There was so much tenderness in the way he held her, so much love, that Kate felt tears sting her eyes.

"I'm tired," Kate said as the door closed behind them. "I think I'll get ready for bed."

"I'll be in as soon as I've locked everything up," Drew said. He set her guitar case in the living room.

They sounded just like an old married couple, Kate thought as she made her way to the bedroom they'd shared for the past two weeks. It was so easy to forget that it was all a charade, an elaborate game they were playing to keep her alive.

She went into the bathroom and took a quick shower. The bedroom was still empty when she entered. Drew had probably stopped to watch a bit of the late news. Kate wondered suddenly if there'd come a time when *she* was part of the news, but she quickly shoved the thought away. There was nothing to be gained by thinking like that.

And yet it wasn't possible *not* to think of how her life had changed. Today she'd finally faced the fact that she could never go back to her apartment, never call it home again. Tonight she realized that there were other things she'd given up, things she'd never even thought of.

She was sitting on the side of the bed when Drew came in, running a brush through her hair, her eyes focused on nothing at all.

"You were quiet tonight," Drew commented as he toed off his shoes in front of the closet. Kate blinked once or twice, as if having trouble shifting her thoughts. She shrugged lightly.

"I was just thinking about how close Jane and Bill are. They've been together so long, it's almost like they're two halves of the same person." Kate shook her head wonderingly. "I can't imagine what it must feel like to be that close to someone."

Drew paused in the act of unbuttoning his shirt and looked at her. There'd been an odd little ache in her voice, a kind of yearning.

"I guess after twenty years together, you tend to get pretty close to someone."

"Not always. My mother and I lived together for eighteen years and we were never more than reluctant roommates. She couldn't wait until I was old enough for her to get on with her life." There was no bitterness in her words, just acceptance of what had been.

"Well, Jane and Bill seem happy together," he said, choosing not to comment on her relationship with her mother. He was afraid if he said anything, it would be something harsh. It struck him as ironic that *he* should feel critical of someone who was incapable of love.

"It's wonderful about the baby, isn't it? They're so happy about it." Kate's voice was wistful.

"Two o'clock feedings and all," he agreed. He pulled his T-shirt off over his head and was reaching for the snap at the waist of his jeans when she spoke again.

"I'll never be able to have children, will I?"

"Why not?" Drew's head came up, his eyes sharp and questioning.

"Because I'm never going to be safe again. I'll always be looking over my shoulder, wondering if Davis is about to catch up with me, to punish me for speaking up."

"Don't think like that." His voice was sharper than he'd intended, made so by the image her words conjured up.

"If I ever had a family, they'd be in danger, too," she continued as if he hadn't spoken. "I couldn't live with that, couldn't live with the idea that something might happen to a child—my child—because I'd testified against Davis."

Drew covered the few feet between them and took hold of her shoulders, drawing her to her feet. His grip was uncomfortably tight.

"Your life isn't over just because you're testifying."

"Not over. Just…changed." She forced a smile she didn't feel and lifted her shoulders in a shrug, the movement hampered by the pressure of his fingers. "Hey, I'd probably make a lousy mother, anyway."

The small wobble in her voice was hardly audible, but Drew heard it. His fingers tightened on her shoulders for an instant and then he pulled her forward to lean against his chest, slipping his arms around her back. Anger tightened his throat, choking off anything he might have said. It was a self-directed anger.

He hadn't given much thought to what it was going to cost to nail Davis. He'd known that Kate was putting her life at risk. That was the reason for his being here, to protect her. But he hadn't really thought beyond the trial, beyond the anticipated pleasure of hearing Davis declared guilty.

He was only now realizing just how large a price Kate might have to pay for having a conscience. More than he'd ever wanted anything in his life, he wanted to be able to tell her that she was wrong—wrong about not being able to go back to her old life, wrong about having to look over her shoulder. But it would have been a lie.

"It's going to be all right, Kate." It was a promise he had no power to keep and they both knew it. But it made him feel a little less powerless to say it, made her feel a little less frightened to hear it.

"Maybe we'll get lucky and Davis will offend some hardened criminal once he's in prison and our problem will be solved," Drew offered.

Kate's snort of laughter was muffled against his chest. She wondered if he knew he'd linked them together—maybe *we'll* get lucky. It made it sound as if he planned on being around after the trial, as if whatever it was they had together wasn't going to end the instant they set foot inside Los Angeles County.

"I won't let anything happen to you, Kate."

Another promise he might not be able to keep, but it didn't matter. What mattered was that he cared enough to make it. And caring could become loving, given time and nurture. She was willing to provide the nurturing, but she had the sad feeling that time might be denied her. But there was nothing she could do about it now. Now all she could do was what she'd been doing for weeks—live only in the moment.

And pray that moment would last forever.

She felt his breath against her forehead and closed her eyes, letting him tilt her head back against his shoulder. His mouth brushed over her eyelids as if drying the tears she refused to shed. He tasted the soft curve of her cheek, the hollow behind her ear, the delicate line of her jaw. By the time his lips touched hers, Kate felt as if he'd soothed all her hurts, smothered all her worries. As long as Drew was kissing her like this, nothing else seemed to matter.

She shifted in his arms, her arms lifting to circle his shoulders, her fingers burrowing into the thick black hair at the back of his neck. Her mouth opened to him, her tongue coming up to fence delicately with his. Drew flattened one hand against her lower back, urging her closer, letting her feel the pressure of his arousal through the layers of cloth that separated them.

In the short time since they'd become lovers, Kate thought she'd experienced just about every nuance of lovemaking possible. Drew had made love to her gently, almost coaxing her response, drawing out each moment until she thought she'd go mad. He'd also shown her that sex could be fierce and quick and just as satisfying. Tonight he made love to her with such tenderness that it brought tears to her eyes.

He eased her nightgown over her head, discarding it in a soft white pool on the carpet. His fingers trailed lightly over her breasts, his thumbs just brushing the taut peaks but not lingering to satisfy. He let his hands slide over her warm skin, the light, skimming touch setting fire to nerve endings she'd barely known existed. And all the while, his mouth lingered on hers, stealing away what little breath she had.

Somewhere in the back of her mind, Kate thought that she shouldn't let him distract her with sex. But she dismissed the thought. Tonight she wanted—needed—his touch, as if it could reaffirm her belief that things could work out. She thought of how foolish it was to lie to herself.

But it wasn't long before she wasn't thinking anything at all.

Drew eased her down onto the bed, bracing one knee against the mattress as he lowered her. Supporting his weight on his arms, he kissed her, a light, teasing kiss that added fuel to the fire burning low in her belly. He nibbled his way down the length of her throat, pausing to let his tongue feel the flutter of the pulse at its base.

Then his lips were brushing over her nipples. She arched, her fingers digging into his shoulder in a silent plea. She thought she felt him smile against her and then his mouth was opening over her, drawing her inside.

His fingers brushed over her stomach, finding the triangle of dark, curling hair at the top of her thighs. Kate whimpered softly as he found the moist heat of her. He switched his attention to her other breast, laving the nipple with his tongue before drawing it into his mouth. And all the while, his fingers were discovering the hidden secrets of her.

She moaned a protest when he left her and then felt his hands close around her hips. She arched, her thighs opening to cradle his hips, her body aching to be filled. But what she felt was not the hard pressure of his masculinity. It was a soft kiss, delicate as a butterfly's wing yet sending shock waves through her body.

"Drew!" Whether his name was protest or welcome, she couldn't have said. Her hands came down, her fingers burrowing into his hair. But if she'd intended to push him away, the intention flew out the window when she felt his tongue against the very heart of her.

She arched into his intimate kiss, her breath leaving her on a sob. She felt as if she were slowly breaking into a thousand different pieces. Never in her life had she imagined the intensity of the sensations he sent rocketing through her.

He played her as if she were a fine instrument, gauging her reactions perfectly, making her shiver with pleasure and sob his name as wave after wave of sensation washed over her. And just when she thought she couldn't stand another moment, he showed her how wrong she was.

He rose above her, his hands braced on either side of her head. Looking up into his face, Kate felt hunger stir anew, though she'd have sworn it wasn't possible. Reaching between them, she closed her fingers around his tumescent length, feeling a wave of feminine triumph when he shuddered at the sweet pain of her touch.

Her eyes locked on his, she drew him forward. He rested against her a moment, barely touching her, teasing them both with the thought of what lay ahead. And then he thrust forward, sheathing himself in her welcoming body.

Kate closed her eyes, drawing her legs up to cradle him more fully, savoring the feelings of completeness. This was what she'd spent a lifetime waiting for.

It could not last long. The fever heat couldn't be sustained. The heat built with each movement, the fire growing hotter and hotter until it was scorching. And then the flames burst out of control, consuming them, completing them, joining them fully.

Kate cradled Drew's heavy weight against her, closing her eyes against the sting of tears. She loved him. Heart and soul, forever and always. How much time did they have left? A week, a few days? Long enough for him to come to love her?

Please, God, just a few more days. A few more memories to store up against what might be a lifetime without him. Surely that wasn't too much to ask.

Chapter Ten

Drew was wide-awake before the echoes of the first ring had faded. The phone rang again, a sharp electronic demand for attention, shattering the quiet. A glance at the clock told him it was not quite seven. Not an hour at which anyone was likely to be calling to try and sell something.

"Whaisit?" Sleep blurred the words together as Kate lifted her head from his shoulder.

"The phone," he said. A third ring punctuated his words.

She blinked and he felt the sudden tension in her body as she registered the early hour and obviously came to the same conclusion he had about the caller's identity.

"It could be a wrong number," she said.

Drew didn't bother to answer her. He knew as well as she did that it wasn't a wrong number. Rolling away from her, he swung his legs over the side of the bed and picked up the phone in the middle of the fourth ring.

"Hello."

Let it be a wrong number, Kate prayed, crossing her fingers in a childish plea for good luck. *Please, please, please. Not now. Not after last night. Not when she was just starting to believe he might come to love her. No man could make love to a woman with such tenderness if he didn't feel something for her. Just a little while longer. A few more days. A*

*week. She just wanted a little more time. That wasn't so much
to ask for.*

But it was more than she was going to get. Drew wasn't
hanging up, wasn't suggesting that the caller might have
made a mistake in dialing. He wasn't even mentioning that
six forty-five was a ridiculous hour for a phone call.

Feeling as if breathing suddenly required a conscious effort, Kate sat up, drawing the sheet up over her breasts, staring at Drew's back, listening to his end of the conversation.
It was brief and told her very little. He said "yes" twice,
stopped and listened and then said, "Tomorrow." There was
another pause and then he repeated the word, his tone flat
and hard.

"Tomorrow." There was another pause and then, "Fine."

Kate watched him hang up the phone, her eyes following
the motion of his hand as if it were important that she see
the receiver settle into the base. For the space of several slow
heartbeats, Drew didn't move. He sat with his back to her,
his hand still on the phone. It was so quiet, she almost
thought that it was possible to hear the rush of blood in her
veins, the thrum of it pulsing in her temples.

Finally he turned to look at her. She felt his eyes on her,
but she couldn't seem to shift her gaze from the plain black
phone on the night table. It was a stupid place to put a phone,
she thought. Why did people put phones next to their beds.
No one wanted to wake to the shrill jangle of it ringing. And
you weren't even alert enough to hold a decent conversation
if it did wake you. Not that Drew had sounded anything less
than coherent. But she wouldn't have expected anything...

"They need you back in L.A. tomorrow."

The flat statement sent her thoughts skittering in a thousand different directions. But they all came back to one resting place.

It was over.

Just what "it" was, she couldn't have said. Her time with

Drew, the whole charade. Her life. One of them or all of them. She wasn't sure it mattered.

She drew a deep breath and looked at him at last. All the gold seemed drained from her eyes, leaving them dull green and lifeless. Her mouth twisted upward as if struggling for a smile, but it couldn't quite make it.

"I guess I'd better get started packing," she said.

Drew opened his mouth and then shut it without speaking. There wasn't anything to say. He watched Kate bend down to lift her nightgown from the floor where it had been discarded the night before. She pulled it over her head, letting it drop around her hips when she stood.

He'd never understand what it was about that plain white cotton nightgown that always made him think of hot nights and hotter sex. If he never saw her again, he'd always remember that nightgown. The sound of the bathroom door closing behind her cut the thought off.

If he never saw her again.

Drew closed his eyes, afraid that the words just might be prophetic. Even more afraid that his life wouldn't be worth living if they were.

IT TURNED OUT TO BE amazingly easy to dismantle the facade they'd created. Kate packed her things, feeling as if it had been a hundred years ago that she'd first done this. That had been another woman, someone she hardly knew anymore.

She stopped, her fingers tightening on the half-finished quilt top she'd been folding. It wasn't just the possibility that Davis might try to extract revenge for her testimony that made it impossible for her to go back to her old life. It was the fact that she'd changed. She wasn't the same Kate Sloane who'd carefully built herself a cozy little nest in that apartment.

After spending all her life moving from place to place, never feeling as if anywhere was really home, she'd been determined to create a home for herself. And she thought she'd accomplished that. Surrounded by things she'd chosen, staying in one place as the months and years rolled by, she'd thought she finally had what she'd always wanted—a home.

It was only now that it was lost to her that she realized it had been more cocoon than home. She'd wrapped herself in quilting fabric and domesticity and told herself she was content. And perhaps she had been. But she'd only been half-alive.

Falling in love had shown her how incomplete her life had been before. Home wasn't just a place, it was a feeling. It was a feeling of completeness, of being whole. With Drew she was complete.

The most annoying thing about truisms was that they were almost always true. Home, at least for her, really was where the heart is. Her heart was with Drew. She only wished she knew where his was.

BY TWO O'CLOCK, they were on the road. The keys to the house had been returned to Jane. Drew had explained that his mother was ill and they were rushing to her bedside. Jane had been sympathetic and said that she hoped his mother recovered quickly and that she'd take care of the garden until they returned. Kate bit the inside of her lip until she tasted blood, hating the lies.

She couldn't stop herself from looking at the little house as Drew backed the car out of the driveway. She'd known some of the happiest moments of her life here and she'd never see it again. She hoped Jane would remember to water the roses and the tree she and Drew had planted—God, was that only yesterday?

Blinking against the sudden sting of tears, she turned her eyes resolutely forward, refusing to look back.

THEY SPOKE VERY little. Drew kept his eyes on the road, as if driving took up every bit of his concentration. Kate didn't even bother to get out a quilt block to work on, though her tote was at her feet. The handwork had helped soothe her nerves on the drive up the coast, but it was going to take more than that to distract her this time.

Before, they'd taken a roundabout route north, hoping to discourage anyone who might have followed them. This time, Drew picked up Highway 5, right through the middle of the state. It was a route known for its speed rather than its scenic attractions. Staring out the window at miles of nothing, Kate tried very hard not to think of anything at all.

She must have succeeded fairly well, because somewhere around the middle of the state she managed to fall asleep. When she woke, it was dark and Drew was pulling off the highway. Sitting up, Kate brushed her hair back from her face and rubbed her eyes, feeling disoriented.

"Where are we?"

"Ventura County. We'll spend the night here and go into L.A. in the morning. Lavery is meeting us at the courthouse."

"We could finish the trip tonight," she pointed out, glancing at the clock in the dashboard. They were just above Los Angeles.

"I told Lavery we'd be there tomorrow." He flicked on the turn signal and turned into the parking lot of a motel that had a vacancy sign flashing out front.

"Did he want us there today?" Kate asked, remembering his side of the phone conversation and his adamant repetition of the word "tomorrow."

"I figured tomorrow was soon enough."

And that was all the explanation she was going to get, Kate thought, reading his tone. He wasn't going to tell her why he'd decided that tomorrow was soon enough. Would she be a fool to hope that part of the reason he'd insisted on the extra few hours was because he wanted to spend them with her?

"You hungry?" he asked as he shut off the engine.

"I guess I should be." Kate ran her fingers through her hair, putting it in slightly tousled order. There was a hollow feeling in her stomach, but she didn't think it had anything to do with hunger.

"There's a coffee shop. Why don't you order us something while I get a room."

Kate ordered bowls of soup and added a sandwich for Drew. The food arrived at the same time he did and they ate in near silence. Kate kept thinking about how little time was left. A few hours and they'd be back in Los Angeles.

Drew paid for their meal and they walked to the room he'd rented, still without speaking. Kate's thoughts tumbled one over the other. What if he handed her over to his boss or whomever was in charge of witnesses at a trial and then just disappeared from her life forever? What if he was immediately given another assignment?

The room was typical of a motel. Beige walls, beige carpets, beige bedspreads and curtains. There were two cheaply framed floral prints on the wall, but they were swallowed up in the sheer beigeness of their surroundings. Not that Kate would have noticed if it had been the Ritz. She wasn't interested in their surroundings, wasn't interested in anything but what was going to happen tomorrow.

"I love you." She hadn't planned to say the words, hadn't even realized that was what she was going to say when she opened her mouth.

They had stopped at the car to get what luggage they'd need for the night. Her tote and Drew's duffel hit the floor with soft thuds as if his fingers had just gone numb. She stared at his back and felt no regret at having finally said what had been locked inside her for weeks.

"I love you, Drew. I don't expect you to say it back. I

just had to tell you how I felt. I don't know what's going to happen tomorrow, whether or not I'll see you after that. I don't even know whether or not you'll *want* to see me. And it's okay if you don't." She forced a smile as he slowly turned to face her.

"Kate—"

"Really, it's all right if you don't," she rushed into speech, terrified of what he might say—of what he might *not* say. "I'm not telling you how I feel to make you feel guilty or obligated. It's not your fault I fell in love with you."

"Kate—"

"And don't tell me all about how I'm just imagining it because we spent a lot of time together and I had to depend on you to protect me. Because I thought of that. And that's not what this is. But I don't expect anything from you. And I'm not going to make any demands."

"Kate, I—"

"And you don't have to worry about me making any kind of scenes or letting anyone find out about what happened between us. I know it would get you in a lot of trouble. So once we get to L.A., I'll act like nothing happened between us."

"Kate, would you—"

"I'd just like to ask one favor." She knew she was babbling, but she couldn't seem to stop talking. If she slowed down, he might say something. And, at the moment, that scared her more than anything. "I guess the police are still going to want someone to protect me and I'd like it to be you. I don't know if I can make requests like that, but I could just tell them it was because I'm used to you. Like an old shoe."

"An old shoe?" Drew had momentarily given up trying to get a real response in. He was watching her with those ice blue eyes, his expression unreadable, as usual.

"Of course, maybe you'd rather I *didn't* ask if you could

stay with me. Maybe you'd like to go on to something else. I wouldn't mind.'' Her voice trembled slightly on the bald-faced lie, but she steadied it immediately. ''I know you've got a career to think about and I wouldn't—''

Drew stopped her by the simple expedient of pulling her into his arms and covering her mouth with his. For an instant, Kate was stiff in his hold. But a heartbeat later, she'd melted against him, her fingers curling into his shirt, clinging to him as if he were the only solid thing in the world.

Passion flared quick and hard. Suddenly the layers of clothing that separated them were too much to be tolerated. Drew's hands were impatient with Kate's shirt and she heard a seam rip. Her own fingers were occupied with trying to work his belt buckle loose.

Since the early-morning call that had destroyed the fragile facade they'd created, tension had been building in each of them. Suddenly everything had shifted. Nothing was what it had been. The past was a fantasy and the future an uncertainty. Only the present mattered, only the feel of Drew's hands on her skin, the welcome pressure of his body on her as they tumbled to the bed.

They made love like lovers long parted, still half-dressed, clothing wrenched open and pushed out of the way. Kate cried out a welcome when Drew's hard strength filled her. Drew groaned at the feeling of her soft warmth cradling him.

It was quick and hard, ending much too soon and yet leaving shock waves that seemed to go on forever. Kate clung to Drew's shoulders, listening to the ragged beat of his heart, feeling him still a part of her. He hadn't said the words, hadn't told her he loved her. But surely he'd told her with his body. He couldn't make love to her with such hunger if he didn't love her.

She shifted slightly, drawing her knees up against his hips to cradle him more fully, her fingers tracing the length of his spine under his opened shirt. She caught her breath as she felt him stir inside her, his hunger no more sated than her own.

They managed to get the rest of their clothes off this time, stripping back the covers to tumble onto the cool sheets. It was slower but no less powerful. The waves of completion were harder, deeper, seeming to rock endlessly through her body.

Kate's nails dug into his back, her neck arching as she was swept up on the crest of a wave and then plunged wildly into the heart of a storm. Drew's mouth swallowed her sobs of pleasure, his own body taut and hard above her.

Afterward Kate fell asleep as quickly and easily as a child. The day had taken a toll on her and she mumbled sleepily as Drew gently pulled away from her and settled on the bed, drawing her to his side. She was asleep instantly, her head snuggled into his shoulder, one leg thrown across his hips.

Sleep did not come as easily to Drew. He stared up at the dark ceiling, hearing her tell him she loved him. Hearing his own silence in answer.

Why hadn't he said something? Anything. Why had he stood there like a wax dummy, listening to her, seeing the fear and need in her eyes and not saying a word. Because the words he should have said had stuck in his throat, refusing to come out.

I love you. Three one-syllable words. What could be easier?

What could be harder?

THE WORDS DIDN'T COME any easier in the cool light of morning.

They'd awakened in the night, reaching for each other, making love with a kind of quiet desperation. Afterward Drew cradled Kate against his chest, wanting to give her the words she needed to hear and unable to force them out.

THE DRIVE TO L.A. was quiet. Each was wrapped in their own thoughts. Kate felt as if there were a million things she wanted to say before it was too late, but she couldn't think of any of them. She'd expected to feel self-conscious with him this morning, expected to feel uneasy that he hadn't responded to her declaration of love. There was none of that.

When she thought about it, she knew it was because, in her mind at least, he had answered her. He'd answered her with his body. And if it was naive of her to believe that he couldn't have made love to her the way he had if he didn't love her, then she was content to hold on to her naiveté.

They reached the outskirts of the sprawl that was Los Angeles and Kate felt her stomach tighten. The glass of juice and roll she'd had for breakfast suddenly felt like brick. Soon they'd be meeting with Lieutenant Lavery and Drew would be handing over his responsibility for her. Only, she'd already bet her heart on being much more than just a responsibility to him.

She slid a glance sideways at his profile. There was nothing to be read, unless she could read something significant in the fact that his jaw seemed made of granite or in the little muscle that ticked restlessly at the outer corner of his eye.

Sensing her eyes on him, he took his gaze off the road long enough to send her a quick look. At least she no longer had to worry that her heart might be in her eyes, she thought. Her mouth quirked in a self-deprecating smile. She'd always been a lousy poker player, anyway.

"We're almost there." Drew's quiet announcement sent a jolt of panic spiraling through her. Her fingers knotted together in her lap and she took a deep breath, trying to still the frantic beat of her heart. He flicked on the turn signal and turned into the parking lot.

"The courthouse is about half a block that way," he said, nodding his head to their left. "Just in case Davis has people waiting for us, we'll park here and go in a back way. I called in a favor this morning and someone will be waiting to let us in through the basement.''

''Okay.'' She couldn't make it seem real. He was talking about the possibility that someone might be waiting to kill her. She'd had weeks to adjust to the idea, but it still didn't seem to have any direct application to her.

She reached for the door handle, but Drew's hand caught her forearm. Turning back to look at him, she saw his eyes, bright and fierce with an emotion she didn't quite dare to name.

''It's going to be all right, Kate. *You're* going to be all right.''

''I know.'' She didn't know anything anymore except that this man had become her life. She tried to force a smile, but Drew leaned across the car and kissed her, quick and hard.

''I'll stay with you as long as they'll let me. Lavery may insist on assigning someone else to protect you, but I'll do my best.''

''Thank you.''

''It's what I want.'' He pulled open his car door and got out before Kate could ask if *she* was part of what he wanted.

She got out of the car. Drew was waiting for her at the rear fender. His eyes scanned the half-empty parking lot, looking for anything that seemed out of place. Apparently he was satisfied with what he saw because he set his hand against Kate's back and urged her forward.

She'd never felt so exposed in her life. The parking lot seemed more like the Gobi Desert, huge, empty and exposed. She wanted nothing so much as to reach out and take hold of Drew's hand, holding it for comfort. But of course she couldn't do anything of the sort.

From now on, she had to think of him as a police officer. He'd never said anything about it, but she didn't doubt that if anyone ever found out they were lovers, he'd almost certainly lose his job. There'd be no explaining how right it had been, that he hadn't taken advantage of her.

So she walked beside him, trying to look as calm as he did, wishing she could turn and run for the safety of the car and then take the car and leave the city behind forever.

Drew could feel her trembling, could sense her fear. He wanted nothing so much as to put his arm around her, hold her close and tell her that she never had to be afraid of anything again. Even better would be to take her back to the car and just get in and drive away. To hell with Davis. Let someone else be the sacrificial lamb on this particular altar of justice. All he cared about was Kate, keeping her safe.

"There's an alley just past that building on the right. We'll cut through there and come in behind the courthouse."

"Okay." Kate barely heard him; she was too busy trying to force enough strength into her knees to keep her upright.

"Detective Hunter?" The man stepped out from behind a van. Drew pushed Kate behind him, his hand reaching inside his jacket for his shoulder holster. Seeing the blue uniform the man wore slowed the motion, but he didn't relax his stance.

"I'm Officer Williams, Detective." He looked very serious, very official. Drew's hand remained inside his jacket, though he'd not yet drawn his gun. His eyes skimmed the area behind the officer.

"What are you doing here?" he asked at last.

"Lieutenant Lavery sent me to escort Ms. Sloane to the courthouse. He was delayed."

"Delayed? What happened?"

Kate obeyed the subtle motion of his shoulder and edged farther behind him. She didn't know what was wrong. Officer Williams looked genuine. He looked just like the policeman who'd visited her elementary class one year and talked about traffic safety. He had the sort of square-jawed, not-too-handsome face that inspired trust.

"The lieutenant had car trouble on the way here. He radioed the station and asked that someone be sent to meet you." Williams's hand moved slightly, a hardly noticeable motion that happened to put it a little closer to his holstered gun.

"The hell he did." Drew reached back with his left hand, catching Kate's shoulder and shoving her between two parked cars. Caught off balance, she stumbled and fell to her knees, feeling the hard asphalt scrape her skin through her slacks. There were shots—two, three? She threw her hands over her ears as the sounds seemed to echo inside her head.

And then Drew was beside her, grabbing her arm, shaking her, demanding to know if she was all right.

"I'm fine." She blinked, looking past his shoulder to focus on the uniformed leg she could see in the gap between the cars. It was ominously still.

"Is he dead?" She realized she'd whispered the question, a ridiculous precaution considering the amount of noise the shots had made.

"I don't know. He won't be bothering us again." Drew was levering fresh bullets into the clip on his .38, unconcerned with whether or not Williams was dead. "Lavery didn't send him. He wouldn't risk sending someone else, but if he had, there's a code. And this guy didn't know the code."

"Maybe he forgot." Kate hardly knew what she was saying. She couldn't take her eyes from that leg. "He looked like a real policeman."

"He probably was." He ignored her gasp of shock. "This was clumsy. They must not have had much time to set this up." He frowned at a dent in the gray door behind Kate's head. "We'll go back to the car. Get the hell out of here. Then I can get hold of Lavery and find out what happened."

"Are there more of them?" Kate was pleasantly surprised that her voice was level.

"Probably. Stay down. We'll try to stay between the cars. If I tell you to do something, you do it immediately. Don't stop to question me."

"Okay." She nodded, acknowledging the logic of that.

Drew would have liked to say something to erase the fear from her eyes, but there was nothing he could say.

Keeping to a crouch, Kate followed Drew as he eased his way around the parked cars. Adrenaline pumped through her, keeping screaming fear at bay, keeping her head clear. Once they were out of this, she would probably collapse completely, she thought, but for the moment she was holding on to her control, even if it was only by the skin of her teeth.

"Damn."

She crept up behind Drew, looking over his shoulder at the gap between them, and the welcome familiarity of the sedan they'd parked just a few minutes before. There were ten yards of bare asphalt between them and safety. It looked like a thousand.

"We're going to run for it. You go first. I'll be right behind you. Open the driver's door and slide over into the passenger seat. Get the key in the ignition." He reached into his pocket and pulled out the keys, pressing them into her hand. "I'll be right behind you."

"Okay."

"Don't stop if you hear shooting, and if something happens to me you keep going."

"But—"

"No. There're no buts. If something happens to me, you take the car and drive like hell. Go to the courthouse. Drive up the damn steps if you have to. Lavery will show up."

"Drew, I—"

"Just do it." He took hold of her upper arm, urging her in front of him, giving her no time to tell him any of the hundred things she wanted to say. "Keep as low as you can and run as fast as you can."

"Drew—"

"Now!"

And somehow she was running across the hot asphalt, hearing Drew's footsteps behind her. Or was that the pounding of her own heart she heard? They were going to make it, she thought. Just a little farther.

She heard a shot and the windshield next to her suddenly had a neat little hole, surrounded by a spider's web of cracks. Despite Drew's orders, she turned. Drew had stopped, dropping to one knee in a classic pose, arm out, the gun an extension of his hand. She saw him fire and jerked her head in time to see a body tumble from the top of the van where Williams had been waiting for them.

"I told you to keep going," he snarled, rising to his feet and starting toward her. Before she could find the words to defend herself, she saw a movement behind him.

"Behind you!" Drew spun, bringing up his gun. But the movement wasn't quick enough. Kate saw the impact of the bullet as it struck him in the chest. She screamed and before the sound had died, another shot struck him. He fell, tumbling back behind the front fender of a car. She was beside him in a minute, oblivious to the fact that a third bullet shattered the headlight a split second after she passed it.

Grabbing Drew under the shoulders, she dragged him a few feet until he was completely behind the car, not even feeling the strain on her arms and back as they took his weight.

She eased him down as gently as she could, unaware that she was sobbing under her breath. Blood was already soaking his jacket, making an ugly black stain on the gray linen.

"Dammit, Kate, I told you not to stop." His voice was stronger than she'd expected. Probably shock prevented him from feeling the pain. But that would wear off shortly. She had to stop the bleeding.

"I've never been much good at obeying orders," she told

him. She pushed open his jacket, feeling faint when she saw the spreading stain on his white shirt.

"Well, you're going to obey this one." He reached up to catch her hand, his grip stronger than it had any right to be. "You're going to get in that car and get out of here. That guy is still out there. He's just looking for an angle to get a shot. Now go."

"No." Her eyes met his. Tears streamed down her cheeks, but there was hard determination in her look. "I'm not leaving you."

"Do as I say."

"Shut up. You're wasting your energy." She was ripping open his shirt as she spoke. "I love you, and I'm not leaving you here to bleed to death in this filthy parking lot."

"Please, Kate. Go. Please."

It was harder to fight him when she heard the weakness in his voice. But she couldn't leave him. She set her jaw.

"No."

The shock was wearing off and Drew could feel pain settling in his chest. In contrast, his left arm was numb. He was badly wounded. Maybe fatally, he thought, with complete clarity. There was nothing Kate could do here except get herself killed trying to save him. The thought of dying didn't frighten him half as much as the thought of something happening to Kate.

"You stupid little idiot." He gathered every bit of his energy and put as much contempt as he could into his voice. "I don't love you. I don't even particularly like you. You were just convenient. It helped pass the time. You don't mean a damn thing to me. Now get the hell out of here."

He saw Kate's eyes lift to his face, but his vision was starting to blur, making it impossible to see her expression. Now she'd go. She'd leave and he could at least hope that she'd get to safety.

And then she smiled at him, the radiance of the expression penetrating the fog that was starting to swallow him.

"You must love me at least a little or you wouldn't be trying so hard to get rid of me."

"I love you a lot," he said, feeling despair swallow him. "That's why you have to go. Please, Kate. Please." The last word was hardly audible.

Kate froze for a moment, her eyes on his face. But there was no time to analyze what she was feeling. No time to savor the fact that Drew had said he loved her. She heard a sound, the soft scuff of leather soles on a hard surface.

Lifting her head, she saw a tall figure step into the gap between the cars. His back was to the sun and she could make out nothing more than an outline. Her hand dropped to the asphalt, her fingers closing around the butt of her gun. Her purse was lying somewhere in the parking lot, dropped and forgotten. But she'd had the gun in her jacket pocket. She'd set it beside Drew when she'd opened his jacket and now it came into her hand as naturally as if she'd been handling it all her life.

She saw the man's arm moving, lifting toward her. There was a glint of sunlight on a gun barrel and then she lifted her hand. Pointing the gun like a finger, the way the instructor had said, she pulled the trigger. Once. Twice. A third time. And then there was nothing to shoot at. He'd fallen back on the ground and he wasn't moving.

Kate lowered the gun slowly, feeling nothing but a vague hope that it was over, that this was the last of them.

"I told you I'd do what I had to if the time came," she said. But when she looked down at Drew, she saw that he was unconscious. Blood still pooled from the wounds on his chest, spreading at a frightening rate.

"Don't you dare die on me, Drew Hunter," she muttered under her breath. Ripping buttons in her haste, she stripped her blouse off, folding it into a pad and pressing it against the wound that seemed to be bleeding the most. She could hear the wail of sirens nearby.

She knelt beside Drew, oblivious to the fact that she was just wearing torn slacks and a bra, keeping the makeshift pressure pad against his chest, waiting for the police to find them and praying that it wouldn't be too late.

It couldn't be too late.

IF SHE LIVED HERE for a thousand years, Kate didn't think she'd ever get used to the fact that it rained in the middle of summer and the temperature didn't go down even a degree. Ninety degrees and ninety percent humidity was a tough adjustment to make after living in Southern California's dry desert heat.

But then she was finding it hard to adjust to almost everything about this move. She just didn't feel like adjusting, she admitted to herself as she eased her car into her parking space. She stared at the concrete wall in front of her, making no effort to get out, though with the engine off, the air conditioning vanished and the car almost immediately became a steam bath.

It wasn't that there was anything wrong with New Jersey. At least, there was nothing wrong with it that wouldn't have also been wrong with any of the other forty-nine states.

Drew.

She closed her eyes against the pain in her chest. There didn't seem to be much reason to adapt to the new life that had been provided for her, not when she felt dead inside. The only thing that made it possible for her to keep going was the knowledge that he was all right, that he'd survived the shooting and was going to make a full recovery.

Sighing, she got out of the car and pulled the bag of groceries from the passenger seat. Wrapping her arm around it, she made her way up the steps to the first level of apartments. Her apartment was at the far end from the garage and she supposed it would make a miserable trip when winter came. The thought didn't bother her.

Sooner or later, she'd surely snap out of this depression. After all, she had a lot to be grateful for. Lester Davis was in prison, serving a lengthy term as a result of her testimony as well as that of one of the gunmen he'd hired to kill her. She'd been given refuge by the Witness Protection Program. She had a new identity, a new job and a new life in a new city. Drew was alive and healthy somewhere.

And probably well on his way to forgetting her, she thought bleakly. Maybe she'd only imagined him saying that he loved her. In the stress of the moment, she could have imagined almost anything. And it didn't really matter, anyway. Even if he did love her, it didn't change the situation, which was that he had a life, a job, a career. And he couldn't have any of those things with her. Not anymore.

Her own life was on hold. In a way, she felt as if she was just marking time, waiting for Davis's men to find her, waiting to become a news story, like poor Joseph Smithson. She shook her head and pushed away the morbid thought. She was alive and she'd been given a chance to build a new life. She had to be grateful for that. And if that new life seemed like an empty shell without Drew, then she was just going to have to learn to live with it.

Blinking back tears, she hefted the bag a little higher on her hip and struggled to find her key. She fitted it into the lock and shoved the door open, sighing as she stepped into the air-conditioned comfort of her apartment. She didn't bother to switch on any lights, relying on the muted illumination of sunlight through the drapes as she made her way to the kitchen.

She'd just set the bag on the counter when she heard someone speak her name.

"Kate."

She froze, feeling as if she'd fallen through a time warp.

A few months ago, another state, another apartment. The same voice. Only he'd called her Ms. Sloane then. She closed her eyes for a minute, telling herself that she was hallucinating. She'd spent too many lonely nights lying awake fantasizing about Drew finding her. Afraid of having the charade that was her life found out, she'd isolated herself, living in her memories. That's all it was.

"Kate." She shuddered and closed her eyes, feeling as if her sanity hung by the thinnest of threads. "Look at me, Kate." There was tenderness in that impossible voice.

"No."

"Why not?"

"Because I've imagined you too many times. And always, when I open my eyes, you're not there. I don't think I could bear it again."

There was a whisper of movement behind her and then she felt hands close over her arms, strong and hard. And real. He turned her to face him but she kept her eyes shut, childishly afraid to open them.

"Look at me, Kate. I'm really here this time."

Hesitantly she lifted her eyelids and stared into Drew's familiar ice blue eyes. He looked just as she remembered him. Thinner, maybe, with new hollows under his cheekbones, evidence of how close he'd come to dying, of how long and hard the recovery had been.

"Drew?" She lifted her fingers to his face, needing to feel the reality of him. "You're here."

"I'm here. I came as soon as I could. You didn't think you'd get rid of me that easily, did you?"

"I didn't know. I wasn't sure you didn't want to be gotten rid of."

The tangled sentence made him cock one eyebrow, his mouth quirking with humor.

"I didn't want to be gotten rid of," he told her. His hands

slid from her shoulders to her back, pulling her closer. "I don't plan on ever being gotten rid of."

"How did you find me?"

"By twisting a lot of arms, calling in every favor I was ever owed and breaking the law half a dozen times. I love you."

They were the words she'd dreamed of hearing. She closed her eyes, savoring them, even as she knew she had to send him away.

"You can't love me."

"Why not? Because I was too stupid to admit it before this?"

"It's not that." She twisted out of his arms, backing a few steps away, knowing she had to rush the words out now, before she let her hunger for him drown out her common sense.

"I'm in the witness program, Drew."

"I know that. Why do you think it took me so long to track you down? I wouldn't have been able to find you if Lavery hadn't been willing to pull a few strings for me." He smiled and reached for her, but she edged away.

"I have a new identity. A whole new life."

"I know what the witness program is, Kate." His smile had faded, his eyes taking on a wary look. Was it too late? Was there no place for him in this new life?

"Then you know I can't go back to L.A. Not as long as Davis is alive."

"I'm not asking you to go back." He reached out and caught her hands, drawing her forward, despite her half-hearted resistance. "I'm staying here."

"You can't. You've got a life in California. A job. Friends."

"I don't have a life without you." He wrapped his arms around her, holding her close, feeling relief wash over him. She was trying to send him away for his own sake. "If you have to make a new life, we'll make it together. There's nothing in California that I can't live without. But I can't live without you."

She hesitated, torn between her need to believe him and her fear that he'd come to regret his decision.

"You can't give up everything for me."

"I already have."

"You'll end up hating me," she whispered.

"Not in this lifetime." He caught her hand, putting it against his heart. "It took me a long time to admit it, but I need you, Kate. I love you and I need you in my life. Don't ask me to leave."

"I should."

"What does your heart say, Kate? What does it tell you to do?"

She closed her eyes, knowing she was about to take the biggest chance of her lifetime. When she opened them again, they were almost pure green and filled with love.

"My heart says I'd be a fool to try and get rid of you."

"Listen to it, Kate." His mouth was only a whisper away from hers. "Listen to your heart."

As if she could do anything else, Kate thought, lifting her arms to draw him close.

**He didn't know she was his bodyguard,
and she wasn't cut out to deceive.**

NOT WITHOUT LOVE

Roberta Leigh

CHAPTER ONE

REES DENTON banged his fist on the boardroom table. 'I don't need a bodyguard and I won't have one. Never! Is that understood?'

'Understood but not agreed,' said Sir Andrew Seymour, chairman of Engineering 2000, and the other directors around the table murmured their agreement. 'Be sensible, Rees. You can't ignore these threats on your life.'

'Whoever made them is a crank,' Rees said irritably.

'Cranks are the ones to watch out for,' put in a balding man with glasses. 'History shows—'

'I don't give a damn what history shows!' Rees cut in, his dark eyebrows drawn into a frown. 'The police can handle it.'

'They are,' Sir Andrew intervened. 'But they need more time. They're working through the passenger list and checking all next of kin. But whittling down the suspects takes time, and this crank, as you call him, could strike any moment.'

'I fail to see how a bodyguard will help,' Rees said obstinately, smoothing back his thick black hair with a strong, well-manicured hand.

'They are specially trained for this kind of work,' another director explained.

Rees reflected on this, then shook his head. 'No, I won't have my every move monitored. I'd feel like a kid with a nanny.'

Resigned glances were exchanged and throats cleared.

'Be sensible, Rees,' Sir Andrew reiterated. 'It's your life we're talking about. The man's dangerous.'

The chorus of endorsements was louder than before. This threat to the life of their managing director had them worried, coming as it did so soon after the crash of the plane which had only just been fitted with Engineering 2000's special 'grey box', devised by Rees to make flying safer.

Most people in the situation in which he now found himself would have immediately agreed to protection. But Rees Denton wasn't 'most people'. Not only was he a brilliant inventor, organiser and negotiator— invaluable assets to the company—but, like most individualists, he was also obstinate.

He stood up, all six foot two of determined muscle and grace, and scanned his fellow directors with piercing dark eyes. 'No guard,' he reiterated. 'That's my last word on the subject. Now, I suggest we get down to the business of the day and waste no more time.'

For the next hour the meeting continued, and as soon as it was over Rees departed, giving pressure of work as his reason for not lunching with the board, though the directors knew quite well that he merely wished to avoid further discussion on a subject he had declared *verboten*.

'We can't let him get away with it,' the vice-chairman stated. 'If anything happened to him...'

'He's not a man you can order around,' Sir Andrew said. 'But you're right. We have to do something.'

'What do you propose?'

'I'm not sure.' Sir Andrew's voice was as smooth as the silver-grey hair brushed back from his high forehead, which gave him the look of a professor rather than that of the astute City man he was.

But Sir Andrew was very sure indeed, for he had known the fuss Rees would make, and had allowed for it, determined to get his own way by stealth if necessary.

As soon as lunch was over, he went to his office and put in a call to Murray Guardian of Guardian Security, who had been recommended to him by a senior police officer at Scotland Yard. A brief word explaining the urgency of the situation, brought him an appointment to see Murray Guardian within the hour, after which, well pleased with himself, he ordered the chauffeur to bring round his car.

Julia Winterton put down the receiver and breathed a sigh of relief. Murray had agreed to see her at four, and if she was lucky he would have another assignment for her. But no more acting nursemaid to the rich and spoilt. She had made it quite clear that, if Guardians couldn't give her the kind of job for which she had been trained, she would leave. But she wanted to give Murray another chance first. Not only was it the ethical thing to do, but she hoped she could twist his arm!

She looked at her watch. It was too early to leave, but she would rather sit at Murray's for the next hour than twiddle her thumbs here. With a cursory glance in the mirror, she left her Sloane Street apartment and took the elevator down to the plush foyer—a tall, willowy girl with long, blue-black hair, and a Miss World body.

Twenty minutes later she was waiting in Murray's reception-room, a smile on her beautifully curved mouth as she remembered how nervously she had waited to see him on that first occasion six months ago, knowing that female security guards were still a rarity, and hoping he wouldn't dismiss her out of hand because she was a model.

But modelling had bored her once she had reached the top, and though the money was fantastic, and her ego massaged every time she walked down the street and someone recognised her from the front cover of Harpers, Tatler or Vogue, she had eventually begun questioning whether the constant battling against sex-hungry males who considered models easy game was worth it all.

It had been a suave City type who had been the last straw.

A gentleman during dinner and dancing at Annabel's, he had become a sex-mad octopus outside her front door.

'Bloody hell!' he had exclaimed, when she had levelled him to the ground with a karate chop. 'Where did you learn *that*?'

'I have four brothers,' she had said nonchalantly. 'And they thought I should know how to protect myself!'

He had departed fast, and, though the incident had been amusing in retrospect, it had reinforced her dissatisfaction with her present life. Women were still the butt of sexual innuendo and harassment, no matter what they did, but some professions were more vulnerable to it than others, and show business and modelling were two of them. But what else could she do, and where would she find a man interested in her as a person and not primarily as a bedworthy partner?

After careful deliberation, she concluded that the first thing to do was to change her occupation. The very next day she had read an article in *The Times* about security guards, and had known instantly that this was the work she wanted to do. Careful enquiry told her that the best company was Guardian Security, and within two months of seeing them she had become a fully trained member.

Her hope that a different career would bring romance into her life had not materialised, for apart from Murray Guardian himself, who oddly she couldn't think of romantically— though he fitted the bill more than any man she knew—there had been no one. But there was still the challenge of the job. If only Murray would *give* her a challenge instead of asking her to act as nanny to a host of ludicrous people. Like the oil baron's son she had escorted from his home in Texas to Eton, his new school in England.

Concordeing across the Atlantic to Dallas, the man next to her had wasted no time putting a pudgy hand on her arm.

'Going on vacation?' he had asked.

'No. I'm on a job. I'm a bodyguard.'

He chuckled. 'Whose body you guarding?'

'Mine.'

'I'd guard it better if you'd let me.'

'I doubt it. I'm a gold medallist in the martial arts.'

That had quickly put paid to *him*, and after seeing gum-chewing Henry Hackenburg Junior safely ensconced in school she had been sent to watch over a sheika, in London for the summer, and seemingly intent on buying out Harrods. Carrying her parcels, her jewellery and her money—no cheques, all cash—Julia had thought long and hard about resigning, for which reason she was now waiting to see Murray.

If he didn't utilise the expensive training he had given her, she would apply to one of his rivals, and if they offered her similar tame assignments she would return to modelling. Yet, even as she said this to herself, she knew she could never go back to the fashion world. Indeed, if it hadn't been for Chris she would never have entered it. Funny, she hadn't thought of him in years.

Blond, blue-eyed Chris, friend of her oldest brother, who had spent most weekends on their estate, and endeared himself to her family by being as fanatic about fitness as they were.

Though she was the only girl among four brothers, she had not been spoilt. On the contrary, they had expected her to join them in all their sporting activities. She had enjoyed being 'one of the boys' until she had fallen in love with Chris, but the day he called her 'kiddo'—which happened to be her eighteenth birthday—she had known it was time to change her image. After all, what was the point having wide-spaced violet eyes and silky black hair if the man you were crazy about saw you as 'kiddo'?

A heart-to-heart talk with her mother resulted in her being sent to London for a three-month beauty and modelling course, and her decision to actually become a model had been met with stoical acceptance by her parents.

Her meteoric rise had astonished even herself, though by this time Chris had married and gone abroad, and she was hard put to it to remember she had ever had a crush on him.

The sound of Murray's door opening brought Julia back to the present, and she looked up as he emerged with a tall, distinguished-looking man in his late fifties. Watching them talking in low voices at the door, Julia remembered how nervous she had been the first time she had met Murray Guardian.

'Miss Winterton?' He had come forward to greet her as she had entered his office, and she had instantly liked him. Average in height, this strongly built man in his mid-thirties, with his dark gold hair and piercing blue eyes, had exactly epitomised her idea of someone who owned and ran a security company.

He had waved her to a chair and sat down at his desk which, like its owner, lacked pretension, as did the rest of the furniture in the room, being dark oak and functional.

She had felt comfortable sitting opposite him, for, though his look had been appraising, it had also been respectful. He had clearly been intrigued that someone looking like a model—she hadn't yet told him she was—should want to become a bodyguard.

'Tell me about yourself,' he had said, leaning back in his chair.

'I've been modelling for nearly four years, and want a change.'

His eyebrows had risen. 'It would certainly be *that*.'

'I know.'

'The training's tough, and I fail thirty per cent.'

'You're not putting me off, Mr Guardian. I grew up with four tough brothers who treated me like a fifth!'

'Then there should be no problem.' He smiled. 'How old are you?'

'Twenty-three.'

'Exactly the right age. Store detectives are in great demand.'

She remembered how aghast she had been. 'Store detectives? But I thought I'd—'

'Guard someone from a terrorist attack?'

'Well, yes—no, not exactly.' But she hadn't expected to peer around dress rails in department stores either!

'Take it or leave it,' he had said crisply. 'I've plenty of other candidates.'

Realising she had expected too much, she had capitulated. Once she had proved herself, she could be demanding. Till then, she would keep her mouth shut!

'I'd like to train,' she had said firmly.

'Good. Report here Monday, eight-thirty, with your suitcase. You'll be spending the next six weeks at my country house in Sussex. Good luck.'

It had all sounded so cut and dried, but then security work couldn't afford any beating around the bush. It required nerve, courage, and physical stamina. All of which she had in plenty.

There had been fourteen of them on the course, thirteen men and she the only girl. Murray's country house was a rambling old place set in ten acres, and at times it seemed as if they crawled over every one of them! Still, they were a fit lot, having been hand-picked, a fact that Murray never let them forget as he put them through a gruelling course in self-defence, attack, and undercover work.

Unbelievably, Julia graduated top of her class, and the amused glint in Murray's eyes when he had told her had made her more determined than ever not to be assigned 'female-type' jobs once she had some experience under her belt.

Murray had thrown a party for them that evening in the

large oak-beamed reception-room, and she had worn the one dress she had brought with her for this occasion—a violet silk to match her eyes—and let her long, silky hair flow down her back in an ebony swathe.

Every head had turned at her entrance, and it had been *her* turn to be amused. Men were still men, she had thought, and a pretty woman still a target.

Next day Murray had called them in separately.

'Much as I'd like to give you the kind of assignment you want,' he had said to her without preamble, 'I can't.'

'You mean you were serious about my working in a department store?'

'Yes. You deserve better, but many of our jobs require muscle, and even those that don't invariably state they want men.'

'That's discriminatory and against the law,' she had protested.

'I know. So they don't put the request in writing. But if I send a woman, I won't get the work.'

Accepting this, Julia took what was offered, and for six months fumed and fretted her way through a variety of tedious assignments—Henry Hackenburg and the sheika among them—until she had finally had enough.

Hence her coming here today to have a showdown with Murray.

Almost as if he sensed it, he gave her a warm smile and paused in front of her to introduce her to the man beside him. 'Meet my star pupil,' he said. 'Julia, Sir Andrew Seymour. She's the only person on any of my courses who graduated with a hundred per cent pass.'

'Well done.' Sir Andrew was plainly astonished, and gave her such an appraising look that Julia was startled. And at his age, too!

'Wait for me in my office, Julia,' Murray said. 'I'll be with you in a moment.'

Julia did as she was bid. Now that confrontation was imminent, was she prepared to go to another agency if Murray didn't give her what she wanted? Before she could decide, he had returned and perched on the side of his desk.

'Out with it.' He smiled. 'You've something on your mind, haven't you?'

She nodded and told him, and though he appreciated her views, as he always did, he was unable to offer a solution. 'I'm always putting your name forward,' he said, 'but in the final event, it's the clients who make the choice.'

'Then you should start re-educating your clients!'

'Do you have another job *I* can do?' Murray asked, mouth curving. 'If I do as you suggest, I sure as hell won't be able to carry on here!'

'President Reagan's guarded by women as well as men,' Julia asserted.

'I deliver what I'm asked for,' Murray reiterated. 'I—' He was interrupted by the telephone, spoke into it, then glanced at Julia. 'Sir Andrew wants to see me again. Hang on, will you?'

He strode away, returning a few moments later with Sir Andrew.

'My meeting you was extremely fortuitous, Miss Winterton,' Sir Andrew began, and Julia, though she smiled politely, inwardly fumed. If he wanted her to watch over his wife or grandchild, the answer would be no! Didn't Murray ever learn?

But what Sir Andrew wanted of her had nothing to do with his family, and as she heard of the death threats his managing director was receiving her hopes started to rise. Yet there was one question she had to ask, even though she knew it was hardly a tactful one.

'*Was* Mr Denton's invention in any way to blame for the crash?'

'Absolutely not.' Sir Andrew spoke from total conviction.

'It may not make flying a hundred per cent foolproof, but it goes a long way towards it. Forgive me if I don't go into the technical details, but—'

'There's no need,' Murray put in, giving Julia a hard look. 'Sir Andrew wants you to guard Mr Denton until the police discover who's behind these threats.'

'Unfortunately Rees won't accept police protection—won't accept *any* protection, in fact.'

'Why not?' Julia asked.

'He says it will curtail his freedom.'

'What we suggest,' Murray said, pretending not to notice Julia's astonishment, 'is that we guard him without his knowing it.'

Julia's beautifully arched eyebrows rose. 'How?'

'We'll arrange that you stand in for Mrs Williamson, his personal assistant,' Sir Andrew answered before Murray could. 'She's been with Rees for years and is very worried for him—as we all are. We'll get her to say she has to go to Canada to see her mother who is very ill. Rees won't suspect anything because he knows the woman recently had an operation.'

'You seem to have worked things out very well.' Julia smiled. 'But it will only give me a legitimate reason for being with him during the day. What about the evenings?'

'He works late,' Sir Andrew replied.

'And when he doesn't work late, and weekends? What then?'

Both men looked flummoxed, though it was Murray whose brow cleared first. 'You'll have to charm him, Julia; make him so besotted over you that he won't want you out of his sight.'

Sir Andrew chuckled. 'That shouldn't be difficult, if you don't mind my saying so, Miss Winterton. Rees has an eye for the ladies, and you're extremely eye-catching.'

Julia wasn't sure she liked where this might lead. In fact,

she was darned sure she didn't! And she wanted to get her position quite clear before deciding whether or not to accept the job.

'Even if Mr Denton finds me attractive, I can't see him wanting to date me all of his spare time.'

'I don't see why not,' Sir Andrew said jovially. 'Rees is very single-minded, and when he sets his sights on a lady, he—well, he's rather inclined to pursue them.'

'And catch them, I suppose?'

Only then did the two men see where Julia's questions were leading, and though Murray couldn't hide a grin, Sir Andrew looked distinctly uncomfortable.

'My dear Miss Winterton, I wasn't suggesting... Believe me, nothing was further from my mind.'

'I'm sure not,' Julia replied evenly, 'but it's very much in mine. I like the sound of this job, Sir Andrew, but there's a limit to what I'm prepared to do in order to get it.'

'Oh, come on, Julia,' Murray said. 'You held your own in the modelling world, so I'm sure you can hold it with Mr Denton.'

Julia was sure too, but she resented having to use her femininity in order to get this assignment. Anyway, what sort of man was Rees Denton? Only an idiot would discount the threats he had been getting. He sounded macho to the point of stupidity—probably considered it a sign of weakness to worry about his safety.

'Come on,' Murray urged again. 'Mata Hari had no trouble, and I can't see you having any either!'

Julia smiled at Murray's confidence in her, though her resentment remained. But she had asked for a challenge, and Rees Denton certainly presented one.

'When do I start?' she asked.

'Tomorrow,' Sir Andrew answered. 'Rees is shut away in his laboratory today and most of tomorrow, which will give me a chance to speak to Mrs Williamson and brief her. I'll get her to say you're the daughter of a friend of hers, and insist you're just the person to take over from her while she's away.'

'But I've never worked in an office in my life!'

'Mrs Williamson won't leave for a couple of days. That should give you plenty of time to learn the ropes.'

Wow! Julia thought. Two whole days to learn to be a personal assistant. Next, he might suggest she study for three and start running the company! Maybe she should tell Murray she had been joking when she had said she was tired of oil barons' sons and child tennis stars! Except Murray wouldn't appreciate the joke.

'Everything settled, then?' he asked, as if guessing her thoughts.

'Yes,' she mumbled.

'Then I'll tell Mrs Williamson to expect you at four tomorrow,' Sir Andrew stated. 'If anything bothers you at any time, don't hesitate to come and talk to me.'

'It's better if Julia talks to *me*,' Murray put in. 'Mr Denton might suspect something if he sees you and Julia in cahoots.'

'Quite right. I hadn't thought of that.'

Knowing the interview was at an end and that Murray would want to get down to the financial aspect, Julia said goodbye and went to the door. She felt Sir Andrew's eyes on her, and knew he was still assessing her, wondering if she could handle Mr Denton—which Murray was probably wondering too. But she'd show them both. Not wishing Rees Denton any harm, she hoped she would have a chance to use her training, for it would be marvellous to prove to Murray once and for all that she was as good as any man—if not better!

An hour later she was back in her apartment, looking through her clothes and trying to decide what to wear for her meeting with her new boss. One thing about modelling—it had given her a sense of style, but whether hers would be

suitable for attracting the roving eye of Mr Denton was another matter.

Her hand stopped at a mauve silk Armani suit and, taking
it out, she held it against her and looked in the mirror. Thick-
fringed violet eyes stared back at her, and lowering them
seductively she lifted her long, raven tresses atop her head
and pouted her lips—*à la* Mata Hari. But this was the eighties, and an office *femme fatale* wouldn't be so obvious.
Maybe she should start off with a bun and heavy spectacles,
and gradually graduate to the temptress. But that would take
time, and Rees Denton could be lying in a pool of blood by
then!

Maybe she'd just be herself. After all, she had never had
any trouble attracting men in the past, and Mr Denton, obstinate and foolhardy though he was, was still a man!

Padding into the bathroom, she slipped off her clothes and
turned on the shower, enjoying the feel of the cool water
needling her skin and forming rivulets between her creamy
breasts and down the length of her willowy frame. Her long
raven hair wound itself around her shoulders like a swathe,
and she pulled it back and plaited it quickly before soaping
herself.

What sort of man was her new client? she wondered again.
From what Sir Andrew had let drop, he was pig-headed and
macho, both of them characteristics she could do without.
Still, she must not start off prejudiced, for as Murray had so
frequently said during her training: 'Many of the people
whose safety we protect may not be the kind we would
choose as friends, but we're there to guard them, not judge
them, so never, ever allow your emotions to become involved.'

Unhappily, this dictum didn't apply here, Julia admitted
as she turned off the shower and wrapped herself in a pink
towelling robe. She *had* to form a judgement of Mr Denton
in order to make herself attractive to him, as well as to enable

her to keep him at arm's length. No easy task, come to think of it, to blow hot one minute and cool the next.

Stop thinking of it, she admonished her reflection as she dressed for a dinner date with a girlfriend. Tomorrow was only a few hours away, and before jumping to any further conclusions about her charge she must first meet him. Only then could she map out a plan to lure him into her net and, if necessary, render him harmless!

CHAPTER TWO

PROMPTLY at four next day Julia arrived at the ten-storey bronze and steel structure in Docklands that housed Engineering 2000.

The interior was equally sparkling, and, as she walked across the white travertine marble floor to the mahogany reception desk in the middle of it, her eyes were drawn to the bank of wall-climbing elevators.

Hardly had she given her name when she was directed to Elevator Three and instructed to go to Room Fifty on the tenth floor. This turned out to be an elegantly furnished office, supervised by an equally elegant Mrs Williamson, a forty-year-old woman who was the epitome of the perfect personal assistant. Julia's confidence plummeted as she wondered how she could possibly follow in such footsteps. Bearing in mind Mrs Williamson was supposed to have personally recommended her to Mr Denton, he would expect her to be pretty damn good. Some hope, when she had never worked in an office in her life!

'I can't tell you how relieved we are to have you,' Mrs Williamson murmured. 'I'm only sorry you have to be here under false pretences.'

'So am I,' Julia said. 'But I've handled far more tricky situations.' Surreptitiously she crossed her fingers.

'You shouldn't find your work here too difficult,' Mrs Williamson went on, assessing her frankly. 'Basically you'll be attending to the more mundane matters, so Mr Denton can concentrate on the important ones.'

'Mundane matters?' Julia questioned.

'Such as keeping tabs on his meetings and appointments,

holding the media off his back, dealing with as much of his mail as you can without bothering him... You'll soon pick it up.'

'Oh, sure,' Julia said with bravura, not sure at all. And there was still the matter of making him fall for her and holding him off at one and the same time!

'Mr Denton often works late,' Mrs Williamson continued. 'Which means you often stay behind with him. But that should fit in very well with why you're here,' she said with a conspiratorial smile, before rising and going to the adjoining door. There was a quiet exchange of words as she put her head around it, then she turned and beckoned to Julia. 'Mr Denton will see you now.'

Nervous as a schoolgirl being summoned to the head, Julia walked into the managing director's office. Except no managing director—outside of a Hollywood romantic epic—ever looked like this, she thought, as a six-foot, dark-eyed Adonis, with strong, patrician features and thick ebony hair, came towards her with panther's grace, an easy smile and hand outstretched.

'Sit down and tell me about yourself.' His voice was deep and resonant, his gesture spare as he waved her to a chair and sat opposite her.

Julia's nervousness increased. She had met many good-looking men in the course of her career, but never one quite so handsome and charismatic. She knew he was waiting for her to speak and could have kicked herself for not finding out what Mrs Williamson had told him about her. She could hardly give herself a false curriculum vitae and find it differed drastically from what he had heard.

'Well?' he asked abruptly, his deep-set, dark eyes narrowing as they regarded her.

'I'm the daughter of a friend of your personal assistant,' she said in a rush.

'So I believe.' He leaned back in his chair, still keeping

his eyes on her. 'I understand you haven't done this kind of work before, but as you've come with Mrs Williamson's recommendation, that's good enough for me.'

'It's really a matter of common sense, I think,' Julia murmured, feeling her way.

'Not quite. You need to know the names of the people I'm always available to, and the ones I avoid like the plague.'

'I'm sure Mrs Williamson has a list for me,' Julia said easily, 'and I've a good memory.'

He eyed her keenly. 'You don't look a fool,' he said. 'In fact, you look good enough to be a model.'

He meant it as a compliment, she knew, but it wasn't one she appreciated, having deliberately changed her career in order *not* to be judged on her looks. Drat the man! Why was he staring at her like this? Anyone would think he was taking an inventory of her! As his eyes continued roaming over her face and body, she was hard put not to disclose her true identity and see *his* face!

'Don't you like my saying you look like a model?' he asked, correctly reading her irritated expression.

'It's simply that I consider them witless,' she shrugged. 'I mean, how intelligent do you have to be to pose in front of a camera or mince down a catwalk?'

'Not intelligent at all,' he agreed, so readily that she longed to hit him.

'Do you know many, Mr Denton?' The instant she asked the question, she regretted it, for it was too personal coming from someone being interviewed for a job.

'A fair number,' he replied, and gave her such a devastating smile that she regretted he was a client. But he was and, bearing in mind Murray's rule, she would do well to remember it. Except that it was her duty to entice him, a duty that seemed less onerous by the minute.

'You're from London?' he asked.

'Yes. But with Cornish grandparents.'

'Same here. My great-great-grandfather was Spanish, though. Came over as a smuggler, fell in love with an inn-keeper's daughter and turned honest!'

Julia laughed. She had wondered about those Latin looks of his, for in all else he seemed decidedly English. Eton and Oxford, she guessed.

'You'll have to do a fair amount of overtime,' he went on. 'I frequently work late and expect you to stay.'

'I don't take shorthand,' she said quickly.

'I rarely give it. My letters are too technical even for an above average secretary. So I use the dictaphone, which gives Mrs Williamson time to use her dictionary!'

Julia hoped he wouldn't ask if she could type, for though she had taken a computer course—during a three-month spell at the beginning of her career when work had been slow— she had subsequently not had time to use it.

'Do you have a boyfriend?'

His question startled her and, aware of it, Rees Denton's wide shoulders lifted. 'No ulterior motive, Miss Winterton, simply that if you stay late, I don't want irate young men barging in to see you. Most of the work I do here is highly confidential.'

'Here?' she echoed, looking around his sumptuously fur-nished office, with its silver-grey carpet, teak desk and black leather chairs.

'Yes, here,' he replied, and, pressing a button on his desk, enjoyed her amazement as the wall to his left slid back to reveal a drawing office, small, but elaborately equipped.

'How clever,' she murmured.

'Not really.' His smile drew attention to his beautifully shaped, sensuous mouth. 'It's simply that I've an aversion to clutter. I like everything in its place, where I need it, when I need it.'

Julia wondered if that applied to his women too, and had the feeling that the female of the species was needed only in his bed. He was too assertive, too sure of himself to need them anywhere else.

She saw him glance at his watch, and she rose.

'Sorry to rush you,' he apologised. 'But I've a date this evening and have a lot of work to get through.'

Even as she reached the door he was engrossed in a file on his desk. Somewhat disconcerted at how quickly he could refocus his attention, she went into the outer office.

'How did it go?' Mrs Williamson enquired.

'I just about passed. I shouldn't think he suffers fools gladly.'

'Only the ones he's dating,' the older woman smiled.

Julia instantly had an impression of lovely dumb-bells falling like nine-pins around him, and though it irritated her, she knew his susceptibility could make her task here that much easier.

She was still mulling this over when she returned to her apartment, and as she closed the front door the telephone rang. Wondering if it was Mr Denton to say he had changed his mind and didn't want to engage her, she reached to answer it.

'Julia, this is Chris.'

For a split second she couldn't place the whimsical voice, then all at once she did, and couldn't keep the astonishment out of hers as she repeated his name. 'Chris? I don't believe it. Where have you sprung from?'

'I'll tell you when we meet. I hope it can be soon? I saw some fashion photographs of you in a magazine last year and was very impressed.'

'A lot's happened to me since then,' she said. 'But I'd love to see you. Do the boys know you're back in England?'

'I spoke to Rob an hour ago—that's how I got your number.'

Julia was surprised, and with a premonition of the answer that was to come, said, 'How's your wife?'

'Fine, I think. We divorced six months ago.'

'And you suddenly remembered a scrawny girl with a ponytail!'

'Particularly when she grows up to look the way *you* do. What about it, Julia? When may I see you?'

'I'm rather tied up at the moment.'

'A boyfriend? I know you aren't married or Rob would have told me.'

'No, no boyfriend,' she said, 'but I—I've just taken on a job that—' She stopped, knowing she dare not explain, and uncertain what to say. In the end she agreed to meet him at Le Suquet for dinner. It was one of the best fish restaurants in town, and noisy and crowded enough to preclude intimate conversation. After all, how well did she know Chris? He hadn't bothered with her as a teenager, but with these glossy pictures of her as a model firmly fixed in his mind he might now be entertaining far different ideas.

It was an amusing thought, particularly when she remembered how she had once vowed to show him what he had missed! Well, here was her chance. Except it didn't seem important any more. But what the hell! It would be fun seeing him again.

Slipping into a hyacinth-flowered silk dress that deepened the blue in her eyes, she wound her blue-black hair into a coil on the nape of her neck, recollecting how Chris had liked to tug her lanky ponytail. Donning matching blue pumps, she surveyed herself in the mirror. A touch of pink to her cheeks and mouth completed the picture, and, even if she said so herself, she looked a dream. Pity she couldn't look it for someone else. But who? And where to find such a man?

Chris was waiting for her outside the restaurant, tall, blond and handsome as she remembered. Yet not quite as she remembered, for there was no charisma, no force of personality, just a good-looking, fair-haired man. But, if she was disappointed, Chris's look of astonished delight showed *he* wasn't.

'You're beautiful,' he murmured, 'much more beautiful than your photographs.'

'It's lovely to see you.' She brushed his compliment aside and tried not to draw away as he took her arm in a proprietorial gesture and led her into the restaurant.

Even here, where many pretty women congregated, Julia still drew all eyes. But she was used to it and able to ignore it as she draped her wrap over the back of her chair and concentrated on her companion.

'Hey,' she said, 'stop staring at me like that.'

'I can't help it. You're so different. The ugly duckling's become a swan.'

'I was never an ugly duckling,' she reminded him. 'Just the usual scrawny teenager.'

'Sorry!' he grinned. 'But do you think *I've* changed as much as you?'

'Hardly at all.'

'Do you remember the crush you used to have on me?'

'Teenagers don't have much sense,' she laughed, and was amused to see him look put out. 'Tell me about yourself,' she said quickly, knowing that most men—most people, come to think of it—enjoyed talking about themselves.

She didn't have to ask him twice, for he launched into a blow-by-blow account of what had happened to him since they had last met: his marriage and a job in Sydney which hadn't lasted due to his wanderlust. But he always managed to find something that suited him better, though not better enough to anchor him, and after his sixth move in five years, his wife had tired of the travelling and left him, after which he had drifted some more before returning to London and another excellent job.

'This one I'm really going to stick at,' Chris said. 'Bairstow and Marsh are a top advertising agency, as you know, and with Bob Marsh himself rooting for me, the only way I can go is up.'

'Providing you don't get another attack of wanderlust.'

'A girl like you could turn itchy feet into sticky feet,' he said, leaning across the table. 'You will let me see you again, won't you, Julia?'

She stared into his eyes, waiting to feel that special lift of excitement that always seemed to elude her. As it eluded her this time. 'If I'm free,' she parried. 'I'm starting a rather difficult job and I'm not sure how busy I'll be.'

'I won't take no for an answer.' Chris raised his wine-glass to her and Julia raised hers in response. As she did, from the corner of her eye she saw a man on the far side of the room lift *his* glass to her too, and her heart did a flip-flop as she recognised Rees Denton. What a coincidence! Yet from tomorrow it wouldn't be, for from then on she would have to find out where he was going *every* night and make sure she was to hand. How much simpler her task would be if *she* were his date. No, not 'if', 'when'. For only when she was close to him could she properly protect him.

Under cover of her conversation with Chris, who was happy to go on talking about himself, she surreptitiously watched Rees Denton and the girl with him. A pretty girl who kept patting her curly, blonde hair and simpering up at him. What, for heaven's sake, could an intelligent man like Rees Denton have in common with an idiot like that? Unless it pleased him to know he didn't have to put himself out to please *her*. Well, if *that* was all he wanted... But how was *she* supposed to act stupid when she wasn't?

'You're not listening,' she heard Chris say.

'I'm sorry.' Quickly Julia focused on him as he started asking her what she had been doing in the years since they had met.

'The usual sort of thing,' she said vaguely. 'Some work

for a couturier house in Paris and Rome, and then mainly photographic modelling.'

'And at the moment?' Chris asked. 'You said you were doing something difficult.'

She hesitated, then decided to be honest, hardly amazed by his look of incredulity as he heard her out.

'A bodyguard? You? I can't believe it,' he exclaimed.

'Because I'm a woman?'

'Partly. But more because you're—well, you're just not the type. You don't look it, for one thing.'

'All the better to fool people, as the wolf said to Red Riding Hood!'

He chuckled. 'Well, you could certainly have fooled me. Who are you protecting now?'

'You know very well I can't tell you.'

He looked disconcerted, and Julia hurriedly switched the conversation back to himself, which soon restored his humour. It didn't do much for her own, however, for he was not the most scintillating conversationalist and she was soon bored out of her skull. None the less she feigned interest, staring into his eyes and careful not to look Rees Denton's way again. Though, when she finally left the restaurant, a quick glance across the room showed his table occupied by another couple. No prize for guessing what Rees Denton was doing at this moment, nor with whom!

'When can I see you again?' Chris asked as their taxi drew to a stop outside her apartment house and he helped her out.

'Give me a call,' Julia parried.

'I will,' he warned. 'I won't let you escape me again.'

Vowing to keep her answerphone switched on, she lightly kissed him on the cheek, marvelling that she'd ever broken her heart over this blond, handsome giant who now left her completely cold.

That night she dreamt of Rees Denton, a jumble of images that fast receded as she stretched and yawned and opened her eyes to the morning. Throwing off her duvet, she went to the window to let in the daylight and some sanity. She had some tough weeks ahead of her, and must concentrate her energies on not only being an efficient personal assistant, but also the sort of dumb *femme fatale* that Rees Denton found appealing. Yet how to combine an efficient PA with the kind of girl who jumped on a chair if she saw a mouse?

The secret was not to be obvious. She didn't have to look or act the clinging vine for Rees to sit up and take notice of her. Just a hint of helplessness would do. After all, what made a man feel important was to make sure he didn't feel threatened. That was it. She would pander to his every whim and make it clear she considered him the most intelligent, superior being she had ever met. That would soon have him eating out of her hand!

She twisted her hair into the smooth bun she had worn yesterday, then, deciding it suited the PA image but wasn't quite what she wanted, she wound it into a braid and pinned it on top of her head, carefully pulling out a few tendrils to soften the effect. Pleased with the result, for it gave her a Regency air, she padded into the bathroom to dress.

CHAPTER THREE

THE CHANCE to try out her new persona came sooner than Julia anticipated, for on her way up to Rees Denton's office suite the elevator stopped on the third floor to let him in.

'Good morning,' he smiled, the whiteness of his teeth accentuated by his tanned skin.

'Good morning,' she said, moving to the door, poised to step out when the elevator stopped again. But when it did, the doors didn't open, and a glance at the indicator panel showed it had come to a standstill between two floors. She pressed the button, but nothing happened.

'Let me,' Rees Denton said, and tried again without success. 'Damn! It's never done this before.'

Julia glanced up at the roof. The elevator had a false ceiling and she was certain it would undo easily to give access to an emergency exit. From there, it should be possible to reach the exit doors of the next floor. Quick as the idea came to her, so she discounted it, knowing that fate had presented her with a golden opportunity of showing this man how helpless she could be. Without further ado, she gave a pathetic little squeak and flung her arms around his neck.

'I'm frightened,' she cried. 'What if it falls? What's going to happen to us?'

'Nothing that pressing Emergency won't remedy,' he said gently, and, disengaging her arms, did so. Julia was glad she hadn't remembered the Emergency button herself or she would have found it hard to make her frightened act look genuine.

'I'm s-sorry to be so silly,' she whispered. 'But I suffer from claustrophobia.'

219

'That can be frightening.' His voice held sympathy. 'Why didn't you use the stairs?'

'Up all those flights? Anyway, I can't bear heights either.'

'Not even when you're *inside* a building?'

She gave a fearful shiver. 'Sounds silly, I know, but I keep remembering I'm leaving the ground far below me and—and my feet turn to lead.'

'You should stick to a job on the ground floor, then.'

Was he laughing at her? she wondered, and, studying him through her lashes, saw his face held no expression whatever. But what a handsome face it was! His eyes were dark and bright, his skin clear and glowing with health, giving no indication that he might have had a pretty active night. Her imagination began working overtime and she was glad when the elevator gave a jerk and then glided up to the top floor.

'Mrs Williamson must be wondering what's happened to me,' Julia said as they walked together down the corridor. 'I wouldn't like her to think I'm late on my first morning.'

'I'll see she doesn't,' he replied, and paused as they reached the door of his office suite.

She waited for him to open it, but he blocked the way to prevent her moving past him. 'Are you doing anything tonight, Miss Winterton?'

'Why? Do you want to work late?'

'I'm not anticipating it. But I'd like to take you out to dinner.'

'To dinner?' Julia had difficulty hiding her triumph. Her little-girl act had paid off quicker than she had anticipated; either that, or he was a pushover for a pretty face.

'Do you already have a date?' he asked, noticing her hesitation.

'No, but—'

'Then what's the problem?'

'I've never dated my boss before.'

'There's always a first time.'

Still she hesitated. He obviously wasn't used to women saying 'no' to him, and she would have enjoyed giving him his come-uppance. But she was here for one reason only—to protect this Lothario—and her preferences had to take second place to her duty.

'I'd like to go out with you, Mr Denton, but I'm not dressed for it.'

'You look fine to me.'

'You think so?' she asked coyly.

'I wouldn't say it if I didn't mean it.'

'Do you always say what you mean?'

'Not always,' he said silkily.

'Then how will I know whether to believe you?'

For an instant he looked nonplussed. 'I'm sure you'll manage,' he answered. 'Most women have a highly developed sense of self-preservation which enables them to know when they're being lied to.'

'Lots of wives don't,' she countered, her expression bland. 'One is always reading terrible stories of husbands playing fast and loose and their wives being the last to know.'

'Yes—well—I wasn't talking about wives,' he said. 'Just girlfriends.'

Julia made herself give a girlish giggle, thinking this was the easiest way to change the conversation, and wondered how many times she would have to use it as a ploy.

Rees Denton stepped back to let her precede him into the office, then walked through it into his own, explaining to Mrs Williamson over his shoulder why they had both been delayed.

For the rest of the day the older woman showed Julia what she would have to do in the office, and, though assured that the job wasn't arduous, by six o'clock Julia was in no mood to agree. Apart from taking innumerable telephone calls, she was expected to liaise with the laboratory, the design department and the factory. Mr Denton, she learned, was a high-powered man in a high-powered position. He had a workforce of a thousand men and countless numbers of important clients who all wanted him to solve their particular engineering problems. No wonder Sir Andrew considered his safety to be of prime importance.

'Why are you frowning?' Mrs Williamson asked when the telephones had finally ceased ringing and they were both relaxing in an office that had miraculously gone quiet.

'I'm wondering how to handle the security side of my job. If I often have to take confidential documents from one office to another, Mr Denton will be left unguarded.'

'You're right,' Mrs Williamson ran a hand through her sleek grey hair. 'I'll arrange for you to have an assistant that you can call on.' She scribbled some names on a pad and passed it across to Julia. 'Either of these girls will be happy to help you.' Mrs Williamson stood up and glanced around the room. 'I wonder how long I'll have to stay away from here?'

'Hard to tell,' Julia shrugged. 'But whoever is making these threats against Mr Denton will have to make a move sooner or later, and he knows that the longer he leaves it, the more chance there is of the police laying a trap for him. Anyway, I thought you were going to Canada to see your mother?'

'That was a ruse Sir Andrew dreamt up. My mother's gone on a cruise with her second husband, and wouldn't appreciate a middle-aged daughter playing second fiddle!' Mrs Williamson went to the door leading to Rees Denton's office. 'I'll go in and say goodbye.'

When she emerged she was pink-eyed and carrying a black crocodile cosmetic case. 'What do you think of this?'

Julia's eyes widened as she saw its suede interior was filled with a complete line of Estée Lauder products. What a stupid gift to give a woman who didn't appear to use anything other than lipstick and powder. But, bearing in mind the elaborately made-up creature she had seen with him last night, he probably assumed every woman longed to cover her face with goo.

'It's a wonderful present,' she said diplomatically.

'I can't wait to try everything,' the older woman confessed. 'It's always been a secret dream of mine to have the complete Lauder range, but it seemed too extravagant to treat myself to it.'

Julia silently apologised to the man. Seemed he knew his personal assistant better than she did!

'Are you leaving with me?' Mrs Williamson asked as she reached for her coat and saw Julia still at her desk.

'No. I'm staying until Mr Denton goes.'

'Of course. How silly of me.' She looked over her shoulder, then whispered, 'How will you disguise yourself when you follow him?'

'I won't even try,' Julia grinned. 'I'm not a private eye! But keeping tabs on him *isn't* going to be easy. That's our big problem at the moment, though I've managed to solve it for tonight.'

'How?'

'He's asked me to have dinner with him.'

'I see.'

The dryness of the tone made Julia defensive. 'It's the best way we could think of to keep tabs on him. In the normal course of events, I never date clients.'

Mrs Williamson looked apologetic, as if knowing Julia had guessed what had been going through her mind. 'Such a pity Mr Denton's complicating things with his silly attitude. So much easier if you could tell him who you really are and do your job properly.'

'I've every intention of doing my job properly,' Julia asserted—and of making sure Rees Denton doesn't behave *im*properly, she added to herself, though when he entered her office an hour and a half later, as immaculate as though he had just showered and changed, she wished for the first time that she had met him socially and could be herself. The thought did not please her, for, though she wouldn't be happy working for a client she disliked, it could complicate matters if she liked one too much. Reminding herself that in her real persona, Rees Denton wouldn't fancy her—how could he, when he liked simpering 'yes'-women, more famous for their beauty than their brains?—she also saw it as a warning not to let her emotions run away with her. This was an assignment pure and simple, and when it was over their paths would no longer cross.

'Sorry to keep you waiting,' he said, not looking in the least sorry, 'but I got caught up with a problem and didn't realise how late it was.'

'It's only seven-thirty,' Julia said, though in the normal course of events she would never have waited an hour and a half for *any* date, no matter how gorgeous. 'Where are we going?' she asked as they descended to the basement parking and his low-slung black Ferrari.

'I've booked a table at Tante Claire.'

Julia was impressed but did not show it, for Tante Claire was a three-star restaurant and one had to book weeks in advance. However, remembering the role she was playing, she gave a simpering smile. 'You must be very influential to get a table there at such short notice.'

'I dine there so often, they always give me preference.'

'How lovely to be so well-known.'

He gave her a sharp look, but she kept hers wide-eyed and innocent, and he relaxed. 'If you'd rather go somewhere else...' he murmured.

'Oh, no! I'd be crazy not to want to go *there*,' she cooed. 'I've heard it's beautiful.'

'So are you,' he smiled, holding the car door open for her to slide into the passenger seat.

She didn't answer, nor did he talk again as they drove to

the restaurant. As far back as her teens, when she had driven with one or other of her brothers, she had been aware how differently people controlled a car, and how much of their character they disclosed when they did. Like Rees Denton, for example, who handled his with confidence and ease, never exceeding the speed limit, which must be difficult in a car that touched a hundred and twenty before you could count to five, never overtaking unless the road was absolutely clear, yet giving one the feeling that if need be he could drive this superb piece of mechanism to its utmost limit and still look as nonchalant about it as if he were doing a steady thirty.

When they entered the restaurant, Julia received the usual appreciative male glances. But there was a difference, for she received intent female glances too, as her companion was assessed and sighed over. It wasn't surprising though, for it was not only his looks that attracted attention, but his air of command. She wondered if he had always had it, or whether it came with success, and debated whether she dared ask him about himself or whether it was too much out of character in the part she was playing. She thought of some of the model girls she had known, in particular the silly ones who had been nothing more than clothes-horses, and knew they would never have been sufficiently interested in a man to find out what he thought and how he felt—other than how he thought and felt about them!

They were shown to a corner table, and Rees Denton immediately asked her what she would like to drink.

'*You* decide,' she simpered, for though it was a rule that a Guardian Security officer did not drink on the job, she intended putting him through the hoop.

'Don't you have any preference?' he asked.

'Not really.'

'Well, let me see—gin and tonic?'

'I hate gin and tonic.'

'Vodka?'

'Ugh!'

'A whisky, then.'

'I never drink whisky.'

'How about some wine?'

It was just what she fancied, but she resisted the temptation. 'I don't really like alcohol,' she lied, and had the pleasure of seeing a spasm of irritation cross his face. Equally quickly she batted her long lashes at him, and his eyes widened as if they had actually struck him!

'A fruit juice, then?' he asked gently.

'Lovely,' she breathed.

She behaved with equal stupidity over the menu, but not by a flicker did Rees Denton show irritation at having to explain every item to her. Even when he had to listen to her inane conversation all evening he kept his patience, and she decided he was too good to be true. Except he liked his women dumb, didn't he? She stifled a smile. Who would have guessed that security work included acting stupid? It needed guts, fitness and fire, but *stupidity*?

'Where do you live?' he asked as they drained the last of their coffee.

'Sloane House,' she said without thinking, and only when she saw one dark eyebrow rise in astonishment did she realise it was far too expensive an address for any personal assistant, however well paid, to afford. Her brain raced. 'I— er—I'm staying there rent-free. The owner's gone abroad and I'm house-sitting for an old lady.' That would at least explain away the lovely antique pieces and the fine Stubbs that hung above her mantelpiece, a present from her parents on her twenty-first birthday.

'Very clever of you,' Rees Denton said. 'I know it's hard finding decent accommodation at an affordable rent.' He signalled for the bill. 'Your place or mine?'

The inference was obvious, and in the normal course of

events Julia would have made it plain it was neither place! With swift realisation she acknowledged that this job wasn't going to be a walkover, and that it would require all her finesse to keep this man at bay without antagonising him.

So what to do now? If she invited him into *her* apartment, he would have to return home alone, yet if she went to his he was sufficient of a gentleman to drive her home afterwards. Deciding to cross that bridge when she came to it, she simpered, '*Your* place.'

Only when they were in the car did she realise she didn't know where 'his place' was. What if he lived out of town, miles from a cab rank? Still, if he came on too strongly, she could be even stronger. She mustn't start thinking she was the simpering fool she was pretending to be. She was perfectly capable of taking care of herself. In fact, she was trained to do so, and could hold her own with a man twice her size and weight.

Twenty minutes later they entered the Dockside apartment block where he lived, only a few streets away from the bronze façade of Engineering 2000, and took the elevator up to his tenth floor penthouse.

Julia stifled a gasp as they entered the domed, marble-floored hall and Rees turned on the concealed lighting. It suffused the entire area in a mellow glow, lighting up a central glass table banked with flowers, as well as the living-room beyond. She had not pictured his home like this, imagining it would be masculine and sombre, rather than so designer-decorated.

There was glass everywhere; from the mirrored walls to the multi-faceted screen that partitioned the living and dining areas, where the only concessions to warmth were the soft leather chairs surrounding a black glass and steel dining-table.

But she was being unfair. For the living-room itself was welcoming and warm, despite the angularity of its shape, with silk-textured fabrics in shades of ivory and peach up-holstering the deep settees and armchairs, as well as the walls.

But it was the wall of glass at the far end that drew her, for through it she had a spectacular view of the river, gleaming like a black satin ribbon. She could well imagine the daytime picture, and wondered if she would see it. But she would definitely have to, *day and night*, if she wanted to keep Rees alive.

'Stunning, isn't it?' he said behind her, taking the wrap from around her and kissing the side of her neck.

'Stunning,' she echoed.

'It's even better by day.' He pointed to the telescope on a tripod in the corner. 'I only wish I had more time to use it. But what will you have to drink?'

'Orange juice.' She moved away from him and perched on the edge of an armchair.

'Again?'

'I was brought up on orange juice,' she said innocently.

'But you're a big girl now. You should try living dangerously.'

'Why? I'm happy as I am.'

'A little danger adds spice to the gingerbread.'

'I hate gingerbread.'

He gave a mock sigh. 'I give up on you, Julia.'

'I'm glad to hear that, Mr Denton.'

'Rees,' he corrected. 'Why do you find it so hard to say?'

'I don't. But you're my employer and it doesn't seem—'

'Right? How old-fashioned of you! These days people are on first-name terms the moment they meet. But to get back to what you said just before. Why were you glad when I said I give up on you?'

Julia hesitated. She wanted to say 'because you're a devilishly handsome man and I think you'd be a devil to love, and give any girl crazy enough to fall for you a lot of heartache'. But she knew she couldn't be honest, for she had to inveigle herself into his life and spend as much time with him as possible. Which would be all too easy to do, she knew, noting the gleam in his eye. But if she did, where would professionalism end and her own emotions take over? It was a question she dare not answer, for as of now her professionalism was at stake, and that meant having to disregard her personal feelings.

'Do you really want me to give up on you?' he repeated.

'Perhaps you shouldn't be such a fast worker,' she murmured. 'You're inclined to—to rush a girl off her feet.'

'Once I know what I want, I don't see the point in beating around the bush.'

'And I'm the particular bush you want to pick?'

'Yes,' he chuckled. 'A very decorative one, too.'

'But most bushes are perennial and you only want annuals. Or perhaps I should say monthlies.'

'Very clever, Julia. You're not so dumb, after all!'

'My mother's a keen gardener,' Julia said hastily, knowing she had to watch her tongue. 'Anyway, a girl doesn't have to be all that clever to see through you, Mr Denton.'

'Rees,' he reminded, handing her an orange juice.

Accepting it, she glanced round the room. 'Did you design all this yourself?'

'No. A friend of mine did.'

'Someone you know well?'

'That's an odd question.' He seemed amused by it.

'Only because I don't think it suits you.'

'Most people think it matches my personality exactly.'

'Well, I don't. It's too artificial, and you're very much a cards on the table man, with a firm set of principles.'

'Indeed? I've been told I can be devious, subtle and ruthless.'

'Only when you have to be. But by nature you prefer being honest.'

'That's a charming compliment, Julia. I shall treasure it.'

She pretended unawareness of the humour in his tone, but she had decided—on the spur of the moment—to let him think she saw him as an honourable man who would appreciate her innocence, in the hope that this would encourage him to actually do so!

'You know, there's something in what you say,' he murmured. 'I'm not quite the big bad wolf this décor implies. So you needn't perch on the edge of that chair like a nervous sparrow. After all, *you're* not quite what you seem, either?'

Her heart leapt into her throat. Oh, lord! He had guessed what she was. But how? 'I—I'm not?' she queried.

'Definitely not. When Mrs Williamson recommended you, she informed me you were a highly capable PA, and that being the case, you can't be the innocent you pretend.'

'By innocent, I suppose you mean virginal?'

Rees was momentarily nonplussed. 'Well, yes.'

'That's stupid reasoning, if you don't mind my saying so. Why can't a successful career girl also remain a virgin?'

'I suppose she could if she were fat and ugly. But you're a beautiful, sexy girl, and I don't believe I'm the first man who has lusted after you.'

This was pretty straight talking, and Julia longed to tell him exactly what he could do with his lust! But she had to tread carefully.

'I'd never go to bed with a man unless we were in love with each other. I'm not interested in casual sex.'

'Nor am I.' Rees came to stand in front of her. 'Casual sex is too dangerous. Anyway, one-night stands are boring when you're over thirty.'

It was a good line, but she didn't believe him. How could she, when she had done her best to be inane and trivial? 'You'd find *me* very boring,' she pouted.

'I find you an enigma,' he corrected. 'The glowing reference from Mrs Williamson doesn't tally with your—er—your—'

'Intelligence?' This time she finished *his* sentence. 'It's easy for me to be a good assistant, because I regard my boss as my child and do everything I can to mother him.'

'Mother him?' Rees was staggered.

'All the time. Mother him, protect him, make sure he has everything he wants when he wants it.'

'Well, you know what *I* want!' He reached for her, and with an effort she made herself stay where she was and not hit out at him. 'Julia, darling, why waste time talking when we can be—'

'We can't,' she cut in. 'It's the wrong time of the month.'

It was an effort not to laugh at the expression on his face, and she made a mental note to recount it to Murray. For the first time since accepting this assignment, she saw it might have its funny moments.

'That's a very good excuse,' he said, stepping away from her. 'But only a temporary one. Now, drink up and I'll take you home.'

'There's no need. I'll get a cab.'

'I'll ring for one,' he said promptly.

She had expected him to argue and, when he didn't, was irrationally disappointed, for it showed he wanted her for one thing only. When she hadn't given it to him, he couldn't wait to be rid of her. Yet, had he taken her home, she would have had to follow him back in her own car to make sure he wasn't attacked, so it was all to the good that he was such a swine!

He put down the telephone and picked up her wrap.

'You're not angry with me?' she asked softly as he draped it round her.

'Of course not.'

'Then you'll ask me out again?'

'Of course,' he said politely.

That means he won't, she thought, and tantalisingly licked her lower lip with the tip of her tongue. 'I'm sorry I had to say no to you.' She felt rather than saw his interest reawaken, and hid her triumph.

'Don't give it a thought,' he said huskily. 'There'll be other occasions.'

Thankfully the buzz of the intercom signalled the arrival of her cab, and she walked quickly through the hall to the elevator.

'Don't bother coming downstairs with me,' she said as he went to follow her into it. The assassin could be lurking outside, and he would be far safer if he stayed in his high-tech ivory tower.

'Don't be silly,' he replied. 'Of course I'll see you down.'

She thought wildly. 'No, you mustn't. I don't want the cab driver to know I'm leaving a man's apartment.'

Rees gaped at her. 'In this day and age?'

'I'm sorry, but that's the way I feel.'

'You could always tell him you were taking dictation!'

'I don't think he'd believe me,' Julia said primly, and pressed the button.

Only as the door closed did she allow herself a huge grin. It was fun acting dumb, and might become even funnier, though she was determined that the laugh—when it finally came—would be on Rees Denton.

Mind, it wasn't going to be easy holding him off, and if the worst came to the worst she would come clean and tell him the truth. But for as long as possible she would maintain her charade, and hope that, before it grew too difficult to play, the person threatening his life would be safely behind bars.

CHAPTER FOUR

NEXT morning in the office Rees reverted to his role of managing director, neither by word nor gesture indicating he had taken her to dinner the previous night and asked to go to bed with her.

She knew he would pose the question again, but for the moment she put it from her mind and concentrated on keeping alert, hoping she might notice someone or something suspicious. The police believed, as did the directors of this company, that a bereaved next-of-kin was behind the death threats made to Rees, but Julia was still watchful of all the personnel around her, deciding it was better to be safe than sorry.

Guarding Rees during the day would present little problem, for as his assistant she could accompany him most places. Not that she would need to when he was in the building, for he was always with other engineers and technicians or his fellow directors. And, since his lunches were generally working ones, her real problems would only start when his working day was over.

Apart from a meeting with Sir Andrew that morning, where Rees had introduced her to him, and Sir Andrew had greeted her as though she were a complete stranger, he had remained at his drawing-board in his office. So without worry, she put her head around his door at lunch time to say she was off to the canteen and would be back within the hour.

'Don't rush,' he replied. 'I'm lunching with one of the engineers and don't expect to be back before three-thirty.'

'Does that mean you'll be working late tonight?'

'I doubt it.'

Julia went off to the canteen, then decided to stretch her legs and go for a walk instead. She could always munch an apple or two on the way. Singing softly under her breath, for it was a lovely day and this was, after all, her first job of any importance, she sauntered down the steps of the building and had almost reached the last one when she espied Rees climbing into a sleek red convertible, an equally sleek blonde at the wheel. The same blonde she had seen dining with him at Le Suquet the night before last.

Lunching with one his engineers, was he? The lying toad! No wonder he had said he wouldn't be back till half-past three. There was no prize for guessing how he would be occupied!

She was on the verge of telling herself it was none of her business what he did with his life, when she recollected that it was. Dammit, she was here to protect him, and that meant watching him the whole time. But how could she? She was no Peeping Tom!

She was still mulling over the problem when she re-entered the office, though it was after four before Rees came in, his step jaunty.

'Had a good lunch?' she asked icily.

'Very.' He paused by his door. 'Why the glacial tone?'

'I beg your pardon?'

'No need to do that,' he said jovially. 'Just tell me why you've gone frigid on me.'

Knowing she dared not, she contented herself with a shrug.

'Dog-in-the-mangerish, are we?' he went on. 'Funny, I'd never have taken you for the jealous type.'

Even as she looked up indignantly, he had closed the door behind him, and Julia was sorely tempted to walk out there and then, except she wasn't one to leave a sinking ship. Hell, Rees was the rat, not her! But, regardless of this, she didn't want him shot down in cold blood.

Promptly at six he walked into her office. 'Still angry, Julia?'

'I never was,' she replied, looking up coolly from her word processor.

'In that case, will you have dinner with me again tonight?'

She almost obliterated a whole paragraph. 'Dinner with you?'

'Yes, and forget about Dawn.' He perched on her desk.

'Dawn?' Julia made her voice rise on the question, though she knew exactly who he meant, for the name suited her to a T.

'The girl you saw me with today.'

'I didn't—'

'You did,' he corrected. 'I saw you out the corner of my eye.'

'How odd. I thought they were both fixed on your ladyfriend! She's certainly pretty enough,' Julia made herself add.

'And pretty dumb.'

'You think the same of me,' Julia said sadly.

'Not quite. *You* make me laugh.'

Oh, but he was quick off the mark! Julia couldn't help admiring him, even though she knew his expertise came from a great deal of practice.

'Do you like notching up new conquests on your belt?' she asked blandly.

'I've never done it on a belt, sweet Julia. On a bed, on a couch, on a rug, on a—'

'No more!' she cried, clapping her hands to her ears. But his answer showed her all too clearly that if she didn't infiltrate herself into his life she'd be spending a whole lot of hers pacing the pavements outside elegant houses or apartments, watching curtained windows! Yet there had to be a way of getting close to him without being too close for comfort, though as of now she couldn't think of one.

'So what's it to be?' he asked impatiently. 'May I see you tonight or not?'

'If not, will it be with someone else?'

'Definitely. I'm in the mood for dancing. So it's you or Dawn or anyone else who's free.'

'Not very choosy, are you?'

'I happen to be very choosy,' he replied loftily. 'All the women in my little black book are highly desirable.'

'And willing,' Julia added.

'Of course. But I make it a policy to take no for an answer.'

'Would you put that in writing?'

'Certainly not!' He leaned across the desk, one lean finger coming up to tilt her chin. 'Don't take life so seriously, sweetie. It's all a game, and you and I could play very nicely together.'

'I'd rather dance,' she said pertly.

'Then go home and change and I'll pick you up at eight-thirty.'

That meant he would be driving home alone, parking his car below the block where he lived—and a damned big, eerie car park it was, too—then going up in the elevator which might stop at one of the floors to let in his assailant. Oh, no! it didn't bear thinking of. She had to find a way of being with him far more than she was.

'Why don't I go back home with you and wait while *you* change?' she suggested. 'Then you can drive me home and wait while *I* change. It will save me going on the train.'

He looked surprised by the suggestion. 'I thought I'd shower and have a rest.'

'You still can. I don't mind watching television.'

He narrowed his eyes at her. 'You're a funny girl, Julia.'

'No, I'm not. I just suffer from claustrophobia, and I'd rather sit in your car than in the tube.'

'Ah,' he said ruefully. 'For a minute I thought you were making a pass at me!'

'I'd never do that. I'm a good girl, Rees.'

His mouth twitched, but his voice was serious as he answered, 'I'm glad to hear it. In fact, I think you'd be very good.'

She lowered her eyes to hide the amusement in them, and gave him full marks for never giving up.

Back in his apartment he was as good as his word, giving her a large glass of fresh orange juice and then leaving her to watch television while he went off to shower and rest.

'I'll only sleep for an hour,' he assured her, 'then I'll take you home to change.'

'You can sleep for longer,' Julia said quickly, thinking how marvellous it would be if he slept away the whole evening, and saved her from simpering and giggling away the next four hours. But it was not to be, for, saying he would be fit as a fiddle after a short nap, he took himself off.

Alone, Julia relaxed, switching off the television and quietly sipping her fruit juice before wandering around the apartment. She wasn't being idly curious, she told herself. It was simply sensible to know the lie of the land: to see where entry could be made, and which part of the apartment was more vulnerable than another.

In the event, the security was excellent, with alarms fitted to all windows and doors, which could be activated when Rees was out or asleep, and twenty-four-hour alarms on the back and front doors. But no security, however strong, could prevent a determined person from gaining entry, and for this reason she couldn't help being uneasy as to Rees' safety when he was here in the evenings and at weekends. She would ask Murray if he had any suggestions. In fact, she might as well talk to him now. But first she had better make sure Rees was asleep.

Tiptoeing down the marble corridor to his bedroom, she

put her ear to the door. Then, to be safe rather than sorry, she gingerly turned the handle, praying the door wouldn't squeak. But it glided smoothly open—naturally it would in such a luxury apartment—and she had her first glimpse of Rees in bed.

It was seven foot wide, its bronze, fan-shaped headboard matching the bronze and smoky-grey glass bedside-tables. The carpet was darker grey, thick and luxurious, and was complimented by pearlised blue-grey walls, lacquered at least ten times, Julia guessed, to give them such wonderful irides-cence. Heavy satin curtains were so identical in colour to the walls that it was only the thickness of the material that brought them to the eye.

They were undrawn, and she saw the darkening sky and the gleaming lights of the lamps on the riverbanks. But, beautiful though the room was, it was Rees who held her attention, his body half covered by a light duvet, patterned in grey and bronze silk. Unable to stop herself, she tiptoed closer, then stopped suddenly, colour flaming her cheeks as she realised he was sleeping in the raw. Still, the duvet cov-ered the essential parts of him, and anyway she'd seen her four brothers in the nude often enough. But Rees wasn't her brother. Also, he had his own brand of good looks. Not the outdoor type, like Jack and Mark and Rob, nor tall and rangy like Dean. No, Rees' physique was less obvious, though equally strong and masculine, with wide shoulders and smooth chest tapering to a narrow waist. His thighs and loins were covered, thank goodness, but he'd flung out one leg restlessly, and she glimpsed the sinewy muscles of his calf and a beautifully formed foot.

In repose he looked younger, less hard-bitten, and there was an unexpected softness to his mouth. Normally set in sardonic lines, it showed gentle curves in sleep; nor had she noticed how long his lashes were and how translucent his lids. They were shadowed blue, and she knew that he drove himself too hard, working and playing with equal fury.

She wished she knew more about his background, then instantly wished she didn't. Murray was always warning them of the dangers of becoming emotionally involved with their clients. 'Liking them too much won't help you take better care of them. On the contrary, it could be the reverse. You must at all times remain calculating and aloof. Calculating in the sense of weighing up what the assailant might do and how you can best circumvent it.'

Remembering this, she walked out of the bedroom and softly closed the door, then returned to the living-room to dial Murray.

To her dismay she learned he had gone abroad to meet a client, which meant that her problem was still hers to solve, and she was cogitating on it when the soft glow of the lights around her brightened, and she swung round to see Rees coming towards her.

As always, she was struck by his looks. Beautiful almost, except that was too feminine a word for a man of such virile masculinity. He looked as rested as though he had slept the night through rather than only an hour, and as he poured himself a whisky—small amount of alcohol and large amount of soda water, she noted—she admired the fluid movements of his body, enhanced by his superlatively cut dark blue suit. His white shirt made his tanned skin appear darker, and as his eyes narrowed as they rested on her she suddenly imagined him in satin doublet and hose, striding the deck of a pirate ship.

Irritated by her fanciful thoughts, she shook her head, and he burst out laughing.

'What's funny?' she asked.

'You,' Rees said. 'I haven't posed any questions yet, but you're already saying "no"!'

She laughed too and rose, and he led the way out.

The rush-hour traffic had long since gone, and in less than half an hour Julia was unlocking her own front door and ushering Rees into her home. No, not mine, she reminded herself. I'm house-sitting and I'd better not forget it.

'Nice place,' Rees commented, crossing the small, square hall and following her into the sitting-room. His eyes took in the several beautiful pieces of antique furniture, the glass shelves either side of the fireplace that held her budding collection of art deco vases and bowls, and the Stubbs above the mantelpiece. It was this that commanded his attention, and he strode over and stared at it.

'Marvellous,' he murmured. 'Your old lady must be well off.'

For an instant Julia thought he was referring to her mother, then realised he meant the mythical old dear she was supposed to be house-sitting for. Oh, lord, she hoped she hadn't left any tell-tale evidence of her own real self lying around! She was reading a book on Modern Philosophers at the moment and, if Rees glimpsed it, it might arouse her curiosity. Her eyes darted around the room and she saw the book in question lying on the settee.

'I must rest for a minute,' she exclaimed, and, flopping down on the corner of the couch, managed to slip the book under the cushions.

'If you're too tired to go dancing, we could stay here,' Rees said, promptly sitting beside her.

Instantly she jumped up. 'I'm fine now.'

His startled expression nearly made her laugh, and she headed for the door. 'Now it's your turn to watch telly,' she called over her shoulder. 'I'll be as quick as I can.'

'There's no hurry,' he replied, and she glanced across at him uncertainly. But he meant it, for he was leaning back, relaxed and at ease, and she suddenly realised this was one of his strengths, an ability to switch off completely and slow himself down.

Pity she couldn't do the same, she thought, as she raced through a shower and into fresh underthings. Only when it came to a dress did she hesitate. She had so many lovely, sophisticated clothes to choose from, yet didn't think this would suit her simpleton image. But what the hell! Even dumb-bells could dress in a sophisticated manner, and she reached for a stark, black crêpe. A wisp of nothing in her hand, on her body it was quite something, caressing every curve and indent of her slender but luscious body, whispering deliciously against her long legs as she slipped on high-heeled black sandals and picked up her purse.

If she needed confirmation that she looked sensational, Rees' look of stunned appreciation more than gave it as he rose slowly to his feet and moved towards her.

'You're quite the most beautiful girl I've seen,' he said huskily.

'Clothes maketh the woman,' she quipped.

'Not in your case. I bet you'd look even better without any!'

She made herself giggle. 'Naughty, naughty. You mustn't say things like that to me.'

'I could say a lot of other things if you'd let me.'

'Well, I won't. And if you don't behave yourself, I won't go out with you.'

'I promise to be as good as you want me to be.'

'Very good,' she said, and, twining her hand through his arm, urged him out.

Driving across the West End to Marco's, the latest place to dine and dance, Julia wondered how she could bear to go on playing the dumb brunette, fearing that if she was too boring she might turn him off. Yet she couldn't suddenly become clever. Maybe she would let herself be less silly. After all, bearing in mind Mrs Williamson had recommended her, Rees shouldn't be surprised if she occasionally showed a flash of sense.

'Why the sigh?' He broke into her thoughts.

'I was thinking of you,' Julia said honestly, 'and wishing I could be more relaxed with you.'

'You mean you aren't?' He seemed genuinely surprised, and taking heart from it she nodded.

'From your reputation, I think you like women who do as they're told and don't give you an argument. And that's not me.'

'Then argue with me,' he chuckled.

'You won't ask me out again if I do.'

'You're maligning me, Julia.' He slowed at a red light. 'You make me sound as if I think of one thing only.'

'Don't you?'

'Definitely not. I appreciate good conversation, and if a woman can hold her own with me, then—'

'I'm so happy you said that,' Julia cut in before he could elaborate. He had given her the opening she wanted and she took it with both hands. 'It's wonderful to meet a man who's willing to talk to me as an equal. I so want us to be friends.'

'So do I,' he said fervently.

'I mean real friendship,' she persisted. 'Not one with sexual undertones.'

The Ferrari spurted forward almost as if in anger, and Julia put a hand to her mouth to hide a smile. '*Will* you be my friend, Rees?'

'Of course. Though you know I'd like more than that.'

'I know. But don't rush me.'

'You have my promise.'

Julia's eyes glittered. The sucker! He had made a statement and she intended nailing him to it.

'I think you must have gone out with some very peculiar men in your time,' he said suddenly. 'You talk as if we're all just waiting to pounce and seduce.'

'The ones I've met *are*,' Julia retorted with genuine feeling.

'I'm not one of them,' Rees asserted, and Julia, glancing at his face, saw he really believed what he was saying. But then, maybe he didn't need to pounce or seduce. He was handsome and eligible enough for the woman to do the pouncing!

For the rest of the evening Rees' behaviour was faultless, though he did hold her a shade too close when they were dancing, and let his fingers linger around her waist as he led her back to their table. But his conversation was strictly impersonal, though occasionally his eyes, glowing like dark coals, said much more.

It was after midnight before he brought her home. And though she said goodnight to him firmly in the car, he was beside her in the elevator as she went up to her apartment.

With her key in the door, she said goodnight to him again, and once again found him beside her in her hallway.

'It's far too late for you to come in for a drink,' she protested.

'I agree. And a drink isn't what I have in mind.' Gently he pushed her into the living-room.

'I'm too tired to talk.'

'Me too,' he said, lowering his mouth to hers as he drew her down with him on to the settee.

Anger flared in her and she held herself aloof from his touch, hoping that if she remained motionless he would get the message. But he was too aroused to receive messages, too intent on his own wants to realise she did not want it at all. So much for his promise!

'You're so beautiful,' he breathed against her lips, as his hand traced a feathery path down her back to her waist, rested there a second, then moved up to cup one breast. 'Beats me why I haven't seen you around before.'

'Maybe because I don't go around.' Julia managed to avert her head. 'Please, Rees, it's late and I want you to go home.'

'Come with me.'

'No.'

'Then let me stay here. I promise I'll only hold you.'

Lord, the times she'd heard that! She pushed against his chest, but he wouldn't budge. 'Rees, go,' she insisted. 'You're breaking your promise.'

'No, I'm not. I'm only holding you and kissing you. A prosaic little kiss between friends.' Tilting her chin, he turned her face to his, and, before she could protest, covered her mouth again. His touch was gentle yet firm, his tongue edging out to savour her lips. Feeling its warmth, she trembled, and the pressure of his mouth grew more insistent, forcing hers apart to give him entry.

She tried to draw back, but as she did he bent with her, and she found herself lying on the cushions with Rees' body covering hers. Through the thin silk of her dress his arousal was all too evident, the throb and heat of it pressing against her thigh. But she experienced none of the anger she normally felt in this sort of situation; instead she was overcome by a sudden longing to draw him closer, to touch her hands to the perfect symmetry of his face, with its broad brow and high cheekbones, to let her fingers knead the muscles of his neck and shoulders, lose themselves in the dark whorls of hair on his chest which she could feel through his fine cambric shirt.

Aware that her resolve was slackening, Rees' kiss deepened, his tongue in her mouth performing the action that the throbbing muscle between his legs so ached to do. As she ached to let him, Julia acknowledged, and was instantly horrified with herself. Rees was a client. She dared not have an affair with him. More important, he was a womaniser, out for what he could get. Dammit! He barely knew her, yet he was falling over himself to get her into bed. Anger dissolved her desire and she longed to throw him out. Even as she tensed to do so, she knew she was duty bound to protect his life, and that she would have to protect her honour in a more subtle way. She racked her brains to figure out how, when she remembered a trick she had learned from Murray to deter unwanted males.

Clasping Rees close in a play of passion, she put her arms around his neck and gently stroked the back of it. At her touch, he groaned deep in his throat, and for an instant she hesitated, reluctant to hurt him, yet accepting she had no choice. Her hand continued its stroking, moving gently backwards and forwards across his neck. Then carefully she pressed.

As if stung by a viper, Rees shot off the settee. 'What the hell was that?'

'What?' she asked innocently. 'Did I do something?'

'*Do* something?' He glared down at her, nursing the back of his neck. 'Stop looking at me with those big eyes of yours! You know damn well what you did.'

'I was only stroking you. Did I scratch you, then? Let me kiss it better.'

'Don't touch me!' he said, though he sounded less angry and more puzzled.

Poor Rees. He didn't know what had hit him! Still, she hadn't pressed as hard as she could have done, so he had been let off lightly!

He kneeled down beside her and she tensed. 'Let me stay with you,' he murmured.

'It's so late.'

'Then we'll go to bed.'

'I can't. I told you it's the wrong time of the month.'

'You said that last night.'

'And I'll have to say it again tomorrow!' Delicately she licked her lips, knowing it was a gesture that never failed to arouse a susceptible male, and Rees, assertive and in control in his business-life, seemed to be a pushover sexually.

She was proved right, for desire flared in the dark depths of his eyes, and though he still looked regretful he accepted her reason for refusing. Gently pulling her to her feet, he kissed her on the forehead, then reached for his jacket, which he had flung on the chair.

'I'll see you down to your car,' Julia said as he reached the front door.

'Don't be silly.'

'But I'd like to.'

He didn't argue, though when she wanted to walk outside the foyer and see him into his Ferrari, he shook his head. 'That dress barely covers you.' He smiled. 'You'll freeze if you go out.'

She nodded as though agreeing with him, but when he opened the car door she was beside him, her body shielding his, did he but know it!

'Get back inside,' he ordered, giving her a gentle push.

She stepped away from the car, and as it roared off into the night she dashed across the road to where she had parked her own, sending up a prayer of thanks for having had the foresight not to garage it.

Because Rees didn't know what car she drove, she was able to follow him closely, donning a rain-hood to partially hide her face in case he glimpsed her through his rear-view mirror. She had watched many car chases on film, and found it far less easy than it looked, for Rees always managed to make the lights before they turned red, forcing her to cross against them. Eventually they reached Dockside, and she watched the Ferrari disappear into the underground parking.

Would he notice her if she followed him inside? Yet no way could he be left unguarded in that vast, cavernous place, and she drove swiftly down the ramp, praying that curiosity wouldn't make him pause when he saw a car close on his heels. But she was in luck, for he parked on the far side, close to one of the elevators, and disappeared into it as she slowly cruised past, head lowered to hide her face.

As the elevator door closed behind him, a shadow moved,

and she stopped with a squeal of brakes and dashed out. But there was no one there. She looked around and, still unsatisfied, headed for the exit door, taking the stairs two at a time to the lobby, where she was able to get another elevator that took her swiftly to the penthouse floor.

Stepping into the corridor, she found it empty, and she tiptoed to Rees' door and put her ear to it. All was silent. But that didn't mean someone couldn't be in there with him, brandishing a silencer! Heart hammering, she stood listening, but the silence continued—which could mean nothing or anything! Reluctantly she returned to her car, thankful she had a telephone there and could call him.

'Yes?' he said into the receiver.

'It's me, Julia. I was checking to see you arrived home safely.'

'Sweet of you, but unnecessary. I'm a big boy.'

She made herself giggle, and with a husky 'goodnight' put down the receiver. At least he was safe, but there would be other nights when it mightn't be so easy to keep tabs on him, and she knew it was a problem she had to resolve if she didn't want a dead man on her hands.

CHAPTER FIVE

FIRMLY ensconced in Rees' employ, Julia had to keep reminding herself it wasn't for real. Although she had never worked in an office, the typing course she had taken during a temporary lull in her modelling career was now invaluable, and her natural intelligence helped her cope with Rees' many appointments, as well as keeping at bay all the people he did not want to see. If only it were as easy for her to keep his would-be assassin away from him!

Julia used every possible pretext to stick as close to him as possible, afraid that if she didn't she might find him lying in a pool of blood and she grappling with a maniac!

It was a good thing Murray was not party to her thoughts, for he would have laughed himself silly, or else been furious with her. After all, a bodyguard should be cool and calm, not go around double-checking doors, locks and windows every few hours, nor bite her nails with fear when Rees had lunch in the directors' dining-room, or spent hours in the laboratory on the third floor, or drove to the company's engineering works outside London.

Indeed, when he was there, he was probably safest of all, for the factory was heavily guarded to prevent their designs being copied or stolen, and, as Sir Andrew himself had told Julia on one occasion when Rees was out of earshot, not even a fly could get through their security.

Rees never referred to the threats made against him, but she knew they had all been made via the telephone, and one afternoon, when she had been working for him for nearly two weeks, she casually asked him whether the voice was male or female.

'Who told you about the calls?' he asked tersely, swivelling round from his desk to glare at her.

'Mrs Williamson,' Julia lied.

'Then forget it. I've more to do with my time than waste it talking about some madman.'

'But was it a man's voice or a woman's?' she persisted.

'How do I know? It was a whisper.'

None the wiser, Julia left him. Rees had informed her he was working late this evening, and with her dictaphone cleared of all his letters, thanks to the help of the capable secretary Mrs Williamson had arranged to help her, Julia had little to do except twiddle her thumbs. But not wishing Rees to know, for he assumed she did all his typing, she sat at the word processor aimlessly tapping the keys, and was wondering whether she dared bring a book with her to read, when the telephone rang.

Rees must have been expecting a call, for he picked it up the same time she did, and before she could replace it, she heard a whispering voice. Immediately her hand stilled, and she listened in, her heart racing madly as a low voice—male, she was sure—uttered its spine-chilling threat.

'Your days are numbered, Mr Denton,' it said. 'If you think you can get away from me, forget it. I know your every move.' Click and silence.

Without thinking, Julia rushed into Rees, but, far from finding him white-faced and shaken, he had resumed work, his sleek dark head bent over some technical drawings.

'Rees!' Julia said urgently. 'That man wasn't joking.'

'So?'

'So what are you going to do?'

'Carry on studying these drawings, if you'd be kind enough to let me. If I took notice of every maniac who—'

'But you must!' she cried.

'I *must* have a cup of coffee, with one of those shortbreads

Mrs Williamson has tucked away in the tin in the bottom drawer of her desk!'

Exasperated, Julia glared at him, determined to say something to penetrate that thick skull of his! 'You can't ignore that lunatic, Rees!'

'I can and will. Now, stop over-reacting.'

'Only if you stop under-reacting, or are you so intent on preserving your macho image that you're willing to behave like a fool?'

With a deep sigh Rees flung down his pen and swivelled his chair to face her. In dark, hip-fitting trousers and pale blue shirt, sleeves rolled to the elbow to show muscular arms, he emanated an intense aura of strength which was, in an odd way, heightened by his silky, dark hair, dishevelled where he had run his fingers through it.

Julia noted all this in one swift glance, and though she personally wanted a man to have more than just looks, she could not help conceding he was most girls idea of Prince Charming, even though at the moment he was acting more like Prince Irritable!

'OK, Julia,' he said, leaning back in his chair and giving her his version of undivided attention—slightly mocking, as if talking to a child. 'What do you suggest I do?'

'Employ a bodyguard.'

'That's definitely out.'

'Then do you know someone who could be with you the whole time?'

'My little black book is full of numbers,' he chuckled.

'It's no laughing matter,' she said crossly.

'It is, when you start flapping round me like an agitated hen. Anyway, I wouldn't burden my friends with such nonsense.'

'Then let *me* stay with you and watch over you,' she said, grabbing at the chance.

'*You?*' For a long moment dark eyes held violet ones, hers

pleading, his slowly starting to gleam with mischief. 'Well, well,' he drawled, 'now you're really talking. So you're willing to stay with me night and day to protect me, is that it?'

Julia bit her lip. What joy to wipe the look of smug anticipation from his face. But, having got this far…

'Yes,' she stated firmly. 'I'm not as fragile as I appear.'

'Care to put it to the test?'

It was a temptation to say 'yes' and use her hard-won skill as a karate expert to throw him to the ground. But she couldn't allow herself such luxury—at least, not if she wanted to go on working for Guardians—and she contented herself with looking rueful as she murmured, 'I'm not offering my strength, Rees, only my alertness. I know I'm not clever, but I've excellent eyesight and hearing, and I—'

'You also have perfect teeth and a wonderful body,' he cut in, then rose from his chair and came over and put his arms around her. There was no love in the gesture, nor sexuality, just warmth and thanks as he hugged her close then released her.

'It's a sweet suggestion, Julia, and I'm touched by it. But you mustn't worry your head about that call. I think I know why that person is making it, and in a way it's understandable.'

'You mean because they lost someone in that plane crash?' Julia said without thinking. Then, seeing his surprise, added quickly, 'Mrs Williamson mentioned it. She felt I should know.'

'Seems everyone in the company knows.' Rees returned to his chair and picked up his pen. 'Do me a favour and forget it. I've a deadline and can't waste my time talking about stupid threats.'

Sighing, Julia went to make him a cup of coffee and one for herself. After that call, she needed it. Strange how the reality of a situation differed from the way one imagined it would be. Her training as a Guardian had equipped her for most emergencies, and threatening calls had been part of it. But actually hearing a person utter a death threat in cold blood had made *her* blood run cold, and the lurid images she had had of Rees struggling, dying or dead, now held a grim reality.

She didn't blame him for being amused when she had offered to watch over him, for since meeting him she had done her best to hide her intelligence. Yet somehow she *had* to be with him night and day. His life was at stake, and guarding him her first priority.

If only she knew what he would say if she told him her true identity. Had she established a good enough relationship with him to do so? After all, he had made it plain he was attracted to her, and though she knew that this week he had seen Dawn as well as a rather ravishing redhead—having sat in her car with a headscarf and dark glasses as she followed him—she was sure that if she herself gave him any encouragement it would bring him straight back to her. But to do so would imply something she was not prepared to give, even in the interest of her job, which left her back at square one.

She took Rees' coffee into him, with two shortbreads as requested, and received an absent-minded thank you. Rees at work had no time for flirtation, which pleased her, not only because it saved her tedious parrying, but because it showed a side of him she liked.

Sipping her coffee, she realised she had reached an impasse and needed Murray's advice. Making sure she wasn't overheard, she called him, deeply disappointed to learn he was still abroad. But, reflecting on it during the afternoon, she was rather glad she hadn't managed to contact him. Rees was her responsibility, and if she ran to Murray every time the going got tough he would interpret it as weakness, the last thing she wanted him to think of her. That being the case, she was still left with the million-dollar question of how to guard Rees at all times!

As if on cue, the door between them opened, and he stood on the threshold, stretching his arms above his head, and stifling a yawn. 'I'm packing it in for tonight. But you should have gone home ages ago. I told you I wouldn't need you.'

'I thought perhaps you might.'

'Can't bear to leave me, eh?' he teased.

'That's right,' she said, and, though it wasn't quite the truth, it wasn't that much of a lie either, for he looked so vulnerable standing there that she longed to go up and push away the fallen lock of hair from his brow, and smooth the lines from his face. His defences were down and she was seeing a side of him she hadn't seen before: the soft core behind the strength and genius. Startled by her thoughts, she hurriedly opened a drawer and pretended to search for something, so he wouldn't see her face.

'By the way,' he informed her, 'I'm flying to San Diego tomorrow.'

Startled, she looked up. 'That's rather sudden.'

'I know. But some of our new machinery is being installed in a factory there, and I want to inspect it for myself.'

'How long will you be away?'

'A few days.'

'I'm coming with you,' she said promptly. No way was she going to let Rees out her her sight. The assassin could be at the airport, on the aircraft, ready to strike at any time!

'Not that again,' Rees muttered. 'Much as I appreciate your concern, I assure you it's needless.'

'No, it isn't. Anyway, I've always wanted to see San Diego. I've heard it's a beautiful city. Please let me come with you, Rees.'

He shook his head, and in desperation she used her ace. 'It will give us a chance of being alone together. Wouldn't you like that?'

His eyebrows rose, dark silk lines above those arresting eyes of his, eyes which could spark with anger, grow frosty with disdain, gleam with amusement or glow with desire, but which she doubted had ever lit with love. For that was a word Rees didn't acknowledge. Not that he had ever said so, but his entire life-style—and he was already in his mid-thirties—indicated it.

'I hope you know what you're letting yourself in for,' he drawled. 'I'll be busy during the day, but there'll be the long evenings for you to entertain me.'

'Won't you be seeing business people and—and things like that?' she asked quickly.

'Not if you're with me.' The side of his mouth curved in a smile. 'If you want to change your mind, I'll understand.'

'No, I don't. I'm coming with you!'

'You've a kind heart, Julia,' he said unexpectedly.

'Why do you say that?'

'Because you've been keeping me at arm's length since we met, and now you're offering yourself to me on a plate! You're only willing to go to San Diego with me because you're worried for my safety.'

Julia took advantage of his perception, hoping that if she admitted he was right, it might keep him at bay. 'I just—I just don't want anything to happen to you,' she murmured.

'I don't want anything to happen to me, either! But as I said earlier, you're taking that call too seriously.'

'And you're not taking it seriously enough. So if you don't mind, I *will* come with you.' She took the bull by the horns. 'And I'll stay around tonight until you go back home. Unless you've a date with Dawn?'

'How do you know I've been seeing her?'

Caught out, Julia improvised wildly. 'Well, you've left *me* alone, so I assumed you were still dating her.'

'I've no date with anyone tonight,' Rees grinned, 'so we'll have a quick meal and I'll hit the sack.'

'What time is your plane leaving for San Diego tomorrow?'

'Noon. Why?'

'Because I want to be on the same flight, if possible.'

'Are you sure you know what you're doing?'

'Yes.'

'OK, then.' He chucked her under the chin. 'But don't say I didn't warn you!'

'I can defend myself,' she asserted, and when he grinned even more broadly hoped she wouldn't have to resort to another of Murray's self-defence tricks to prove it!

Rees was as tired as he had said, and they had a quick meal at a new restaurant nearby—a French bistro that was surprisingly good, which had opened to serve the newly built houses and apartments.

'Five years from now Docklands will be a real community,' Rees said, as he heartily demolished a delicious *coq au vin*.

'It isn't the sort of place to bring up children,' Julia commented.

'Maybe not. But that makes it even more perfect for me. There'll be no brats squealing about the place.'

'Don't you like children?'

'In their place. And that will never be mine!'

She might have known, Julia thought gloomily. A man bent only on pleasuring himself wouldn't want the problems of marriage and raising a family, even if the problems could be smoothed over by his wealth.

'You don't hide your displeasure too well,' he teased, and she glanced up from her plate to see him watching her.

'I was thinking what a lonely old man you'll be.'

'I'm sure I'll always find someone to take care of me. And if I can't, I'll arrange for a couple of anonymous telephone calls and death threats!'

'Don't expect *me* to come running,' Julia said pertly. 'By then I'll be living in a rose-covered cottage with a doting husband and grandchildren around me.'

'All women are the same,' Rees grumbled. 'They can't think of love without commitment. It must be bred in their bones. Even the majority of feminists ease up on their convictions when they get to their late thirties.'

He was deliberately laying himself open to argument, but Julia knew better than to rise to the bait. Had she been dining with him on a purely social basis, she would have had no hesitation in cutting his comments to shreds. But, since it was her duty to make herself desirable and necessary to him, she swallowed her chagrin.

After dinner, she made no demur when he headed for his apartment. However, once in the foyer, she stopped and asked the porter to get her a cab.

Rees made no effort to hide his amusement. 'Come up for a drink first, and I'll drive you home myself.'

'No. That man might be lurking outside. I'll feel happier if I know you're safe in your apartment.'

'But *you* don't feel safe there!'

'Should I?'

'Definitely not.' Rees hesitated. 'So think twice about San Diego!'

'I'll feel differently there,' she lied. 'In England I'm more—more inhibited.'

Rees's reply was cut short by the arrival of a cab depositing another resident, and Julia rushed to tell the driver to wait, then insisted on going up with Rees to his apartment and waiting while he unlocked his front door and switched off the alarm system.

'Don't forget to put it on again before you go to sleep,' she cautioned.

'You really take these threats seriously, don't you?'

'Because I'm sensible. And it's a pity *you* aren't.'

'I'll be very sensible tonight,' he assured her. 'I don't want to die before our trip to America!'

Ignoring this, Julia blew him a kiss, and headed back to the foyer.

'Julia,' Rees called, and she paused and glanced back. 'I understand your fear for my safety,' he said softly, 'but I'm perfectly capable of looking after myself, and I don't like possessive women.'

'I don't want to possess you,' she said sweetly. 'Only to make sure you're alive and well.'

'And able to perform?' he enquired silkily. 'I promise you won't have any complaints on that score!'

Colour flooded her face and, furious with herself, Julia stepped into the elevator, Rees' laughter ringing in her ears. Drat the man! San Diego looked like becoming their battle-ground, and she had to steel herself for it. Rees had endless charm and was ruthless enough to use it to his advantage. But she could be ruthless too, and when it came to her emotional safety she knew how to put up the barricades.

Only when she was in her own living-room did she slump in a chair and relax. One more night safely over. Maybe when this job was finished she would settle for another sheika! It would certainly be less wearing on her nerves.

The purr of the telephone had her reaching for it, and she was delighted to hear Murray's voice.

'I've just flown in from Rome and heard you were trying to contact me,' he said. 'How are things?'

Concisely she filled him in, aware of his interest quickening when she told him of the telephone call she had listened into earlier that evening, and that she had persuaded Rees to take her with him to San Diego.

'You'll still be faced with the same problems when you get back,' Murray stated, 'unless you move in with him, of course. If Denton weren't so pig-headed, this whole ridiculous charade could be avoided.'

'I know. But I'm managing to cope, though I've had a few nerve-racking moments.'

'Oh?' Murray's tone was interested. 'Care to fill me in?'

'Not particularly,' she chuckled, 'but I will. Rees has his pick of adoring females, but at the moment seems intent on picking *me*.'

'That's what we planned on,' Murray reminded her. 'But don't do anything you don't want to.'

'I won't,' she said drily. 'Anxious as I am to protect our client, I'd rather be a store detective than go against my principles.'

'There won't be any more store work for you,' Murray said crisply. 'I've had a letter from Sir Andrew, singing your praises, and from now on you'll be up front with the men.'

'Honestly?'

'Absolutely.'

'That's the best news you could have given me,' she said happily. 'I can't wait till this job's over. Much more of Rees Denton, and *I* might end up as his assassin!'

CHAPTER SIX

JULIA was so delighted she had managed to talk Rees into letting her accompany him to the States that she barely slept the night, and was so tired next day that she dozed for most of the flight. Not that this seemed to bother Rees, for he was absorbed with a stack of documents and only woke her as they came in to land.

It was early evening when they arrived, having flown over the Pole to Los Angeles, where they had changed planes.

As she had anticipated, it was a beautiful city, with wonderful homes set in the hills high above it, and equally wonderful ones ranged along the shore, with a view of the tossing blue-grey Pacific Ocean. There was always a faint breeze here to lessen the heat, and it blew soft tendrils of hair across Julia's face as they drove from the airport to their hotel.

She had hoped they would be staying in one with a sea view, but found it to be in the heart of the city itself, though it was set in beautiful gardens where fountains shimmered among the palms and oriental shrubs.

But she hadn't come here to appreciate the views, the climate or the buildings, only to safeguard the dynamic man beside her. No easy task, she suspected with dismay as they entered a lobby teeming with people. But she was happy to see they had been booked into a suite, both their bedrooms opening into a charmingly furnished sitting-room. When she had called the hotel yesterday to say she was coming, she had asked for a bedroom next door to Rees', and wondered whether *he* had made another call to request the suite. But she was not about to look a gift horse in the mouth, and she accepted the change of accommodation without comment.

She was unpacking her case when she felt herself being watched, and looked up to see Rees lounging against the doorjamb. He had discarded his jacket and shirt, and she saw his broad shoulders owed nothing to his tailor. Although he was a swarthy man, his dark skin had a golden glow. Sun-kissed, she thought, and had a sudden desire to touch his silk-textured skin.

Watch it! she warned herself. This man can be dangerous to your peace of mind. On the other hand, one of the reasons she had changed jobs had been in the hope of meeting some-one she would like, and there was no point pretending she didn't like Rees. In fact, it was a liking that could grow into something deeper. But she dared not allow it, for he had his future cut and dried, and it didn't include any of the things she held dear.

'If you aren't too tired,' he said, 'we can go out to dinner. There's a wonderful restaurant in—'

'Let's dine here,' she cut in, thinking it safer.

He knew the reason instantly, and went to argue. But she looked at him meltingly and had the pleasure of watching him nod agreement.

What a powerful weapon physical attraction was, she thought soberly, as she showered and dressed. It made the strongest person weak, and the weakest strong. It gave hope, and it could equally cause despair. Yes, like most emotions it had a good and a bad side, and had to be treated with respect and caution.

Rees was waiting in the sitting-room when she came in, the sensuous movement of his lower lip showing he was not unmoved by the lovely picture she made. Beautiful, no mat-ter what she wore, she was breathtaking at her best, and tonight she was definitely at her best, her white crêpe dress skimming her body and barely hinting at the curves beneath, yet somehow making one intensely conscious of them as she sauntered forward in her best model-girl walk.

'You look perfect,' Rees said huskily, breathing in the scent of her as she stopped in front of him. 'So perfect, I'm almost afraid to touch you in case I find you're only a dream.'

Oh, lord! she thought. And this was *before* dinner!

'You look pretty good yourself,' she replied, and he certainly did. His silver-grey suit of some thin silk material was as superbly tailored as his business clothes. Yet it had a casualness about it that spoke of the best Italian tailoring. It really was a pity he was intent on staying single.

All eyes were riveted to them as they entered the hotel dining-room—the women to Rees, the men to her—and though Rees, no slouch when it came to taking out a lovely girl, must be used to having his dates admired, he seemed vaguely irritated by the stir she caused.

'If that guy at the next table doesn't stop staring at you, I'll punch him on the jaw!'

'You wouldn't,' she said quickly.

'No, I wouldn't,' he agreed with the faintest of smiles, 'but I do find it annoying.'

'Doesn't it make you feel good to know your choice of companion is admired?' she asked with genuine curiosity.

'I already know I have excellent taste in women, and I don't like us being the centre of attraction. It cramps my style.'

'I haven't noticed,' she teased. 'You're doing very well.'

'I'll do better when we're alone.' He reached under the table and placed his hand on her thigh.

She forced herself not to tense, and was not sure quite what she would do if his hand travelled to a more intimate place. But in this she had misjudged him, for, though she knew Rees to be a wolf, he was a wolf only in his lair, and he withdrew his hand almost immediately, making her realise it was merely a gesture of intent.

But it was an intent not to be ignored, and it almost made

her chicken out from what she had to do. Yet what price a passionate clinch or two if it helped save Rees' life? Surely that was more important than... But she dared not finish the question, and to keep it at bay she stood up and drew Rees on to the floor.

An excellent combo was playing languorous music, and he took advantage of it to hold her close, his hands curving her body into his as they moved slowly in time to the beat.

'If I didn't know you better,' he murmured, 'I'd say you were trying to seduce me.'

'I'm coming between you and a bullet,' she retorted.

He laughed. 'For the first time I'm grateful to this madman. Without him, I'd never have got you here.'

'Don't count your chickens.'

'Why not? Anticipation can be as good as the feast.'

Anticipation is all you're going to get, she thought mutinously, and decided there was nothing more irritating to a woman than an over-confident man. But then, why shouldn't he be over-confident when his little black book was bulging with names?

'I'm hungry,' she said, pulling away from him and leading him back to the table.

'Me, too,' he replied. 'How about oysters or caviare? Both are excellent aphrodisiacs.'

'Oh, dear,' she said in a puzzled voice. 'I didn't know you were in need of it.'

Thinking she was teasing him, he started to smile; then, seeing her face—which with a supreme effort she kept serious—he looked dumbstruck.

'I certainly *don't* need it,' he declared. 'I was being funny.'

'You've an odd sense of humour, then.' She saw him bite back a retort, and knew her stupidity was annoying him. All to the good. She was only beginning! Unthinkingly, she reached for her wine-glass.

thetically. 'But it s-seems *you* aren't. I'm s-sorry I misunderstood you.'

'So am I.' Belatedly aware of the tremor in her voice, Rees' own grew gentler. 'I never believed that in this day and age a sophisticated girl would regard going to bed with someone as a proposal of marriage.'

'I've never pretended to be sophisticated,' Julia gulped, enjoying herself so much she didn't mind prolonging this conversation, and awarding herself a gold medal for having come up with this fantastic idea. 'I've always told you I'm old-fashioned.'

'You're archaic!' he retorted.

Her violet eyes lifted to his as she carefully covered herself with a silk sheet. 'But I love you, Rees, and I thought you loved me.'

He went to speak but seemed to find it impossible, and Julia decided not to give him time to find a way out of a situation she intended to use to her advantage. Yet not just to *her* advantage, but to his too, for what she now planned would enable her to stick as close to him as glue to a stamp.

'Maybe we shouldn't be in such a hurry,' she went on. 'Maybe we should try it out first.'

'Try what out first?'

'Living together.'

'*Living* together?' His tone was incredulous.

'To see if we're compatible.' She hung her head as if in embarrassment. 'I don't mean compatible in bed. That must wait until we're quite sure we're right for each other. But first we must make sure we get on in every other way.'

'Get on?' Rees still looked bemused.

'That's what I said.' Julia dared not meet his eyes for fear of laughing. 'We'll have a purely platonic relationship. Almost the real thing, but not quite.'

'"Not quite" being the operative words,' he muttered.

'Don't be angry with me, Rees,' she pleaded.

'I'm not. I'm astonished.' He shook his head. 'Just when I think I'm getting to know you, I find I don't.'

'That's all to the good,' she beamed. 'It means I'll never bore you.'

'That's for sure,' he said drily. 'In fact, keeping up with the way your mind works is a full-time occupation, and highly exhausting.'

'You're exhausted because of jet lag.' Julia bounced off the bed, still clutching the sheet around her. 'Goodnight, Rees darling. Sleep well.'

'I'd have slept better with *you*,' he said wryly, and went out.

Alone, Julia danced a little jig, only stopping when she stumbled over the sheet. She would never forget the look on Rees' face when she had pretended she had thought he wanted to marry her. If only there had been a hidden camera in the room! Still, he had played into her hands and made her job much easier, for which she was highly delighted!

CHAPTER SEVEN

DETERMINED not to oversleep, Julia set her alarm, and was waiting in the sitting-room, showered and dressed, when Rees entered it at eight-thirty.

He stopped in surprise at sight of her. 'Why are you up so early?'

'To go with you to your meeting.'

'I don't need an assistant with me.'

'I didn't come here for that reason,' she stated matter-of-factly. 'I came to protect you.'

He burst out laughing. 'You? You couldn't protect a butterfly.'

'You're right. They're too easy to catch. But the madman that's threatening to kill you might be waiting in the corridor. Or outside the hotel.'

'That's not logical,' Rees said impatiently. 'We're pretty sure he's British, and he's hardly likely to kill me in a strange country, where he would be far more noticeable. In fact, I don't know why I didn't think of it yesterday and stopped you coming with me.'

'Because you wanted to get me into bed, and thought you'd stand a better chance here.'

Rees had the grace to colour. 'Honesty must be your middle name.'

'It was nearly my first name,' she said ingenuously. 'My mother's a keen gardener, and she says honesty is a lovely flower.' Head on one side, Julia appraised him. 'I wonder what she'd have christened you?'

'A garden implement,' Rees said wryly. 'Something like a rake!'

Julia's laugh was genuine, though so far this morning none of her conversation had been. But it was fun playing Miss Dumb-bell, provided she managed to get in a few digs at this Lothario, who had brought her here for the sole purpose of seducing her. She fumed at the very idea, then firmly pushed the thought aside, remembering Murray's dictum never to let personalities come between her and her work.

For the next two days Julia did not leave Rees' side, though several times during their first morning together he had tried to persuade her to go sightseeing and enjoy herself.

But she would have none of it, and after a second try Rees gave up on her, and with ill-concealed irritation accepted her presence, though he insisted she tell no one that his life had been threatened.

Julia had never seen Rees with his managing director's hat, for in London he was more the inventor-cum-engineer. But during these few days he met with the heads of various large companies and showed a grasp of complex financial matters that left her reeling in admiration.

On their second and third nights, Rees had business dinners, but luckily as his PA she was included in them, though he did his best to ignore her. Since their discussion in her bedroom, he had remained strictly impersonal, and each night when they returned to their suite he went directly to his room. She had a vague suspicion he even locked his door!

Although she was happy to go along with his behaviour for the moment, it made no difference to her master plan which she intended putting into action the moment they returned to London. One day, when she had stopped working for Guardians, this entire episode was going to make a marvellous after-dinner story!

Their departure was delayed by an unexpected order for more of Rees's grey boxes, and it wasn't until the following Sunday, seven days after leaving Heathrow, that they returned to it. A car was waiting to meet them and, recognising the chauffeur as another Guardian employee, Julia was content to let Rees drop her off at her apartment first.

He bade her a curt good morning and said he would see her in the office on Monday and, watching the back of his dark head as he was driven away, she could sympathise with his frustration. She had alternately blown hot and cold with him, and though she had reached the peak of infuriating behaviour in San Diego he had taken it like a man. An annoyed one, admittedly, but one with sufficient control not to try to coerce her into changing her mind. But then, why should he? As he had once said, he had never found there to be a shortage of willing women.

No sooner had she unpacked than she called Murray and outlined her new strategy.

'Wish I could see Denton's face when you confront him,' he said when he had stopped laughing. 'Keep me posted on what happens.'

Smiling with anticipation, Julia went to the cupboard for a larger suitcase and began packing all over again, at the same time working out the story she was going to spin Rees.

An hour later, two cases at her feet, she was ringing his doorbell. There was no answer, and she grew nervous. The porter on duty had assured her Mr Denton was in, and had only allowed her into the penthouse elevator because he recognised her. So why wasn't Rees answering? She rang again and was wondering whether she dare pick the lock and run the risk of setting off the alarm, when the door was flung open by an irate Rees, his skin glistening damply, his body partially covered by a short, navy towelling robe.

'You!' he exclaimed, then saw the cases. 'What the—'

'It's the best way,' she cut across him.

'Best way to what?'

'To see if we're compatible. That's why I'm moving in with you.'

'Moving in with me? *Here?*' Surprise gave way to astonishment. 'I don't remember asking you.'

'Not in so many words,' she agreed, keeping a smile
clamped to her mouth. 'But you implied it, didn't you? The
night you came into my room and undressed me.'

'You can't be serious!' He tightened the belt of his robe,
but not before she had caught a glimpse of a muscular thigh
lightly flecked with dark hair. 'Look, Julia, I'm afraid you
misunderstood my intentions. You're a lovely girl and I—
well, I fancied you like mad. But there was nothing more to
it than that. As I've already made plain to you, I have no
intention of *ever* marrying.'

'But I thought you loved me.' Julia puckered her face, but
could not manage to squeeze any tears from her eyes, though
she screwed them up tightly. 'You couldn't have kissed me
the way you did if you didn't feel something for me.'

'I could have done a lot more than kiss you without being
in love with you,' he snorted. 'Dammit, this is the nineteen
eighties, not the eighteen eighties! Now, be a good girl and
go home. If you wait till I change, I'll drive you back.'

'I can't go back.' She launched into her prepared story.
'When I walked into the apartment this morning I found Mrs
Elton there. The owner,' she explained. 'The woman I was
house-sitting for. She wasn't due back for several months,
but her plans changed and—and she doesn't need me any
more.'

Rees' mouth set in a tight line. 'She can't throw you out.
Didn't she engage you for a specific length of time?'

'No. She said she would be away three months, but we
didn't bother about a contract.' Seeing no softening of Rees'
expression, Julia played her trump card. 'I think one of the
neighbours must have written and told her I'd left the apartment—when I went with you to San Diego. That's probably
why she came back and was so horrid to me.'

'Didn't you tell her *why* you came with me?' Rees demanded. 'I know it was misguided of you, but you did it with the best of intentions. Would you like me to have a word with her?'

'It won't do any good. She's terribly obstinate.'

'Like some others I know,' Rees muttered.

'Anyway, I think it was fated to happen. I'm sure I'm meant to stay here instead, so I told her I was quite happy to go because I was moving in with my fiancé.'

'You *what*?'

'I see now that it was a mistake,' Julia snivelled, 'and I'm sorry for not realising you were only amusing yourself with me.'

This time she managed to squeeze out some tears, though they were tears of rage when she thought how fast and loose he played with women, and what pleasure it would be to give him his come-uppance at the same time that she was guarding him. It would make her job doubly worth while!

'Don't cry,' Rees said curtly. 'That's a woman's favourite weapon.'

'I haven't any weapons to use against you.' Julia cried harder. 'But I've nowhere to go—and—and I came here because I thought you loved me.'

'Don't you have any friends?'

'None I can stay with.'

'Why not move into a hotel until you find yourself an apartment, or another house-sitting job?'

'Those sort of jobs aren't easy to come by. And it might take me weeks.' She raised tear-drenched eyes to his, her long lashes glittering with moisture. 'Can't I stay here for a little while, Rees? Now I know you don't love me, I promise I'll keep out of your way as much as possible.'

He looked as if he were about to refuse, and she held her breath, realising that if he said 'no', she would have no choice but to go. But she was counting on his not being as hard-bitten as he sounded, and when he gave a heavy sigh and reached out for her cases she knew she was right.

'Just till you find somewhere else,' he stated.

'Oh, thank you,' she breathed tremulously, and followed him down the marble-floored corridor into a beautifully appointed bedroom with its own small terrace and breathtaking view of the Thames and London beyond it.

'What a lovely room!' she exclaimed, genuinely delighted to find it less starkly modern than the rest of the apartment, with hand-painted French furniture, a delicately sprigged carpet in pale green and pink, and matching curtains and duvet.

'This isn't a bit like the rest of your home,' she couldn't help saying.

'It came from my father's house,' he said curtly, the set of his mouth precluding her from further comment or questions.

'You have your own bathroom,' he went on, pointing to a door behind her. 'And if there's anything you require, ask my housekeeper. She comes in on a daily basis.'

'I can't see myself needing anything,' Julia smiled, and spun round on her heel. Her full skirt lifted, giving him a better view of her shapely legs, and seeing the way his eyes went instantly to them she said firmly, 'No funny tricks, Rees. Now I know you don't love me, my staying here is purely a platonic arrangement.'

'Most definitely,' he agreed, and stalked out.

Julia tiptoed to the door and inched it open to watch him return to his bedroom. A moment later she heard his shower come on. Only then did she call Murray.

'I never thought you'd get away with it,' he chuckled.

'Nor did I, to be honest. He put up a fight to begin with, and then sort of caved in.'

'He was probably scared you'd make a scene or start telling everyone he'd tried to seduce you.'

'I'd never have done that.' Julia was shocked.

'*You* wouldn't,' Murray said, 'but the character you're playing might well have done, and he could have found himself getting some unwanted publicity.'

'You think that would have worried him?'

'Not in the normal course of events, but I had a word with Sir Andrew after you called me earlier—I thought I should put him in the picture—and he told me that as of now, Rees is going to be Mr Whiter than White in order to clinch a fantastic deal with Bargett Engineering. Seems that Bargett himself is devoutly religious, and won't do business with anyone whose lifestyle he disapproves of. Hence Rees being careful not to step out of line until contracts have been exchanged.'

So *that* accounted for his easy capitulation! Julia thought wryly, and here she was thinking he had taken pity on her! Still, it had given her the 'in' she required, so who was she to complain? But once he had signed the contract, she would be out on her ear. If only the police could find the assassin before then!

'I appreciate the way you've put your heart into this assignment,' Murray said into the silence. 'No male security guard could have done what you have.'

Julia couldn't help laughing. 'Certainly not with a womaniser like Rees!'

'He's no worse than most bachelors of his age and position. You're too tough on him.'

'I don't think so.' Julia's cool tones were quickly picked up by Murray.

'OK, so you're telling me to mind my own business.'

'No, I'm not. But you're a bachelor too and you're bound to defend Rees.'

On a note of laughter the call ended, and as she unpacked and placed her clothes in the capacious wardrobe she reflected on what Murray had said. Her four brothers, good-looking all, had played the field as hard as Rees, but the three who were now married had proved themselves ideal husbands. Except that Rees wasn't interested in changing his single status.

She tried envisaging him as a husband, coming home each night to talk over the events of the day with his wife, to share a meal, maybe help stack the dishes in the dishwasher. All the hundred and one mundane chores that went to make up a life together. She shook her head. Rees would never fit into that kind of picture. He was a love 'em and leave 'em type, ready to forget the old when someone new appeared. But would a girl who had been loved by Rees forget *him*?

Disturbed at where her thoughts had taken her, Julia clamped down on them. Falling for Rees was the last thing she wanted. She would as soon fall for a boa constrictor!

Julia settled into Rees' apartment more easily than she had anticipated. She left for work with him in the morning and returned with him in the evening, the two occasions when he was most at risk. For the first few evenings he had worked late at the office and been too tired to go out socially afterwards. Which was all to the good as far as she was concerned.

It was only when he remained home for the fourth and fifth evening that the penny dropped. Of course! Rees intended leading an exemplary life until the deal he was working on was completed and signed. No wonder the telephone numbers in his little black book remained unrung, and he was content to eat the dinners Mrs Hartley left prepared for him, before she departed each afternoon at five.

Julia, careful to keep out of his way once they were home, prepared herself a quick snack and ate it in the kitchen, closing her senses to the delicious smells wafting from the dining-room where Rees was enjoying the cordon bleu dishes which he had only to heat in the microwave.

It wasn't until the end of the week that she suddenly wondered if Rees had given any thought to the possibility that

Mr Bargett might discover he was sharing his home with his assistant, who happened to be a rather comely young female.

However, she had no intention of asking him, and was smiling to herself when he strolled into the kitchen as she was making a sandwich, and brusquely told her Mrs Hartley had prepared enough dinner for two.

'Unless you prefer sandwiches,' he finished, glancing at the bread and cheese in her hand.

'What are you offering instead?'

'Veal cutlet in asparagus creamed sauce, gratin potatoes and fresh broccoli, followed by peach pie.'

'That's an offer I can't refuse.' Julia whisked the bread back into the bin and the cheese into the refrigerator, and nipped smartly ahead of Rees into the dining-room.

Eating at the glass and steel table, with Rees opposite her, and behind him the glorious panorama of London, she wondered what it would be like to be married to this man. Physically exciting, as she knew to her cost, mentally stimulating too, but emotionally barren, for Rees was basically a loner.

She found herself curious to know something of his background, but did not see him taking kindly to being cross-questioned, and wondered if Murray knew anything about him. Yet she wouldn't ask Murray either, for he was a perceptive man and she didn't want him assuming she had any feeling for Rees other than on a purely professional basis.

After all, when the person threatening him was caught, she would step out of his life and never see him again. The knowledge should have delighted her, yet it didn't, and pondering why, she admitted that in an odd way she had grown to like him—inasmuch as it was possible to like a man who regarded women only as sex objects.

That evening set the scene for the next week. Julia would re-heat the dinner Mrs Hartley had prepared, and she and Rees then ate together, sometimes in the dining-room, sometimes in the more intimate atmosphere of the kitchen, if black granite worktops and steel cabinets and fittings could be called intimate. It was more like an operating theatre, Julia thought as she took a bowl of fluffy white rice out of the microwave and set it on the table, its shape following the unusual bow window that formed a dining nook.

'Seen any suitable accommodation for yourself?' Rees asked, taking a bottle of Chablis from the refrigerator.

'Heaps. But nothing affordable.'

'I'll give you a raise.' He filled her glass and his own, then motioned her to help herself to the chicken casserole.

'It won't do much good once Mrs Williamson comes back and I'm looking for another job.'

'You shouldn't have difficulty finding one. You're an excellent assistant. Quick, efficient and with plenty of initiative.'

Julia hid a grin. The last part was certainly true! 'So I take it you'll give me a good reference?'

'You can write it yourself, and bring it in for me to sign.'

'That would be dishonest,' she said in shocked tones.

He grunted and heaped his plate high. 'Mmm, this smells good. If you'd like Mrs Hartley to prepare something special for the weekend, by all means tell her.'

'I rather fancy lobster salad for Sunday lunch. Unless you'll be out?'

'I'm staying home for the next few weeks,' came the firm answer.

Julia waited for him to explain why, and was not surprised when he didn't. Even Rees, cynic that he was, was not going to admit he was playing a part in order to clinch a business contract.

'Of course, if you'd like to cook something yourself,' he went on, 'I've no objection.'

'I'm quite happy for Mrs Hartley to do it.'

'But don't you *enjoy* cooking?' he persisted. 'I've been told this is a fabulous kitchen to work in.'

'I'm sure it is—if you like working in kitchens. But I don't.'

'You *can* cook, though?' he ventured. 'I mean, if you had to, you could whip up something delicious?'

'Nutritious,' Julia corrected. 'I doubt it would be delicious. My soufflés fall flat, likewise my sponge cakes; my pastry is hard as a brick, and my omelettes are fine for soling shoes.'

Rees raised a silky, black eyebrow. 'I'm amazed you don't mind admitting it.'

Only then did it dawn on Julia that she had been answering out of character. Well, out of character to the ingenuous 'I'll only go to bed with the man I marry' girl she was pretending to be, but very much in character with her real self. But it was too late to backtrack, and she had to plough on as best she could.

'I suppose all your ladyfriends are great cooks in between their busy career-girl lives?'

'They are, as it so happens. Most of them love cooking.'

'Because they see it as a way to a man's heart. Even in this day and age. But I'd never pretend to be what I'm not.' Julia could not cross her fingers for they were holding her knife and fork, so she crossed her legs instead. 'But when I marry I'm sure I'll be good around the house.'

'As long as you're good in the bedroom, don't worry!' Rees grinned wolfishly, and Julia promptly put down her fork.

'That's not funny.'

'Too right. I was serious. If a man finds a woman compatible with him in bed, he'll accept her being a poor housekeeper.'

'Would you?' Julia questioned sweetly.

'I wasn't talking personally,' Rees said. 'As you know, I'm not interested in marriage. Which is why I asked whether you've found some place else to live. The sooner you leave here, the sooner you'll forget me and start making another life for yourself.'

Julia longed to throw a plate at him. Conceited swine! Yet she could hardly blame him when she had appeared on his doorstep, cases in hand, ready for a platonic trial marriage.

'There's no point making another social life for myself while I'm seeing you every day in the office. But once Mrs Williamson is back and I can leave you, I'll be able to forget you.' She picked up her fork and resumed eating, stopping as she became aware of Rees watching her intently.

'Anything wrong?' she asked.

He shrugged. 'Unrequited love hasn't affected your appetite.'

She swallowed hastily. 'I think I'm getting over you. There's nothing like living with a man for opening your eyes to his faults.'

'Indeed?' Rees' voice was dry. 'And what faults have you suddenly discovered in me?'

Ready for the question, Julia returned her answer as fast as Steffi Graff a poor serve. 'You're impatient, untidy, tetchy in the morning until you've had your coffee, and generally short-tempered after midnight.'

'That's because living like a monk goes against my temperament. God, if this contract—' He stopped, and she reached for her wine-glass and pretended she had not heard.

Lying in bed that night, she knew Rees couldn't continue this celibate existence much longer, and was not surprised when, at six next evening, he announced he was leaving the office and going out to dinner.

Would it be with Dawn, she wondered, or the gorgeous redhead whose name she had still not discovered? Or maybe the elf-like brunette he had dated three times in succession before they had gone to the States? But whichever, he would soon be off with the old and on with the new, for he saw safety in numbers.

Sitting beside him as they drove home, she wished he was not going out tonight. She enjoyed their evenings together, particularly since he was treating her as a friend, careful to say nothing which she could construe as another proposal of marriage! Yet he was not a man to whom aloofness with the opposite sex came easily. He was very tactile, and frequently put a hand on her arm or across her shoulders. Nor could he help appraising her each morning when she came out of her room, his varying expressions showing quite clearly whether or not he approved of her outfit. Indeed, he was knowledgeable about women's fashions, and she found herself dressing to please him, liking it when his eyes lit with appreciation.

As soon as they entered the apartment, he disappeared into his bedroom and she went into hers, changed into a tracksuit and made for the kitchen and a cup of coffee, debating whether to trail Rees herself tonight or see if Murray had someone free to do it. She heard the telephone tinkle several times, and after the fourth occasion he appeared at the kitchen door, his expression distinctly irritable.

'No one's free,' he said abruptly. 'There's some big charity ball on tonight, and they all seem to be going to it.'

'Poor Rees,' Julia commiserated falsely. 'You shouldn't have left it so late before ringing.'

'I've never had this trouble before.'

'Well, we're all getting older,' she said brightly, and seeing his eyes spark with temper, added, 'At least the girls are, and they probably don't like sitting around waiting till you deign to call.'

'There's no deign about it,' came the curt response. 'I often don't know until the last moment if I'll be free.'

'*I* wouldn't hang around waiting for a man to call me.'

'Not even me?'

'*Especially* you.'

'You fall out of love fast, don't you?' he sneered.

'Maybe I was never in love with you. All I know is I—'
She stopped and looked down demurely. 'I'm still very fond
of you, but—but in a sisterly way.'

'That's all I need,' he groaned.

'You should be pleased. When you thought I wanted to
marry you, you got in a dreadful panic.'

'Because I didn't want you to be hurt,' he came back at
her quickly, 'and I'm delighted to hear you aren't. Though
I must say I didn't think your emotions were so shallow.'

Julia's temper rose. 'Would you have been happier if I'd
pined for you for ever?'

'Don't be silly.'

'Then why are you cross because I'm not?'

'I'm not in the least cross,' he said between gritted teeth.
'Now, for God's sake go and get ready.'

'Ready for what?'

'Dinner at the Ritz.' He waited for her to look pleased,
and when she didn't, said sharply, 'What's wrong now?'

'I don't like being a last resort.'

He opened his mouth to say she was not, then obviously
thought better of it. 'You're a beautiful girl, Julia, as I've
told you many times before, and I would be delighted to be
seen with you.'

'Even though you think me silly and naïve?'

'You're not always silly and naïve. Only sometimes. But
we're getting away from the point. I didn't think of asking
you out because I wasn't sure you'd want to come with me
now you've decided you don't love me.'

'You don't have to be in love with someone to go out to
dinner with them,' Julia said as if she were speaking to a
child. 'After all, *you* don't love me, yet you're asking me
out.'

The logic of her comment made him roll his eyes heavenwards, and stifling her laughter she walked out of the kitchen.

'Where are you going?' he called.

'To change, of course. You wouldn't want me to go out with you in a tracksuit!'

Sensing this might be their last date, she decided to take his breath away, and, peeling off her clothes, reached for a new set of undies, pure silk and costing a fortune, even though she had managed to get them wholesale—one of the perks of being a model. But she was a great believer in looking as good on the inside as the outside, convinced it helped boost the morale. Then she ran her eyes expertly over the dresses in her wardrobe, regretting she had only brought a small number with her. But at least she had had the sense to bring one eye-catcher, and she slipped into it and zipped it up. It was in red, a colour she rarely wore in summer. But it was as defiant as her mood, and anyway, come the winter, she would be guarding someone else, and Rees would be dating heaven knew who.

Her patent shoes and bag were black and shiny as her hair, which tonight she wore loose and curly, having given it a quick tong. It was very much an innocent pre-Raphaelite look, which contrasted wickedly with the daring cleavage of her dress which plunged almost to her waist, though the material was so skilfully cut that it gave only a tantalising glimpse of her full breasts.

When she swayed into the living-room, Rees's silence spoke volumes. But his hand on her elbow as he guided her into the elevator was unusually solicitous, as though she was something fragile that might break, and he ushered her into his car in the same manner.

He was looking pretty delectable himself, his perfectly cut dinner-jacket enhancing his lithe body, and making her aware of its latent strength. For a man who spent so many hours poring over a drawing-board, he was in excellent shape. But then, he got his exercise bouncing up and down on a bed!

They reached the Ritz and, leaving his car to be parked by a porter, they entered the hotel.

It was not one Julia knew well, and she was enchanted by the restaurant, with its rococo décor and the wide windows that opened on to a flower-filled terrace. It was a room designed to make the best of a woman, the lights muted and rosy, the furnishings pastel.

They were shown to a table by the window, but Julia, ever mindful of Rees' safety, and conscious of the many vantage points on the terrace where an assassin could hide, shook her head and pointed to one in the corner of the room.

'But this is the best table, madam,' the waiter said, shocked that she should decline it.

'I have hayfever, and the flowers on the terrace will make me sneeze,' she lied.

Instantly they were shown to the table of her choice, though Rees' faintly suspicious regard showed he had not swallowed the reason she had given.

'My apartment's full of flowers,' he murmured, 'and you haven't sneezed once.'

'This table is much more romantic,' she invented. 'We're not overlooked and—you can put your hand on my knee without anyone watching.'

He did it too, his fingers warm on the top of her thigh, and she jerked back, colour flaming into her face.

'Sorry, darling,' he drawled, 'but you did suggest it, and I got carried away.'

'That's exactly what you'll be, if you try it again,' she asserted, and he grinned mischievously.

'So tell me the real reason you want to sit here.'

'Because it's safer for you. I haven't forgotten that man's telephone call, even if *you* have.'

The sudden stillness of his body told her she had surprised

him, but, being Rees and determined to play the macho man, he ignored her answer and beckoned the waiter for the menu and the wine-list.

'I don't see you as a Ritz type,' she said when, their order given, they sat sipping champagne. 'I picture you at night-clubs and discos and smart restaurants.'

'The Ritz is a very smart restaurant,' he countered, the side of his mouth quirking with amusement.

'I know, but it's more—' She searched for the right word. 'More decorous.'

His laugh rang out, drawing several eyes to him, the male ones appraising, the women's lingering. 'I'm sorry you see me as such a rake, Julia,' he said when he could speak, 'but that's only because you're so naïve.'

'Sorry,' she said, tossing back her champagne. 'I'll try not to bore you to death.'

'You'll never do that.' He paused, head to one side, almost as if he were mulling over what he had said, which he was, as his next words proved. 'To be honest, you're the least boring female I know. But I'm damned if I can figure out why.'

It was the first compliment he had paid her that she thoroughly liked. Used to being told she was beautiful, sexy, alluring, she couldn't ever remember being paid this particular compliment, and wondered if Rees knew what a lovely one it was.

'Do your other girlfriends bore you, then?' she asked carefully.

'I never thought so until now, but comparing them with you, I suppose the answer is yes. You seem to be three different people, so I never know where I am with you, and which one I'm going to encounter: the efficient PA, the little homebody—even though she can't cook—or the enchanting, sexy girl I'm out with tonight.'

'Let's see if I can guess which one you prefer,' she said sarcastically.

'You might be wrong.' His eyes ranged over her, but his expression was enigmatic. 'They say variety is the spice of life, and you're such a variety of people that I think it must be part of your charm.' He raised his glass. 'Let's drink to that, shall we? To the three faces of Julia. Each one more intriguing than the next.'

Pleasure coursed through her. It was rather like coming in from the cold and finding oneself in a room with a log fire. It was a fanciful simile, but she could think of none that more aptly described her feelings. Rees was a charmer all right, and she would do well to remember that charmers also knew how to keep their emotions intact.

But what do I care if it isn't lasting? she thought. It's nice at the time, so I might as well enjoy it.

Yet she could not quite give herself over to the mood, for she was constantly on the alert for Rees' safety. Still, they had their back to the wall so he could only be attacked from the front. Her eyes scanned the nearby diners, but they all looked innocent enough. Well-groomed, well-heeled men and women happily enjoying themselves. Yet she dared not lower her guard for a second, for even in the most unlikely places danger could threaten.

But the evening was uneventful from a security point of view, though emotionally she found it disquieting. She was liking Rees more and more, and wished she could truly be herself with him. Yet, if she were, he'd swiftly set about seducing her, which would bring her back to square one!

It was not until they were sipping their coffee that Rees surprised her by asking her about her background, and she decided to be as truthful as she could, without disclosing the real nature of her current job.

'I was born and brought up in the country,' she said casually. 'My father's ex-army turned farmer, and I have four brothers. When I was a child there was lots of laughter and teasing, trees to climb, rivers to fish and swim in, and the usual things one does in the country.'

'Sounds delightful.'

'It was—is. I miss it terribly.'

Rees leaned forward. 'So what brought you to this wicked city?'

'An urge to spread my wings.'

'And now you've spread them?'

'I'll fly a little longer. But one day I'll head for home. What about you?' she asked.

'A country upbringing like yours, though there the similarity ends. I have no siblings, and when I was nine my mother went off to Monaco with her tax exile lover. My father was killed in a car accident shortly afterwards.' He paused a moment before continuing, 'I never believed it was an accident as the coroner said. My father was a first-rate driver and knew the road too well to overshoot the bend.'

'You think he…' Julia's voice trailed away and Rees nodded.

'I think he didn't want to go on living after my mother left. He had loved her since they were in kindergarten together, and couldn't contemplate life without her.'

Julia was shocked. 'But he had you. Surely for your sake…'

'I wasn't compensation enough.'

Another question hovered, and Julia had to ask it. 'What happened then? Did you live with your mother?'

'She was too busy. By that time she had left her lover and opened an art gallery in New York. She flew over to see me once at school and charmed all the boys, even though she was wearing the most ridiculous hat.'

Julia could picture the scene all too well. The shy schoolboy, deeply missing his mother who, looking like an exotic bird, had suddenly presented herself to him. 'You loved her, didn't you?' she said softly.

'I suppose I must have done.' Rees' eyes were hooded, his face a mask she could not read. 'She's still running a gallery, but in Boca Rotan—a resort for the rich in Florida,' he explained.

The very lack of emotion in his voice spoke of a much deeper emotion that he would not release, that he might not even be aware of, and Julia's heart ached for the nine-year-old boy who had to come to terms with the knowledge that his mother had put her lover before him, and that, even when he was left fatherless, she had made no move to accept her responsibility.

'Where did you live after your father died?'

'I spent my vacations with my paternal aunt and uncle.'

He vouchsafed no more, and Julia did not press him. But what he had said had painted a bleak picture that explained why he was the cynical man of today, who was never going to become dependent on a woman.

'Don't go all dewy-eyed on me.'

Rees' voice, resonant and curt, broke the silence and shattered her mood. But it did not shatter the conclusions she had come to about him. Ruefully she acknowledged she had stepped away from the platonic relationship which Murray considered essential between a Guardian and the person they were protecting, and had now become emotionally as well as professionally caring of Rees's safety.

Too caring, she thought soberly, knowing that, for her own peace of mind, the sooner this assignment was over the better.

CHAPTER EIGHT

'JULIA, is that you?'

'Chris!' She nearly dropped the receiver in surprise. 'How did you know where to find me?'

'Your mother told me you were working for Engineering 2000 and I thought she was having me on. Last time we met you were singing the praises of Guardians.'

'Well...a woman's prerogative and all that.' Hastily she launched into the explanation she had given everyone other than her parents, that security was far duller than she had expected, and also too demanding.

'If that means you aren't so tied up,' Chris said at once, 'I'm glad to hear it. I'm off to New Zealand and I'd like to see you before I go.'

'A new job?' she asked.

'Yes. I think I've hit the jackpot this time.'

She hoped he had. But then, from what she could gather, he was always hitting the jackpot, then coming a cropper. She didn't even bother asking what the jackpot was.

'So when can I see you?' he asked.

'I'm afraid I'm tied up,' she lied. 'We've a sales conference on all week, and I rarely finish before midnight.'

That should put paid to Chris, she decided, paling at the thought of him bringing her back to the penthouse and bumping into Rees. Sure as chickens laid eggs, he'd blurt out she'd been in security work, and it wouldn't take Rees long to guess that she still was, and send her packing. Not that she would be sorry to leave, for, the sooner she was out of his orbit, the better for her peace of mind. Yet what peace would she have if her departure left him open to an assassin's bullet? If only the police soon discovered something concrete. But they were still no nearer finding out who had made the threats against Rees' life, and Julia was coming to the conclusion that only when the man—or woman—made their move against him would they know. She had learned from Murray only yesterday that Rees would soon be signing the all-important American contract, and once he did he would be out on the town again and leaving himself wide open to be struck down.

Already his girlfriends were ringing to find out why they had not heard from him, and she had occasionally gone into his office and heard him sweet-talking them. How furious it made her to see him perusing a document or signing his letters at the same time, his mind clearly not on any of the sweet nothings he was mouthing. And 'sweet nothings' was a very apt description, for nothing was what he felt for Dawn and Clarissa and the countless others whose names she didn't know!

'Daydreaming?' Rees' deep voice made her aware he had come into the office. His cheeks were flushed, and his eyes, always bright, had an extra gleam in their dark brown depths.

'Good news?' she asked, aware he had come from a meeting with Sir Andrew.

'Yes. I'm finalising something tomorrow, and I'll be free to—' He stopped abruptly, as if once again remembering Julia knew nothing about his business deals, nor why he had led such an exemplary life these past few weeks.

'You mean the American contract with that religious Mr Bargett?' she queried, hiding a smile as she saw Rees grow rigid.

'Who told you about it?'

'I have my sources.'

'Who?'

'I also know it's the only reason you let me move in with you,' she parried, striving to look wide-eyed. 'Because you were scared I'd tell everyone you'd played fast and loose with me, and Mr Bargett might hear of it.'

'I most certainly didn't play fast and loose with you!' he grated. 'You childishly assumed that because I wanted to make love to you I wanted to marry you. Dammit, Julia, it's time you grew up!' Upon which remark, he strode into his office and slammed the door.

Julia felt a spark of sympathy for him. No girl in today's world would be as naïve as the character she was portraying, and it had been kind-hearted of him to believe her sob story about having nowhere to live and letting her move in with him. But what was she thinking? He hadn't done it out of kindness, but in order to protect his good name.

But once the deal was concluded he would have no more worries, and she was sure that within the next few days he would tell her to go. Julia's eyebrows knit together in a frown. There had to be a way of stopping him, though for the moment nothing came to mind.

With a sigh she reached for his diary to check on his next appointment. As she did, an idea came to mind and her eyes lit with satisfaction. If Rees asked her to leave his apartment, she would threaten to walk out on her job. This would mean his having to hire someone else, not something a busy man would relish doing, especially when he knew Mrs William-son would soon be returning. Yes, that was her solution.

For the rest of the afternoon she saw nothing of Rees, who spent several hours with one of the senior engineers in the workshop-cum-laboratory that took up the entire basement floor.

It was five-thirty before he returned to his office, his hair dishevelled, his collar loosened, with the look of pleasure on his face he always wore when he had been 'messing about' with machinery.

How like little boys men were, she thought, feeling an

upsurge of affection for him, and resisting the urge to lean forward and wipe off the smut of oil marking the firm chin.

'Sir Andrew would like to see you,' she said.

With barely a glance in her direction, he strode out again, leaving Julia to tidy her desk and wonder how long it would be before they went home.

At six-thirty she was still wondering, and when her watch showed seven, she was convinced he had gone home without telling her. Surely he wouldn't be so mean? Yet why not? He was furious with her and this would be a good way of showing it. As the thought crossed her mind, the door opened to admit him.

'Sorry I'm late, Julia.'

She shrugged and reached for her jacket, a navy silk blazer that complemented her navy pleated skirt and sleeveless, silky white top.

'I like your idea of a business outfit,' he commented drily.

'Navy and white is very serviceable.' Her voice was prim. 'And the blouse is high-necked.'

'So it is.' He eyed her. 'I guess you'd look sexy even in a sack.'

Her heart thumped as if he had given her the most wonderful compliment, but she said nothing and demurely did up the gilt buttons.

'I thought we'd eat out tonight,' he went on.

'But Mrs Hartley's prepared—'

'We'll eat it tomorrow. I'm fed up staying at home.'

Julia's spirits lifted, realising that for these two days at least he wasn't turfing her out. 'I'd just as soon stay home,' she said. 'There's a good programme on television and—'

'We're eating out.'

Accepting the order, she followed him down to the car park, hoping he wouldn't choose a restaurant that left him open to attack.

In the event, they went to another French bistro, a stone's

throw from his apartment, and entering the small room—it held no more than a dozen tables—her apprehension lessened, for she'd have no difficulty monitoring everyone who came in.

To her surprise the owner, a plump, voluble man, greeted Rees like a long-lost friend, and the two men indulged in a long conversation in French which she only just managed to follow. Watching Rees' face light up as he heard the latest exploits of Philippe's youngest son, increased her conviction that he had turned away from love because of his mother and his determination not to be hurt again, and she found herself hoping he would meet a girl who'd touch his heart. There were so many fine things about him, so many springs untapped, that it would be a waste if he lived his life on the surface, eschewing love and commitment lest it lead to pain.

With a start she realised Rees was speaking to her. 'Sorry,' she apologised, 'I was miles away.'

'With whom?'

'No one. To be honest, I was thinking of *you*.'

'Not very pleasant thoughts, by the look on your face!'

'I was actually hoping that one day you'll fall in love.'

'What a morbid wish. You'd better have a drink to cheer you up!'

'Fruit juice for me, please.'

'On the wagon again?'

She did not answer, and concentrated on the menu.

During the meal they chatted idly on a host of subjects, making Julia realise they were never short of things to say to each other. Funny what an easy man Rees was to talk to, when he gave the impression of being aloof and uninterested in other people's opinions. More than any man she knew, his façade belied the inner person, and she was cogitating on this when he almost echoed her thoughts.

'You're a strange girl, Julia—one moment childish, the next perceptive and profound.'

'You keep saying that,' she reminded him.

'And I keep wondering which is the real you.'

'Guess.'

'I wouldn't waste my time. Women can change their moods and beliefs to suit themselves.'

She understood his cynicism, but none the less deplored it. 'You see us as very expedient, don't you?'

'That shouldn't surprise you.'

'Well, it does. It's childish to judge all women on the basis of one.'

'I'm acquainted with quite a few,' he said curtly, 'and I can't say any have struck me as being anything other than vain and self-centred.'

'*All* the women you've met?' Julia countered, and was intrigued when his eyes looked away from hers and he visibly hesitated.

'*Almost*,' he said slowly.

'What happened to her?' Julia asked.

'Who?'

'The woman who was different.'

'She went back to Australia where she came from.'

'Were you in love with her?'

'Who said anything about love?' he retorted. 'I fancied her like mad and—and then I stopped fancying her.' He sipped his wine. 'Why do you always have to talk about my girlfriends? It seems to be your favourite topic of conversation.'

'Because I think it's your favourite occupation!'

'Well, you're wrong. My work comes first with me. In fact, it's my life.'

'How empty.'

'How rewarding,' he countered.

'I'll remind you of that in five years' time, when I have you to dinner in my happy home with my loving husband and adorable children!'

His teeth flashed in a grin. 'How happy I'll be to leave you and return to the peace of my own home, where I can eat what I like when I like, have total control of the television and stereo, with no one to tell me what to do and when to do it!'

The more he said, the more she realised how determined he was to remain a bachelor, a thought which inexplicably depressed her. But only because it seemed a waste of a gorgeous-looking man who had so much to offer. Though not to me, she told herself. We'd fight like cat and dog! I'm too determined and he's too obstinate. Or was it the other way round? But no matter. Either way they were incompatible.

She was aware of him watching her, and, strangely reluctant to meet his gaze, let her eyes roam the room. All the tables were full now, with diners who looked like regulars: couples and families who had come to their 'local' for what they knew would be a reliably good meal.

Her gaze stopped at a table by the door. By the door! An excellent spot for someone wanting to make a quick getaway. She craned to see who was sitting there, waiting impatiently for a waiter to move away. As he did, she saw a gaunt, grey-faced man in his mid-forties. But what alerted her was his menacing stare as he focused on each table, as though looking for someone. Now he was staring at their table, his head coming forward as if for a better view.

Rees turned at that moment to attract the attention of the waiter, and Julia saw the man by the door stealthily put his hand into the pocket of his jacket.

He was reaching for a gun! In one bound she jumped up and flung herself against Rees, knocking his wine-glass from his hand.

'Quick!' she cried. 'Under the table!'

'*What?*'

'Under the table!'

Shielding Rees with her body, she tried to pull him off his

chair. Furiously he resisted her, much to the amusement of the other diners, who assumed she had been overcome by lust. But Julia was beyond caring what anyone thought, intent only on saving Rees' life.

'Get under the table!' she shouted, clutching him round the neck. 'The man by the door—he's got a gun!'

'For God's sake, woman!' Rees bellowed, pushing her away from him and back into her chair. 'That's Franqis, and he wouldn't hurt a fly.'

Julia's mouth fell open. 'Franqis? You know him?'

'Everyone who comes here does. He sits at that table every night, planning how to get even with his wife who ran off with his best friend.' Rees turned round and waved a greeting to the man by the door before turning back to Julia, his eyes brimming with amusement. 'Did you think he was a killer?'

'You've got to admit he looks like one, and he kept staring our way.'

'He probably fancies you!'

'Must you bring everything down to sex?' she said crossly.

'Can you think of anything better?'

Irritably she looked away, still aware of the chuckles around her. What an idiot she must seem. Still, as Murray would say, better safe than sorry. And if Franqis *had* been the assassin...

It was still early when they returned home, and though Julia instantly retired to her room she was too restless and edgy to sleep. After showering and slipping on a housecoat that covered her from top to toe—she was taking no chances with Rees—she wandered into the living-room and found him immersed in papers.

Settling into the corner of a couch, she wondered if switching on the television would disturb him.

'It won't bother me,' he said, as if divining her thoughts, and indicated the remote control pad lying on the table in front of him.

Keeping the volume low, Julia watched the news. She found it difficult to concentrate, too aware of Rees beside her, jacket and tie off, shirt unbuttoned to show a tanned chest.

He was completely oblivious of her presence as he studied the papers on his lap, occasionally pursing his mouth—what a well-shaped mouth it was for a man—and frequently scribbling in the margin, his gold pen glinting against long, lean fingers.

There was not one physical thing about him she would change, she decided, musing how unfair it was of nature to give a man so much and not also give him a desire for marriage!

'I want to thank you, Julia.'

His voice startled her out of her absorption. 'Thank me for what?'

'Offering me your body.' There was humour in his voice, though his eyes remained serious.

'I did no such thing,' she said indignantly.

'Yes, you did—in the restaurant. If François had been out to kill me, the bullet would have hit you in the middle of your delectable back.'

Only then did she realise that, in her desire to protect Rees, she had given no thought to her own safety. But that was what she had been trained for, wasn't it? No, the answer came back. She had been trained to protect her client, but not to put her own life directly in the firing line.

'Of course, accidents will happen, and you may get hurt,' Murray had said during one of their training sessions. 'But your main job at all times is to be watchful and prevent a dangerous situation from arising, not to put yourselves at risk.'

But, as Rees had so rightly said, she had done exactly that, and knew that if necessary she would do it again, for she loved this man. Loved him with all her heart, and could not envisage life without him.

My God! What had she said? Stunned, she was powerless to think. All she experienced were overwhelming feelings whose intensity scared her: feelings of tenderness, passion, admiration, even anger at Rees' blindness in refusing to see so many things that were crystal clear to her.

How blind I was not to know, she thought soberly. But now that I do, what *am* I going to do? At the moment there was only one answer to this question. She would stay with Rees and protect him.

'Nothing to say for yourself?' he murmured into the silence. 'Or do you always go around trying to save your escort's life?'

'When they're as obstinate as *you*, yes!'

Rees dumped his papers on to the table and came to sit on the settee beside her. 'Even though I think you're worrying about me for nothing, I was touched by what you did, especially since you still see me as a seducer out to get my way with you.'

'Not any more I don't,' she said quickly, afraid that if he made a pass at her she wouldn't be able to hide her feelings for him. 'You've—you've behaved in an exemplary manner since I moved in with you. Just like a brother.'

'I don't feel like your brother. I feel I want to be your lover!' Lifting her hair with a gentle hand, he lightly pressed a kiss on the nape of her neck.

His touch sent tremors through her, and he was instantly aware of it and pulled her swiftly into his arms, at the same time pressing her down on to the cushions.

Julia knew she should resist him, but the touch of his hands—like fire on her body—burned away her resolve, and she made no demur as he skilfully unbuttoned her housecoat and buried his face in the softness of her breasts, suckling first one nipple, then the other, till they rose in hard, throbbing points. Only then did his mouth leave them to feather little kisses up her neck, and then higher still to part her lips with his questing tongue, and enter the soft, inner moistness.

With wild abandon she drank him in, breathing in the scent of him, exulting in the feel of his body, the weight of his limbs and the stirring between his thighs. Desire rushed through her like a river in flood, scattering her senses, and she gripped him tightly, thrilling to his muffled groan as his hands slowly explored her, cupping the fullness of her breasts, curving around her hips to grasp her buttocks and raise them till her soft curves pressed tightly against his hard stomach and the throbbing swell of his arousal.

It aroused an answering need in her that couldn't be denied, and she parted her legs and twined them around his hips, uncaring that she was leaving herself open to him, knowing only that she wanted him inside her, filling her with his life force.

'You're beautiful,' he gasped. 'So beautiful, I want to kiss every inch of you...every inch.'

He began to do so, leaving a moist trail down the velvety skin of her thighs and the softer skin where curly dark hair shielded the pulsing bud that no man had ever touched. But she wanted Rees to, wanted to give herself entirely to him, abandon herself to his hands, his mouth, his tongue that was even now penetrating the dark mysterious depths of her virginity. Never had she felt such overpowering desire, such deep longing, and she threshed wildly and arched her body to his.

'Yes, yes,' he cried. 'Let me love you; let me take you.'

Dimly the words penetrated her mind. 'Let me love you, let me take you.' But not 'I love you'. She was only a body to him, a receptacle for his passion; nothing more. She shivered with the pain of it, the knowledge robbing her of all passion and leaving her cold as the grave. What a fitting word, she thought bleakly. The grave of all her hopes...

'No, Rees!' she whispered, and tried to push him away. 'I can't.'

'You can. We want each other,' he muttered deep in his throat and sought her mouth again, his tongue wild within her, penetrating so deeply that it was like the sexual act itself.

She tried to turn her head, but was powerless to move, and instead she made an effort to control the response of her body. But, oh God, how difficult it was when his fingers were playing her as though she were a violin, finding the crevices, the curves, the beating pulse that ached for him.

'Let me enter you,' he gasped. 'Julia, *darling*...'

'No!' she cried. *'Not without love.'*

Her words fell like ice-shards between them, shattering the passion that had almost made them one, and they were two people again, with an ever-widening gulf between them, a gulf that had always been there, though for a brief moment she had almost believed he had crossed it.

'Still clinging to your romantic illusions?' he asked with irony, his words showing how firmly he was entrenched on the far side.

'Yes,' she said, gathering her housecoat around her, and with it her pride. 'I'll never change my mind, Rees. Sex without love is meaningless.'

'Sex without love can be exhilarating, exciting and a wonderful release of emotion and tension.'

'I prefer a hot bath.' She stood up and, though it required an effort, looked him full in the face. 'I'm sure sex without love can be everything you say it is, but *with* love it can give your life a whole new dimension.'

'I'm happy as I am,' he shrugged, and turned away from her.

Heartbroken, she stared at his broad-shouldered back, noticing the proud way he held his head. She waited for him to ask her to move out of his home, and wondered what problems this would create for Murray Guardian and herself. Her mind raced madly, only stopping as Rees spoke.

'You won't need to lock your bedroom door, Julia.'

'I'm delighted to hear it,' she retorted. 'Even *my* love can't last if it isn't nourished, and I've gone off you in a very big way.'

'Then there's no harm done,' he said, returning to his chair and papers.

'Except to your pride.'

'It would take more than a turn-down from *you* to dent that.'

Giving him the last word, she marched from the room. Her bravado lasted only till she was alone, and she sank down on her bed and stared into a future that was going to be very bleak without him. Yet better bleakness than the pain and bitterness she would feel if she compromised her beliefs. Blinking back the tears, she stood up and went to the window.

It was a beautiful clear night, with a full moon in the sky sending a pattern of light across the terrace. Since moving in here she had made sure the terrace lights were kept on till daybreak, pretending she liked to look out of her bedroom window and see the flowers in their decorative urns, when in reality it was to ensure that any trespasser could be seen.

Unlocking the glass door, she walked outside. Though midnight, the air was still warm, and she wandered across to the edge of the patio and looked down at the Thames, dark and gleaming. In a week's time, or a month—surely it would not be longer?—she would be gone from Rees' life, with Mrs Williamson taking over from her in the office, and some blonde, brunette or redhead making her a fading memory in Rees' mind. But it would be a long while before he was out of her own, and for the briefest of moments she was tempted to go to him and let him make love to her, so she would at least have some happy memories as consolation.

Yet, aware that what they shared would only be sex, those memories wouldn't satisfy her for long, and sombrely she left the terrace and went to bed; alone, unhappy, yet strangely content in the knowledge that she had done the right thing.

CHAPTER NINE

NEXT day Rees behaved as though nothing had happened between them. Of course, nothing *had*, Julia reminded herself, piqued that he had so quickly written her off. But then, as he had made abundantly clear, he wasn't going to waste his time trying to seduce the unseduceable!

Telling herself it was for the best, she determinedly matched his mood, and anyone coming into the office and seeing them together would never have guessed that the previous night they had been lying in a passionate embrace, skin upon skin, devouring mouth upon throbbing breasts.

Whether it was on purpose or by intent, Rees was kept inordinately busy that day, going from one meeting to another, and taking Julia with him to nearly all of them to make notes. He appeared to have forgotten she did not do shorthand, and she was hard put to it to get all the salient points down. But luckily she had a retentive memory, and in the apartment later that evening she began adding to the notes she had made. By the time she had finished, her hand was aching, and she flung her pen down with relief. Another day like today and she would take one of the secretaries along with her.

She was still gently massaging her wrist when the telephone rang, and a lilting, feminine voice asked to speak to Rees. But this one had an Australian accent, and Julia, who tried to monitor all his calls, had never spoken to her before.

'You don't sound like Mrs Hartley,' the girl said. 'Are you the new housekeeper or a girlfriend?'

'Neither,' Julia said crisply. 'I'm Rees' assistant, and I *do* mean assistant.'

A warm laugh came across the line. 'I'm Melinda Harrison, and I'd like to speak to Rees.'

'He's in the shower. But I'll tell him as soon as he comes out. Does he have your number?'

'Yes. Tell him I've managed to rent the same apartment—just around the corner from him.'

Julia was replacing the receiver when Rees came in, clad in a towelling robe.

'One of your girlfriends just called,' she said. 'Melinda Harrison.'

'*What?*' Rees looked stunned, then his mobile mouth widened into a smile of pure delight. 'Melinda *here*? In England?'

Only then did Julia recollect Rees telling her that he had fancied one girl above all others and that she had returned to Australia when he had stopped fancying her. But the happiness now on his face belied his words, and Julia was filled with fury, anguish and misery, all of which she belatedly recognised as nothing more than jealousy. Oh, God, she thought, what is this man doing to me? I've always hated jealousy. It's a demeaning emotion and shows a lack of self-esteem. Yet jealousy was what she felt, and there was nothing she could do to stop it as Rees reached for the telephone.

'Did she say where she's staying?'

'She's in her old apartment.'

Swiftly he dialled. No problem about him forgetting the number, Julia thought miserably. It must be engraved on his heart. Hurriedly she gathered her notes together, but Rees was already talking.

'It's wonderful to hear your voice! Why didn't you let me know? Of course I'm free. I'll be with you as soon as I've changed.' His head tilted to one side as he listened, his full lower lip curving into a smile. 'Sure you can,' he said. 'Come over and have a drink with her. Then I'll take you to Annabel's for dinner.'

'Melinda wants to see you for yourself,' he said, putting down the receiver and grinning at Julia. 'She says, knowing my reputation, she doesn't believe you're only my assistant!'

'Shall I take off my make-up and dig out a pair of glasses?'

'Even a false nose wouldn't make you ugly! Just act naturally and let Melinda judge for herself. She's no fool.'

'You amaze me,' Julia retorted. 'Only a fool could go on fancying you!'

Rees laughed. 'Good thing you have a sense a humour. It's one of your better qualities.'

She warned herself to watch her tongue. There was too much at stake—Rees' life—to put a foot wrong.

Tossing her head, she walked out, but, once in her room, paced the floor anxiously. There was no way of preventing Rees from going out with Melinda, and no way of getting herself invited. She could imagine his face if she suggested it! Yet she dared not leave him unguarded, and in desperation she telephoned Murray.

'I don't have anyone free,' he informed her when she told him the problem.

'But *someone* has to watch him.'

'Too right. Will *I* do?'

'Of course you'll do,' she exclaimed. 'But I didn't think you worked in the field any more.'

'Only when there's an emergency. And tonight there is. Shall I pick you up, or will you cadge a lift with Rees and his lady-love?'

Julia was flummoxed. 'Cadge a lift where?'

'To Annabel's, where else? If I'm playing protector for a night, I intend it to be with a beautiful girl in tow. So get your glad rags on, sweetheart. We're dining and dancing together.'

Julia's eyes sparkled at the thought of Rees' face when he saw her at the nightclub with a good-looking man like Murray. Oh, boy, his nose would really be out of joint! Except why should it, when his nose was pointed firmly in Melinda's direction?

'You still there?' Murray asked.

'I was just thinking. Call me back in ten minutes and ask me for a date. That will make it look authentic, because Rees and I were supposed to be staying in tonight.'

With Murray promising to do as she asked, Julia took out the dress she had bought during her lunch break today, a flowery chiffon in pink and violet. It had practically beckoned at her from the window of a boutique, and because she had been filled with miserable thoughts over Rees she had extravagantly treated herself to it. But she dared not put it on yet, not until Murray had called and Rees had overheard the conversation. Picking up a book, she went back to the living-room.

She was half-way down the hall when the doorbell rang and Rees dashed from his room, pulled the door open and a smiling girl into his arms.

Hurriedly Julia turned away, but Rees called her.

'Hey, Julia, come and meet Melinda.'

Summoning a smile, she took the girl's outstretched hand. Prepared to dislike her, Julia instantly felt a rapport. Not only was Melinda stunningly pretty, tall and slender, with hair the colour of corn, but she also had a genuine smile, and a humorous gleam in her big brown eyes.

'Are you really his assistant?' Melinda asked, her voice even more melodious than on the telephone. 'Or is Rees too diplomatic to tell me you're his latest?'

'I've never considered him diplomatic,' Julia said, 'and I'm definitely not his latest.'

'Even though she's living here,' Rees put in smoothly, and Julia, watching the Australian girl, saw the statement had come as a shock.

'I was turned out of my apartment and haven't yet managed to find anything else,' she explained quickly, determined not to let Rees think she wanted to make mischief between him and his lady-love. 'In fact I turned up on Rees's doorstep with my cases and bludgeoned him into taking me in.'

'Chalk that up as a victory,' Melinda said. 'I've never known Rees be bludgeoned into doing anything he didn't want to do.'

'When you two have finished dissecting me...' Firmly pushing them both into the living-room, he went to the bar. 'What will you have, Melinda?'

'The usual,' she smiled, and there was a world of intimacy in the two words as well as in the look that passed between them.

'And you, Julia?'

It was a wonder he had remembered she was there, Julia thought sourly. 'I'll have the usual, too,' she replied, but there was no intimacy in *her* words, and definitely none in the way Rees didn't look at her when he handed her an orange juice and then turned to uncork a bottle of champagne.

Melinda accepted a glass from him and waited while he poured his own.

Julia, anticipating an intimate toast, was even more jealous when Rees simply touched his goblet to Melinda's mouth before drinking from it. Then he caught her hand and drew her down on to the couch beside him.

Julia knew that the decent thing was to leave them alone, but deciding that since Rees had given her an orange juice he did not expect her to sip it in solitary state, she perched on a chair a little distance away from them.

'How come you're back in London?' Rees questioned the girl beside him.

'I'm doing some cosmetic commercials.' Melinda settled back comfortably and crossed one shapely leg over the other.

'How long will you be here?'

'As long as I like. My agent says he can get me masses of work.'

'That's great. At least, I hope it is?'

There was an electric silence between them, as tangible as if a spark had flashed, and then Melinda gave a faint sigh and commented, 'Doesn't my ringing you give you your answer?'

The dark head nodded, and Julia was unable to bear any more. She was half-way to the door when the telephone rang, and she slowed her step.

'Sure,' Rees said into the receiver. 'She's right here.' He held out the phone to her. 'For you.'

'For me?' she asked with pseudo-innocence, then allowed a look of pleasure to cross her face as she heard the voice at the other end.

'Mark, *darling*! I didn't realise you were back in town. Of course I'm free. I've been a real stay-at-home since you left London. I know, darling. I've missed you too.' Julia made herself pause while Murray chuckled at the other end, and then told her to get on with her act. 'I'd love to go to Annabel's,' she said. 'Hang on a moment.' She looked at Rees. 'Mark lives in Highgate, and if he has to come all the way down here to collect me—'

'We can give you a lift, can't we, Rees?' Melinda cut in.

'No problem,' he said. 'But you'll have to make your own way back.'

It was all Julia could do not to throw her drink at him. 'How unusual of you to state the obvious,' she said sweetly, then turned to make her arrangements with 'Mark'.

'If you ladies will excuse me, I'll go and finish dressing,' Rees said.

'Me, too,' Julia added. 'I'd no idea I was going out tonight.'

'Don't mind me,' Melinda smiled. 'I can do with a cat

nap.' She curled up in a corner of the couch, showing more than a glimpse of creamy thigh, then closed her eyes.

Julia walked ahead of Rees down the corridor, very conscious of him behind her.

'I'm glad you've a date tonight,' he said. 'I wouldn't want you to stay at home alone and be bored.'

'That's sweet of you,' Julia said with false sincerity. 'Mark's an old flame of mine.'

'Not a very hot one, or you wouldn't be going out with him.'

'Mark respects me,' Julia said primly.

'He must be under-sexed!'

For answer, she closed the door in his face.

Curiosity to find out more about Melinda gave Julia the speed of lightning, and she was dressed and back in the living-room within ten minutes. Unfortunately Melinda had fallen asleep, her long hair a soft, golden cloud around her.

Julia flung her bag on to the floor, hoping to wake her. It did, and sleepy brown eyes blinked at her.

'I think jet lag's caught up with me.' Melinda yawned prettily. 'I flew in this morning.'

'And you called Rees straight away?' Julia tried to sound disinterested.

'I almost called him from Sydney before I left, but I didn't want to give him the chance to run!'

The girl swung her legs to the ground and lazily stretched. Her every movement was graceful, and Julia, no slouch herself when it came to looks, accepted that Melinda was a natural beauty in the Australian mould: tall, blonde and tanned, with a warmth and vivacity that girls in the southern hemisphere always seemed to have.

'How long have you worked for Rees?' Melinda asked. 'I never thought Mrs Williamson would ever leave him.'

Julia launched into her well-rehearsed explanation for the woman's temporary leave.

'Will you be sorry to go when she comes back?' Melinda enquired.

'No. I'm counting the days, actually.' She decided it was her turn to be inquisitor. 'Have you known Rees long?'

'Four years. But I haven't seen him for eighteen months. We quarrelled and I went back to Australia.'

The girl lapsed into silence, her lovely face sad, and, though Julia was as full of curiosity as a puppy, she didn't feel she had the right to pry further.

'We lived together for nearly two years,' Melinda went on softly, almost as if speaking to herself, 'and then I tried to push him into marriage by giving him an ultimatum. I lost, of course. He said he loved me, but that he'd never marry *anyone*, and I was so angry and upset, I walked out.'

'And you're back to do some commercials?'

'I'm back because I wanted to be. I've as much work in Australia as I can handle. But I needed an excuse to see Rees and find out if there's someone else in his life, or if I can move into it again.'

'Without marriage?' Julia kept her voice even.

'On any terms he'll have me. I nearly married someone else a few months ago, but then found I couldn't go through with it. So here I am.'

Julia was sincerely sorry for Melinda. She obviously cared for Rees, while he, in his inimitable fashion, cared only for himself. But wasn't she judging him too harshly? After all, he made no secret of his determination to stay single, and if Melinda finally accepted this they'd probably be very happy.

'*Is* there anyone else in his life?' Melinda asked.

Julia was tempted to lie, then honesty won the day and she shook her head. 'He's still playing the field, from what I gather.'

Melinda seemed decidedly happier, though Julia's mood swung in the opposite direction. If only I didn't like the girl, she thought, but she's so warm and friendly, it's easy to see

why Rees still cares for her. No way could she see him turning down the chance of having Melinda back. If the girl
played her cards more carefully this time, she might eventually even lead him into marriage.

'I won't make the mistake of pushing him this time,' Melinda said, as if echoing Julia's thoughts. 'Rees never looked
at another girl the two years he was with me, and if I can
settle for that...' She gave the faintest of smiles. 'Perhaps if
we have a child later on, he might change his mind.'

Julia's spirits plummeted to an all-time low, and though
she tried to look uncaring the keen look Melinda gave her
told her she had not succeeded. For a moment she was
tempted to admit she was also in love with Rees, then knew
nothing would be served by doing so. Before the night was
out, Melinda would be in his bed and she herself a fading
memory.

'Ready?' Rees asked from the door, and Melinda went
across to him. Julia was filled with despair. They looked so
right for each other. He tall, dark and handsome, she blonde
and willowy. Feeling like a third wheel, Julia went down
with them to the foyer.

'I intend drinking a magnum of champagne to celebrate
your return,' he said, shepherding Melinda into a taxi, and
then doing so more perfunctorily for Julia. 'So it's best if I
don't drive.'

Julia, ever conscious that she was guarding Rees' life, was
glad he was saved the necessity of parking and could go
straight from the cab into the shelter of Annabel's. With this
in mind, she jumped out of the taxi almost before it had
halted outside the club, and with the open door of the cab
protecting Rees on one side, she was careful to make sure
she shielded him on the other.

Murray had not yet arrived, but he had rung to say he was
delayed, and she was shown to the table he had booked,
which luckily was not too far from Rees'. Flailing herself,

Julia watched him devote his attention to Melinda, sitting close beside her on the banquette and smiling into her eyes. So intently was she watching him that she didn't notice Murray until she felt his hand on her arm, and she looked up, startled.

She was even more startled when she took in his appearance, for she had never before seen him dressed for an evening out. In the office he generally wore navy trousers and sweater, and the few occasions he had supervised her training course, he had worn denims. But tonight he was resplendent in a grey silk mohair suit, his wavy golden hair brushed sleek. A pale blue shirt drew attention to his tanned skin, and made his eyes appear an even deeper blue.

'You look gorgeous,' he said, sliding on to the banquette beside her.

'So do you.'

He appraised her frankly, as if enjoying the sight of her heart-shaped face framed by her lustrous black hair; her slender, yet curvaceous body enticingly covered in soft chiffon. 'You look good enough to eat.'

'Hey,' she said. 'This is a business date, remember? It's not supposed to be for real.'

'Sorry. I guess the sight of you carried me away.'

Teasingly, she flexed her muscles. 'Make sure I don't get you carried away permanently!'

He laughed. 'OK, so let's stick to business. Where's Denton?'

'Three tables to the right, sitting with a gorgeous blonde.'

Murray dropped his napkin to the floor and, bending to pick it up, used the opportunity to check out exactly where Rees was. 'Shall we order and then dance?' Then, before she had a chance to reply, Murray jumped up and pulled her to her feet. 'Sorry, but Denton's dancing and so must we.'

Though tall and broad, Murray was light on his feet, and, without appearing to, adroitly kept on Rees' heels.

Julia tried not to see Rees dancing cheek to cheek with Melinda, and resisted the urge to close her eyes, remembering that she and Murray had to keep them wide open in this ever-moving, ever-changing throng.

The music seemed to go on for ever—slow, smoochy music, when she longed for something bright and brash, for anything to keep Melinda from nestling close in Rees' arms.

'I like the scent you're wearing,' Murray murmured.

'I forgot to put any on,' Julia confessed.

'You mean the lovely smell is you?'

'Stop flirting with me, Murray.'

'I'm doing it to make Denton jealous,' he protested. 'You've still got to stick close to him, you know.'

'Fat chance I'll have with Melinda back.'

'You can always blow your cover and tell him who you are.'

'He'd kick me out. He's the most stupidly obstinate man.'

'Obstinate or not, I think Sir Andrew's reached the stage where he'll give him an ultimatum if I say it's necessary.'

Julia debated whether this might not be the best course of action. With her subterfuge out of the way, she could do her job more easily and, in reverting to her proper role, might convince Rees that her feelings for him had merely been a hoax. Would that it were true! Watching the dark head bent to the fair one, she trembled with longing for him.

Feeling the movement, Murray drew her closer. 'Your feelings are showing.'

About to deny it, she changed her mind. Maybe if she told someone how she felt, she'd get it out of her system. After all, bearing in mind what she wanted from life, she was crazy to love a man like Rees.

'Stupid, aren't I?' she said.

'Denton's even more stupid for not seeing what's under his nose.'

'Oh, he saw,' Julia sighed, 'but he didn't want—except on a temporary basis.'

'You're lovely enough to make any man change his mind about that.'

'Not Rees, and certainly not now Melinda's back. She's the love of his life, you know.'

'You're going to find this job tough,' Murray muttered. 'Especially when they leave here. I hope his bedroom's sound-proofed.'

Julia's cheeks burned, and the images Murray's words evoked were so painful, it was a moment before she spoke. 'He'll probably go back to her place.'

'If he does, I'll take over from you and you can go home.'

'You don't need to wet-nurse me,' she said sharply. 'I'm perfectly capable of doing my job.'

'Too capable.'

'What does that mean?'

'That you've worn yourself to a frazzle guarding Denton. You've lost weight, and there are blue shadows under your eyes.'

'My weight fluctuates,' she lied. 'And the shadows are make-up. It's all the rage to look fragile this season.'

'Rubbish.' Murray gave her a little shake, then wrapped his arms around her again, at which moment Rees turned to lead Melinda off the floor, and saw them.

'Hello, Julia.' He looked directly at Murray, and she casually introduced them.

'Rees, this is Mark Gardner, an old friend of mine.'

'Not as old as all that,' Murray chuckled, and looked at Rees. 'I want to thank you for taking care of Julia when she had to leave that apartment she was in. But now I'm back, I'm going to see if I can make her move in with *me*.'

Julia was astonished and delighted by Murray's imagination, though her pleasure ebbed as Rees nodded and said equably, 'She's free to go any time.'

'Thanks for trying to make him jealous,' Julia murmured when they were out of Rees' earshot. 'But if you don't care about someone, you don't care what they do.'

'Well, nothing ventured, nothing gained. You're worth ten of that blonde.'

'Not true, boss. You're prejudiced.'

For the next couple of hours Julia did her best to act as if she were enjoying herself, though it was a relief when Murray glanced across her shoulder and said, 'I'll call for the bill. Rees and his lady-love are leaving.'

'He generally stays out later than this,' Julia commented before she could stop herself.

'When you've a beautiful and willing lady beside you, it can never be too soon to go home,' Murray chuckled.

'That's hardly a diplomatic comment to make to me,' Julia said brightly, deciding that, since Murray had guessed how she felt about Rees, it was better to wear her heart brazenly on her sleeve.

'I'm a great believer in the cold turkey treatment,' he replied. 'If you're convinced you don't stand a chance with him, you'll start looking for someone else.'

Murray's hand was warm around her waist as he escorted her from the room, and Julia suddenly wished she was his girl, and that Rees Denton meant nothing to her.

As they emerged from Annabel's, the object of her thoughts was being driven away in a cab, and she and Murray raced to his car, parked a few yards away.

'Do you know where Melinda's staying?' he asked, switching on the ignition. 'If we lose the cab, I want to know where to head for.'

'She has an apartment in Dockland Towers, round the corner from Rees.'

'We'll head there,' Murray said, setting the car in motion. 'And then?'

'I'll wait for him to come out, and you can go home and get your beauty sleep.'

Fat chance she had of sleeping, Julia thought miserably. All she'd do was pace the floor and think of Rees making love to Melinda, his mouth exploring hers, his supple fingers caressing her breasts, his strong legs entwined with paler, fragile ones. For the first time she wished she had never quit modelling, that she hadn't become a Guardian, and that she had never met Rees.

But she had, and her only chance of finding peace was to get him out of her system as fast as possible.

CHAPTER TEN

MURRAY drew his car quietly to a stop in the shadows—a few yards from the entrance to Docklands Towers—and switched off the engine. Julia had managed to get the number of Rees' cab as it had pulled away from Annabel's, and they had kept it in sight all the way. Murray was right, Julia thought as the cab drove off, empty, Rees *is* going to stay with Melinda.

'We'll give them five minutes,' Murray said.

Five minutes to lock the door, undress and jump into bed?

'You're very quiet,' Murray murmured when the time had passed.

'Aren't we supposed to be?'

'Hardly, out here,' he smiled, and checked the time again. 'OK, let's go.'

'Go where?'

'To check that they're safe.'

'You don't think anyone is waiting for them inside the apartment, do you?' Julia was out of the car in a flash, with Murray hard on her heels.

'Logically, no,' Murray said, running alongside her. 'But we have to check every possibility.'

They reached the plush gilt and glass entrance, and Murray signalled the porter to open the door for them. He did not do so, but slid back a small pane of glass to talk to them.

Murray held out an identity card, and the man examined it carefully, then opened the door.

'We'd like to know the number of Miss Harrison's apartment,' Murray said. 'She's the blonde who just came in with a man.'

The porter's eyes glowed with appreciation. 'She has 581 on the tenth floor.'

'Thanks,' Murray said, making for the elevator. 'Now we go gashle.'

'Gashle?' Julia was puzzled.

'Zulu for "slowly". I was there for six months.'

'I never knew you'd been to Africa.'

'In our game we go anywhere and everywhere.'

It was good to know, Julia thought. Maybe she would ask Murray to assign her to the Australian outback next time, or the Brazilian jungle. Anywhere, so long as she need never set eyes on Rees.

The elevator stopped on the tenth floor, and they made their way along the thickly carpeted corridor to 581, stopping directly in front of it for Murray to bend his ear to the door.

Julia heard the murmur of voices and, unwilling to eavesdrop, stepped back. But Murray had no such inhibition, and remained where he was, a slow smile creasing his face before he too finally stepped back.

'Everything seems OK,' he mouthed. 'Now, let's see where's the best place to keep watch.'

'We just passed an unnumbered door,' Julia said, making for it and finding it was a broom closet, dark and warm and smelling of disinfectant.

Murray came in with her and they left the door ajar, giving themselves a clear view of Melinda's apartment.

'We don't both have to stay,' Julia whispered.

'I'm enjoying myself,' Murray whispered back. 'It's not often I get to play "I-Spy".'

'You don't need to. I can manage perfectly well on my own.'

'Oh, sure. You just love being on duty twenty-four hours out of twenty-four.'

'It's what I've been doing for weeks,' she rejoined.

'I'm quite willing to send someone to relieve you,' Murray

protested, moving closer to her and banging his shin against a bucket. 'Damn!' He rubbed his leg.

'Go home,' Julia said again.

'No way. *You* go home and get some beauty sleep.'

Fat chance she had of sleeping when all she would be doing was trying not to think of Rees and what *he* would be doing!

'I mean it,' Murray reiterated. 'Go.'

It was an order and she obeyed it.

Back in the apartment, she switched on the television to watch a late-night movie, but all she saw were Rees and Melinda in bed together, and she switched it off again. It was impossible to relax until Rees walked in. But, if he saw her sitting up like this, he'd think she was waiting up for him! Of course, she could always put on her broadest smile and say she'd had such a wonderful time she couldn't go to bed for thinking about it!

Then, amazingly—as if in answer to her prayers—he was in the doorway, smiling and clear-eyed.

'What are you doing up?' he asked.

'Thinking about tonight,' she smiled.

'*Last* night,' he said. 'It's after two.'

'Really? I'd no idea.'

'Had a good time?'

'Mmm, wonderful...'

'You'd better get some shut eye.' He turned away, yawning. 'I'm exhausted. See you at eight.'

As he disappeared, tears stung Julia's eyes. Exhausted, was he? No wonder! How many times had he and Melinda... She jumped up from the couch and rushing to her room, flung herself on the bed and burst into sobs, the sound muffled by her pillow. Damn Melinda and every woman Rees had been to bed with. But, most of all, damn Rees!

It seemed only a moment later that the sound of tapping brought her back to consciousness, and bleary-eyed, she sat up and squinted at her wrist-watch. Nine o'clock! As she swung her legs to the floor, Rees put his head around the door. He was fully dressed, bright and bushy-tailed, and she glared at him sourly.

Ignoring it, he gave her a wide grin. 'Good thing I'm your boss, or you'd be fired!' Only then did he take in her crumpled chiffon dress and mussed hair. 'Why are you still in your glad rags?'

'I must have flaked out.'

'I thought you didn't drink.'

'I wasn't drunk. I was tired.'

'That Mark must be quite a guy. Even *I* didn't manage to make you so exhausted.'

'Don't talk nonsense!'

But Rees was already on his way, calling over his shoulder that he would see her in the office.

Oh, God! That meant he'd be driving there on his own! Galvanised into action, she tore off her dress and dashed into the bathroom. What a sight she looked with mascara streaked down her cheeks and her black hair wild as a witch! But what did it matter in the face of Rees' safety?

Creaming the make-up off her face in one fell swoop, she donned panties and the first dress that came to hand, slipped into a pair of pumps—no time for stockings and bra—and tore out of the apartment, praying she'd find a cab was to hand.

She breathed a sigh of relief as one cruised past her as she reached the street, and, asking the cabby to drive as fast as he dared, she caught up with Rees' car as it turned down the ramp into the parking area of his office building.

Hardly had he stepped from his car when she was beside him.

'Good lord!' He was startled. 'Where did *you* spring from?'

'A gooseberry bush!' Eyes alert, she stuck close to him as

they crossed to the elevator, breathing a sigh of relief as the doors closed behind them.

'Your face is shiny and still streaked,' he remarked conversationally.

Scarlet-cheeked, she rubbed at her skin with a tissue. 'That better?'

'Not much,' he grinned heartlessly. 'You look a real sight—for sore eyes!'

Her spirits rose. 'Do I really?'

He nodded. 'So does Melinda without make-up. Beats me why good-looking women want to plaster their faces with goo.'

Their arrival at their office saved her the necessity of replying, and he went directly into his room, where two senior engineers were waiting for him. It was noon before his meeting ended and she was able to go in to see him, feeling she owed him an apology.

'Sorry I overslept, Rees. It won't happen again.'

'Forget it. There's such a thing as *quid pro quo*, and you've worked late so often...' He leaned back in his chair, swivelling it gently from side to side.

Though his conference had gone on for nearly three hours, he showed no sign of fatigue. But then, he was a demon when it came to work. Only as her eyes met his did she realise he was studying her as closely as she him, a quizzical look on his face that she had never seen before.

'Lunching with the boyfriend, I see,' he murmured.

'What makes you say that?'

He waved a languid arm in her direction, and looking down she saw she was wearing one of her most expensive dresses, peach silk with a narrow pleated bodice and sunray pleated skirt. Heavens, she *must* have been in a hurry, to have picked this one out and not noticed!

'I just grabbed the first dress to hand,' she confessed.

'You didn't really think I'd fire you because you were late?' he said.

'Of course not, but—' She dared not explain why she had rushed, and changed the subject. 'What's on the agenda for this afternoon? Your diary's empty.'

'I'll be in the laboratory, then I'm going to our factory in Kent.'

Instantly she was alert. 'Who with?'

'Not Melinda,' he said gently. 'So stop glaring at me.'

'I wasn't glaring. Anyway, what do I care if you go out with Melinda—except that she's too nice for you?'

He laughed. 'Sweet Julia, always ready to cut me down to size. Didn't your mother tell you it doesn't always pay to be honest?'

'No.'

'Pity.' He rose and reached for his jacket from a nearby chair. 'You can have the afternoon off, if you like. I won't be needing you.'

'Are you going by car?' she asked as he went to the door.

'Helicopter.'

'May I come with you?'

'You don't need to accompany me *everywhere* I go.'

'As your assistant I—'

'Let *me* decide if I want you around.'

'I've never been in a helicopter,' she added, reverting to her little-girl voice.

Muttering beneath his breath, he nodded, and hiding her triumph Julia went with him.

Julia wasn't lying when she said she had never been in a helicopter, though she had flown many thousands of miles during her modelling career, and she was in no way prepared for the motion of this whirly-bird.

Although it was a warm summer's day, there was a strong southerly wind, and the helicopter bounced around the sky like a children's balloon in play. This motion, coupled with the appalling noise of the blades, made her decidedly queasy, a fact which Rees noted with malice.

'Serves you right,' he said as they landed and she stumbled out after him. 'Next time do as I tell you.'

She felt too nauseous to reply, and was glad Rees had elected to have lunch when they landed, rather than before, for her meal would assuredly have hit the ground before she did.

'Do—do you mind if I sit down for a moment?' she whispered, and, not waiting for his answer, sank on to the tarmac.

'You really *are* ill.' Bending over her, Rees took out his handkerchief and dabbed the sweat from her forehead and upper lip. 'Little fool. I bet you didn't even have breakfast.'

She nodded, still too nauseous to speak, and kept her eyes firmly closed so as not to see the ground still heaving around her.

She felt strong hands grip her as Rees lifted her to her feet, and then swung her up into his arms, cradling her effortlessly as he strode across the helicopter pad to the factory entrance.

Only when they reached the lobby did he set her on her feet. 'Lunch first, work later,' he said, as she went to thank him. 'And if you still feel queasy, go to the ladies' room and lie down. I'll be too busy to catch you before you hit the ground again!'

'I'll be perfectly all right when I've had a sandwich.'

And so she was, her natural good health returning once she had some food inside her. For the remainder of the afternoon she followed Rees around the factory floor. Security was naturally tight here, and there hadn't been any necessity for her to come, but something had impelled her, and she didn't wish to analyse it. Watching his camaraderie with the men, it was easy to see why he was well-liked, and she thought again what an unusual man he was: determinedly professional, and a determined playboy.

It was five o'clock before they took to the sky again—luckily windless—and six before they re-entered their apartment. No, not theirs, she reminded herself, *his*. Maybe eventually his and Melinda's, for there was no point kidding herself that the Australian girl would not be moving in with him.

'Seeing Melinda?' she asked casually.

'Yes. Seeing Mark?'

'Of course.' She saw a frown cross his face, and for a joyous moment she thought he was jealous, but his next words dissipated the notion.

'You're not seeing him on the rebound, are you?'

She was puzzled. 'Rebound?'

'From me. Not so long ago you loved me enough to want to marry me.'

'Oh, I've got over that,' she said airily. 'Once I discovered the type of man you were, I knew I'd never be happy with you.' She gave him her baby-eyed look, wondering what he'd do if she flung herself at his feet and told him she loved him. Why, he'd run so fast, his shoes would catch fire!

'I suppose you fancy yourself in love with Mark,' Rees muttered.

'It's funny you should say that,' Julia replied, 'because I—'

'Spare me your reasons,' Rees cut in. 'I'm picking Melinda up in an hour and I want to have a rest first.'

With Rees safely in his room, Julia contacted Murray. 'We seem to be playing the same record,' she apologised, 'but Rees is going out again tonight, and I'm not sure if I should follow him myself or see if you can put someone else on to him.'

'Neither,' Murray replied. 'Fact is, I was about to call you when you rang. The results of the enquiry into the plane crash was made public on the six o'clock news. It's been confirmed it was due to a wing-flap failure and had nothing to do with Rees' invention.'

Relief washed over Julia like a beach at high tide, and she almost cried with joy. 'So whoever has been threatening him knows they're wrong to blame him for the accident?'

'Hopefully. It's a man, by the way. Jack Ledbury. Only an hour before the cause of the crash was announced, the police managed to get to see him—his wife was one of the dead. Apparently he seemed very reasonable, but they're pretty sure he's the one who's been making the threatening calls. They didn't say so to him—merely that they were seeing *all* the relatives of the crash victims to put them in the picture as to the real cause of the accident.'

'So what happens now?'

'They've put a round-the-clock watch on him.'

'Does that mean my job's finished?' Julia asked.

'Not until we hear from Sir Andrew. But there's no need for you to guard Rees tonight.'

'What a relief,' Julia murmured. 'I'll catch up on my sleep.'

'Pity. I was going to suggest a quiet dinner together.'

'I had dinner with you last night.'

'That was in the course of duty. This would be in the course of pleasure.'

'May I take a rain check?'

'Absolutely.'

The call ended, and she ruefully wondered why she had fallen for the wrong man when the right one was available. She and Murray had so many things in common. They liked the outdoor life, they understood each other's work, and he was handsome and intelligent. In fact, it was a damned shame she was unable to fall in love with him to order!

Sliding a note under Rees' door to say she had a date, she took herself off to the cinema and, determined not to be home before he was, sat through the programme twice. Even then it was only eleven, and, tired from her lack of sleep the night before, she went back to the penthouse. There was no reason for Rees to know she had come back early. After all, he never came into her room to check up on her.

Stifling a yawn, she let herself into the mirrored hall, stopping in surprise as she heard the delicate strains of a Mozart concerto. She tiptoed towards her bedroom.

'That you, Julia?'

Damn! What finely tuned ears he had. 'Yes,' she said reluctantly, pausing by the doorway. He was sprawled on the couch and must have been there some time, for he was wearing the towelling robe she knew so well, and there was a stack of documents on the table beside him and a coffee percolator bubbling away.

'Care for a cup?' he asked.

Wanting to store up every possible memory of him—God, what a masochist she was!—she nodded and helped herself, then perched on an armchair near him.

'You're back early,' she commented.

'So are you.'

'I was tired, and Mark was very understanding.'

'What does he do?'

'Do?' She thought quickly. 'He has a—a nursery.'

'I thought that was women's work.'

'Chauvinist!' She stuck out her tongue at him. 'I mean he runs a flower nursery.'

Rees looked amused. 'Gardner by name and gardener by trade?'

She nodded, took another sip of coffee and studied Rees through her lashes.

He showed no signs of fatigue, but then, why should he? Making love to Melinda had probably refreshed him, and he had to be happy when he loved her so much.

'Melinda's a nice girl.' The words tumbled out of their own accord.

'Exceptionally so,' Rees agreed.

'How well do you know her?' Julia asked.

'Don't give me that,' he teased. 'You two didn't talk about the weather when I left you together last night.'

Julia accepted the rebuke. 'She said you'd been good friends and—and that she had wanted to marry you.'

He nodded. 'Melinda's always been honest about her feelings. In that respect she's rather like you. You're a very open person, too.'

Julia swallowed hard. 'I am?'

'Too honest sometimes. It's bad to wear your heart on your sleeve.'

'One can't help the way one's made.' What a platitude, but it was all she could think of to say.

'It's important you know the sort of person you are, Julia. If you do, you won't get hurt.'

'What sort of girl *am* I?'

'Sweet, innocent, surprisingly capable when you set your mind to it, yet obviously preferring a home, husband and children to a career.'

Fat lot he knew! Until his advent into her life, she had never even considered having a home, husband and children, and had believed that her work with Guardians was the most important thing in her life.

From the corner of her eye she saw him set down his cup of coffee and lean back on the sofa, his lids lowered, the dark lashes fanning his cheeks. Even in repose he exuded vitality and command, and she thought what a pity it was that his mother didn't know the person he had become. If she did, she would have to have a heart of stone not to regret her behaviour.

Julia longed to run over and fling herself into his arms, to feel the silken strands of his hair on her palms, touch her cheek to his lean one, rest her mouth on his.

'Sometimes people meet each other too soon,' Rees said

into the silence. 'There's a wrong time and a right time, I guess.'

'And Melinda and you met at the wrong time?' Julia finished for him.

'Yes.'

But now Melinda had come back into his life, and the brooding expression on his face seemed to indicate it might be the right time for him. How ironic if everything she herself had said to him about a wasted life, a lonely old age, was giving him food for thought and reassessment. But life was full of ironies, and the most bitter one would be Melinda moving in with him again. If she did, there was no doubt that Rees would marry her.

CHAPTER ELEVEN

EXPECTING to leave Rees next day, Julia was dismayed when Murray called to say Jack Ledbury had given the police the slip.

'Looks as if he still blames Rees for the accident, regardless of what he said.'

'How could they have let him slip past them?' she exclaimed.

'That's what Sir Andrew's asking the Commissioner,' Murray said drily. 'Look, if it will make you feel easier, I'll bring someone in to help you. Ledbury's a desperate man and you've carried this assignment alone for too long.'

'Thanks for the vote of confidence,' Julia spoke equally drily. 'If my name were Julian would you be offering to send me a partner?'

'Your sex has nothing to do with it. But Rees needs more than one person covering him at a time like this.'

'Ledbury knows better than to try to take him in the office,' Julia said. 'Rees will only be vulnerable when he goes out.'

'Then let's hope he doesn't. He's been told the man's on the loose, so he may act sensibly and stay home. I double-checked the penthouse myself the other morning, and no one can force entry without blowing the electronic alarms installed there. Anyway, let me know Denton's plans. If he goes out with Melinda tonight, I'll send you a partner.'

As Murray hung up, Rees buzzed for her. He appeared completely unperturbed, and gave her a list of calls to make and appointments to arrange. She longed to ask how he felt about Ledbury's escaping through the police net, but, as she was not supposed to know, she dared not do so.

'Wake up!' Rees cut across her thoughts. 'I've been talking to you and you were miles away.'

'Sorry.' Hastily she continued making notes of the things he was asking her to do, and two pages were filled before he stopped. 'This will keep me busy all day,' she commented. 'You aren't going out, are you?'

'No, nanny, I'm not. I've some drawings to check and then I'll be in the laboratory.' He hesitated. 'There's something you might like to know. The findings on the enquiry into the plane crash have been published, and our grey box has been completely vindicated.'

She nodded. 'I heard it on the news this morning. You must be very delighted.'

His only answer was to lift his shoulders, and Julia almost shook him with rage. If he had any sense he'd stay right here in this office till Ledbury was found.

'That will be all, Julia,' Rees said. 'Take all calls and say I'm not to be disturbed.'

Nodding, she returned to her office. She followed Rees' instructions to the letter, and even when Melinda called apologetically explained he wasn't taking any calls.

'One of *those* days, is it?' the girl said sympathetically. 'When he surfaces, tell him I'll call him this evening.'

Julia gave Rees the message when he emerged from his office at lunch time, but he was so deep in thought that she didn't think he had heard, and she followed him down the corridor, careful to step behind a large potted plant—thank goodness there were dozens of them—whenever he looked as if he might stop and turn round.

Once she had satisfied herself he was in the laboratory, she went back to the office to make the rest of her calls, then returned to the laboratory to wait for Rees to emerge. It was boring hanging around for him, but far less boring than escorting a sheika to Harrods! At least here she was doing something worth while. Even so, she was glad when Rees finally emerged at five-thirty, and once again she shadowed him, only showing herself boldly when they were a few yards from his room.

'Are you following me?' he demanded.

'Can't a girl go to the powder-room?'

'Sorry. Guess I'm being paranoid. But everywhere I go you're underfoot.'

'Not for much longer,' she said brightly. 'I'm sure Mrs Williamson will soon be back.'

'What a relief,' he muttered, stalking past her.

She glared at his back, glad of a chance to dislike him, even though she knew it would not last.

Promptly at six he reappeared, jacket over his arm. 'Let's go home,' he said. 'I'm tired.'

Hiding her relief, she reached for her bag and they walked side by side to the elevator.

'Seeing the boyfriend?' he enquired.

'Mark isn't sure he'll be free, but—er—but I want to be available in case he is.'

'Don't make yourself too available, Julia. Men like to do the chasing.'

'Mark's chased me long enough,' she said demurely. 'I think it's time I let him catch me.'

Rees' eyes glittered. From annoyance that *he* hadn't caught her? Julia wondered. After all, it must be galling for a man used to success to suddenly have a failure.

The drive home seemed shorter than usual, and as Rees turned the nose of the car towards the underground parking she experienced a stab of fear.

'Leave the car on the street,' she said quickly.

'What for?'

'You may want to go out.' She said the first thing that came into her head.

'I'm staying in tonight.'

Her breath expelled in relief, though it was short-lived. 'I just remembered, Melinda called you earlier and said she'd speak to you at home. I'm afraid it slipped my mind.'

'No matter. I called her myself before I left the office.'

They drove into the vast area underneath the block, and Julia looked anxiously round, uncaring if Rees noticed, which of course he did. But, though his mouth thinned with annoyance, he made no comment. Luckily his parking bay was near the elevator, and she sent up a silent prayer of relief that it was waiting for them. Even before the ignition was switched off, she was out of the car, ready to shield him.

'Why the rush?' he asked as they entered the elevator.

'I don't like being underground. It gives me—'

'Claustrophobia,' he grinned. 'There are so many things you're scared of, I often wonder what *doesn't* bother you.'

Their arrival at the top floor saved her from answering, and she shot out fast and looked up and down the corridor. From the service elevator at the far end, a middle-aged man in a navy boiler-suit, tool box in his hand, emerged.

'Who's that?' she hissed.

Rees glanced at him casually. 'One of the maintenance staff.'

Knowing he was being watched, the man quickened his pace towards them. 'Just checking the lights in the corridors, sir.'

'That must take you a while,' Julia said.

'Nineteen minutes. Double that if any bulbs 'ave to be changed.'

Rees and Julia walked towards the penthouse door, the man pausing behind them to examine a switch.

Rees had his key in the lock when the man stepped behind them. 'I'd like to come in with you, if you don't mind.' The Cockney accent had gone, and the voice was quiet, cultured and menacing.

Julia's scalp prickled, her worst fears realised. How the hell had Jack Ledbury got into the building? Once the police knew he had left his house, surely they had put a round-the-clock guard on this block?

'You're making a mistake,' she said crisply, and went to swing around, only stopping as the business end of a gun dug into the small of her back.

'I'm not making a mistake,' came the answer.

'Haven't you heard the news?' Rees asked, still facing the door.

'Exonerating that marvellous invention of yours? Oh, yes, I heard it, but I'm not fool enough to believe it.'

'It's true.' Rees's voice was full of conviction, though quiet as the man's. 'The accident was due to wing-flap failure.'

'Don't give me that! We both know that grey box of yours will bring millions of revenue into this country, so it's only natural for the government to exonerate it.'

'It's not up to the government. The Civil Aviation Authority don't cover up the truth, and they're the ones who have issued the report.'

'Whitewash!' Jack Ledbury reiterated. 'Now, open the door carefully. One wrong move and this lovely young lady will get the first bullet.'

Rees did as he was told, and the three of them went into the entrance hall. The lights came on automatically, the domed ceiling above them glowing pink, the recessed lights in the walls casting a pearly radiance on the flowers standing on the circular, steel table in the centre of the floor.

In a few moments Rees might be dead. Julia found the thought unbearable. He was too full of vitality to die in such a pointless manner. He had so much to give, so much to live for. Yet tackling Jack Ledbury was out—his gun would go off before she even raised an arm—so she had to disarm him by catching him off guard.

'Please take your gun away from my back,' she begged in a pleading voice. '*I* haven't done you any harm.'

'You're Denton's girlfriend,' he snapped.

'I'm not. I'm his assistant.' She felt the gun ease away from her back, and very carefully turned.

Seeing Ledbury full-face, Julia's fears intensified. He was pale-faced yet calm, with a glow of determination about him that did not augur well for Rees' safety. She judged him to be in his early fifties—conservatively dressed, with pale brown hair and neat features. The sort of man you would pass in the street without noticing, or if you did, would think of as 'Mr Average'.

She wondered if she should mention his wife, then decided nothing ventured nothing gained. But she would lead up to it.

'What do you do?' she asked gently. 'When you're not waving that gun around, I mean?'

'I'm a civil servant. I was going to take early retirement next year, but your boss put paid to that.' The man's face clouded over, his expression no longer calm. 'Margaret and I were going to move to Cornwall. She loves—she loved the sea and... But all that's finished, and so is my life.'

'I'm sure Margaret wouldn't want you to say that.'

'How do *you* know?' Ledbury said bitterly. 'You never met her.'

'But she loved you, and if you love someone you want them to go on living.' Julia kept her voice gentle, remembering Murray stressing the importance of trying to establish a relationship with the person threatening you. This meant encouraging them to talk, being sympathetic, putting on no pressure. Pressure. Yes, that was the danger, for it could make the knife flash, the finger pull back the trigger, remove the grenade pin. Easy now, she warned herself, easy.

'Was your wife a civil servant, too?' As she asked the question, she was aware of Rees staring at her as if she were off her head, but she was afraid to signal him with her eyes in case Jack Ledbury intercepted it.

'She gave up work when our baby was born. But Mandy died when she was three and Margaret never became pregnant again. I didn't mind, though. It drew us closer together.' Ignoring Julia, he looked directly at Rees. 'She was all I had and you took her away from me. That's why you're going to pay for it.'

'The grey box wasn't to blame,' Rees said firmly. 'It's as perfect as man can make it.'

'No more talk. You're a murderer and you're going to die.'

Julia, trained to sense the infinitesimal movement of muscles, felt, rather than saw Rees tense, as if, like an animal, he was girding himself to spring. But he would be shot before he got anywhere near Ledbury. No man, however quick off the mark, could beat the swiftness of a bullet.

Don't move, she willed him. Don't move. I love you, Rees, I love you.

'Killing Mr Denton won't bring Margaret back,' she said calmly, softly. 'And she wouldn't want you to have his death on your hands.'

'He's got *her* death on his hands!' Ledbury said with such anguish that Julia knew she had to act fast. Delay it a few seconds and Rees would spring—and be shot.

'Why don't we sit down and talk things over?' she said casually.

'Don't talk down to me!' The gun rose.

'I'm not! I understand how you feel.' Her voice was slow, slow, and soft as sigh. 'I really do understand.' Gently, she bent at the knees, twisted sideways in case Ledbury fired— and swooped across the floor in a rugby tackle that brought him crashing down, legs buckling, arms flailing. The gun went off in what seemed like an explosion, and the wall of mirror behind Rees shattered into a thousand scintillating pieces, like a waterfall. In that instant Rees was beside her, knocking the gun from Ledbury's hand and pinning him to the ground before giving him a sharp right to the jaw that rendered him unconscious.

Then he pulled her to her feet, his eyes blazing. 'What a damned stupid thing to do! You might have been killed.'

'And you'd *definitely* have been killed if you'd tackled him.'

'You're mad!' He shook her violently. 'Mad! Why the hell didn't you leave it to me?'

'Five seconds more and he'd have shot you.'

'How do you think I'd have felt if he'd shot you instead?' Rees shouted, still shaking her.

Wriggling from his grasp, she reached into her bag and took out a length of twine. Kneeling beside Ledbury, who was showing signs of coming round, she skilfully tied his feet together, then bound his hands behind his back.

As she did, she was aware of Rees dialling for the police, and when she straightened she found him staring at her as if she had grown another head. Which to him, of course, she *had*. A head that spelt 'bodyguard', a head that showed what a fool he had been!

'I don't believe it,' he muttered. 'You can't be…not *you*.' He glowered at her. 'Why the subterfuge? If you'd told me—'

'You refused to be guarded.'

'I see. So my estimable chairman took the decision himself.' Curving black brows lowered over glittering black eyes. 'I can understand him doing it, but to engage a woman!'

'They guard American presidents, too.'

'A woman,' Rees went on as if he had not heard her. 'Someone like *you*!'

'Why not *me*?' Julia demanded.

'Because you're a bundle of nerves. You don't like confined spaces, you can't bear heights, you hate…' His voice trailed away and he knuckled his forehead. 'It was all an act, wasn't it? Everything you said, your fears, your phobias, were all hogwash!'

'Yes.'

'But why?'

'To make you less suspicious of me.'

Only then did Rees smile, not a very pleasant smile, but one that was almost a sneer. 'You certainly played that part up to the hilt. I suppose all your talk about being turfed out of your apartment was—'

'A lie,' she admitted. 'The Sloane Street place is mine.'

'Did you say *anything* that was true?' he asked in an interested tone.

Only that I loved you, she thought. But I won't embarrass you by saying so. Anyway, you don't want commitment, and why should you, when Melinda has come back and is ready to live with you on *your* terms?

'Well?' Rees asked. 'You haven't answered my question.'

'I said and did only what was necessary for your safety. I'm sorry we had to bring emotions and personalities into it, but it was the only way I was able to be with you around the clock.'

'You're a marvellous actress, Julia.'

It was balm to her pride that he did not know she had ever spoken from the heart. Her eyes roamed over him, enjoying the broad shoulders, the narrow waist, the strongly muscled thighs. 'I'd better pack,' she murmured. 'There's no reason for me to stay here any longer.'

She was on the threshold of her room when he spoke again. 'I assume Mrs Williamson was in on the whole thing, too?'

'Yes.'

'So everybody knew about it except *me*? What a fool you must have thought me.'

'Don't be angry, Rees.'

'Angry that you saved my life? Or angry that you might have been killed by what you did?'

She was wondering how to answer this double-barrelled question, when he spoke again. 'You made a fool of me, Julia, and I deserved it. Sure I'm smarting at the moment, but give me a day or two, and I'll see the funny side of it.' The corner of his mouth twitched. 'Fact is, I'm beginning to see it already. If you—'

The rest of his sentence was cut short by the arrival of the police, and Julia was instantly the professional, giving them a report of the incident and watching with relief as Jack Ledbury was taken away. Only then did she go to her room and toss her clothes in her cases.

When she emerged into the hall, Rees was waiting for her. 'I'll take you home. It's the least I can do.' He hesitated, then came closer to her. Embarrassment was writ large upon him, and Julia knew he was remembering how hard he had tried to get her into his bed, and how she had played him for a fool over it. 'I realise that everything you said to me was part of the performance,' he muttered, 'but I'd like you to know that I—that I meant what *I* said to you.'

'That you wanted to make love to me?' Julia was amazed at how calm she sounded when she longed to hit out at him in fury and jealousy. 'Oh, I knew you meant that. It's the only thing you *do* mean when you talk to a woman!'

As if he hadn't heard her, his hand came out to touch her face, his fingers moving across her brow and down her cheek to linger a moment upon her lips. 'At one time you had me fooled you really loved me.'

'Sorry about that.' She forced a smile to her lips. 'I know the consternation it must have caused you!'

'But how cleverly you held me off.'

'Well, there are only certain things I'll do in the line of duty, Rees, and—er—you-know-what isn't one of them!'

He laughed and reached for her cases.

It was not until he had returned her to Sloane Street, deposited her luggage in her bedroom and bade her a grave goodbye, that Julia realised he had never asked her about 'Mark'. Heavens! He still didn't know 'Mark' was Murray Guardian, the man she worked for. Well, so much the better. If he believed she was in love with another man, he'd never guess her secret.

It was cold comfort, but it was all she had.

CHAPTER TWELVE

Two hours after saving Rees' life, Julia was facing up to the fact that her life was no longer her own.

For a girl who had always been fancy-free, it was chastening to admit that her happiness was dependent on a man who did not even know she existed other than as a beautiful girl he had tried to bed.

'I might as well have stayed a model for all the good it's done me,' she muttered as she stowed away her clothes and then stomped into the kitchen to see if there was food in the refrigerator. Predictably there was none, and she was on her way out to buy some when the telephone rang.

Was it Rees calling to say her departure had knocked him for a loop and he realised he loved her? She nearly tripped in her eagerness to lift the receiver before it stopped ringing, though her 'hello' dimmed to despondency as she heard Murray's voice.

'Why didn't you let me know you'd cornered Ledbury?' His anger reverberated in her ear, but it was no less than she deserved, though how could she tell him that misery at leaving Rees had pushed everything else from her mind? He would be furious with her for allowing personal feelings to interfere with her job, and part of her job was to let him know when her assignment was completed.

'I'm sorry, Murray. It slipped my mind.'

'What's wrong?' Always perceptive where his employees were concerned, Murray instantly heard the wobble in her voice.

'N—nothing. Reaction, I suppose. I'm fine, really.'

'You did a marvellous job,' he continued warmly. 'I'm proud of you.'

Knowing that if he continued in this vein, she would break down, she said brightly, 'All in a day's work, Murray. What's next on the agenda for me?'

'A week off.'

The thought of having nothing to do for seven days was intolerable, but even as she protested he cut her short.

'You've been working twenty-four hours out of twenty-four, Julia, and you owe it to your next client, whoever it may be, to be bright-eyed and bushy-tailed. Take yourself away for a week and enjoy yourself.'

'Very well. But if anything crops up for me before then— '

'A week off,' he reiterated. 'Don't you dare set foot in the office until then. 'Bye, Julia.'

'Murray, wait!' She was struck by a thought. 'Remember when I introduced you to Rees at Annabel's? Well, he doesn't know you're my boss. He still thinks you're my boy-friend.'

'You can always tell him the truth when you see him.'

'I doubt I'll bother. He's so busy with his own life, he couldn't care less about mine.'

'Then he's a fool. Forget him, my dear.'

Determined to try, Julia went home to her parents for the week. The moment she entered her rustic bedroom, built into the eaves of the lovely old farmhouse, her troubled spirits felt soothed. How good it was to be back, cocooned by happy childhood memories, warmed by her parents' love.

Her mother was quick to sense she was not happy, but did not impinge on her privacy by questioning her, and Julia, unwilling to talk of Rees—what was there to say beyond the fact that he had made a pass at her?—made a determined effort to put on a good face.

By the time she left for London, she was able to keep all

thoughts of Rees at bay, except first thing in the morning and late at night, when the image of him, the memory of his voice, his touch, turned her limbs to water.

She drove straight to the Guardians office—having first checked that Murray would be there—and warmed to the sight of his breezy, blond looks.

'You look great.' He enveloped her in a bearhug before returning to his desk. He wasn't in his office clothes, but denims and a fine knit T-shirt, indicating he had just returned from, or was going to, the Guardian mansion.

In the event he had returned, having set up a new course for a fresh batch of recruits. 'I've got myself a partner,' he announced. 'He'll be supervising most of the training, and I'll go down for the last couple of days to test them.'

'I never imagined you delegating authority.'

'Blame it on age.' His face creased with humour. 'I'm thirty-eight, Julia. I want to ease up.'

'Poor old man,' she commiserated. 'Where's your bath-chair?'

'Not that old!' The way his eyes ranged over her gave meaning to his words. 'There's more to life than work, you know. Guardians is highly successful, I've plenty of money in the bank, and I'd like someone to share it with.'

'You won't have to advertise,' she smiled.

'Thanks,' he smiled back, his gaze lingering on her mouth.

Oh, no, Julia thought. Store detective work, here I come, for if Murray fancied her he'd start being protective, and once that happened it was goodbye to anything that smacked of danger.

'What's on your books for me?' she asked, as if unaware of the way he was staring at her.

'That sheika's back in town and—'

'No. Absolutely not.'

'Lord Burrows wants someone to watch over his daughter's wedding presents for ten days. You'd have to pretend to be a friend of the family, so you'll get a chance to wear your glad rags.'

'No,' she repeated. 'What else?'

'Bealeys want someone in their jewellery department for three months. They're doing some internal redesigning and they're worried about security.' Murray paused. 'No like either?'

'Afraid not. Come on, Murray. I'm sure you can do better than that.'

'Don't bank on it. Jobs like Denton's are few and far between.'

'Anything going abroad? There's been a spate of kidnap threats in France—surely that's put business your way.'

'Not so far.'

'Then it looks as if I'll have to go to one of your rivals.'

Murray pulled a face at her, then rubbed the side of chin, brow furrowed in thought. 'Look, I do have something that might suit you, but it means you going to Scotland.'

'As long as it's not guarding pheasants!'

He laughed. 'You might prefer them to the three children you'll be protecting.'

'Kidnap threat, eh?' Julia was vindicated.

'Yes. By a determined father. Their mother is equally determined not to give them up.'

'Why didn't you tell me about this job before?'

'Pure selfishness.' He rose and came round the side of the desk to stand beside her. He exuded strength, vitality and forcefulness, and she was sorry that his blond good looks did not make her heart beat any faster. 'Aren't you going to ask me what I mean?' Murray broke into her thoughts.

'No.'

Their eyes met, and in his she saw regret, ruefulness, and finally acceptance.

'Be ready to leave for Edinburgh in the morning,' he said crisply. 'You'll be met on arrival and taken to your destination. It's a few hours' drive from the city and somewhat isolated.'

Murray had not been joking when he had said the assignment was out in the wilds, for even though Julia had grown up in the country, this was more solitary than she had anticipated; a large castle, beautifully renovated and heated—the young châtelaine was an American heiress—and occupied now by her and her three rumbustious children: a boy of eight and twin girls of eleven.

Quickly Julia settled into a routine, and once she had established her authority over the children, who luckily liked her, she found it enjoyable looking after them.

The best thing about being here was that it was miles from Rees, so there was no possibility of bumping into him in a restaurant or nightclub. On the debit side, the many hours of solitude gave her too much time to think, and she was aware of a continual ache for him, a longing to hear his voice, breathe in the scent of him, touch him.

She knew that one day she would think of him without pain, but even when that time came she would never fall in love again with the same intensity. There was something special about Rees, not merely his looks, which were exceptional, but his strength of character and charisma. She wondered if Melinda would eventually succeed in changing his mind about marriage, and if they were already living together.

The idea of Melinda occupying the room she herself had used was to painful to think about. Then she knew how silly she was being. Rees, sensual man that he was, wouldn't let Melinda sleep down the corridor from him, when she could be in his bed and in his arms.

Only at this point did Julia succumb to tears, racking sobs that brought little relief. But a long while later, as she dried her eyes, she vowed never to cry for Rees again. He was gone from her life and she had to rebuild it without him.

CHAPTER THIRTEEN

JULIA had been at the castle four weeks when one of the maids came to tell her a man was waiting to see her in the library. Knowing it could only be Murray, and wondering if he was here to check the scene for himself, she hurried downstairs, having warned the children with dire consequences if they left the playroom.

The library was in the west wing, and she sped down endless corridors towards it, wondering how anyone enjoyed living in such a vast place, even though it *was* warm as a hothouse.

She opened the library door, her smile of welcome fading as she saw not Murray's rugged frame and blond hair, but the taut, lean figure of Rees. She opened her mouth to speak, but no words came, though he seemed unaware of it as he turned from the window to greet her.

'Hello, Julia. You're looking great.'

His voice was as deep as she remembered, his dark eyes just as bright. He might have stepped from the pages of *Men in Vogue*, so sartorially magnificent did he look in dark grey trousers and greyish tweed jacket, its cut superb, though the ensemble was clearly not new, which only served to add to its distinction. Trust Rees always to look perfect, she thought crossly, and was glad she was wearing one of her prettiest cottons, a soft lilac that deepened the lilac of her eyes.

'Fancy meeting you!' she said, her smile holding no trace of care. 'How did you know where to find me?'

'I rang the Guardian office. Some dragon of a woman refused to disclose your whereabouts, but when I explained

345

who I was and why I wanted to see you, she gave me your address.'

Julia's heart raced. 'You came all the way up here to see me?'

'I had to come to Scotland, as it happens. I'm at Martlett House.' He named a mansion a few miles away that had been turned into a conference centre. 'It was a lucky coincidence, otherwise I'd have had to wait until you returned to London. But I wanted to give you this with my deepest appreciation.' From his pocket he withdrew a narrow, maroon leather box, and put it in her hand.

She opened it, lost for words when she saw a shimmering diamond bracelet. 'It's magnificent!' she gasped, 'but I—' she held it out to him '—I can't accept it, Rees. I did nothing to deserve it.'

'Except save my life. Or don't you think that has any value?'

'I didn't mean that.' She was distressed he had misinterpreted her. 'But it was—it was part of my job. Anyone else in my position would have done the same.'

'Maybe, maybe not. But you were extremely brave. Foolhardy,' he added, and clasped his hand around hers to press her fingers on to the leather box.

His touch burned her like fire, and she was intensely conscious of his nearness, so close to him that she saw the faintest dark shadow along his cheek, showing he had shaved very early that morning.

'Please accept the bracelet,' he persisted. 'It comes with my deepest thanks.'

Aware that to refuse again was ungrateful, she nodded.

'I'd like to see it on you,' he said softly, and, taking the bracelet from the box, clasped it round her wrist. His long fingers were deft, reminding her of how easily they had unzipped her dress and run over her body. Her cheeks burned at the memory and she lowered her eyes to the flashing fire around her wrist.

'I still feel it's wrong for me to accept this, Rees.' She forced herself to look up at him, a longer way than usual, for she was wearing flat sandals.

Noticing her tilt her head, he gave a lopsided grin. 'So the secret of your height was stiletto heels!'

'I'm five foot eight in my stockinged feet,' she flashed back. 'That's no midget.'

'It is when I'm six foot three.'

She moved away from him, saying carelessly, 'How's Melinda?'

'Fine. Busy filming that series of commercials she came over to do.'

'When is she going back to Sydney?' Julia waited tensely for the answer, remembering Melinda stating she wouldn't go if there was the slightest chance of getting back with Rees.

'She's remaining in London,' he said.

Julia's mouth went dry, and it was an effort for her to speak. 'You must be pleased. I know how *I* felt when—when Mark went away and then came back.'

'Ah, yes. Mark Gardner. Still on the horizon, is he?'

'Very much. He—he wants to marry me.'

'I shouldn't think he's the first one.'

'Nice of you to say so.' She edged to the door, yet for some reason could not leave. No, not *some* reason, she thought wildly, a very definite reason. She had to tell Rees that Mark was Murray Guardian, before he discovered it for himself. After all, Engineering 2000 might wish to employ Guardian Security again.

'There's something I'd like you to know, Rees. Mark Gardner isn't his real name. It's Murray Guardian.'

'Your boss?' Rees didn't hide his surprise.

'Yes. When I had to follow you and Melinda to Annabel's, I needed an escort, and he was the only man I could contact.'

'Then he isn't really your boyfriend?'

'He is *now*. That's the funny part of it.' Julia made herself smile. 'I'd always kept him at arm's length because he was my boss, and that night at Annabel's was the first time I'd let him take me out.' She paused. 'It made me see him differently, and—and I realised how I felt about him.'

Rees' mouth curved sardonically. 'I'm glad *some* good came out of this Ledbury affair. Are you going to marry him?'

'I'm thinking about it.'

One hand in the pocket of his jacket, Rees eyed her quizzically. 'I won't ask if all your talk about being an old-fashioned girl was true, or merely an act to hold me off!'

'I'm glad you won't ask, because I won't tell you,' she teased, and opened the door, afraid that if he didn't go soon she would fling herself into his arms and howl like a baby.

Together they walked into the main hall. 'I'll be here for a few days, Julia. If you're free at any time I'd be delighted to take you out.'

'I'm afraid I can't. I'm on duty round the clock.' She saw him to his car, filling him in on why she was here, and he looked so grim that she remembered his childhood had also been torn apart by divorce.

'You'd think parents would know better than use their children as bait,' he grated as he climbed into his Ferrari. 'I'd like to knock some sense into them.'

'I agree.' She stepped back from the car. 'Drive slowly, Rees. Country lanes are full of cattle!'

'I'll try to keep to seventy!'

'Do you good to use your will-power.' Only as the words popped out was Julia aware of their double meaning, and his laugh made her cheeks burn afresh.

'Still frank, I see.'

'Not usually,' she came back at him. 'That was the part I was playing.'

'And very well you played it, too. You certainly had me fooled.'

Thank goodness I did, she echoed silently, and remained where she was until he had driven out of sight.

'Who was that gorgeous hunk of man?' Cindy McAllen, mother of the three children, came out of the drawing-room as Julia closed the front door.

'Rees Denton. I did some work for his company.'

'Don't tell me you didn't fall for him!'

'I didn't,' Julia said abruptly, still fighting back the tears.

'I wasn't meaning to pry, Julia, but I—I guess I'm still a romantic at heart. Crazy, isn't it, when you think how badly Donald's behaved to me?'

Julia was not sure exactly what it was Donald McAllen had done, though gossip backstairs said they had quarrelled constantly. 'There's nothing wrong with being a romantic,' she said aloud. 'And you're still young enough to make another life for yourself, Mrs McAllen.'

'Except that I still love my husband, and I'll never feel the same about any other man.'

It was a statement Julia could endorse, and tears welled into her eyes. Mumbling that she had to be with the children, she hurried to the playroom, where eight-year-old Billy was laying into the eleven-year-old twins.

It was not until later that night, when she was locking the bracelet away and wishing it was as easy to lock away memories of Rees, that she allowed herself to think of him.

So Melinda was remaining in London. It confirmed what she had feared, and sounded the death knell to the faint hope that had foolishly lingered in her heart. Goodbye dreams, she thought sadly, and prepared herself to face a bleak future.

Julia had been at the castle two months when a black Jensen sneaked on to the estate and two burly men rushed from it and headed towards the children, who were cavorting on the tennis court.

Luckily one of the gamekeepers was with her, and while he headed off one man she brought the other one down with a karate chop, then alerted the local police on her walkie-talkie.

A chat to Murray later in the day brought another security guard to help her, but hardly had he settled in when Donald McAllen returned to the castle to talk to his wife, and a reconciliation took place.

Wishing all her cases ended as happily, Julia flew back to London and waited for another assignment. Only routine work was available, and throughout the autumn she was kept busy on unexciting jobs that did not tax her mentally or physically.

Engineering 2000 was in the news, for another major airline was installing the grey box in all their planes, and Julia switched on the television one evening and saw Rees being interviewed on a chat show, his usual incisiveness overlaid by a stunning display of charm which had the female interviewer drooling.

'How have you managed to stay single so long?' she asked coyly.

'At school, I won a gold medal for running.'

The audience roared their appreciation, but the interviewer persisted.

'Isn't there anyone special in your life?'

For an instant Rees looked serious. 'Yes, there is.'

'May we know who she is?'

Only then did the charm momentarily slip. 'Definitely not.'

Unable to bear any more, Julia flicked to another channel, then, bereft of his face, flicked back again. But the conversation was no longer personal, and she tuned out the sound and simply feasted her eyes on him.

It was a feast that gave her emotional indigestion, and she was awake most of the night, aching for him, tossing and turning with unassuaged desire, her breasts throbbing, her loins damp.

Predictably, in the morning she looked a wreck, but, model-girl training to the fore, she emerged into Sloane Street as beautiful as ever, though admittedly her make-up was heavier than usual.

She was between jobs, and she spent the morning shopping, buying a dress she did not need to cheer herself up, though it failed to do so, and debating whether to cut her hair short, which she finally decided against. And it was still only eleven o'clock in the morning!

With a sigh, she headed for the Guardian offices.

Since becoming aware of Murray's interest in her, she had studiously kept out of his way, but she felt so despondent that she decided to change her attitude and go out with any personable man who asked her—Murray included—in the hope that one day someone would ignite a spark in her.

This in mind, she walked jauntily into his office.

'Just the girl I wanted to see.' He rose and came towards her, holding out a photocopy of a letter. The words had been cut from a newspaper and crudely stuck on to a single sheet of cheap notepaper.

Carefully Julia read it. It was anonymous, and threatened the death of its recipient in the most ghoulish, cold-blooded manner.

'Whoever wrote this is a fiend!' she said flatly.

'Which is why we've been asked for one of our top operators.'

Miserable though she was, Julia rose to the challenge. 'Me?'

'You deserve it,' Murray said. 'But there's something you should know before you say yes, and if you decide to turn the job down, I'll understand.'

'Why should I turn it down?' Her eyes narrowed. 'You do want me to handle it, don't you?'

'Even if I didn't, I'd *have* to offer it to you. That's the basis on which...'

For the first time since Julia had known Murray, he was ill at ease, his fingers drumming on the side of the desk as he leaned against it, his eyes avoiding hers. 'The man who's received this death threat is Rees.'

'Oh, no!'

Murray nodded, his expression perturbed. 'He's specifically asked for *you*. He said he's used to you, and he doesn't want anyone strange.'

'What if I refuse?'

'Then he won't have anyone. He'll just take his chance.'

Her anger boiled over. He was still a fool, she thought stormily. 'It wouldn't be Ledbury again?'

'No. He's in a psychiatric hospital. We haven't a clue who wrote this letter. This is the third one, incidentally, and it's worried Denton enough to take notice of it. But as I said, you can refuse the assignment.'

'And leave him defenceless?'

'I'll try to talk him into accepting someone else. Ben's a good guy, and unobtrusive enough not to get under Denton's feet.'

Julia listened despairingly. Regardless of what Murray said, she knew he had no chance of getting Rees to change his mind, and that it was her or no one. But if she said no, and anything happened to him, she would be guilt-ridden for the rest of her life.

'Forget Ben,' she said quickly. '*I'll* do it.'

'Are you sure?'

'I don't have any choice.' Her voice broke and, hearing it, Murray swore under his breath and pulled her against his chest, his arms wrapping around her in a comforting hug. Julia's tears flowed faster, dampening his shirt, but he was uncaring of it and gently stroked her hair, holding her closer still, so that she was comforted by the warmth of his body, and the knowledge that someone understood how she felt and cared that she was unhappy.

'I wish you didn't still care for Rees,' he whispered against her hair. 'I'm much more suitable for you!'

She looked up at him with tear-drenched eyes. 'I'm so sorry, Murray.'

'Me, too,' he said with a lopsided grin. 'But that's the way the cookie crumbles.'

'It hasn't crumbled,' she whispered, 'it's fallen to pieces. He's in love with Melinda and she's staying on in London.' Her tears flowed faster than ever, and once again Murray drew her close.

'Darling, don't,' he said, then looked up startled as the door burst open and Rees strode in.

Julia, aware of steps behind her, moved quickly away from Murray, but kept her face averted, shaking with fear as she heard Rees' voice.

'Sorry to barge in on you,' he was saying in clipped tones, 'but I had a meeting with someone on the next floor and thought I'd drop in to see you.'

'If it's about employing me,' Julia swung round to face him, careful to keep her back to the light lest he saw the marks of her tears, 'then I'm free to start as of now.'

'That won't be necessary,' Rees said. 'That's why I came in. The letter was a hoax.'

'A hoax?' Murray questioned, his tall body leaning forward as if ready to spring. 'You're sure of that?'

'Quite sure.'

'How did you find out?'

'I have my ways, but the upshot is that I won't be requiring Julia's services.'

He regarded her again. The late summer sun streaming through the window deepened his tanned skin, giving added gloss to his shiny, black hair, and those wonderful dark brown eyes, marked by silky eyebrows. Yet it also showed new lines on his face, fine ones around his eyes, deeper ones either side of his mouth. Too many late nights, too much lovemaking, Julia thought bleakly, and glanced beseechingly at Murray who, reading her expression, came light-footed to her side. He did not put his arms around her—that would have been too obvious for Murray—but his very closeness, the protective slant of his body, spoke volumes, and Rees, glancing from one to the other, gave the faintest of smiles.

'Looks like I came in at an inappropriate moment. I'm sorry.'

'No need to be,' Murray said easily. 'Better you than one of my staff!'

Rees went to the door. 'I'll leave you to carry on where you left off!'

'Not in the office he won't,' Julia said, and kept a smile on her face until Rees had closed the door behind him. Only then did she collapse into the nearest chair. 'Thanks for saving my face, Murray.'

'Any time,' he shrugged. 'And now Rees is out of the way, we'll have to find something else for you to do.' He gave a mischievous grin. 'Hackenburg Junior needs to be escorted back to Texas. You do remember Hackenburg Junior, don't you?'

'His name is engraved on my heart!' She sighed. 'Is that store detective job still vacant?'

'Absolutely. For three months at least.'

'Then I'll take it.'

CHAPTER FOURTEEN

WORKING in a store was as boring as Julia had anticipated, and gave her too much time to think. Inevitably she was preoccupied with Rees, for, hard as she tried to forget him, he kept creeping into her mind, robbing her of appetite and putting shadows beneath her eyes and under her cheekbones.

The hazy days of autumn gave way to the crisper days of October, and Julia, walking home late one afternoon, succumbed to the blandishments of a flowerseller, and bought herself an armful of tawny-gold chrysanthemums.

She was arranging them in a vase when Melinda telephoned.

'You sound surprised,' the girl said.

'I am.'

'I was wondering if you're free this evening. I'd like to see you.'

About to plead a headache, an early night, any excuse she could find, curiosity got the better of her, and Julia heard herself agreeing.

'Shall we meet at my place?' Melinda suggested. 'I'm not the world's greatest cook, but I can rustle up an omelette.'

'Why not come here?' Julia suggested, unwilling to go to Dockside and pass Rees' home.

'Fine. I'll be with you about eight.'

In the months since Julia had seen her, Melinda had grown even lovelier. The less harsh British sunlight had made her hair darker, and it was now the colour of a golden guinea. The deeper hue intensified the big brown eyes flecked by gold, which gave her a slightly feline look. Yet she was a friendly feline, with no claws extended as she greeted Julia like a long-lost friend and helped prepare salad, while Julia set out a lavish cheeseboard.

'What a pretty place you have,' Melinda commented as they ate in the dining area of the lemon and white kitchen, and she glanced beyond it to the sitting-room, large and airy, its windows overlooking the green square where trees were already turning to russet.

'It's not bad for London,' Julia agreed. 'I suppose you've settled down completely?'

Melinda's mumble was unintelligible, and Julia let it pass, hoping the girl had not guessed she loved Rees and was trying to be tactful. The thought of being the object of pity was intolerable, and she was wondering how to get over it when Melinda spoke.

'I understand you saw Rees in Scotland?'

'Yes. I was on a job there and he was at a conference centre nearby.'

'Did you like the bracelet he bought you?'

Julia bit back a sigh. So Melinda knew. Not surprising, really. She had probably helped him choose it. 'It's lovely, but far too expensive a gift.'

'You saved his life.'

'All part of the Guardian service.' Julia smiled, and decided she had hedged long enough and would be blunt. After all, she knew what was going on and the sooner it was out in the open, the better for her peace of mind. 'How are things going between you and Rees?' she asked, popping a piece of tomato into her mouth and forcing herself to chew it.

'We're just good friends,' Melinda said drily. 'And I *do* mean friends.'

'I'm sure if you played your cards right...' Why am I telling her this? Julia asked herself angrily. The last thing I want is for Melinda to snare Rees. Yet maybe it would be better if she did. At least then there'd be an end to it.

'I don't *want* to have to play my cards right to get Rees to marry me,' Melinda admitted.

'Then bide your time and hope he'll see sense.'

'I'd live with him even if he didn't see sense! I told you when I first met you that I'd go back to him regardless.'

'Then where's the problem? You're here and he's here, and—'

'He doesn't want me.' Melinda saw Julia's sceptical expression. 'It's true. Randy Rees hasn't laid a finger on me since I came back from Australia, and that's more than four months.'

'You mean he fancies someone else?'

'Yes. Someone he's crazy about.'

'Hang in there,' Julia said sarcastically. 'With Rees's record, he's bound to fall out of love soon enough.'

The golden head gave an emphatic shake of disagreement. 'Not this time. You know what they say about playboys? They play themselves to a standstill, and when they finally fall, they don't recover.'

'Rees, faithful to *one* girl?' Julia scoffed. 'You must be joking.'

'I was never more serious in my life.' Melinda set down her fork. 'Tell me, Julia, how do *you* feel about him?'

'He's charming, intelligent, clever—'

'Are you in love with him?'

The unexpectedness of the question stopped Julia short, and colour burned in her face. 'Of course not.'

'Are you in love with Murray Guardian? Rees thinks you are.'

'I—er—yes.'

'And he loves you?'

'He wants to marry me, but I…well, it's a question of my career, and…you know how it is.'

'I think I do,' Melinda said bluntly. 'You're lying through your back teeth!' She leaned forward across the table. 'I have something interesting to tell you, Julia. You know those anonymous letters Rees was getting?'

'I certainly do. The one I saw was fiendish. If I knew who wrote it I'd—'

'It was Rees.'

Julia gaped. 'Did you say Rees?'

'None other.'

'But why?'

'To get you back into his life. He couldn't think of any other way.'

'If this is your idea of a joke...'

'It's no joke admitting that the man I love is in love with *you*. But I can't bear seeing him so unhappy. He works like a demon and I'm the only girl he sees. And only then because he knows I've accepted that he doesn't want *any* woman in his life if he can't have you.'

'You mean he's told you he loves me?' Julia found it too incredible to believe.

'Not in so many words,' Melinda admitted. 'You know how he hides his feelings, but I suspected it months ago, and this morning I found out for certain.'

'How?'

'Well, the other night I had dinner at his apartment, and the chain of my gold necklace snapped. It wasn't until I went to take it in to be mended this morning that I remembered I'd left it in his living-room. I rang him to ask if I could collect it and he said he'd put it in the top drawer of his desk. But it wasn't there, so I opened the next one and that's when I found the letters.'

'The letters?'

'And the glue and scissors and newspapers that he'd cut the words from. Plus the draft of the last letter he received— a letter he had written to himself!'

Julia was still disbelieving. 'Never! He wouldn't. He couldn't.'

'He could and he did.' Melinda reached for her bag, and from its capacious depths withdrew the draft of a letter and a newspaper article with numerous gaps in it where the words had been cut out. She held them under Julia's nose. 'There! See for yourself.'

Julia's heart started beating erratically. Melinda was right. This letter was a copy of the one Murray had shown her.

'Why would Rees do such a thing?' she asked.

'I've already told you. To get you back into his life. He went to Murray and said he didn't want anyone other than you to guard him. I guess he felt that if the two of you were together, he'd have another chance with you.'

'He soon changed his mind,' Julia said, her spirits plummeting as fast they had risen. 'Murray had just shown me the letter, and I'd agreed to take on the assignment, when Rees came in and said it wasn't necessary because he'd found out the whole thing was a hoax.'

'That's the only part I don't understand,' Melinda confessed. 'Why did he change his mind?'

'Does it matter?' Julia shrugged. 'It's more than two months ago.'

'It still matters to Rees. He's like a walking corpse. He loves you. I'm positive of that. So it beats me why he admitted the letters were a hoax.'

'Looks as if it will have to remain a mystery,' Julia said.

But Melinda would have none of it. 'When Rees told me he'd found out who had written those letters, he said you wouldn't have taken the job anyway, because you were going to marry Murray. Well, if he believed that, it was a good reason for him to abandon his plan.'

Julia cast her mind back to the scene in the office when Rees had arrived unannounced. She had just read that dreadful letter and had started to cry, and Murray had been holding her when Rees walked in. Was that why he had back-tracked on his mad scheme? Because he had seen her in Murray's arms and thought she had finally agreed to be his wife?

'What are you going to do?' Melinda enquired.

'I'm not sure. If Rees cares for me, why didn't he put up a fight?'

'I think he intended to—that's why he went to Scotland. There was no conference, you know. Mrs Williamson let drop that he was visiting a sick aunt!'

'Pity he wasn't honest with me,' Julia muttered.

'Were *you* honest with him? When you left him—after Ledbury was caught—you made it plain that everything you'd said to him had been part of your charade, so he naturally felt you didn't care for him.'

'What else could I have said when you were already on the scene?' Julia defended herself. 'I thought he was in love with *you*.'

'Rees *had* been carrying a torch for me,' Melinda confessed, 'but the night I came back from Australia and he took me out, he realised the battery was flat! Unfortunately you chose that same night to bring your boyfriend, "Mark Gardner" on the scene, and Rees saved face by pretending he still cared for me. But he went to Scotland to see you, and he did write himself those crazy letters, which was such a demented a thing to do, I can only think he's out of his mind with love!'

It was hard for Julia to credit this, for the Rees she knew was always in control of himself. Yet it sounded as if Melinda was right.

'If you *do* love him,' Melinda went on, 'tell him. Unless you're so proud you'd rather you both went on suffering.'

'You make me sound very stupid,' Julia murmured.

'People in love often are. Look at *me*. I'm still crazy about Rees, yet I'm handing him to you on a platter.'

Embarrassed, Julia swallowed hard. 'It's a generous thing to do.'

'I nearly didn't. I told myself if I hung around, I'd get him on the rebound. But then I realised I wouldn't be happy with him on those terms, knowing part of him would always be hankering for you.' Standing up, Melinda reached for her bag. 'Whatever you do, I wish you luck.'

'I don't know how to thank you.'

'Just make Rees happy.'

Alone again, Julia hesitated only for a moment, then dashed into the bedroom and searched out her prettiest, sexiest dress. With shaking hands she freshened her make-up and hair, then raced down to her car.

Not until she was outside Rees' apartment block, did she pause to wonder if he was in.

The porter, at his desk in the elegant foyer, recognised her as she peered through the glass door, and pressed the button to let her in. He had his hand on the intercom to tell Rees he had a visitor, when she stopped him, saying she wanted to surprise Mr Denton.

Succumbing to her brilliant smile, he nodded, and she winged her way up to the topmost floor, trying not to feel a sense of homecoming in case Melinda had got it all wrong. As she faced the black lacquered door with its shiny brass trim, she almost turned tail and fled. Then drawing a deep breath, she pressed the buzzer.

She was on the verge of pressing it again, when the door swung open, and she found herself confronting the man who, only a couple of hours before, she had hoped never to see again.

From the consternation on his face, he seemed to have harboured the same thoughts about her, and again she wondered if Melinda had got her wires crossed.

'Hello, Julia.' Rees' voice was formal. 'This is an unexpected visit.'

'I was passing by.' Only as she said it did she realise how silly this was. How could she be passing by the top floor that was home only to Rees? 'What I mean is I—I wanted to see you.'

He made no move to ask her in, and she stepped past him into the hall.

'I'd like a drink,' she said laconically.

'Sorry.' He sauntered ahead of her with the easy grace she remembered, and with economic movements began to pour out a fruit juice. Mid-flow, he stopped. 'I'm forgetting you aren't on duty. Would you like some wine?'

She hesitated, then said boldly, 'Champagne, please. I'm celebrating.'

He looked startled, then silently went out, returning after a moment with a bottle of Veuve Clicquot.

'Lucky I always keep one on ice,' he commented, opening it so skilfully that the only sound it made was as it bubbled into the narrow champagne flutes. 'As I don't know what we're celebrating, I'll leave the toast to you,' he said, raising his glass.

Julia could not take her eyes off him, mesmerised by his dark good looks. He was definitely thinner—Melinda was right about that—and paler too, which made his hair seem even blacker. She noticed it needed cutting, but decided it suited him longer, and felt her heart turn over as he raked it back with his fingers. He was dressed for an evening at home, his charcoal-grey trousers drawing attention to his lean hips, his matching silk sweater clinging to his wide shoulders.

'The bubbles are going flat,' he said, pointing to his glass. 'What's the toast, Julia?'

'To the man I love.' She raised her glass, then saw he wasn't doing the same. 'Drink up,' she said gaily. 'I don't think he's the easiest man, but he's the most intelligent, charming and sexy one I know. He's also blind, stupid and obstinate.'

'He sounds far from ideal,' Rees commented, still making no move to drink.

'You're right. But when you love someone, you love them warts and all.' Julia saw the tension in Rees' body by the way he gripped the stem of the glass, for his knuckles were white. 'Don't you know what I'm trying to say? Or are you really too obstinate to listen to your heart?'

Slowly Rees set down his glass on the table and moved closer to her, so close that she saw her reflection in his eyes. 'You've said so many things to me that you didn't mean, Julia,' his voice was deep and slurred, as if drunk with emotion, 'so many things that I'm afraid to believe any of them.'

'Well, you can believe this, Rees Denton.' She put down her glass too. 'I love you. I've loved you all along, but I wanted more than you were prepared to give at that time. But now I know you really care for me—thanks to Melinda—so I had to come and tell you how I felt.'

With a throaty murmur, he pulled her into his arms, gripping her tightly as he pressed feverish kisses over her face before finding the moistness of her mouth and draining it with the desperation of a man who had been wandering the Sahara for weeks.

Julia clung to him, giving him back kiss for kiss, moulding her body to his, exalting in the wild surge of passion that stiffened his thighs as her hands caressed his muscled back.

'Julia, Julia,' he said against her lips, an agony of longing in his voice as he drew her down on to the settee and his lap.

She curled against him, her breasts swelling to his touch. 'Unzip me,' she whispered, and he did so instantly, his face suffusing with tenderness as he took a pointed nipple into his mouth, his dark head heavy upon her shoulder.

Heat coursed through her, linking her breasts, her stomach, the throbbing bud between her thighs, and she arched against him in a frenzy of longing. 'I want you so much,' she cried. 'Oh, Rees, I love you, I love you.'

Slowly, as though with an effort, he lifted his mouth from her breast and held her away from him. 'And I love *you*,' he said thickly. 'More than I dreamed possible; more than life itself. I can't believe you're warm and real in my arms. The nights I've lain awake imagining this, aching for you, wanting to make you mine and never let you go.'

'You won't need to let me go. I'm here for as long as you want me.'

'For ever,' he muttered, straining her close to him.

Once again their mouths fused, and in an abandonment of desire Julia slid from his lap and lay back on the cushions, pulling him down on top of her. She revelled in the weight of him, the hardness of his thighs, the swell of his love, and twined her legs around his, vulnerable and open to him.

But he did not take her, and though his breath was heavy and his face had the sheen of sweat on it, he strained away from her. 'Not like this, Julia. What I feel for you is too... We must talk first. Why did you come here? You said something about Melinda, but I didn't follow you.'

Gently Julia told him of her meeting with the girl. She made it as succinct as possible, aware of his skin darkening with embarrassment as she referred to the threatening letters, though he made no effort to avoid her eyes.

'You can see what a fool love made of me,' he confessed when she finished speaking. 'I was so crazy about you, I was willing to do anything to give myself another chance with you.'

'All you had to do was say you loved me.'

'I believed you loved Murray!'

'And you let a rival stop you? I thought a knight fought for his lady.'

'I intended fighting for you—but subtly. Hence those letters I wrote to myself. Then when I walked into Murray's office and saw you in his arms…'

'It's a good thing Melinda came to see me,' Julia said sombrely, pulling him down to her. 'We've so much time to make up for, Rees.'

'I know.' His tongue feathered her mouth. 'These last months have been the most miserable of my life.' He nuzzled her ear, his hair silky against her cheek. 'I've still so much to learn about you.'

'After being with me for weeks?' she teased.

'You were playing a part then, and I still have no idea which is the real you.'

'The woman who loves you, who's willing to live with you on your own terms.'

Silently she vowed not to make the same mistake as Melinda and press for marriage, knowing that unless she compromised she would lose him. Maybe when he realised how happy he was with her, he would forget the unhappiness his mother had brought his father, and stop using her as a yardstick to judge all women. But she would say none of this to Rees—just make him as happy as she knew how. Show him that he was her world.

'You love your career, don't you?' he asked, deftly changing their positions on the settee, so they were lying side by side, and he could look more easily into her eyes.

'Very much. I find it interesting and challenging.'

'Dangerous too. I still wake up in a panic when I think how nearly Ledbury killed you. I've no right to lay down the law with you, Julia, but…' He paused for a long moment, then said firmly, 'If you go on taking the same kind of risks for your other clients that you took for me, I'll never know a minute's peace.'

Loving him as she did, Julia knew she would feel exactly the same if he was doing *her* job, and the admission showed her plainly what she had to do.

'I've no intention of risking my life, darling. In fact I've been considering going back to modelling. Then I'd at least be free to go abroad with you whenever you go. If you'd want me to, that is.'

'If I'd *want* you to?' He pressed her back on the settee. 'I want you with me all the time. I'll be miserable every minute we're apart.' His hands gripped her shoulders. 'I've no right to say this, but—dammit, Julia, do you think you could concentrate on me and give up modelling too?'

Before she could reply, he stopped her. 'No, forget I asked that. I know you enjoy working and... Dammit!' he muttered. 'I never thought I'd be so old-fashioned.'

'Old-fashioned?' She was puzzled.

'Old-fashioned enough to want us to live in the country, a place with a big garden, and dogs and cats and a horse or two.'

'*You?*' She laughed, her creamy throat swelling at the sound.

'Yes, me,' he said fiercely, his lips seeking the graceful curve. 'You've turned all my ideas on their heads. I've had plenty of time to think these last few months, and I've faced a few home truths about myself. I realised I was allowing the bitterness I felt towards my mother to colour my attitude to all women. Anyway, who am I to judge what went wrong with her marriage to my father? Sometimes it's difficult enough to judge one's own actions.' He paused, and when he spoke again his voice was barely audible. 'I went to see her a month ago. I doubt if we'll ever have a normal mother and son relationship, but at least I no longer feel bitter towards her.'

'Oh, darling, I'm so glad for you.' Julia could not stop the tears welling into her eyes, and Rees licked them away.

'About that house in the country,' he said. 'I'm happy to settle for a little weekend cottage.'

'I'm not letting you get out of your first suggestion,' she chided. 'I intend to give up work and concentrate on *you*.'

Delight suffused his face, and she glimpsed an unnatural glitter in his eyes. 'Don't let me talk you into anything you don't want, Julia.'

She wondered what he would say if she told him he had already done so, for in committing herself to live with him, knowing how adamant he was against marriage, she had forsworn her principles.

'I want *you*, Rees. Nothing is more important to me than being with you and loving you.'

'You won't get bored once the novelty wears off?'

'I might go back to painting. When I was sixteen I won a national portrait competition.'

'You're kidding!'

'I'm not. It was a pastel of our gardener's baby. I'm sure there's no shortage of babies in the country.'

'We can always make our own,' Rees whispered into her ear.

No, never, she thought sadly. Children needed the stability that came when a man and woman loved each other enough to make the commitment of marriage.

'Don't you want any?' Rees asked when she didn't answer, raising his head to look into her eyes. 'Or don't you trust me enough yet to marry me?'

'*Marry you?* But you hate marriage!'

'Not to you. I won't rest easy till you're tied and trussed.'

'As a liberated female I refuse to be tied and trussed.'

'How about adored and cherished, protected and sustained?'

'That'll do for starters.' With a cry of happiness she opened her mouth to him, and he drew her close and took what she offered. Her hands moved over his back, delighting in the feel of his muscles, the latent strength of him, the life-force he was longing to pour into her, yet was firmly holding in check.

'Make love to me, Rees. Make me yours.'

'No, Julia!' He jumped up fast. 'I can't. It's against all my principles. You have to make an honest man of me first.'

'I see. That's a pity.'

Straight-faced, Julia stood up and, as she did, her unzipped dress fell to the ground. She stood before him in the briefest of silk and lace panties and bra, and slowly she unhooked the bra and let it drop to the sofa. Then, resting a slender arm on a nearby chair, she stepped out of her panties. She felt her face go hot, but her lowered head, with its fall of silky black hair, hid it from his gaze, though her voice had the faintest tremble in it as she spoke.

'I don't know about you, Rees, but I'm too tired to go home. And as I've slept here safely so many times before, I'm sure you won't mind if I do so again.'

'Not at all.'

Leaving her clothes scattered around her, she sauntered gracefully out. The marble floor was cool to her feet, but she was burning with heat and hardly noticed it. She opened the door of the bedroom she had used, and saw it was exactly as she had left it, even to the paperback life story of Tom Cruise, whom she had pretended to have a crush on during her Bimbo act with Rees. She smiled at the memory, and sank gracefully on to the bed, running her hands lightly over the fine silk duvet cover.

There was a knock on the door.

'Who is it?' she asked languorously.

The door opened, and a tall, wide-shouldered man stood there, totally naked. His face was dark and shuttered, only the eyes—gleaming like jet, showed animation. A thin blue vein on his neck was prominent, as was the erratic beat of a pulse at the base of his throat, where a fine smattering of black hair dappled his chest, then almost vanished into a fine

V lower down his body, but grew thicker again as it partially protected his manhood. A narrow waist merged into strong hips and then muscular legs, and these brought him to the side of the bed, where he stood, feet slightly apart, making no attempt to hide anything.

Pulse hammering in her throat, Julia regarded him gravely. 'Did you want to say something?'

He nodded. 'It isn't only a woman's privilege to change her mind.'

'I'm glad to hear it.'

'I thought you would be.' He knelt on the bed and bent over her, so close that the hairs on his chest rubbed erotically against her breasts, then lowered his body fully on to hers.

'Oh!' she gasped, and strained him close in her arms. 'Oh, Rees.'

'You talk too much!' he growled.

Her tongue licked his lower lip. 'So show me some action.'

Rees did.

Maybe she was safer *without* police protection....

SOMETIMES A LADY

Linda Randall Wisdom

SOMETIMES A LADY

Linda Randall Wisdom

Chapter One

"If you've come to rob the place, you're too late."

Her voice was pitched low enough not to carry to the wrong set of ears, which made it music to this man's acute hearing. Dean slowly inched up from the belly crawl he'd been performing since sliding through a rear window that was smaller than he'd gauged. He swore his back was scraped raw from his wiggling; he'd almost gotten stuck halfway in. The guys at the station and the six-o'clock news sure would have loved *that*—it was the type of event that haunted a man right up to his retirement dinner.

He raised his head slightly and surveyed the area. The main lobby of the midtown bank was the tension-ridden stage of a robbery gone bad. A guard had already been wounded, and ten people were still being held hostage while the police negotiator tried to deal with three unstable kooks probably sky-high on drugs.

"You're awfully calm for a hostage," he commented sotto voce to the woman watching him with a pair of the most beautiful eyes he'd ever seen. Turquoise eyes, strawberry-blond hair, heart-shaped face. Just the kind of woman he wouldn't mind getting to know better. She smelled real good to a man who'd been crawling along a dusty floor. He crept over to a column where he could crouch down, unseen by the robbers brandishing lethal-looking weapons over a huddled group of men and women.

Her lips barely moved as she kept a wary eye on the armed men. "It doesn't do any good to get upset over a situation I can't resolve by myself."

He grinned. "Good girl."

She arched an eyebrow. "The times are changing, my friend. *Woman* is the appropriate term." She looked back down at the man lying beside her, who moaned, shifting restlessly, his bloodstained gray uniform shirt torn open to reveal a wadded-up half-slip used as a compress.

The one-man rescue team hissed through his teeth. "How bad is he?"

"Bad enough. I was able to stop the bleeding, but he's awfully shocky."

Dean rubbed a hand over his beard. "You a nurse?"

Her lips twitched with what looked like secret amusement. "I'm a doctor." She eyed the dark-haired, dark-eyed man who looked like the answer to any woman's dream. The kind who got the blood stirring and the hormones jumping. The kind she preferred to stay as far away from as possible.

He looked properly rueful. "Guess I blew it with my sexist assumptions, huh?" He wondered what she'd say if he told her that she had the most beautiful eyes he'd ever seen and, by the way, was she free Saturday night?

"So what are *you* here for? To take a census?"

He grinned as he pointed to the gold shield clipped to his shirt pocket. "Detective Dean Cornell. I'm your rescue party."

She rolled her eyes. "God help us."

"Your prayers have been answered."

"I don't think so."

"What's going on back there?" A man wearing dark clothing and a ski mask and cradling an automatic weapon against his chest walked toward the woman and her patient—and Detective Dean Cornell.

The doctor showed no outward sign of fear. She had once vowed she would never be victimized by a man with a gun again, and her firm resolve kept her from backing down in abject terror before this animal. "I'm talking to my patient in hopes of keeping him alive. I didn't think you'd want a murder charge added to your list of misdeeds."

"Lady, if you don't want to see that pretty face roughed up, you won't open your mouth again." His voice was strained, high-pitched with either fear or something even more dangerous.

She didn't flinch. "Sorry, I thought you'd want your question answered."

The man stalked back toward the front where his two accomplices paced restlessly, twitching fingers caressing their guns. She watched him, wondering why he seemed so familiar to her even though she couldn't see his face. She dreaded the idea he might have been in her clinic at one time.

For Elise Carpenter it was the perfect climax to a hellish morning. The minute she'd gotten up and realized it was Friday the thirteenth, she should have climbed back into bed and stayed there.

First the automated teller ate her bank card, forcing her to go inside to cash a check and request a new card. Before she finished her transactions, three maniacs ran in, waving automatic rifles and yelling, "Hold up." Between customers screaming, a teller hitting the alarm button, the guard getting shot, and panicked robbers seeing no choice but to hold the people hostage while deciding how to get out of there in one piece, she felt as if she were living a nightmare.

She'd fudged her credentials a bit in hopes of helping the wounded guard and told the robbers she was a doctor. And just as she saw her day going to hell in a hand basket, this overgrown adolescent, looking more like a street person than a cop, crawled into the lobby and announced he was going to save her! She only hoped her daughters in Riverside County and sister here in town wouldn't hear her name on the evening news; thank heavens, her parents were on a cruise.

"Detective, if you have an extra weapon on you, I'm a crack shot," she said softly.

"Sorry, I never carry a spare. You think these guys will surrender to that SWAT team or come out shooting?"

"The latter. While I don't claim to be an expert, I'd hazard a guess two of them are coming down from some heavy-duty drugs and growing more unstable by the minute. The leader is just as unbalanced. Probably even more so. He appears to enjoy intimidating anyone who gets in his way. He's the one who shot the guard."

Dean swore under his breath. "Okay, Doc, remain calm, and we'll get you out of here as soon as possible."

She turned her head slightly and ran into a pair of eyes so dark a brown they were almost black. Bittersweet chocolate, she thought illogically. Good thing she was a *milk* chocolate fan. The detective wore a full beard that was just a bit shaggy, as if he hadn't taken the time to trim it lately. His hair, too, was overlong, and had waves most women would kill for. Hadn't the character ever heard of haircuts?

Still she had to admit that this thug with a badge looked as if he could handle any situation that came long. So why didn't she put her trust in him? Easy. He was a cop. Past experience had taught her police weren't all they were cracked up to be. "Ah, yes, the men in blue to the rescue. It's amazing, I feel safer already."

Dean frowned. Her sardonic tone told him she didn't have much faith in law enforcers. The cop in him noted the hectic rose color dotting her creamy complexion and the glitter in her gemstone eyes; he'd hazard a guess both were indicative of a temper most people would probably duck to avoid. Not him; he never backed down from a good fight. He glanced at his watch.

"I need to count on you, Doc. In a minute all hell's going to break loose, and we're gonna have to pray those people up front hit the deck fast."

"What you're talking about is performing your personalized version of *Die Hard* and taking a chance with people's lives."

"*Saving* lives is more like it."

Dean watched the second hand on his watch, slowly counting down. Precisely as it swept past the twelve, he leaped up.

"All right, freeze!" His eyes widened as the three gunmen, automatics ready, spun around, and he realized his backup hadn't yet appeared. "Sh—!" He dove for cover, rolling over and over as the front door crashed open in a storm of glass and men in uniform came running in, guns drawn.

Thanks to quick thinking and near-precision action, gunfire was kept to a minimum. Elise huddled protectively over her patient and fervently prayed it would all be over soon and she would remain in one piece.

"YOU OKAY, ma'am?" A uniformed officer wearing a bullet-proof vest bent over her.

She ignored his outstretched hand and stood up, dusting her hands against her thighs. "Yes, I'm fine, but this man needs immediate medical attention."

"Paramedics!" he bellowed.

"Oh, damn."

Elise turned at the sound of the disgruntled voice. Her "hero" was sprawled on the floor, mumbling curses and holding his right hand against his left shoulder, which was stained a bright red.

"We have another casualty," she announced crisply. "Why am I not surprised?" she added quietly, hoping none-theless that Detective Cornell was not gravely injured.

Dean looked into Elise's eyes. "I can't stand the sight of blood," he told her just before he keeled to one side and passed out cold.

A tall man in his mid-forties appeared and crouched down next to Dean's prone figure. "Good going, buddy," he said in a gravelly voice. He chuckled, then caught the surprise on Elise's face. "It's just a flesh wound. This guy can handle any situation as long as it doesn't involve his own blood. Then he's a goner."

Elise shook her head. "Some rescuer he turned out to be." She moved away to accompany the paramedics as they wheeled out the wounded bank guard.

WHEN DEAN CAME TO, he found himself strapped to a gurney outside the open doors of an ambulance.

"Hey, Mac," he croaked, trying unsuccessfully to lift his hand out from under restraining straps.

Frank "Mac" McConnell appeared at his side. "Don't worry, buddy, you'll live." He grinned.

"You guys were five seconds late," he accused, closing his eyes to fight the light-headedness overtaking him.

"Your watch was probably fast. That's what happens when you buy cheap merchandise."

Dean turned his head. "Better me shot than you, I guess. If you'd gotten it, Stacy would have skinned me alive."

Mac chuckled. "Yeah, you're right there."

Dean shifted, then winced as white-hot pain tore through his shoulder. "Is the gorgeous doc anywhere around?"

"Yeah, over there."

Dean tried to move, then swore under his breath as shafts of pain whizzed through his shoulder. "Could you ask her if she'd like a new patient? Be sure to tell her what a great guy I am."

Mac shook his head. Trust Dean to use any situation, including a gunshot wound, to get a pretty woman's attention. "I don't know, Dean, she doesn't seem too friendly to cops."

"Oh, come on, she's the best thing I've seen in years. Besides, I don't have a regular doctor. Give me a break. I could be dying here." He hoped he looked suitably pathetic.

"We should be so lucky." Mac sauntered off, catching up with Elise, who was talking to one of the uniformed officers.

With a hopeful gaze, Dean watched Mac talk to her and saw her amused smile as she glanced toward the gurney. She said something else and pulled a card out of her purse, handing it to Mac. Dean didn't like the expression in Mac's eyes when he returned.

"At first she turned you down flat," he said without preamble. "Then she reconsidered and said maybe she *was* the doctor for you." He dropped the business card onto Dean's chest.

Dean craned his neck to decipher the small print on the blue pasteboard. He couldn't. "Meaning what?"

Mac tipped the card. "Read it and weep, my friend."

With the card angled, Dean read: Dr. Elise Carpenter, Doctor of Veterinary Science. Below, in smaller print was her specialty: exotic animals.

"The world is cruel, Mac. Really cruel."

"Were you frightened in there?"

"Did you feel as if they would kill you at any time?"

"Please, look this way?"

"Vultures," Elise muttered to the young officer recording her words, glaring at the press people buzzing all around them.

He looked confused. "Ma'am?"

She sighed. "Let's just get this over with, all right?" Her brow creased in a puzzled frown as she looked beyond the officer's shoulder to the three handcuffed prisoners being led toward waiting patrol cars. Something about the leader of the deadly trio still jogged her mind. Then he struggled briefly, and the sleeve of his sweatshirt slid back to reveal the tattoo of a grinning skull with a coiled snake emerging from the mouth. The tattoo and a scar.

The officer's words became nothing more than white noise as she stared at the tattoo and the scar and old memories exploded in her brain. She was suddenly blind to her surroundings and deaf to the young man's worried-sounding questions as scenes from five years ago flashed through her mind, renewing pain she thought she'd finally put behind her.

The clinic she and her husband Steve had worked so hard to expand...the night they stayed late to tend an ailing macaw...the two men breaking in, looking for drugs...Steven fighting with them, getting shot during the struggle...one of the intruders slapping her around...the seemingly miraculous sound of a police cruiser's siren. She'd fought back, grabbing a scalpel and slashing at her attacker, cutting open his arm, which left him crazy with pain and determined to do worse to her. It all unfolded before her eyes: the frantic ride to the hospital, only to hear her husband pronounced dead on arrival...two hours later, going into early labor and miscarrying the baby boy they'd hoped for after having their three delightful daughters.

Then came the questions, the investigation, the arrests, finally the lineup. She had identified the two men easily, especially the one with the distinctive tattoo on his left arm, now marred by a diagonal slash. And then, because of police error—a "technicality," the wrong name was typed on the arrest report—the man was freed, leaving a bitter widow with three young children to raise.

From that day on, Elise had had no use for the police.

Elise stared at the man, feeling all the anger and all the pain rise up. All the fury of a woman who had lost too much and never had the chance to see justice served. Justice she felt compelled to carry out herself if no one else would do it.

"You bastard!" she screamed, shoving past the stunned officer and running toward the prisoner, murder on her mind. Just as she reached her prey, a strong arm circled her waist, lifting her off her feet and out of the way. "No! Let me go!" She vainly batted at the arm.

"That I can't do, Doc," Mac murmured, stepping back a few paces. "Now, we know these creeps put you through hell back there, but you can't take the law into your own hands."

The pain bursting through her brain left her blind with fury. "You don't understand! That son of a bitch killed my husband and my baby five years ago, and you idiots let him loose!" The anguish flowing through her made her entire body quiver with rage.

Mac uttered a pungent curse as he noticed the television news cameras hungrily recording the scene. "Look, Doc, I think we should go down to the station and get this straightened out." He ushered her toward his car and away from the hungry press eagerly recording every word.

Elise sat stiffly in the passenger seat. The memories had ripped open old wounds and now she couldn't hold back the pain. She clenched her teeth to keep the moans inside. She turned to stare blankly out the window.

"You okay, Doc?" Mac asked in his quiet, gravelly voice as he turned into the precinct parking lot.

She didn't turn her head. "Never better."

He stopped the car and got out, walking around to assist her. Elise noticed the broad gold band on his left ring finger and a gold chain circling his wrist. The chain looked too delicate for such a masculine guy.

"How long have you been married, Detective?" she asked as he guided her toward a side door into the station.

His craggy features softened. "A little over two years. We're expecting our first child soon."

"I was married almost twelve years when I had to explain

to my three children that a crazed drug addict had killed their father and their unborn baby brother,'' she said in a quiet, deadly monotone. "Then I had to explain to them that the man responsible wouldn't receive the justice he deserved because the police had had to let him go. All because someone couldn't spell."

Careful not to react visibly, Mac winced inside. He didn't have to look hard to see why Dean was attracted to the woman. She was lovely, with strawberry-blond hair pulled back in a French braid, delicate features and bright turquoise eyes that had seen too much horror for any one lifetime. She also had a cool, touch-me-not manner, which probably attracted his partner the most. He made a mental note to call the hospital to check on Dean as soon as he could get away to a phone. First, though, he had some bad news for good ol' Captain Anderson. Tomorrow's glowing headlines featuring the department's neat easy capture of the bank robbers was going to turn into something very messy unless they could contain the secondary story—fast.

"SHE *WHAT?*" Captain Anderson's face was so red Mac wondered if the man would keel over from shock.

Mac rubbed a hand wearily over his face. Maybe Dean *had* gotten the better deal by being shot. At least he didn't have to sit in on this. Mac doubted his butt would be in one piece once this business was finished. "She's the widow of a veterinarian killed five years ago by one of the prisoners. Seems he got off due to a clerical error, and how she's out for blood—his *and* ours. And not necessarily in that order. The press got an earful when she recognized him." He waited for the explosion.

He didn't have long to wait. The captain paced back and

forth, haranguing the world in general, Dean and Mac specifically.

"Where is she now?" the captain asked once he ran out of steam.

"She's at my desk calling her sister." He smiled wryly at his superior's look of fury. "Captain, she's not under arrest. She wanted to assure her sister she was all right, since the woman has probably seen the story on the news."

"I want her in here, now."

Mac pushed himself out of the chair. "You got it." He hoped he could stick around to see Captain Anderson and Dr. Carpenter faced off. Somehow he doubted the doctor would be intimidated.

As soon as Elise entered Captain Anderson's office, it was clear who would dominate the conversation.

"Captain, I've given my statement, identified the robbers and insisted on double-checking your men's paperwork to insure there are no mistakes *this time*," she began without preamble. "Now I'd like to go home and say a few prayers that you don't screw up the arrest."

The older man's jaw worked furiously. He glanced down at her statement. "Mrs. Carpenter."

"*Dr.* Carpenter."

He took a deep breath. "Doctor. I'm sorry you've had to face your husband's alleged killer more than once."

Her eyes were turquoise chips of ice. "*Alleged?* Captain, I watched the man turn his gun on my husband and shoot him in the head. The overhead lights were on, so there was no mistaking the shooter's identity. His face and that tattoo have been firmly etched in my memory. I only wish I had used my scalpel on his throat instead of his arm. Then we wouldn't be having this conversation right now. You let him get away this time, and I'll tell the press a story that will make your name mud." Her voice was soft and dangerous. "A story that will give your superiors in city hall something to think about."

Captain Anderson's face darkened with fury. "I don't appreciate being threatened, Dr. Carpenter."

She didn't back down. "I never threaten, Captain Anderson. I only state the facts." With that, she spun on her heel and stalked out of the office.

"You!" The captain pointed his finger at Mac, who lounged near the door. "Keep an eye on her and find out when that idiotic partner of yours will be fit to return to work."

Mac straightened up and touched two fingers to his forehead in salute. "Gotcha."

He walked out and found Elise greeting a woman who looked so much like her they had to be related. Elise noticed Mac and quickly strode over to his desk.

"Detective, I know I've been a bit of a bitch, and I apologize for taking it out on you." She stuck out her hand. "Thank you for putting up with me."

"No apology necessary, Doc. I enjoyed watching you make mincemeat out of the captain in there. We don't get to see that happen too often."

Her lips twitched. "You know, with a little effort and some spit and polish, you and your partner might just pass in polite company." With that, she left.

"AH, COME ON, it's only a flesh wound." Dean knew he was whining, but he couldn't help it; he hated hospitals almost as much as he hated the sight of his own blood. "I'll go home and go straight to bed, I promise."

The doctor writing on his chart looked at him with disbelief. "Give me a break, Detective. I know you guys only too well. You're staying here overnight for observation."

Dean groaned with impatience. "But I have a dog to feed!"

"You do not." Stacy McConnell walked into the room—actually, waddled, since she was close to eight months pregnant. "You hate animals."

"Stacy." He winced as he pushed himself up into a sitting position. "How did you know I was here?"

She grinned. "You were on the evening news, my dear. They said you were unconscious from loss of blood, but I knew better. You passed out once you realized the blood was yours, didn't you?" She dropped a stack of comic books onto his bed. "Here, I brought you some reading material." She rested her hands on the chair arms and slowly lowered herself downward, glancing with gratitude at the doctor, who gave her a helping hand. "Thanks. Sitting isn't as easy as it used to be."

"You didn't *drive* down here, did you? Mac'd bust a gut if he thought you drove here by yourself."

"No, Janet dropped me off. I left a message for Mac that he could meet me here." She covered his hand. "How are you feeling?"

He grimaced. "I just want to go home."

"Dean, a five-year-old would be acting more mature than you are right now," Stacy remonstrated, smiling at him with affection.

"I don't care. I want out of here!"

"Wouldn't you rather check out the nurses?" Mac walked in, pausing to kiss his wife before perching on her chair arm.

"The only woman I wanted to check out turned me down flat."

Mac grinned. "Ah, yes, Dr. Carpenter. The lady's something else."

"Watch it, bud." Stacy elbowed him in the midriff. "Remember you're a married man."

He pretended great pain. "I meant for Dean here."

"I should hope so."

"What happened?" Dean demanded, sensing he'd missed something.

Mac quickly filled him in, including the episode in Captain Anderson's office.

"Oh, man, I miss all the good stuff," Dean moaned, trying, without much success, to turn over. He glared at the IV that impeded movements. "The old man must be having a coronary over all this."

"He was popping antacids like they were candy when I left. We're to keep on top of this, and if anything goes wrong, our heads roll."

Dean wasn't worried. "He's been threatening us with that for years."

"Yeah, but the lady has some pretty nasty ammunition. The public likes nothing better than learning the police screwed up. And this was one big mess. I pulled the file to see what we're in for. It should have been cut-and-dried if it hadn't been for some idiot who typed in the wrong name."

Dean was hopeful. "At least I'll get to see her again."

"Her and her three kids."

"Three?" Stacy chuckled. "Dean, our never-ending child here, should get along with them beautifully."

"Unless they're like their mother. Not to mention that Dr. Carpenter looks upon the police the way a dog looks at fleas—a nasty problem that should be eliminated with all due haste."

Dean was undaunted. "So I'll show her that not all fleas are nasty."

"HERE, I THINK after the day you've had, you need this." Kristen Davis, Elise's sister, handed her a glass of wine.

Elise lay back in the hot tub, sighing as jets of water pummeled her tense muscles. "Thanks. Once I'm out of here, I'm going to down this wine like it was water."

"Just be grateful that Mom and Dad weren't around to see you on the eleven-o'clock news."

She threw back her head, moaning, "That's all I would have needed! Mom would have been horrified and crying over the terrible ordeal I'd gone through, and Dad would have ranted and raved about the ineptitude of the police department. And I would have been sitting here seriously thinking about leaving the country for the next ten or twenty years."

"Oh, I don't know," Kristen interjected. "Between their looking forward to their cruise and going on about the real reasons behind my divorce, I suspect they'd pretty well used up their parental energy for this year."

"You wish." Elise shook her head, then sobered as the day's events resurfaced in her mind. "I cannot believe that slime would show up in my life twice." Bitterness laced her voice.

"Hey," Kristen pointed out, trying to lighten Elise's horror, "at least you met a good-looking man in the process, right?"

Elise gazed fondly at her perpetually optimistic sister. Though just as horrified and indignant as Elise at the thought of Steven Carpenter's killer on the loose to kill again, Kristen had informed Elise the moment she met her at the police station that at least the detective who'd driven her there was cute.

"You know who I mean. The one who said goodbye to you. Those macho, rugged types are so-o-o sexy! And that voice! Elise, it sent shivers down my spine. A voice like that should be illegal."

Elise sighed. "Oh, Kris, I know you believe in looking on the bright side, but I honestly can't handle it right now. I had to face Steve's killer today. The man almost took more lives because of inept law enforcers. As for Detective McConnell, sorry, sister dear, but he's married—and happily, judging by his expression when I asked about his wife. Besides, the last person you'd want anything to do with is a cop."

"Considering some of the creeps I've dated in the past, they can't be any worse." Kristen was philosophical about her divorce.

Elise had a sudden image of a dark-eyed detective with a rakish grin and the haircut and temperament of a juvenile delinquent. She wondered if he was all right. While gunshot wounds weren't her specialty, she had known his wasn't fatal—probably just a flesh wound that would require a few stitches and bed rest. She wouldn't be surprised if he already was trading phone numbers with all the nurses on his floor.

Kristen studied her sister with a look Elise knew only too well.

"No."

Kristen blinked. "No, what?"

"Please, Kris, it's been a rough day. I love you dearly, but the fact that there isn't a man in my life is not my idea of a fun conversation right about now." Elise rotated her neck in hopes of easing the tension.

"As far as you're concerned, there's never a good time."

"Oh, come on, Kris, you know I've tried to date but each time was a complete disaster."

"You didn't give them a chance!"

"A chance? One guy was allergic to the animals. Another thought a vet would be a great drug connection. And let's not forget that production control manager from your company who got so miffed when Baby insulted him that he informed me my children's emotional growth would be stunted by their bizarre home life."

Kristen waved a hand. "Well, Baby does get pretty insulting if anyone dares to refer to her as a bird. It's your fault for raising her like a child. She's positive she's human and that all the other animals are *her* pets. That bird is strange, Elise. Very strange."

She smiled. "She's not strange, she's special. How many women get a hand-fed blue-and-gold baby macaw for a wedding present?"

Kristen shook her head, used to her sister's preoccupation with exotic animals. "Did you get hold of the girls?"

Elise nodded, her expression sober once more. "They were worried after seeing the news, but I assured them everything was fine. Myrna said she was going to take them out to dinner and the movies tonight and not to cut my time short at the conference. Keri, likewise told me that she'd keep an eye on Lisa and Becky."

"Ten to one those three are ecstatic Myrna is staying with them. I'm sure they're doing everything you don't allow them to and they plan to live it up as long as possible," Kristen teased.

Elise pushed herself up and out of the hot tub, sitting on the edge as she reached for her glass of wine. "Funny, if I hadn't decided to miss the conference's opening speeches, I would have missed seeing that slime caught again." Her features turned grim. "I want to see that bastard behind bars. I'm not going to allow Steve's killer to get away again."

"Elise, don't even think of anything that smacks of vigilantism," Kristen warned. "Let the police do their work."

"Then they'd better not screw up again."

"HEY, LOOK, it's the hero returning from the wars!" came the announcement from the squad room.

Dean bowed several times as he made his way to his desk. "Thank you, thank you, men. But no big deal, obviously, since four days later and I'm back in the trenches. Just a flesh wound. Nothing to worry about."

"Is that why you passed out cold the minute you saw the blood?" one uniform joked.

"Once I have full mobility back, I'll take you to task for that remark." Dan tossed his sheepskin-lined denim jacket onto his chair before heading for Mac's desk. After a bit of searching he found what he was looking for: Dr. Elise Carpenter's statement and a bit of personal information.

Too bad she didn't live in the area. Still, Lake Elsinore over in Riverside County would make a nice drive. Thirty-seven, widowed, three daughters, ages sixteen, twelve and seven. Lucky he was pretty good with kids, although most of the kids he dealt with were rough-and-tumble boys.

"Better watch it, Cornell, or you'll end up as soppy as that partner of yours," he muttered to himself.

"Be prepared, old buddy."

Dean looked up, wisecrack ready, but his smile disappeared when he saw his partner's grim expression.

"Something tells me I'm not going to like what you're about to say."

"Heads are going to roll," Mac announced. "And ours will lead the procession."

Cold entered his veins. "What happened?"

"Dr. Carpenter's favorite man walked out of the county jail this morning and hasn't been seen or heard from since."

Chapter Two

"Thank you for giving me a ride, Andrew. I guess that battery I bought for my car wasn't as good as the mechanic said it was." Elise forced a stiff smile to her lips. Standing on her sister's front stoop, she dipped her head, rummaging through her purse for her keys, eager for the safety of the house.

An arm slung itself heavily across her shoulders. "You know, Elise, the evening doesn't have to end." Whiskey-scented breath wafted unpleasantly across her face. "It's still early."

"Yes, it does have to end, and while you think it's early, I don't." She wiggled out of his loose embrace, using what her daughters called her this-is-my-final-warning voice.

When she left the hotel where the veterinarians' conference-closing banquet was held, she didn't expect her car to refuse to start. Tired and ready for a relaxing bath and bed, she'd eagerly accepted Dr. Andrew Marsh's offer of a ride after he'd looked under her car hood and pronounced the battery dead. Still tired from the past few days' events, including the bank robbery, the reporters and the conference, she'd noticed too late that Andrew had drunk too much that evening to be a completely safe driver. It had become especially obvious when one of his hands kept finding its way to his passenger's knee during the short drive from the hotel to Kristen's.

"In fact," she added now, "I think you should seriously consider calling a cab to return you to the hotel."

He swayed forward, his eyes glazed from the alcohol he'd consumed. "Then I'll have to come inside to call, won't I?" He looked at the darkened windows. "Looks real cozy. Your sister out for the evening?"

"She's most definitely home, and she would not appreciate an unexpected visitor." She tried to insert her key in the lock and bat Andrew's hands away at the same time. "Andrew, do you mind!"

"Not at all, sweetie. C'mon, just one little kiss." At almost any other time Elise might have found his pucker laughable. Right now, though, she only thought about slapping it off his face.

"Andrew, get your hands off me this minute or you'll find yourself practicing surgery with both arms in slings," she threatened.

"Aw, come on, Elise, loosen up."

"Hey, buddy, the lady told you to get your hands off her. I suggest you do as she says."

Both Elise and Andrew turned at the unexpected interruption from the shrubbery along the front of the house. The foliage parted to reveal Dan Cornell and Mac McConnell. Both were dressed in faded jeans and denim jackets and looked as if they should be straddling Harleys instead of protecting the public.

"I don't need this," Elise moaned softly, looking skyward.

"Who do you think you are?" Andrew protested, all puffed-up drunken swagger. "We're having a private conversation here."

Dean's chilling smile should have sobered up the inebriated doctor faster than a cold shower and hot coffee would have. He pulled out a leather wallet and flashed a badge. "We're the fuzz, buddy. Maybe you'd better run along before I slap you with a morals charge." He scowled at the man. "Of course, if you get back behind that wheel, a DWI would be impossible to avoid."

Elise lifted her eyes to the sky and silently counted to ten. She was *not* happy about this.

"Elise is going to call me a cab." Andrew moved a step closer to her as if seeking protection from these scruffy-looking men.

Mac spoke up. "There's a 7-Eleven at the corner with three pay phones, friend. I suggest you use one of them. I'll even give you a quarter."

"He can call from here," Elise inserted, not about to let these buffoons take charge. By now she was so angry she could chew nails. Who the hell were they to tell people what to do? Her eyes flashed fury as she first directed her ire on Dean then moved on to Mac.

Andrew scurried down the walk, keeping one eye on the two men still standing there. "No wonder nobody can get close to you, with bodyguards like these macho jerks," he called out, determined to have the last word before practically running down the street.

Hands braced on her hips, Elise spun around and faced the two detectives with all the fury her three daughters prayed they would never incur.

"You idiots, what do you think you were doing just

then?'' She kept her voice low in deference to the neighbors, although she wanted nothing more than to scream. "That man is a colleague who throws a lot of business my way. You treated him like a common criminal!"

"Yeah, and it appeared he expected to be paid for all that business he sends you, too," Dean replied, unfazed by her temper. In truth, he was dazzled by it, along with seeing her slender body dressed in a bronze silk sheath and cream wool coat. The perfume she wore tonight was heavier than the one he remembered from the bank and packed a powerful wallop. Her reddish blond hair was twisted up in an intricate knot, revealing the slender column of her throat, which was adorned by a tricolor twisted chin. Her high heels matched her dress and did wonderful things for a pair of legs he decided he could look at forever.

Elise eyed the suggestive saying on Dean's T-shirt with faint disgust. "You don't get out often, do you?"

"Down boy," Mac murmured in his gravelly voice before Dean could respond to Elise's comment.

Dean reluctantly pulled himself back to the business at hand. "Dr. Carpenter, we'd like to come in and talk to you."

"Detective, do you know what time it is?"

"Yes, ma'am, we do. We've been waiting for you for the past two hours. We wouldn't be here if we didn't feel it was important."

"Amazing how something so important had you lurking in the bushes," she muttered, pulling the screen door open with such force it almost came off its hinges before she unlocked the inner door and thrust it open. The two men were on her heels as she stormed into the living room.

"We're sorry if we ruined your date," Dean told her without a hint of apology. He privately thought that kind of man wasn't right for someone like this lady.

"It wasn't a date. I was at a conference; I had a dead battery, and Dr. Marsh offered to drive me home." She shrugged off her coat and draped it over the back of a chair. "Let's cut out the small talk, shall we? Exactly why are you here? It's been a long day and an equally long evening. The sooner you tell me why you're here, the sooner you're gone and I'm catching up on some much-needed sleep."

Mac and Dean exchanged a telling look. One Elise didn't like.

She stiffened. What if... "What is it? Is it something about my daughters? Just tell me, dammit!" Her voice was raspy; her stomach rolled. If anything had happened to one of the girls, she doubted she could go on.

It had been decided beforehand that Dean would be the one to break the news. Gently. But after seeing the terror etched on her face as she demanded reassurance her daughters were all right, he knew he had to blurt out the truth and not waste any time. "As far as we know, your daughters are just fine, Dr. Carpenter. The bad news is that Carl Dietrich got loose."

Her face froze, but her brilliant turquoise eyes blazed fire. She swallowed the bitterness that rose in her throat. No, it couldn't happen again! She blinked rapidly to keep back the tears that burned her eyes and firmed a mouth that trembled with emotion. For a moment her hand sought support, but she snatched it back. She refused to lean on anything.

"Who screwed up the paperwork this time?" Her voice was raw with feeling. Her fists were clenched at her sides.

"Nobody, Doc," Mac said. "He escaped from the county jail."

"He escaped?" she hissed. "What happened, did somebody forget to lock his cell? Or did he just say, 'Hey, guys, I don't belong in here. Why don't you let me out, okay?' Naturally, they went along with what he said and escorted him to the front door. Right?"

Dean drew in a deep breath. He'd expected her to be angry. In this situation, anyone would be upset. He didn't expect to hear such deep pain coupled with such vivid bitterness. He felt her pain. For a cop who prided himself on his lack of emotion on his cases, this was highly unusual. He prayed he wasn't losing his edge; that was dangerous for someone in his line of work.

"Dr. Carpenter, we're sorry we have to bring you this kind of news," he said. "We don't know why it happened, only that it did. Somehow Dietrich walked out of the jail. We have an APB out, and we plan to pick him up as soon as possible."

Her harsh laugh held no humor. "Spare me the platitudes, Detective. Because of a clerical error he was freed the last time. Because someone wasn't doing his job, he strolled out of the county jail. And don't try to tell me any different. I read the papers. I know what goes on. And this time a man who beat the system before got a second chance to do it again. Why should I expect anything better? You people haven't done anything right yet. You couldn't even time storming the bank correctly!"

Dean winced at the accusation.

"I can just hear your cop reasoning now!" she fairly shouted, tossing her silk clutch bag onto the couch. "So you lost a prisoner. Hey, no problem. You'll be able to replace him with another in no time, right? What's one prisoner to you?"

"This one is pretty important, not only to us, but to the bank," Mac pointed out. "Banks don't appreciate guys trying to withdraw funds that don't belong to them."

"And I don't appreciate men killing my husband and murdering my unborn child," Elise said quietly. "Two murders he can't even be tried for. Whose husband or wife will he have to kill before he's finally brought to justice?"

Neither man had an answer, but she didn't expect one. She walked around the room, passing her hand over the back of a chair.

"I gather you came here to tell me that my testimony is no longer required?" she said quietly.

"He'll be caught, Doc," Mac assured her.

She raised her head. It wasn't until then, with the lamp backlighting her, that they could see the sheen of tears in her eyes. Tears she didn't want them to know about.

She couldn't look at either of them. But turning away didn't help, either. "Will he? To date, your track record hasn't been very good. I'm sure you'll understand if I don't thank you for your news or offer to show you to the door." Only a stirring in the air told her someone was behind her. The faint scent of soap teased her nostrils. Something in the back of her mind told her it was Dean Cornell standing behind her, not Frank McConnell. The tiny click of the door latch and the silent presence behind her told her she Dean were now alone.

"Dr. Carpenter, we will find Dietrich, I promise," Dean murmured. "And while I know we're not your favorite people, I want you to know you can call Mac or me if anything comes up. I'll leave you my card." He placed it on the back of the chair.

"You don't understand," she whispered, closing her eyes.

"I didn't want to go through this hell a second time, and now, if you do your jobs right—for once—I'll actually have to go through it a *third* time. That's why I'm angry."

Although he knew she couldn't see him, Dean nodded his understanding. He deeply regretted all that had happened. Ironic, that the woman who fascinated him so much was brought into his life in such a tragic way. A part of him wanted to track down Carl Dietrich and lay the man's head at Elise Carpenter's feet. He also wanted to reach out, touch her arm, reassure her. But he sensed if he offered her anything in the way of comfort, she'd probably hit him.

Though Elise continued to face away from the detective she felt a wholly unfamiliar urge to simply lay her head on his shoulder and cry. To let someone else do all the worrying for once. And Dean Cornell had very broad shoulders.

She thrust the betraying thought out of her mind with the stern reminder that, broad shoulders or not, good-looking and all-around sexy or not, the man was a cop. A stupid, bungling, incompetent cop. Still, a tiny voice reminded her, he was pretty brave in that bank. She had to give him credit for that.

"I'm very tired, Detective," she finally murmured, afraid if she turned around she might do something foolish. Like throw herself into his arms. "Please go."

Dean let himself out of the house and walked to the car, where Mac stood waiting.

"She's in a lot of pain over this." Dean pulled open the driver's door and slid behind the wheel. "I just wish I could do something for her."

"I thought you already had that planned."

Dean winced. "Yeah, but that was before I realized there was more to her than just a pretty face. She saw her husband shot in the head and then was beat up so badly she lost her baby. If that patrolman hadn't decided to investigate, she might have been killed, too. Then we let her husband's killer walk, and when we book him on something else, he just ambles out of jail as if he was only visiting. No wonder she hates cops. Right about now I don't like us much, either.''

''How about we do something to make us look good in the lady's pretty eyes?'' Mac suggested. ''Why don't we check out her car at the hotel?''

With the ease of a longtime friend and partner, Dean immediately picked up the line of thought. ''You think Mr. Personality had something to do with her dead battery?''

''Could be.''

''Then you're right—it might not hurt to check it out.''

UNABLE TO SLEEP, Elise stood in the kitchen, nursing a glass of wine she didn't want, when Kristen stumbled in, wincing under the bright overhead light. Her gaze fell on the wineglass.

''I gather the Bobbsey Twins told you about Dietrich.'' She opened the refrigerator, drew out the wine bottle and poured a glass for herself before sitting down at the table across from her sister. ''I invited them to wait inside, but I guess they feel more comfortable lurking around in the dark.''

''It was better when they hanged bank robbers without benefit of trial,'' Elise grumbled, tracing the rim of her glass with her fingertips. She glanced at the manicured nails that had to be kept at a serviceable length because of her work. ''Steve always hated guns, but I felt he should keep one at the clinic for nights he worked late. He used to say no one would bother a veterinary clinic. That assumption cost him his life.''

''Most people who plan to use a gun against an intruder end up shot with it themselves.'' Kristen pointed out. ''Let it go, Elise. Let the boys in blue do their job.''

Her lips tightened. ''It appears I have no choice on that point. I have a practice to return to, along with three daughters to look after. But that doesn't mean I have to like it.''

Kristen sipped her wine. ''I guess this wouldn't be the time to tell you that I think Detective Cornell is quite a man. I never liked beards before, but his suits him—along with that scrumptious hair that hasn't been cut any time recently. A man like him could tempt a woman to dial 911 on a regular basis.'' Her lips tipped in a leer.

Elise couldn't help smiling. Her sister was well-known for her penchant for clean-shaven men in three-piece suits who would never dirty their hands on mundane tasks. ''I'm sure the man in question prefers nubile nineteen-year-olds who don't have one original thought in their heads to a woman who won't see thirty again.''

''Thanks for that thought, Elise! Not seeing thirty again is bad enough without you driving the nails in even deeper.''

''Well, really, didn't that T-shirt he wore tell you something about the man?''

Kristen only giggled.

Elise shook her head. ''Kristen, a man like that would bring a woman nothing but trouble.''

''Yes, but that kind of trouble a woman wouldn't mind handling. And if you were the least bit honest with yourself, you would admit the same thing.''

Elise pictured Steve. Tawny hair always kept short because he thought that would stave off the early baldness the men in his family suffered. Aqua eyes that readily showed laughter. He loved his wife, his family and his work, though not always in that order. A man who had no enemies. Yet that hadn't stopped him from getting killed. Nor did it stop his widow from having to sell the practice they'd worked so hard to build, when she couldn't bear to enter the offices again. Her move to Riverside County was as much for her own sanity as to try to give her daughters a new life without so many painful reminders. It had worked until now.

"If you don't mind, I think I'll drive home in the morning instead of early afternoon. After Myrna's had my girls for four days, I'm sure she'll be only too happy to return to normal life," she said. Then she groaned as her memory bank kicked in. "As soon as I get my car fixed, that is." She filled her sister in on the evening's events, including Dean's intervention. "I dread to think that story Andrew will tell the others."

Kristen wrinkled her nose. "Detective Cornell was probably right—the man was looking for payment for all the business he's sent your way over the years. I always thought he was kind of sleazy."

"But he has a lot of influence in this field. As for sleaze, I'd say it's a toss-up between Andrew and Detective Cornell as to who's worse."

Kristen finished her wine and stood up, yawning. "The cop's no sleaze. Besides, I think he has his eye on you."

Elise remembered his penetrating gaze. "That's his problem."

Kristen smiled. "No, sister dear, I do believe that's yours."

"COME ON, lazy, you've got to see this!"

Elise groaned, pulling the covers over her head. "Go

away," she mumbled, kicking out at the weight on the side of the bed.

"Elise, there's a surprise for you in the driveway."

She rolled over onto her back and pulled the covers down enough to barely open one eye. "What time is it?"

"A little after six."

The comforter covered the eye. "Come back in four hours."

Insistent hands continued the torture of pushing her out of bed. "I swear, Elise, you're as bad about getting up as ever. If you don't get up this minute, I'll pour a pitcher of cold water on your head."

Elise muttered uncomplimentary things about her sister as she slowly unfurled the comforter. She knew Kristen well enough to fear she would follow through on her threat.

"I hope the day will come when you find a man as sadistic as you are." She sat up on the edge of the bed, pushing her hair from her eyes. "What is so important that it can't wait until the sun comes up?"

Kristen grabbed her hand and pulled her to her feet. "This." She practically dragged her to the window.

Elise peered sleepily between the drapes, started to turn away, then turned back for a better look. "That's my car!"

"I know."

"How?"

Kristen's grin threatened to split her face. "I think I have a good idea. There's a piece of paper under the windshield wiper."

"You couldn't have gone out and gotten it?"

Kristen grimaced. "Do you know how cold it is out there right now?"

Sighing, Elise dragged on her robe and walked outside. Her Pathfinder—freshly washed and waxed, judging by the shine on its dark red surface—sat sedately in the driveway as if it had been there all night. She plucked the folded sheet of paper from under the windshield wiper and carried it inside. Kristen was already in the kitchen brewing coffee.

"What does it say?" she asked eagerly.

Elise unfolded the paper and read the dark scrawl aloud.

"No dead battery, only disconnected battery cables, I'm sure courtesy of you know who. From now on, make sure all your doors are locked, and don't keep your spare key in such a logical place. Even if it did keep me from having to hotwire your ignition. P.S. You owe me $12.95 for the wash and wax."

Elise chuckled.

Kristen snatched the paper out of her hand and quickly scanned it. "It's not signed."

"It doesn't have to be. Only a policeman would warn you to lock your car doors to protect against theft after he'd already commandeered it."

Kristen continued studying the paper. "It might prove interesting to have his handwriting analyzed."

"They'd probably say he should be locked away for the good of the public." Elise's eyes didn't leave Kristen's movements as she placed the paper on the table.

Kristen didn't miss her sister's intensity. "You're more interested in the man than you'd like to admit."

"Kris, the man has three strikes against him. He has an adolescent sense of humor, and he looks as if he's just climbed out of a ragbag."

"And the third?"

She looked grim. "The third and worst, he's a cop."

"It's as if the creep disappeared off the face of the earth." Dean stood in the kitchen doorway watching Mac grab two cans of beer out of the refrigerator. He accepted the one Mac handed him. "One of our sources should have had something for us by now."

Mac nodded before drinking deeply. "Yeah, and it worries me that they don't."

"You thinking what I am—that he left the area?"

"Seems possible." Mac led the way into the living room and gestured to one of the chairs.

Dean settled down, his legs stretched out in front of him. He rested the can on his flat belly. "We should have told her about Dietrich's threats against her."

"And have Anderson on our asses for sure."

"Dietrich said he'd go after her." Dean shifted his weight. "I think he meant it."

"You know the rules. We have to wait for a complaint before we can act on it. Plus, the lady lives out of our jurisdiction. All we can do is concentrate on tracking down Dietrich and make sure he stays put this time." Mac set his beer aside and stretched his arms over his head. "I'm getting too old for this. I should say the hell with it and put in for retirement. They've had more than twenty years of my life. I should be able to do what I want now."

"I've heard that story before."

The two men looked up to find a heavy-eyed Stacy standing in the hallway. She rested her hands on her distended belly. "Do you two realize what time it is?"

Mac held out his arms. "Sorry if we woke you, honey."

Stacy walked slowly. "I'm too heavy for you."

"Nah, you're still a light bundle."

With his help, she arranged herself in his lap, his hand splayed across her belly in a caressing motion. With more than a little envy, Dean watched the love flowing between them. Years ago, he'd decided marriage and family life weren't for him. He knew the divorce statistics among the police force and didn't want to be part of them. But watching Stacy and Mac, he thought more and more about finding a special woman and giving it a try.

Stacy kissed Mac and drew back, her nose wrinkled in disgust. "It's not even light out, and you two are drinking beer?"

"It's made from grain," Dean pointed out.

She shook her head, laughing at his logic. "You guys are hopeless."

"You could always adopt me and turn me into a better person."

"I think we already have. You already eat most of your meals here, and I seem to find more and more of your clothes in the laundry. If this keeps up, you're going to have to take a turn with the washer and dryer, Cornell," she warned in mock threat, relaxing under Mac's massage of her lower back. "I swear, McConnell, this kid of yours is going to be a soccer player." She rested her head against his shoulder.

He lifted his hand, the gold bracelet glinting at his wrist. The bracelet had once graced Stacy's ankle, a visual reminder of her less than perfect past, until the time she let go of the memories. Now Mac wore the bracelet as a reminder of their future together.

"I wish I could help."

"Believe me, you will when you're with me in the delivery room."

Dean was amused to see his partner's face pale. While Mac hadn't said it out loud, Dean sensed his friend wasn't too sure about being there when his child was born. It seemed Mac didn't have such a strong stomach after all.

"If you two are going to get soppy, I'm leaving," he announced.

"Up yours, Cornell," Mac said amiably.

"What time do you guys have to be in to work?" Stacy asked.

Mac glanced at his watch. "About an hour and a half."

"Were you able to talk to Dr. Carpenter?"

Dean nodded. "Something tells me she won't be sending us a Christmas card this year."

Mac and Stacy exchanged a telling look. She slowly climbed off his lap.

"Let me fix you two some breakfast," she offered.

"Pancakes?" Dean asked hopefully. "With plenty of butter and syrup?"

She smiled at him. "All right."

"And bacon, crisp?"

"Who's married to the lady?" Mac demanded.

"You are, but it's me she really loves," Dean confided.

"Your latest batch of clean clothes is in the guest room chest of drawers," Stacy told him. "Why don't both of you take your showers while I start breakfast."

Mac's gaze didn't leave his wife's retreating figure as he watched her make her way slowly into the kitchen. Worry was etched on his face, and along with the worry, such love that Dean felt as if he were intruding on something private.

He's seen a lot of changes in his partner over the past two

years. Mac's loner personality had expanded to include a special woman, and he laughed and joked more with the others. He even took Captain Anderson's tantrums better. The two men's friendship hadn't diminished because of Mac's marriage. Stacy treated Dean like a brother and cheerfully bullied him whenever she got the chance. Dean found himself part of a family, which only got him thinking more and more about making one of his own.

"I love that lady so much," Mac breathed. "I don't know what I would do if anything happened to her."

"Nothing's going to happen," Dean was quick to assure him. "The guys at the station have the routine down pat. They should, since seven of them have become new fathers since the first of the year. Nothing's going to interfere with you being at the hospital to see my godson coming into the world." He set his can of beer aside. "You think Dr. Carpenter's going to thank us for returning her truck?"

"After she reads the note you wrote? I doubt it."

"A woman alone at night should lock her car doors!"

"That isn't the part I'm talking about."

Dean nodded in understanding. "I wanted to get her attention."

Mac grinned. "I'm sure you did. I'm just not sure it'll get you the kind of attention you're hoping for."

"Yeah, I should have left off the cost of the wash and wax."

"If you guys want some breakfast, you'd better get your showers taken within the next five minutes," Stacy called out.

"Only if you scrub my back, darlin'," Dean called back.

"In your dreams, Cornell!"

He grinned broadly. "That's where you already are."

"HEY, CORNELL," the desk sergeant sang out, holding an envelope above his head as Dean and Mac entered the station that morning. "Got something for you. A lady just left it. A real looker, too. Nice legs."

Dean grabbed the envelope and walked on by. "You need to get out more, Stan."

"I try to. Thing is, my wife objects," he chortled.

"Comedians, they're all comedians," he muttered, heading for his desk, then stopping short. "You say she just left it?" He looked down at the envelope. The faint hint of something warm and exotic wafted upward to tease his nostrils. The kind of scent that got a man thinking of silk sheets and a roaring fire. His name was written on the front in a neat feminine script. It may have been unfamiliar, but he still knew who'd written it.

Stan nodded. "Not more'n a minute ago."

Dean raced for the door, slapping it open with one hand and descending the steps two at a time. One glance at the adjoining parking lot located his quarry.

"So you didn't forget about me after all, did ya, Doc?" he called out.

Elise was in the process of closing her car door when she heard him. "One thing you should know, Detective, I always pay my debts," she returned sweetly, slamming the door shut. The engine started up with a muted roar, and the window rolled down as she drove past him. "Have a nice day!"

"Would it have hurt her to stop and just talk?" Dean groused, watching the small truck travel down the street.

"Your hormones are showing again, friend," Mac growled, walking up behind him. He spied the envelope Dean clutched. "What did she leave you?"

"I hope her telephone number, but I doubt it." He tore

open the envelope, revealing a rectangular piece of pale blue paper. No note, no phone number, just the muted picture of whales crashing the ocean waves, partially obscured by the numbers neatly written across it—$12.95—and the signature, Elise A. Carpenter. In the corner marked *memo,* it read, *for services rendered.* Dean's shoulders shook with laughter.

"It is a shame I won't see the lady again. I'd say we could be a perfect match."

Mac shook his head. "Yeah, just like Little Red Riding Hood and the big bad wolf."

Chapter Three

"It's time to get up. It's time to get up. It's time to get up in the morning!" The raspy voice intruded on what Elise considered the quality sleep she wanted to continue for at least four more days.

"Go 'way," she muttered, pushing at the offender, who merely screeched and hopped away a couple steps before coming back to nip her bare shoulder.

"Fud up."

"Fud up yourself, you mangy kid." She opened her eyes to find the black feather lines decorating the dark eyes of a blue-and-gold macaw peering into her face. "Baby, there are times I hate your alarm-clock routine."

"Mama, Mama," the bird chanted, grabbing several strands of hair with her beak and pulling back on them slightly, intent on grooming her mom to a macaw's high standards.

Elise groaned. "Baby, go find Keri," she told the macaw. "Go get Keri."

"No."

She sighed as she rolled over. "You are so obnoxious." She pushed herself upward.

"Mom?" A tall slender teenager stood in the doorway. "Sorry. Baby got away before I could stop her. She's missed you."

Elise nodded as the macaw huddled closer to her side. "That's okay. I should go in early to the clinic anyway." She pushed wayward strands of hair away from her face, wincing as she heard strident sounds from the front of the house. Ah, home sweet home, she thought to herself. "Hey, you two, give it a rest!" she hollered in their general direction.

Two more girls soon appeared, both wearing murderous expressions.

The taller of the two spoke up first, determined to present her side of the case. "Mom, she wrote all over the front of my notebook!"

The smaller one's face scrunched up in anger. "It's my notebook!"

"No, it's not!"

"You said I could have it."

"Did not!"

"Did so!"

Elise put two fingers in her mouth and released a shrill whistle guaranteed to wake the dead.

"Honestly, Mom..." Keri looked as if her mother had done the unforgivable.

"It's the only thing that works with these two." Elise faced her middle daughter. "Lisa, did you give Becky your notebook?"

The girl shifted uncomfortably under her mother's gaze. "Not exactly."

"Either you did or you didn't. Which is it?"

"Well, I want it back," she wailed.

"That's tough, sweetheart. If you gave it to Becky, it's hers, and she can do anything she wants with it." She turned to her youngest. "And no more quarreling from you either. I didn't come home to listen to you two fight."

Keri urged them out of the room, suggesting they eat their breakfast. "They were upset after they saw that news report," she said quietly. "Since then they've been fighting and obnoxious like this."

Elise gestured Keri closer to the bed until she sat on the edge. A disgruntled Baby was set on the headboard, which already displayed macaw chew marks. Elise wrapped her arms around her eldest daughter.

"It's all over, sweetheart," she assured her, rocking her gently. "I'm back, and it's all over."

"Except the man who killed Daddy is free again."

She released a deep breath. "Yes, but the police will catch him."

"Do you really believe that?"

At that moment, Keri sounded more six than sixteen, the child needing reassurance from the one adult she could trust completely.

"No, honey, I don't," Elise said finally. "But I keep saying it in hopes it will help me feel better. So let's put this all behind us and get on with life, okay? We did it before, we can do it again. Right?" She smiled, kissing her daughter's forehead.

Keri managed a faint smile. "All right." She held on to Elise tightly, as if her touch was crucial. "Florence went into hibernation."

Elise laughed softly. "The same place?"

Keri nodded. "Where else but under the guest room bed? I'm just glad she gave up on the living room fireplace for her winter quarters. We couldn't build a fire for the first two years we were here. Henry's in the coat closet."

"It wouldn't be so bad if we didn't have two tortoises who snore." Elise released her daughter and stood up, reaching for her robe. She glanced at the bedside clock. "Your bus should be here soon."

"If you'd let me use the car, I could drive all of us to school and we wouldn't have to wait for the bus," Keri said slyly.

"We'll discuss it when you can pay for your own car insurance." Elise held out her arm for Baby to step onto.

"Mama, Mama," the macaw crooned, nuzzling her.

"Come on, Baby, let's get some breakfast," Keri offered, holding out her arm.

The macaw glared at her, ruffling her brilliant blue and gold feathers and staying put on Elise's arm. "No. Fud up."

Keri rolled her eyes. "I swear, that's all that bird says. When she's not demanding to be let out, she's telling everyone to shut up. She's so spoiled!"

Elise stroked the bird's feathers in a grooming motion. "She still misses your dad. She loved him a great deal." She recovered. "Come on, Baby, you can take a shower with me."

While Elise showered, Baby sat perched on top of the cubicle, singing a bawdy ditty at the top of her lungs—something she only did in the shower. While Elise stood under the stream of hot water, she thought of the many mornings Steve would bring Baby in to shower with him.

She had been surprised when he presented her with a baby macaw for a wedding present. From the beginning the newly wedded couple had treated the genial bird like one of the family, hand-feeding her, talking to her and, Elise guessed, spoiling her rotten. Now Baby was convinced she was human and got belligerent if anyone tried to tell her differently. The bird bossed the rest of the family and other pets as if she were head of the household.

When Steve died, the macaw grieved right along with the rest of them. Finally, after months of moping and mournful silence, she started to bounce back to her usual bratty self. From then on, Baby joined Elise at the clinic and bossed whoever happened to be in earshot. Elise was grateful for that return to *some* kind of normalcy in their lives as she struggled to rear her sixteen-, twelve-and seven-year-old daughters as best she could.

"Baby, I wish someone had told you you couldn't sing worth a damn," she informed the bird as she toweled off and dressed in jeans and a pale green-and-cream-colored soft flannel shirt. Feeling somewhat restored and more like her old self, she headed for the kitchen.

"Mommy, I can't find my blue jacket," Becky complained, jumping out of her chair and running to her mother. She wound her arms around Elise's legs.

"Since I haven't been here for the past week, I'm not sure I'd know where it is, either," she replied, bending down to kiss the top of her head. "I'd suggest you'd try looking in your closet first."

Becky sniffed, clearly not happy with that idea. "Lisa probably took it."

"Why would I want that crummy old jacket?" Lisa asked.

Elise fixed her middle daughter with a daunting stare. "Tonight, we'll have a talk about attitude."

She grimaced. "She's always accusing me of taking her crummy stuff!"

"Well, honey, you have given her reason to," Elise observed with gentle logic, thinking fleetingly of Kristen's house with its bubbling spa and peace and quiet.

"The bus will be here in five minutes. Off with you." Myrna, the Carpenters' housekeeper and part-time surrogate mother, began distributing lunch bags and book bags and herding the girls out the door. A goose's honks followed the girls' chatter as they left after kissing their mother goodbye.

Elise gratefully accepted the cup of coffee Myrna handed her. "I'd run away from home, but with my luck, the kids would only track me down."

Myrna's back was to Elise as she stood at the stove, whipping up eggs and checking on bacon cooking in the microwave oven.

"You're probably right," the housekeeper chuckled as she slipped a piece of toast to a waiting Baby.

"Thanks for looking after the girls while I was gone. I really appreciate it." Elise dug into the food Myrna set in front of her.

"Nonsense, you know I enjoy it."

"Yes, but lately I feel as if I should offer you combat pay. If it isn't Keri upset over Lisa daring to intrude on her two shelves in the medicine cabinet, Lisa is furious with Becky for entering her room without permission and Becky is angry at Keri for refusing to help her with her homework." She rubbed her forehead. She wasn't surprised that a headache was cropping up. After everything else that had happened over the past few days, a headache was a minor inconvenience. "There are days when I feel as if I were living in a war zone."

"Mama, Mama," Baby croaked, climbing up one of the chairs and eyeing Elise's food with a hungry gleam.

"No," she said firmly.

"Baby, you already had your breakfast," Myrna reminded the bird.

The macaw snapped around and glared at the woman. "Fud up."

Myrna rolled her eyes. "Who had the nerve to teach her that?"

Elise laughed. "She just came up with it one day. The best explanation I can come up with is she heard it from television, since I never said 'shut up' to anyone."

"It's not just that. It's the fact that she doesn't believe she's a *b...i...r...d.*" Even though Myrna spelled out the last word, Baby turned her head to glare suspiciously at her.

"See what I mean?"

"She'll be happier back at the clinic, where she has more people and animals to boss." Elise picked up her plate and carried it to the sink. She glanced at the large wall clock. "Where I should have been five minutes ago."

It took Elise another ten minutes before she could leave the house and walk down the driveway to the building just off the main road that held the Carpenter Avian and Exotic Animal Clinic. She looked over the two acres she'd bought five years ago, grateful that she was able to have her home and business on the same piece of property. While the area was far more rural than Pasadena had been, it held a peace she had sought five years ago and enjoyed now.

The house in the rear had been remodeled to suit the family and the house in the front turned into a clinic that did a booming business. Elise marveled that people were willing to drive sometimes an hour and a half to see her. While she knew avian and exotic animal veterinarians were not as plentiful as those dealing with felines and canines, she still couldn't believe her patient load kept increasing.

Because she knew where she was going, Baby hated what she considered the indignity of making the short walk to the clinic encased in a pet carrier. As a result, she threatened Frances, the watch goose, and Herman, Frances's mate, with extra vehemence. The family dogs—Bailey, a harlequin Great Dane, Duke, a tan-and-black German shepherd, and Kola, a malamute husky—greeted Elise with high-pitched barks quickly silenced when she threw them their favorite treats.

"Not nice," Baby informed Elise when she was first put into the carrier.

"I don't care if you don't think I'm nice. You know the rules. No creature with wings leaves this house without being in a carrier," Elise replied, releasing the latch. "Besides, I'm sure Donna has missed you these past few days."

"Hey there, boss." A young technician dressed in surgical greens lifted a hand in greeting as Elise opened the back door. "How was the conference?"

Elise walked into an enclosed aviary off the waiting area, where Baby, along with a few other birds, spent their days. She left Baby preening on top of a tall dome cage and headed for her office. "The usual. How about here?"

"No emergencies, although Mrs. Harper called again." Donna's hazel eyes glinted with laughter.

Elise cursed under her breath. "She's still in a snit?"

"More than ever. As far as she's concerned, her darling little Robin is a girl, not a boy, as you informed her after the surgical sexing."

Elise thought of the Rosy Breasted cockatoo who was more spoiled than Baby, hard as it was to believe. "I told her as long as she wanted to keep Robin as a pet and not put her out for breeding, there was no reason to put the bird through the stress of having it sexed," she muttered. "But, no, she insisted she wanted to know her little girl was really a little girl. You'd think the end of the world had come just because her little girl is a little boy. And a mean one, at that. That beak can nail a person with deadly accuracy."

"She's insisted you made a mistake, and she wants a second opinion."

"A *what?* That procedure is hard enough on a bird once, but for someone to demand it be done a second time..." She shook her head in frustration at the problems some of her clients offered her. "Did you give her some names?"

Donna nodded. "That's why she called. The other doctors all refused to perform the procedure a second time. She was told that if you said she was a male, she was a male. End of discussion."

"What's on the books for today?"

"Cheryl said you're going to love today. First up is a monitor lizard with a nicked tail. He'll be here in about ten minutes. And Althea is coming in. Sean said she has a slight temperature. He's afraid she might have eaten a bad mouse." Donna stared up at the ceiling, ticking the list off on her fingertips.

Elise tightened her lips to keep from laughing. "Eaten a bad mouse?" she choked.

Donna nodded, her own lips kept just as tight. "He wondered if snakes can get salmonella from bad mice. I told him I'd ask you."

"Thanks a lot," she muttered. "I could have settled for treating cats' fur balls and giving rabies and distemper shots to dogs, but, no, I wanted to treat exotics. To work in a field that's sparsely populated. What do I get from it? A woman screaming that I can't read the sex of her cockatoo correctly and a man worrying about his python eating a bad mouse. Don't you have anything good to tell me?''

"The electric bill was down fifteen dollars from last month.''

ELISE THREW HERSELF into the blessed routine of work as she treated a cockatiel who'd pulled a blood feather and needed his wound packed before he bled to death, and examined a little boy's rabbit who'd supposedly swallowed the child's nickel. She went from one examination room to another, pleased to be back where she felt most comfortable and where the hours passed most easily. By the time the day wound down, she felt tired but happy with herself.

"Long day," Donna commented from her slouched position against the hallway wall.

Elise nodded. "Anyone else out there?"

Donna shook her head. "So far, so good. Some man called for you when you were with a patient but wouldn't leave his name. He said he'd call back.''

Elise shrugged, her thoughts elsewhere. "Then let's lock up for the night. Is the answering machine on?''

"Cheryl turned it on before she left.'' Donna ran her fingers through black spiky hair. After she made sure all the instruments had been sterilized and put away, she grabbed a sweatshirt, which she pulled on over her surgical greens.

Elise chuckled. "You really don't mind leaving here looking like that?''

"Hey," Donna intoned dramatically, "we get animal blood, bird poop and other disgusting stuff all over us. Why not wear something easy to clean? I prefer these to jeans.'' Her dark eyes twinkled. "Besides, Gary says they're kinda sexy.''

For a brief moment, a dark-bearded man came into Elise's mind's eye. He probably consider them sexy, too, her brain told her. She ruthlessly pushed Detective Cornell from her thoughts, glad she'd never have to see him again.

As Elise walked back to the house with a grumbling Baby in her carrier, she felt a faint prickling of unease lodge between her shoulder blades. The sense was so strong, so thick, she had to forcibly resist the urge to turn around. If she didn't know better, she'd swear she was being watched, but she told herself it was nothing more than her imagination. Why would anyone be watching her? Still, the feeling refused to go away. In fact, it intensified. She tightened her grip on Baby's carrier and forced herself to keep her stride normal even though the impulse to run for the house and lock the door behind her was so strong she almost shook with it.

She didn't breathe a sigh of relief until she reached her front door. When she closed it behind her, she made sure to secure the dead bolt. Even it if was nothing more than an attack of nerves, she wasn't going to take any chances. While Frances and Herman were excellent watch geese and the dogs were semitrained, they weren't infallible. She even peeked out between the folds of the curtains, as if she might find the reason for her unease in the middle of the yard.

"Myrna left a chicken-noodle casserole in the oven," Keri informed her from her post on the couch, books spread out in front of her on the coffee table. The television set blared, making Elise wonder how her daughter got anything accomplished with the noise level so loud.

She walked over and turned down the volume. "Didn't I say no MTV until the homework was done?"

"It is done. I'm just getting ahead in a couple of my classes."

"I think I used that excuse when I was in school. Where's Lisa and Becky?"

"Lisa's working on her science project, and Becky's in her room." Keri marked the page and closed the book lying in her lap. "Someone called for you."

Elise remained still. She told herself to act normal, act as if nothing were wrong, as she opened the carrier and released Baby, who promptly waddled toward her cage and climbed inside. "Oh? Who?"

Keri shrugged. "He didn't say. He just said he'd call back. He's probably selling something, although he did ask for you by name."

Elise wanted to believe that but couldn't bring herself to agree with her daughter. Two calls for her in one day, one at the office and the other at her home, both times from a man refusing to leave his name. She didn't like it. She felt the lump in her throat grow.

"Why don't you set the table while I freshen up." She forced herself to speak normally. Nothing was wrong, her brain insisted. So why this feeling? Why calls for her with the caller refusing to leave his name? And why did she feel as if she were waiting for the other shoe to drop?

"It's Lisa's turn to set the table this week."

"Fine, then ask her to do so."

Elise quickly washed up and changed her clothes, then stopped to check the locks on all the bedroom windows on her way back to the living room. She tried to tell herself she was being paranoid, but it didn't work. She glanced out a window. "If you don't watch yourself, next thing you know you'll be looking under the bed for the bogeyman," she chided herself.

Elise ate little of her dinner and concentrated so hard on

a reassuring appearance of normalcy for the girls that she had a headache by the time she checked on her sleeping children before practically crawling to her own bedroom. No matter what, she couldn't shake the feeling that something *was* wrong. She felt uneasy that the man with no name hadn't called back. Unless, as Keri suggested, he was nothing more than a phone solicitor selling carpeting or performing a telephone survey on what brand of coffee she drank. She resisted the urge to turn on all the lights to banish even faint shadows in room corners and to turn on the floodlights outside to keep away unseen enemies. Instead, she assured herself that if trouble came to her door, she'd give trouble back in spades.

By the time she dropped into bed, she felt ready to stay there for several days. Sleep didn't come easy, but eventually her weary body overtook her worried mind and she sank into blissful oblivion.

"MOM! MOM!"

Her oldest daughter's frantic whisper slowly made its way through her sleep-fogged brain.

"What?" She reached out to turn on her lamp, but Keri's hand stayed her action.

"Don't turn it on," she whispered. "There's someone walking around outside."

Elise shot upward, her earlier fears back with a vengeance. "Are you sure?"

Keri nodded, then whispered again when she realized her mother couldn't see her. "Something woke me up, and when I looked toward my window, I saw a figure walk past." Her voice trembled. "Mom, I don't hear Frances and Herman or the dogs. What if something happened to them?"

Elise reached for the phone. When no dial tone greeted her, she cursed under her breath.

"Are Lisa and Becky still asleep?"

"Yes."

She silently blessed the Fates for giving her a daughter who didn't panic easily. "Keri, the phone's dead." She could feel her hand crushed in the young girl's grip. "I'm going to go to the gun cabinet and get out the rifle. I want you to wake Lisa and Becky, take them into your room and make sure they remain quiet. Lock the bedroom door, and don't let anyone in but me. If you hear anything, take your keys, go out your window and run for the clinic. Hopefully, that phone line hasn't been cut, also. Lock that door behind you and call the sheriff's office. Tell them what's going on and remain there until help comes."

"I'm not going to leave you," Keri insisted.

"Yes, you are," Elise said firmly. "I need you to look after the girls for me. Do this for me, Keri. I'm counting on you."

In the dim light she could see the girl's downcast head.

"All right." The words were barely audible.

Elise gave her a quick hug and jumped out of bed. "All right, go now."

Elise took several deep breaths before she made her way down the hall. She had just reached the living room when she heard Keri hushing Lisa and Becky's frightened whispers. Elise reached the locked wooden cabinet, quickly unlocked the door and pulled out a rifle, which she easily loaded in the dark. She didn't have any doubts about her ability. She had practiced many times with her eyes closed. She wasn't about to allow anything as mundane as darkness to hamper her.

When something thumped against her front door, she jumped, then quickly regained her senses. Someone had climbed the fence surrounding the property, silenced the geese and dogs and cut her telephone lines. She wasn't going to allow that person to get away with it.

Then, just as suddenly, an explosion of light flared in the front yard, and she heard the roar of a motorcycle.

Deafening herself to her daughters' screams, Elise kept the rifle close to her body as she cautiously eased the front door open. What she found on the doormat turned her stomach.

"Mom?" Keri ventured from nearby.

"Get back, Keri," she ordered hoarsely, scanning the yard but seeing nothing other than the shadowed figures of the geese and the dogs lying in the middle of the yard.

"But, Mom..."

"Get back!"

Her daughter's gasp sent her spinning around.

"Keri, go back to your sisters."

"What is it?" the girl cried out from behind the protective mask of her hands over her mouth.

"A squirrel. I'll take care of it."

"But Frances and Herman? The dogs? Are they...?"

"I don't know yet. Go back to Lisa and Becky. I'll check on Frances and Herman."

"What if someone's still out there?"

"No, whoever it was is gone now," Elise could say with conviction. The unease she'd felt all evening had dissipated. As she stepped over the slaughtered rodent, she noticed a sheet of paper underneath. Two words were written—in red. She dreaded to think what had been used for ink. And a blurred thumbprint was the signature. A name wasn't necessary. She stared at the words, seeing the threat.

I'm back.

Chapter Four

"Are you sure this note was written by Carl Dietrich, Dr. Carpenter?" the deputy asked as he continued jotting down his report.

She silently counted to ten. How many times would she be asked the same ridiculous questions!

"If you sent that print to the Pasadena police department, I'm sure they could verify it," she replied. Why weren't they doing more than just looking around the grounds? The formerly locked gate now lay in the road, two groggy geese were recovering from drugged "treats," and three dogs had been felled by tranquilizer darts. Fear and anger warred within her. "Talk to Detectives Dean Cornell and Frank McConnell in Pasadena. They can tell you all you want to know about the situation."

The deputy didn't look up from his writing. "Do you feel you might be in any danger, Doctor?"

"My phone lines were cut, my animals drugged, this disgusting 'message' was left on my doorstep and my children were terrorized. Oh, no, I don't feel threatened. Why on earth would I?" Sarcasm dripped from every word. "The man who killed my husband and unborn child is running around loose after leisurely walking out of the county jail where he was being held for armed bank robbery. He also knows I'd like nothing better than to see him strung up by his..." She paused to take a calming breath, reading the expression in the deputy's eyes. "Don't you dare think I'm hysterical, Deputy. That's one luxury I never allow myself. Now, I do intend to do everything possible to protect my daughters, with or without your assistance." The expression on her face told him loud and clear what she thought of his assistance.

"Dr. Carpenter, don't try anything foolish," he warned.

"Then get the bastard who's terrorizing me!"

"It could have been a bunch of kids. Some of the wilder gangs have been known to pull stunts like this."

"You talk to Detectives Cornell and McConnell. I don't think they'll agree with you." She wondered what the two men would think if they could hear her basically begging for their help. "And if you won't contact then, I will."

"They have no jurisdiction in Riverside County."

"I don't give a damn if they're from Mars," she said through gritted teeth. "Don't mess with me, Deputy. Just do what I suggest or I'll talk to someone who will."

The man's features turned to stone. He clearly didn't like being told what to do by this or any woman. "Lady, I'm only trying to do my job."

"Then make sure you do it right."

By the time the deputy sheriff and crime lab team left the property, it was dawn, and Elise felt as if she'd been up for days. She fixed a pot of hot chocolate and sat the girls at the kitchen table.

"We have some new rules," she began without preamble. "From now on, you will be driven to school by either Myrna or myself. You are not to go to a friend's house after school without one of us taking you there and picking you up, and you are not to answer the phone here at the house. Let the answering machine pick up the calls. Don't go off anywhere, even with a friend. I know you won't like these restrictions, but for the time being, they're necessary.''

Becky climbed into Elise's lap and wrapped her arms around her. ''Is Frances and Herman dead, Mommy?''

She hugged her youngest. ''No, darling, they're just sleeping. They'll be fine in a few hours. And the dogs will be waking up soon, too.''

''I wish you'd shot the creep who did it,'' Lisa said with bloodthirsty glee.

Keri looked at her mother with a wisdom beyond her years. ''What else are we going to do?''

Elise drew in a deep breath. ''We're going to watch out for ourselves, because the way the police are treating the situation, I doubt they're going to be much help. I'll look into having a security system installed in the house. I really should have done so a long time ago.'' Her face settled into grim lines. ''And if that creature dares to step foot on this property again, I will shoot him down like the madman he is.''

''HEY, CORNELL, Captain Anderson wants to see you,'' one of the men shouted. ''He's about to have a coronary, so I suggest you don't waste any time.''

Dean groaned. ''Oh, man! I just got in. Does he have to ruin my day first thing?'' He threw some papers onto his desk.

''Better you than me.''

''Yeah, yeah.'' He looked around. ''Mac in yet?''

''No, his wife had a doctor's appointment. With her being

so close to her due date, he wanted to take her. Besides, Anderson asked for you."

Dean sighed. "I should have read my horoscope this morning. It probably would have told me to stay in bed." He headed for the frosted glass door and knocked.

"Come in, Cornell." Captain Anderson's usual sour expression appeared to have soured even more overnight.

"You wanted to see me, sir?"

"I talked to a Detective Lieutenant Santee over at the Riverside County Sheriff's station in Lake Elsinore earlier today. It appears Dr. Elise Carpenter told them to call either you or McConnell. Since you two weren't in, I took the call."

Dean seethed inside. How many other calls had Anderson intercepted in the past just to make him or Mac look incompetent? He wouldn't put it past the man.

"Considering everything, I'm surprised Dr. Carpenter would suggest we be contacted."

"I doubt she would have if it hadn't been for an attack on her home last night." Captain Anderson shook his head. "The sheriff's office feels it was just some kids playing one of their sick jokes, and I tend to agree."

"What happened?"

He looked down at the paper in front of him. "Someone cut her phone lines, drugged her watchdogs and left a slaughtered squirrel on her front porch. Probably kids high on drugs doing their thing. There was also a note left there, written in the squirrel's blood, saying 'I'm back.' A bloody thumbprint on the paper turned out to be smeared too much to get a match."

The back of Dean's neck tingled madly. "Has this kind of thing ever happened in her neighborhood before?" Dean questioned tautly.

"I didn't ask, and Santee didn't say."

Dean leaned forward, planting his hands on the desk. "Dietrich made some pretty nasty threats against the lady, and from what we've seen of his record, this could be something he'd pull just to give her a good scare before moving in for the kill."

"If Dietrich had any brains, he'd be in Mexico by now."

"If you and this Santee feel it has nothing to do Dietrich, why are you bothering to tell me about it?"

The older man looked at him as if he were a bothersome insect. "Because I told Santee I would pass it on to you, and I don't want you saying you don't receive your messages." Hostility radiated outward.

"I'd like to go down there and talk to Dr. Carpenter."

"It's out of our jurisdiction."

"It could have something to do with our case," he argued. "What's wrong with going down there to check things out?"

"Waste of time. If you have any questions, talk to Santee on the phone. There's no need to talk to the woman."

Dean bit back the hot words that threatened to erupt. The last thing he needed right now was to be bumped down to pounding a beat. "Fine, I'll do that."

He wasted no time in putting through the call, grateful he could talk to the man immediately. Detective Santee filled him in with excerpts from the deputy's report and a later telephone call from Dr. Carpenter.

"The lady was very insistent on our contacting you, even though we still feel the work was nothing more than a bunch of kids out to stir up some havoc," he explained. "I checked into this Carl Dietrich, and I can see why she's worried, but it still doesn't check out."

"This creep is capable of anything," Dean replied. "Especially from the sounds of the note left with the squirrel and the bloody thumbprint. Too bad it was too smeared to help out. While he was an unwilling resident in our local jail, he made some pretty nasty threats against the doctor, so I believe he'd do it. What kind of protection are you giving her?''

"Detective, what happened isn't serious enough to offer her anything more than a few more drive-bys during the night. And she's lucky to get that. We just don't have the manpower.''

Dean ground his teeth in frustration. ''That's not enough.''

''If Dr. Carpenter wants anything more in the way of protection, she'll have to arrange for it herself.''

''Have you met the lady?''

''No, but my deputy said she met him at the door with a nasty-looking shotgun that she looked prepared to use if necessary.''

A pair of hot-tempered turquoise eyes seared Dean's memory. He thought quickly as he scanned the calendar. ''If it was Dietrich out there that night, and I seriously think it was, would you be amenable to our sending someone down to kinda look after her? If we work together on this, we might be able to catch Dietrich and keep him put away.''

''I don't see much problem on my end, but between you and me, I don't think your captain will go for it.''

Dean grinned. ''Are you kidding? If I volunteer for this special duty, he'll run home and pack my bags for me!''

''ARE YOU SURE about this?'' Mac slumped in a chair, watching Dean sort through a jumble of clothing.

''Sure, why not?'' He held up a wrinkled chambray shirt. ''Does this look clean to you?''

Mac shook his head. "Ol' buddy, you've turned into a slob in your old age."

"My cleaning lady quit."

"What number was she?"

"I lost count after thirty-six. Stacy promised to find someone for me, but she said I'm too well-known." He stuffed some T-shirts into a duffel bag.

Mac brushed the top of his Coke can against his mustache. "Does the doc know you're going out there to protect her from whatever goes bump in the night?"

"Nope, I figured it would be better if I just show up on her doorstep. That way she can't do anything about it."

"She can throw you out on your ass."

Dean hesitated. "Not after I explain I'm there to catch Carl Dietrich for her."

"So far the police haven't done too good a job of keeping the guy on ice," he drawled. "I don't think the lady will exactly welcome you with open arms."

Dean pushed his duffel bag off the chair and dropped down into the seat. "I've got a feeling about this, Mac," he said quietly. "A bad feeling. Dietrich is out there with the idea of scaring the hell out of the lady until he's got her so unhinged it will be a snap to finish the job. He's playing with her now, but it won't be long before he makes his final move. I plan to be there when he does."

"And leave me without a partner. With my luck, Anderson will stick me with Carlton." Mac grimaced.

Dean shook his head. "You're taking your vacation time soon so you'll be home when Stacy's baby comes, and with the way Anderson feels about us, it's better if I'm not around. Although I must admit, driving him crazy always makes my day." He grinned, his teeth flashing white between his beard.

"You should have seen his face when I gave him my suggestion. He still doesn't believe it's Dietrich down there, but he's seen too many of our hunches come through, and he doesn't want me to be right and have it come out that he ignored my suggestions. Besides, I think he was happy to know we'd both be out of his thinning hair for a while." He gathered up some equipment while Mac grabbed his duffel bag. "I'm just sorry it took a week for me to catch up on my work before I could leave."

Mac helped him carry his things out to his truck. "Still, you know my number, and I'm always available for backup." He tossed the duffel bag into the back.

Dean nodded. "Yeah, I know. But for now, you just concentrate on keeping Stacy happy," he said quietly, sticking out his hand. "And call me the minute my godchild enters the world."

The two men shook hands, then embraced, as if both friends sensed that life was changing for all of them.

"MOM, YOU HAVEN'T SIGNED the permission slip yet!" Lisa waved the sheet of paper in front of Elise's nose. "If I don't take it in tomorrow, I won't be able to go to the zoo."

Elise hesitated. While things had been quiet the past few days, she still felt uneasy every time she or one of the girls left the house. "Lisa, I don't know."

"But everyone else is going!" she wailed. "You can't not sign it."

She pressed her fingers against her forehead in hopes of stopping the headache that had been lurking there all day. "Lisa, I am the mother here. I can do anything I darn well please."

"It's been over a week, and nothing more has happened.

Plus, I'll be with my class and two others. I won't go off by myself, I promise,'' she whined, clasping her hands in front of her. ''Please, Mom.''

''Mom, if you don't let her go, she'll just make our lives miserable,'' Keri told her. ''You know she will.''

''If she tries, *I'll* be the one to make *her* life miserable,'' Elise stated emphatically, glaring at her middle daughter. ''All right, I'll sign, but you remember what you've promised. No wandering off by yourself.'' She scribbled her name and the date at the bottom of the slip before she could change her mind. As if sensing her mother's thoughts, Lisa swiftly buried the paper in her book bag.

Elise knew she couldn't wrap her daughters in cotton for the rest of their lives even if she wanted to. ''I realize you think I'm being unduly paranoid, but for now I feel more comfortable taking precautions,'' she said quietly.

''The sheriff seems to think we're okay,'' Keri said, more to reassure herself than to reassure her mother.

''The sheriff's deputy also thought I was nothing more than a hysterical woman.'' Her head snapped up when she heard the sound of a truck engine getting closer to the house and the dogs' excited barking. ''Don't tell me Cheryl forgot to lock the gate when she left,'' she muttered, running for the gun cabinet.

''Mom, it might not be anything.'' Keri's eyes were large.

''Yes, and then again, it might be.'' She pulled the rifle out. She halted in the midst of loading it when she heard a familiar voice cursing Frances and Herman's frenzied honks.

''Hey! Damn! Ow, cut that out! Hey, Doc, come here and rescue me!''

She lowered the rifle. ''After everything else that's happened, why am I not surprised?'' She walked over to the door and pulled it open. The floodlights illuminating the front yard brought Dean Cornell into sharp relief. She noticed he had one hand on his rear, with an agitated Frances standing behind him. "Detective Cornell, fancy meeting you here." A tiny part of her wanted to laugh out loud at the picture before her. Another part wanted to say how happy she was to see him. Still another part wanted to escort him off the property. Right about now, she wasn't sure what part to listen to.

"Call off the goose, please," he growled. "Between that beaked monster going for my butt and the dogs heading for my b...crotch, I could end up as a chewed-up soprano here."

"They don't appreciate uninvited visitors."

Dean eyed her rifle. He wasn't sure if it was loaded and didn't want to chance finding out the hard way. "Detective Santee didn't call you about me?"

"Was he supposed to?"

"The coward," he muttered. "I'm here to offer you police protection."

"Police protection. How interesting." She raised an eyebrow. "You're out of your jurisdiction, Detective. Pasadena is seventy miles away from here."

"Is he the guy from the bank who fainted when he got shot?" Lisa whispered, peering around Elise's back. "Is he really a cop, Mom?"

Keri sniffed with disdain. "He looks more like someone off the streets." She walked away, clearly uninterested.

"Sometimes it helps to blend in." Dean looked at Elise. "Look, Doc, it's simple. You had a nasty incident. You were smart enough to tell the authorities here to call us about that note you received. While they might not have believed you,

Mac and I did. And we figure Dietrich is going to strike again. When he does, I want to be here.''

''I can't believe your captain allowed you to come down here, even if the sheriff's department allowed you to cross lines.'' She didn't budge from her post in the doorway. She was having enough trouble dealing with the fact that the first man in years to catch her attention was with the police force. Even as scruffy as Dean Cornell looked, with a goose hovering behind him and a German shepherd guarding him from the front, he still looked good enough to pounce on. No wonder people told her she needed to get out more!

''Are you kidding? He was ecstatic to see me go. Mac is taking some vacation time to be with his wife before their baby is born, so he didn't mind my being gone, too. Can't say I mind being here.'' His dark eyes swept over her from head to toe, the midnight gleam telling her he didn't mind what he saw one bit.

Elise still had trouble taking it all in. ''So why didn't Detective Santee contact me about this?''

''Probably because he's a chicken at heart. Considering your previous dealings, he wouldn't have any trouble figuring out what your response would be.''

''And he's right, you can just climb back into that rattletrap you call a truck and head on home, because I'm more than capable of protecting my children,'' she informed him, aware she was grasping at thin air. No one knew how much that night had shaken her up, how difficult it had been for her to sleep because she feared the next time there would be more than a note written in animal blood. It didn't take an expert to tell her Carl Dietrich wasn't sane and that she might not be able to protect the girls next time around. Still, a stubborn part of her refused to admit it to this cocky guy standing before her.

In the wink of an eye, Dean was on the porch and had snatched Elise's rifle out of her hands and backed her against the doorjamb, with the gun muzzle nestled neatly against her throat. He ignored the frightened cries behind him and the goose honking its agitation. Finally he lowered the gun and stepped back.

"Yeah, you're protecting them real good. Just like you protected yourself just now." His eyes bored into hers. Compassion warred with realism in the dark depths. "Next time it might not be me taking away that gun, and the next person just might decide to use it instead of teaching you a lesson."

Elise's face could have been carved from white marble. "You've made your point, Detective." She refused to show him how his graphic lesson had unsettled her. "I'm just a helpless mother of three children who can be wrestled to the ground by anyone bigger."

"Kick him where it counts, Mom!" Lisa shouted.

Elise didn't turn her head. "Lisa, if I hear one more word from you, I will dig out that permission slip and burn it. All of you, back inside."

"Mom, what if he's right?" Keri spoke up. "We don't want you hurt. And he looks as if he can handle anything that comes along."

Dean didn't look away from Keri. "Face it, Doc, you've got me as a houseguest whether you want me or not."

She nearly ground her teeth in frustration. "For how long?"

"For however long it takes."

For a split second, Elise felt as if there were two meanings to his words...and she wasn't sure she was ready for the second one. Then she pulled herself together with the only defense remaining to her: sarcasm. "Where *do* you buy your clothes, Detective Cornell? At one of those trendy little boutiques called Bikers R Us?"

He glanced down at the death's head outlined in glittering paint against the black fabric. "You really have a problem with my wardrobe, don't you? I'll have you know my mother bought this for me."

Elise didn't dare look at the jeans that fit him so tightly she wondered how he could even breath. She didn't want to look at him at all. He brought back feelings she preferred to keep repressed. She did some rapid thinking. The guest room wasn't exactly quiet during this time of year, thanks to Florence's snoring. In fact, her entire household had never been known for its peace and quiet. As far as she knew, this man was the consummate bachelor. Twenty-four hours in a household of squabbling girls and snoring turtles and loudmouthed macaws should be more than enough to do the trick. Yes, she'd just sit back and see what kind of man he was.

"Since I can't get rid of you, I suppose I'll have to show you to the guest room," she said finally.

Dean looked wary at her too-easy capitulation. "Yeah?"

She gestured inside. "Come on."

He hopped off the porch and ran to the truck, pulling his bags out of the back.

"Girls, it's past your bedtime," Elise announced once she stepped inside.

Keri gaped at her. "Now?"

"Now."

Sensing this was no time to argue, they hurried to their rooms.

Elise turned to Dean, who had paused on the threshold

and was warily gazing around as if expecting to be attacked again. "I'll show you to your room." She took the rifle and replaced it in the cabinet, locking the door and palming the key.

He watched her with a nod of approval. "The lock on your front gate was a snap to pick. You need something a lot more heavy-duty."

She found her jaw tightening again and concentrated on relaxing it. "It's nice to know our police officers have the same skills as the crooks they're paid to catch."

Dean grabbed her arm and spun her around. "Hey, that's how we stay alive,' he tautly informed her. His grip on her arm tightened as the light scent of her perfume reached his nostrils. He took a moment to compose himself. "Look, Doc, you've got some cute kids, and I don't want to see them crying because I have to tell them they don't have a mother anymore."

Elise could feel his fingers burning into her skin. Why did he have to be so damned attractive? she silently railed at herself. "Let go of me," she said, her lips barely moving.

He released her, one finger at a time. "I've had a long drive on top of a long day. I'd like to get some sleep," he said quietly.

She inclined her head and led him down the hallway. She opened the door and flipped the light switch to turn on the bedside lamp.

Dean entered the room and looked around, pausing once to check the windows. "Good locks, but they could be better" was all he said. He stopped in the middle of the room, a frown creasing his brow. "Am I overtired, or do I hear someone snoring?"

She resisted the urge to smile with satisfaction. "Under the bed."

Dean bent down and flipped up the covers. "What the hell?" His head snapped back up. "There's a turtle under here!"

"To be precise, Florence is a tortoise, and she's just gone into hibernation," she explained coolly.

"How am I supposed to sleep in here with this?" His eyes narrowed. "Oh, I see. I'm *not* supposed to. It's a good thing I can sleep through anything when I'm tired enough, because this critter sounds like a freight train." He dropped his duffel bag onto the bedspread.

"The bathroom is next door," Elise went on in her touch-me-not voice. "All I ask is you stay out of the way between seven and eight-thirty when the girls are getting ready for school."

"What about you?"

"I have my own bathroom." She realized her mistake the moment she said it.

Devilment danced in his eyes. "Perhaps I should share yours, so the girls and I won't have to worry about running into each other."

"I don't think so." Behind her back her fingers gripped the doorknob with frantic desperation. "And another thing, Detective. I have three girls who aren't used to men being around the house at all hours. I would appreciate your watching your language and manners. I've tried to teach them not all men are Neanderthals. Please don't show them differently." She turned to leave.

Dean dropped down onto the bed. "I can live with that. Oh, Doc?"

She turned her head, her eyes snapping the question before she voiced it. "What?"

"Did anyone ever tell you you smell so sexy it wouldn't be difficult to hustle you off to a dark corner for some heavy-duty necking? And that those jeans of yours show off a great butt? I'm talking world-class here."

Elise's fingers tightened on the doorknob. She looked furious, ready to slam the door if it hadn't been for her daughter.

Dean grinned, fully aware of the waves of fury rolling in his direction. "There, I've gotten it all out of my system." He held up his hands. "Good night."

"Good night," she spat.

"Oh, and, Doc, if you hear anything suspicious, feel free to wake me up. After all, that's what I'm here for." His words followed her out into the hallway.

A seething Elise followed her usual routine of checking all the doors and windows before heading for her bedroom. She checked the impulse to lock her door. She never knew if one of the girls might wake up and need her. Right after her father's death, Becky had suffered serious nightmares, and for the past week they had begun to recur. When that happened, she would come into her mother's bedroom and climb into bed with her. Plus, Elise felt Dean's words were more teasing than serious.

"At least I hope so," she murmured, standing in the bathroom and turning on the shower.

Dean cocked his head when he heard a shower running. For a moment, he visualized the very proper Elise A. Carpenter standing naked under running water. The picture sent interesting impulses to his libido.

He whistled between his teeth. "Damn, and here I told Mac this would be a breeze."

With the idea of Elise in the shower still running through his mind, he took the time to check out the rest of the house. He noted the new locks on the doors and windows, the precise location of the gun cabinet, even the book bags lying on the coffee table waiting for their owners to snatch them up in the morning and dash off to school. The house wasn't fancy but comfortable, the furniture well suited for a household with children. The kind of place a man could put his feet up and not be yelled at for doing so. At the same time, he knew he wouldn't find a speck of dust anywhere.

"Fud up," a raspy voice grumbled from one corner.

Dean spun around, crouched in a defensive position. Then the shadowy outline of a tall dome cage caught his attention. He walked over and carefully lifted one corner of the covers. He could swear the macaw he faced was glaring at him.

"Fud up," the macaw informed him, snapping her beak at him.

He dropped the cover. "You got it, bird."

He stepped back a pace as the macaw screeched, then called him a name he didn't think a bird in this all-female family would know. Deciding retreat would be a good idea, he returned to the room to gather up his toothbrush and toothpaste, more than ready for bed.

In no time he was lying in one of the most uncomfortable beds he'd ever known. Dean preferred extra-firm mattresses, and this one was more like a featherbed.

"She did this on purpose," he muttered, punching his pillow and turning onto his side. His eyes had started to drift shut when a light but steady droning sound vibrated into his head. He uttered a pungent curse and rolled over onto his other side.

"Geese that think a person's rear is fair game, dogs that go for the other side, birds that insult you and a tortoise that sounds like a jet engine." He punched the pillow even harder. "The woman is a sadist."

"YOU STAY OUT of my stuff!"

"You said I could use it!"

"Did not!"

"Did so!"

"Give it back before I punch you good!"

"Will not, it's mine!"

"Becky, give it back to me right now or else!"

"Mom, they're at it again!"

Dean's eyes flew open and he stalked into the hallway to find out who was waging war just outside his room.

"What the hell is going on here?" he roared, not in the best of moods after having only two hours of what he might call decent sleep.

Lisa and Becky turned their heads and lifted them at the dark-visaged image of wrath standing over them.

"Wow," Lisa breathed, her mouth dropped open.

"Mom said you have to—" Keri skidded to a stop, her own mouth dropping open in shock. Elise was right on her heels. Luckily she was able to maintain her composure. Which wasn't easy. Dean Cornell stood there wearing nothing more than a scanty pair of bright red briefs that barely covered the essentials.

"Mom, she took my glue!" Lisa wailed.

"Kitchen," she said tersely.

"Mom!"

She stared them down. "Both of you. Now."

Grumbling, the girls headed toward the front of the house.

"Detective Cornell, just last night I explained about your being careful in this house." Elise concentrated on looking only at his face—a challenging task, considering how good the rest of him looked...and how much of it was bare. "That means I not only want you to watch your language, but please don't leave your room until you're properly dressed."

He crossed his arms over his chest and leaned against the doorjamb, looking all too relaxed. "I am properly dressed."

Before she could help it, her eyes flickered downward and lingered a scant second longer than they should have. "I wouldn't call that properly dressed."

His grin did strange things to her insides. "It is when I normally sleep in the raw. I wore the underwear as a concession to this all-female household."

Elise could feel her face growing hot. "Breakfast is in ten minutes. Don't be late." She turned on her heel and walked away, her back so stiff a steel rod couldn't have competed.

"I doubt this is anything they haven't seen before," he called after her. "Hell, even the Disney Channel shows men in their underwear."

Elise was prepared to commit homicide.

"Wow, he looks better than some of those guys on TV," she could hear Lisa enthusing in the kitchen. "I thought most cops had beer bellies, but he sure doesn't."

"He's crude," Keri sniffed, lifting her juice glass to her lips.

"Enough," Elise ordered, walking into the room. "Detective Cornell is here to do a job." She poured herself a cup of coffee. Right about now she was in need of a shot of caffeine. The sight of the obviously virile Detective Cornell felt embedded in her brain.

"It's amazing how one pair of red briefs can leave such a lasting impression on some people's minds," Myrna said under her breath, then looked the essence of innocence when Elise glared at her. It was a well-known fact that the older woman, like Kristen, felt it was time for Elise to add a man to her life.

"Hopefully, he won't be here long enough for us to find out," she said stiffly, downing the hot coffee without a whimper and pouring herself another cup. "The last thing we need is an unwanted guest who acts like the typical heavy-handed cop."

Dean appeared five minutes later, looking incredibly sexy in rumpled jeans and a dark red sweat shirt with the sleeves hacked off. For a split second Elise wondered what color his underwear was this time.

"I'm Myrna, the housekeeper," the woman standing at the stove introduced herself. Tall, thin, with salt-and-pepper hair curled around her face, she looked like the kind of grandmother who baked cookies every weekend. Dean instantly liked her forthright manner. "Hope your appetite is better than most of these kids with their eternal diets."

He grinned. "I eat anything that's not moving."

"Then we'll get along fine."

Elise rolled her eyes, then glanced at her watch. "Hurry up, girls." She turned a cool gaze on Dean. "Either Myrna or I drive the girls to school."

"I'll do it from now on." He gulped the cup of coffee Myrna handed him.

"We haven't had any problems so far."

"No, but if you are the target, you might feel better if you aren't with them if anything happens,'' he explained, grabbing a piece of bacon and chomping on it. One look at Elise's stiff features told him she didn't appreciate his obvious logic. Nor that she would have to admit he was right.

Keri looked for one adult to the other. She didn't like the way this conversation was going.

''Mom, he drives a truck that should have been junked fifty years ago. I can't be seen in that thing.''

Elise sighed. She didn't bother arguing with him, because she knew she'd lose. ''Go with him.''

''All *right!*'' Lisa shouted, jumping up.

Becky was more cautious. ''He's not going to yell at us again, is he?''

Dean dropped a hand on top of her head. ''No, princess, and I'm sorry I yelled this morning. After listening to a tortoise snore all night, I wasn't ready for the Civil War to be fought outside my bedroom door. I promise it won't happen again.''

She flashed him a smile that resembled her mother's. ''Okay.''

Keri stood up and walked into the other room for her books. ''If any of my friends see me in that—that piece of junk, I'll just die.''

''She's at that age when life itself is traumatic,'' Elise explained.

''I'll fix you breakfast when you get back,'' Myrna offered.

He grinned. ''I won't turn it down.''

Dean soon discovered chauffeuring three girls was an experience in itself.

''This is so embarrassing,'' Keri grumbled, huddling near the door since she would be dropped off first. ''If you don't mind, I'd prefer you leave me at the corner." *Where no one can see me getting out of this* was left unspoken.

"I do mind." He was unperturbed. "Your safety is my business, sweetheart."

She turned her head and glared at him. "I am not your sweetheart."

Dean grinned. "I see you take after your mother."

"Do you have your gun with you?" Lisa asked. "If someone stopped us, would you shoot it? Have you killed anyone?"

"You've got a bloodthirsty imagination," he chuckled.

She looked him up and down. "You sure don't look like the cops on TV."

"That's because he's a real one, Lisa," Keri informed her with her bored, lady-of-the manor tone, as Dean privately dubbed it.

The one who captivated him the most was little Becky, with her big eyes, more aquamarine than turquoise, and her short strawberry-blond curls. Right now, she looked up at him as if he were a type of being she'd never encountered before.

"And what about you, Becky?" he asked. "What question do you have to ask me?"

The tip of her tongue appeared for a moment as she thought long and hard. "How come your underwear has lumps in it?"

Dean was grateful to be at a stop light, because he found himself almost choking. When he looked at the innocent face of the little one who'd voiced the provocative question, he found himself the subject of Lisa's curious gaze and Keri's smirk that said *Get yourself out of this one!* Yep, she was like her mother, all right. He fell back on that time-honored reply all men give when asked dangerous questions by small girls.

"Ask your mother."

Chapter Five

"I see you survived driving the girls to school." Myrna set a filled plate in front of him.

Dean hungrily eyed the food and dug in immediately. "Keri crept out of the truck, afraid someone might see her." He picked up a warm blueberry muffin and buttered it liberally. "Lisa ran out of the truck shouting at the top of her lungs that she knows a real cop, and Becky still isn't sure of me."

"Poor little thing," Myrna clucked as she sat down across from him with a cup of coffee in her hand. "She's not used to having men around here."

Meaning the lady doesn't have overnight guests, he decided. He liked that idea.

"I understand Dr. Carpenter's clinic is the front house on the property."

Myrna nodded. "Elise was lucky enough to find a house where she could work close by. She concentrated on settling the girls in first before she opened her clinic."

"How long have you been with her?"

"Four years and ten months." She studied him closely as

he mopped up egg with a bit of his muffin. "Ready for seconds? Are all your appetites this hearty?"

Dean couldn't remember the last time he'd blushed, if ever, but this woman appeared to have the capacity to bring that trait out in him. "I tend to burn a lot of calories in my business," he muttered, ducking his head. "It depends on who you talk to about the others."

Myrna laughed loudly and slapped his arm as she got up. "Honey, I'm just happy to see someone enjoy his food. I love cooking, and I love to watch people eat the results." Within moments, Dean had two more muffins in front of him and four more strips of bacon. "Now, you continue with your interrogation. This is fun." Her hazel eyes sparkled.

Dean chuckled. "Nothing throws you, does it?"

"Not much."

He sobered. "She could be in a lot of trouble, Myrna. This guy is not working with a sane mind, and he's targeted the doc as his next victim."

She nodded. "What can I do to help?"

"Give me the information she's going to be too hardheaded to give me," he urged. "That's the only way I can protect her and the girls."

Myrna smiled. "The girls are just as pigheaded as their mama."

"Yeah, I already found that out." He silently wondered what Elise was going to think of him if Becky remembered to ask her about his lumpy underwear. Not accustomed to dealing with members of the opposite sex under the age of consent, he had been thrown for a loop by Becky's innocent question.

"Keri's a good girl—she's just at that age where everything is a major production and appearances are all—

important. And Lisa's coming to the age when she's going to have to decide whether she wants to continue being a tomboy or take that next step to being a girl. And Becky, well, she's a little doll.'' She beamed, for all the world like a proud grandmother. ''She can sit there obstinate like her mama and sisters, then give you this glowing smile that makes you forget why you're angry at her.''

''And the doc?'' he asked casually. But his inflection didn't get past the keen-minded housekeeper. ''What about her?''

''Elise is stubborn, feels the need to do everything herself and not have to depend on others. She works entirely too hard, but she feels she's doing it for the girls. And she doesn't feel too guilty since her clinic is on the property and they have access to her any time they need her. Considering her husband's violent death, they've all managed very well.'' She released a soft sigh. ''Until now. Having to be reminded that that horrible man is in the area waiting to—'' She shook her head. ''It isn't fair.''

Dean popped the last bit of muffin into his mouth. ''That's why I'm here.''

A smile touched her lips. '''Pears to me you're here more to shake up the family then to protect them.''

''Yeah, well, in my line of duty, I'm not used to having to watch my language because of three impressionable girls,'' he said ruefully.

''They'll keep you on your toes, all right.'' She chuckled, standing up and snagging his plate to carry it to the sink. ''What will you do today? Other than make yourself a nuisance under my feet?''

Taking the more than subtle hint, he likewise stood up and stretched his arms above his head. ''Look over the clinic, talk to the staff and see if they've noticed anything out of the ordinary.''

"Elise won't like that. She considers the clinic her kingdom, and none dare try anything she doesn't like. And it's already obvious she doesn't appreciate your being here.''

"She doesn't have to appreciate my being here. She only has to understand it's for a good reason. Besides, I can be just as stubborn as she is.''

Myrna turned around to lean back against the counter, her arms crossed over her chest. "I have an idea things are going to turn pretty interesting around here. I'm glad I'll be around to watch the fireworks.''

Dean recalled his first impression of Elise: instant attraction, then amusement at her imperious manner, and now, well, now he wasn't too sure what he thought about her. Except that she was still a lovely woman, even if she did tend to treat him with queenly disdain.

"She doesn't want you here, and she'll fight you every step of the way.'' Myrna didn't mean it unkindly as she easily read his thoughts. "But she does need you here, and somewhere inside her, that bothers her a lot.''

Dean nodded in agreement. "I've been treated worse. I have to admit it will be a challenge to prove to her just how necessary I am. Not to mention that I'm an all-around nice guy.''

"Cheryl's the receptionist, and Donna's the head AHT down there—animal health technician, to the layman,'' she clarified.

"Gotcha.'' He paused at the back door. "Uh, would you be able to keep that homicidal goose away from me?''

"I thought cops weren't afraid of anything.''

"We're not, but no one I've known has come up against a butt-biting goose, either."

Myrna followed him onto the back steps, holding a bowl of grain in her arms. "When she and Herman head for the bowl, you head for the clinic. Frances, Herman, breakfast!" she called out.

To Dean's surprise, the two geese ran toward the steps, their wings outstretched, honking merrily at the sight of food. One goose eyed him suspiciously, and he quickly backed up against the post, much to the housekeeper's amusement.

"Go on," she urged. "You're safe for the moment."

He quickly made his escape. While he walked across the lawn and down the driveway to the front building, he scanned the surroundings. Houses were sparse in this area, and the mountains looked closer than he knew they really were. His senses told him there was nothing to worry about, but he also knew that could be temporary. He made a mental note to call Detective Santee and make an appointment to stop by the sheriff's station that afternoon. And to give Mac a call to see if he'd learned anything new. Even though he'd taken time off until Stacy had the baby, Mac had promised to continue tracking down any promising leads.

When Dean pushed open the heavy glass outer door to the clinic, he felt as if he had stepped into another world, one with an incredible noise level. Several people sat in the chairs ringing the waiting room, some holding cages in their laps. One woman was reading a magazine while a large tortoise rested on a skateboard in front of her. A boy in his late teens sat in a corner holding a narrow leash with a large iguana on the other end. One end of the waiting area boasted a glassed enclosure with several cages that barely contained several screaming tropical birds. He recognized the blue-and-gold macaw who'd told him off the night before.

"May I help you, sir?" A spritely woman stood at a waist-high counter, her eyes questioning since he'd walked in without an animal.

He quickly skirted the clients and their "pets," aware he was under their scrutiny as he flashed his badge. "Uh, yeah, I'm Detective Cornell. I'd like to see Dr. Carpenter."

She hesitated. "She's with a patient right now." She lowered her voice. "I understand why you're here, Detective, but you have to understand she has a very full schedule."

His smile indicated he understood—and he wasn't about to back off. "I want to see her now. I don't think her patient would object."

Another woman appeared. This one was dressed in surgical greens and sported a short, spiky haircut. "So you're the one who's got her eating nails." She grinned. "I'm Donna. It's okay, Cheryl, I'll take him back." She turned and gestured over her shoulder. "Come through the side door there."

The first thing Dean noticed was that the examination rooms he passed didn't look at all that different than the ones in a regular doctor's office, except that the "patients" waiting there were rabbits, reptiles and exotic birds.

"The doc doesn't seem to lack for patients," he commented.

"The ownership of exotic pets is increasing every year," Donna replied, leading him to the rear of the building. "Elise also has an excellent reputation in the field. Word of mouth is better than advertising." She eyed him consideringly. "You don't seem too comfortable."

He shrugged. "I'm not used to being around so many animals."

"Donna!" Elise's voice sounded strained. "Donna!"

Both took off on a run, Dean drawing his gun from under his sweatshirt, where he kept it nestled against his back. Donna pushed open the swinging door and stopped short.

"Althea!"

Dean skidded to a stop. He didn't expect to find a python wrapped snugly around Elise's upper body. Her face was bright red as she gasped for air.

"Get her loose," she panted.

Donna immediately headed for Elise, working her fingers around the large snake, and, with a bit of grunting and heaving, she soon freed her boss.

"What got into her?" Donna placed the coiled snake on the examination table.

"Beats me," Elise rasped, collapsing against the counter. "She got it into her head to hug me, and I couldn't get my hands free to work her loose. Luckily, she wasn't squeezing too hard. The last time she tried this I ended up with two broken ribs."

"I knew I shouldn't have left you alone with her." Donna shook her head with self-disgust.

Elise watched Dean's defensive stance. "Althea isn't armed, Detective. You can put the gun away."

"I'm not so sure." He eyed the now-placid reptile with suspicion and kept a healthy distance.

"Don't tell me you're afraid of a simple python?" A faint hint of amusement laced her voice.

"I wouldn't exactly call anything that could crush a person as easily as a grape 'simple.'" He glared at her. "That thing broke your ribs once and you still try to handle it by yourself? You're nuts!''

''I think I'll check on your next patient.'' Sensing the hostile vibrations coming from both parties, Donna hurriedly exited the room.

''Surely you had white mice or a lizard or two when you were a child,'' Elise commented.

He shook his head. ''Not even a dog or cat.'' He didn't tell her that where he grew up pets were a luxury one didn't even dare to consider. That was something he didn't talk about to anyone. Only Mac knew, and even he'd never heard the entire story of Dean's less-than-ideal childhood.

Elise draped the python over her arm and stroked the head, smiling at the tongue flickering out. ''Althea was just showing her affection the only way she knows how.''

''I thought that's how pythons captured their prey.''

She nodded. ''They do, and instinct causes Althea to squeeze us a bit too much at times. She's been domestically bred, but that hasn't hampered her abilities one bit. Actually, she's a sweetheart most of the time.'' She looked up at him. ''Now, do you care to tell me why you've burst into my place of business?''

''I want to talk to your staff.''

Her lovely features hardened. ''No.''

''I'm not asking, Doc. I'm telling.''

''They have nothing to tell you.''

''The day of your unwanted visitor, your receptionist received a call from a man who wouldn't leave his name.''

Elise took several calming breaths, so as not to transfer her agitation to the python. ''Which she already told the sheriff. There's nothing more she can tell you than she's already told them.''

"They might not have asked the right questions."

Bright turquoise eyes warred with dark brown. In the end, neither gave an inch or looked away. It was a standoff.

"You can talk to them at the end of the day and not before. As you can see, I have a great many patients to attend to, and I don't like to keep them waiting too long. It creates undue stress on the animals."

"Why don't you have another doctor in here to take off some of the strain?"

She had been thinking about that for the past year, when it appeared her practice was growing faster than she'd expected. "You have to find the right person first."

"I'll be back a few minutes before five," he stated.

"We close at six."

Dean silently counted to ten. "Whatever." He turned toward the swinging door.

"Detective, there's a rear door you can use." She gestured behind her.

Dean noticed the cages and kennels obviously used for animals kept overnight, as well as a lot of unfamiliar equipment whose use he couldn't fathom. Beyond that was a door. He tried the knob and discovered it turned easily. He flashed Elise an accusing look.

"It's unlocked."

"I come in that door in the mornings. I usually don't relock it because no one other than staff uses it."

He stalked over to her until they stood toe to toe. "Listen carefully so I won't have to repeat myself. This door is to be locked at all times. You are not to let anyone in—I don't care if it's the president of the United States. In fact, I'll arrange to have a peephole installed in it."

Elise's neck was bent back so far she could feel the slight

strain on her muscles. Her flaring nostrils picked up a hint of soap and clean male skin. The cop didn't need any of those men's colognes advertised so heavily; he was potent enough on his own, she thought irrationally. She schooled her features to remain cool and composed but found it more difficult than usual. Darn this man! He'd already caused her enough mental anguish, and he hadn't even been there for twenty-four hours!

"You're disturbing my work, Detective." She silently damned the husky catch in her voice.

He couldn't miss the faint rose flush to her skin, the slight fog in her eyes and the voice that brought to mind a darkened bedroom. His own respiration turned rough with reaction. She wasn't wearing any perfume today, but then again, she didn't need any. Not when her own fresh scent was so evocative. He wanted to find out if that lush mouth tasted as good as it looked and if her skin was really as soft as it appeared, but some rational part of him told him this wasn't the time.

"Goodbye, Detective," she whispered.

"I have a name, you know."

"Yes, but this is a professional situation we're in."

"Is it?" He moved closer until she could feel the heat of his body. "Why don't you try my name? It's easy to say. I'll even make a deal with you—I'll say yours, and then you can say mine."

She didn't consider it that great a deal, and her expression told him so.

"Elise." He waited. "Your turn."

"No." She couldn't. She wasn't about to allow this dark-haired hellion to intrude on her well-ordered life any more than was strictly necessary. And she certainly wasn't going to allow him into her equally well-ordered sanity.

"Elise," he murmured again. His eyes tracked several strands of hair curled along her cheek to her lips. His fingers itched to move it, but he dared not. He was here on business, dammit!

"Dean." It came out huskier than she wanted.

He showed no satisfaction at her capitulation. He merely stepped back and turned to walk out the rear door. "Lock it," he tossed over his shoulder.

Out of his potent range, Elise could only collapse against the examination table. She brushed a stray hair from her face and saw that her hand was trembling. Quickly straightening her shoulders, she marched out of the room. Work had always soothed her mind before; she could only hope it would now, too.

She glanced out the window and noticed Dean standing in the crisp air. His chest rose and fell with deep breaths. She was perversely pleased to note he appeared as affected by the encounter as she.

"So this is what they call protective custody," she murmured, turning away.

"AS YOU CAN SEE, you have more information about Dietrich than we do." Detective Santee, a man in his late forties, gestured toward the sheaf of papers in Dean's hand. Dean had arranged to meet with him that afternoon before he picked the Carpenter girls up from school. "All we have is Deputy Webster's report and what he just told you."

Dean nodded, thinking about the young man he had just unmercifully grilled. He knew he'd acted like the tough city cop, and after Webster's crack about women who tended to imagine things, he hadn't been able to help himself.

"You were a little rough on the kid," Detective Santee commented.

"He deserved it," he said. "We have a major witness whose life was threatened, and when she tells him what happened, he acts as if she's the type to look under her bed every night. She must have been uneasy that night, probably even frightened, and he didn't offer her one shred of compassion. Hell, he even tried to pass it off as a PMS attack!"

Santee held up his hands in surrender. "Hey, I'm on your side," he assured Dean. "And I agree with you. Webster's a good cop, has good instincts, but he needs work on his bedside manner, so to speak. Public relations isn't his forte."

"No kidding." Dean tossed the papers onto the desk. "Dietrich must be in the area. I can't understand why your men haven't been able to rout him."

"We checked every hotel from the five-stars down to the dives. He could be hiding out with friends, even camping somewhere. CHP—" he named the California Highway Patrol "—has been on the lookout for him and his motorcycle, too. Nothing."

Dean exhaled a sigh of frustration. "With all our resources you'd think we could come up with one lousy creep," he muttered. "Something's not right here."

"He could have left the area," Santee suggested.

Dean shook his head. "No, he's around. I feel it in my bones."

"I didn't think you knew all that much about him."

"I have his file, and I know his type. He's getting his kicks out of outwitting us. I'm sure he knows who I am and exactly why I'm here. My captain wanted me to act like the doc and I were 'old friends,' if you know what I mean, but I knew she wouldn't go for that. We don't exactly get along." Now there was an understatement, his brain jeered. "Course, the captain tends to forget that Dietrich saw me crash his little party in the bank, and I doubt he'd forget my face all that easily."

"Yeah, I know what you mean. And we've all heard stories of that kind of bastard deciding to get even."

The two men traded a few stories and parted as friends. Santee even gave Dean his home number in case he needed to get hold of him after-hours.

"By the way, what's your first name? Or is it a state secret?" Dean asked.

The man smiled. "Nothing I care to divulge to the public."

"Not even a fellow cop?"

"Especially a fellow cop. Stories like that tend to remain with you until the end."

Dean stuck out his hand. "I'll be in touch."

"And I'll let you know if I hear anything."

DEAN REACHED Becky's school just as classes were released for the day and found the little girl waiting in the building's doorway, as he'd instructed her when he dropped her off that morning. Presenting him with a shy smile, she climbed into the truck and they headed down the street to pick up Lisa and Keri. Lisa was easy to find. Keri wasn't. He finally tracked her down at the football field, where she was watching the team practice. By then his temper was not at its best.

"You were told to wait in front," he grumbled, guiding her to the truck with a none-too-gentle hand.

She jerked her arm away, only to have it captured again. "I am not a child to be scolded, Detective Cornell," she snapped.

"Hey, Keri, are you okay?" A boy about her age stepped in front of them.

Dean had to respect the kid for having the courage to go up against a clearly cranky adult male. "Everything is just fine," He growled.

The boy looked suspicious. "Who are you?"

Dean pulled out his badge. "Good enough for you, kid?"

The boy reddened and stepped back. By then, Keri looked mortified.

"It's all right, Brian," she muttered.

"Are you sure, Keri?" he asked.

She nodded, her cheeks by now flaming red. "Yes, I disobeyed the detective's instructions." She clutched her books against her chest and walked swiftly toward the waiting truck, where Lisa and Becky had been avidly watching the entire scene.

"Hey, kid." Dean stopped the boy. "You've got guts. I'm proud of you."

He looked puzzled. "For what?"

"For seeing a friend who might be in trouble and being willing to step in and make sure she was all right. A lot of people would probably just look the other way. You're all right." He held out his hand.

Brian reddened as he grasped the older man's hand. "Well, it's just that Keri's so pretty, and things do happen," he mumbled, staring down at his feet. "We know her mom has been having problems with some bank robber."

Dean caught on immediately. The young rescuer had a crush on the cool Keri!

"I'll put a good word in for you," he assured the boy. He paused. "Do you see her a lot during the school day?"

He nodded. "We have three classes together, and we both belong to the language club."

"Then do me a favor? Keep an eye on her. Make sure no man, other than a teacher, ever approaches her or tries to take her off school grounds. If you see anyone suspicious hanging around her, call me at Keri's house, and if you can't reach me, call a Detective Santee with the sheriff's department."

Brian's eyes widened. "No one's going to hurt her around here, Detective," he fervently assured him.

Certain he had an ally, Dean smiled and headed for the truck.

"Are you through with your macho act now?" Keri demanded as he climbed into the truck. "After that display I'll never be able to hold my head up in school again. They probably think you were arresting me for something."

He chose to ignore her tantrum. As much as he hated to admit it, she had a point. His anger had pushed him to be a little too hard on her, but he doubted she was in the mood for an apology just now. He certainly wasn't. He tried the next best thing. "Hey, that Brian has a good head on his shoulders. And it was pretty cool of him to stand up to me like that." He turned on the ignition. "A real brave kid. You should feel honored he tried to save you from what he thought was suspicious activity."

Keri lifted her chin higher, her expression icy enough to turn Dean into a Popsicle.

Used to the cold shoulder from half the Carpenter women, Dean merely shrugged and pulled away from the curb.

"You know what sounds good to me?" he said casually as he scanned the shopping areas on either side of the busy main street. "An ice-cream sundae."

Becky's eyes widened. "Really? I didn't think grown-ups liked them very much. 'Cept Mom, and that's only every few weeks when she says she's going through her chocolate-or-die phase."

Dean swallowed a chuckle at Becky's description.

"Well, I might not feel like chocolate-or-die, but there's times I like good old-fashioned hot-fudge sundae. Any decent places around here?"

"Not a lot, but there is one," Lisa drawled.

"My treat." Dean pressed home his advantage as he took in Lisa and Becky's excited expression. "I gather Keri isn't fond of hot fudge."

She didn't turn from her studied pose of looking out the window as if the scenery were vastly entertaining and the company equally boring. "Chocolate isn't good for you. It causes nasty blemishes, not to mention that it rots your teeth," she said haughtily.

Dean wasn't about to give up now. "No problem. You can have strawberry."

Chapter Six

"Do you have any idea what you've done?"

Dean puffed out his cheeks and exhaled noisily. He spun on his heel to face a furious Elise bearing down on him.

"No, but I have an idea you're going to tell me."

She looked at him as if the idea of murder were very appealing. "Where shall I start? Your telling Becky to ask me about your damn lumpy underwear?"

"I figured you would prefer the answer came from you rather than from me."

"And your manhandling Keri on the school campus? Was that something I would also prefer?" she angrily demanded, furious because he was right. She *would* prefer answering Becky's question herself. Who knew what *he* night say? So she launched her next missile. "According to Keri, you acted like a Neanderthal with her. For all we know, she'll have bruises on her arm tomorrow!

His features turned to granite. "Look, Doc, I didn't ask much, only that those kids be waiting for me just inside the front door. I didn't want them wandering off. But your little Miss Keri decided those rules didn't apply to her and was out in the back drooling over the football team. There's a maniac on the loose who might decide to get to you through your kids, and she would have been a perfect target. She's going to have to learn that if she doesn't follow my rules, she'll have to pay the piper. Just because she wants to act cool doesn't mean she has to act stupid, too.''

His cold, matter-of-fact words deflated Elise's anger. ''Keri may be a little headstrong, but she isn't stupid.''

''If you can't drum into her head what we're up against, I'll play the heavy each and every time, and her precious feelings be damned,'' he said softly but firmly, starting to turn away.

''Wait a minute, Detective, there's one more thing.'' Elise's voice was sweetness over acid.

He closed his eyes. Something warned him this was the killer. ''Now what? Did they say I drove too fast? Ran a stop light? What?''

''You took the girls out for ice cream.''

''It was early enough that I didn't think it would spoil their dinner,'' he defended himself. ''If you're pissed because I didn't ask your permission, I'm sorry. I was just trying to get to know them better in a more relaxing atmosphere.''

''Maybe so,'' she said quietly. ''The thing is, you allowed Becky to order the super-duper hot-fudge sundae.''

''Yeah, and she ate every bite. Frankly, I was surprised a little kid like her could handle something that large.''

Elise shook her head. ''That's just it. She couldn't. Becky's super-duper hot-fudge sundae left her with a super-duper stomachache. Right now, she's in bed convinced she'll die at any moment. Actually, I think she's hoping she will.''

Dean winced. ''Look, I'm sorry. I should have realized

that much sugar could put away an adult, much less a little girl.''

"Lisa goaded her into it?" Elise guessed.

He grimaced, remembering the exchange in the ice-cream parlor. "She told her she couldn't handle one, and Becky said she could."

Elise's face softened in a tiny smile. "Lisa is good at that kind of thing. She loves to challenge Becky because she knows her darling little sister is the perfect victim for a dare."

Dean shifted uneasily. "Look, Elise, I'm sorry. I guess I blew it. I'm afraid my past experience didn't cover this type of situation."

By now all of her anger had dissipated. "You didn't know." She shifted from one foot to the other, gnawing on her lower lip. "I'm sorry for jumping down your throat like that. It's just that..." She took a deep breath. "All of a sudden my life is turned upside down, and I can't seem to control anything anymore. I'm more worried about my children being in danger than I am about any harm coming to me. They're all I have left," she finished quietly.

Dean swore silently. He could see the naked pain in her eyes. She had already lost her husband and unborn child to this maniac. And after that trauma, she had somehow found the courage to go on to make a new life for herself and her children. If something happened to one of them because of this animal, he knew she would never be the same again.

"Next time I won't let Becky order the super-duper hot-fudge sundae," he vowed.

Elise allowed herself a little smile. "Fine." She turned away.

"Hey, Doc." Dean's voice stopped her. She looked at him

over her shoulder. "Thanks for not peeling a strip off my hide."

She smiled. "You do it again and I'll do more than peel a strip off." She headed to her bedroom.

Dean watched her until the door closed after her. "It must be in the genes," he muttered. "Only a mother can have a grown-up man quaking in his boots."

"Boots you shouldn't be wearing in a house where I've just vacuumed the carpets," Myrna scolded, walking out of the bathroom with an armload of laundry. "Tell me something, does your whole apartment look like the same kind of war zone you've left the guest bedroom looking?"

He flushed. "I guess I'm not real big on neatness," he admitted.

She snorted. "Son, you have clothes strewn all over that room, and I don't intend to pick them up for you. I put a basket in a corner for your dirty clothes, but the clean ones should be put away." She directed a glare at him. "Around here, everyone keeps their room clean or is punished appropriately."

"No dessert?"

"No food."

"Mac arranged this, I just know it," he muttered, heading for his room. He had an idea if his room wasn't picked up pronto, there would be no place set for him at dinner. Of course, if Elise Carpenter had anything to do with it, he wouldn't even have a room! The moment he entered he winced at the steady snoring coming from under the bed. "Yep, Mac arranged this and is having himself a good laugh."

DEAN LEARNED a lot about the Carpenters during dinner. Elise patiently listened to each girl talk about her day at school, and if there were homework problems, she promised to help them after dinner. He noticed that while Keri didn't act like his best friend, she'd ceased her obvious cold-shoulder treatment. Now she just acted as if he didn't exist. Lisa still pushed for police stories, the bloodier and gorier the better. Becky stayed in her room with a bowl of soup for her upset stomach.

"Lisa, if you ask about shoot-outs one more time, you will leave this table and figure out your history homework yourself," Elise said finally. "One, it is not appropriate dinner conversation, and two, Detective Cornell might not care to discuss people he's had to shoot during his career."

Dean sent her a look of gratitude, impressed with her sensitivity. He didn't like talking—or even thinking—about the people he'd had to shoot, even if it was in self-defense.

"Luckily, movies and TV are finally showing that a cop's life isn't all that glamourous," he said slowly, staring down at his roast beef and mashed potatoes swimming in rich brown gravy. Myrna sure knew the way to a man's heart. "Most of the time it's a lot of legwork, phone calls and talking to countless people just to chase down one lousy lead. It's a lot of all-nighters drinking cold coffee and eating greasy hamburgers. I'd have an ulcer right now if it wasn't for the fact that I have a cast-iron stomach. Or maybe have no taste buds left."

"You can say that while eating my roast beef?" Myrna asked tartly.

He flashed her a smile. "No, I sure can't. If I keep on eating like this while I'm here, I'll probably gain fifty pounds."

Elise's gaze dropped, taking in the sweatshirt fitting snugly over broad shoulders and a washboard-flat stomach. She doubted there was once ounce of fat on his entire body. When she raised her eyes she found Dean gazing at her, a hint of laughter in the dark depths. Embarrassment threatening to flood her, she quickly glanced away. By now she knew better than to silently dare him to say anything. With his outrageous personality, he would probably do more than just say something. Deciding that cowardice was for once the best tactic, she quickly applied herself to her meal.

"Lisa, you'll help with the dishes tonight," she announced once dinner was finished.

"It's Becky's week!" the girl protested.

"Since she's sick due to your little game, you'll take her place. In fact, you can finish out her week." Elise rose from the table. "Feel free to watch television or listen to the stereo, Detective."

"Actually, I have some homework of my own," he admitted. "Captain Anderson expects daily reports."

"Give him my regards." Her smile indicated the opposite.

"Yeah, I can imagine he'd like that." Dean headed for his room to pick up the notebook where he kept his summary of what he'd learned so far. Which wasn't very much. As far as he was concerned, writing reports was on a par with having teeth drilled. And having a captain who insisted on seeing every *t crossed and i* dotted, along with each report handed in on time or else, didn't help.

"I have a typewriter you can use if you'd like," Elise offered.

His eyes lit up. "I'd like."

Elise led him into a small home office where a typewriter stand was arranged next to the desk that held a personal computer. "It has a correcting feature," she explained, whipping off the typewriter cover. "And there's typing paper in the bottom drawer if you need any."

Dean looked at the miraculous electric typewriter with relief. His typing skills weren't the best. "Great, thank you." he sat at the desk, then looked up, cocking his head to one side. "You're great with those girls."

His praise warmed her. "It probably helps that I was a girl once upon a time."

"No, it's more than that," he said quietly. "You really listen to them. So many parents nowadays don't bother to listen to their kids, to find out what they're feeling and show genuine interest in what they do, but you do. You really care, and it shows."

She lingered by the desk, trailing her fingers across the top. No dust married the brightly polished surface, thanks to Myrna. "A single parent has to try harder, and I've always taken my family seriously."

"How come you never remarried?" He inwardly winced, fearing his question might be too indelicate. "A pretty lady like you must have men knocking down her door."

"Most men are leery of a woman with children," she said frankly. "Not to mention I have a career that's very demanding and I haven't met a man I felt was the right one. I'm happy with my life."

Dean looked around the room, taking in the pictures of the girls and a framed photo of a younger Elise standing next to a lanky blond man with a broad smile. Behind them was a large sign proclaiming the building Carpenters' Exotic Animal Clinic. Privately Dean thought the man looked a little too easygoing for a firebrand like Elise. Perhaps that side of her personality hadn't been prominent then. He liked the idea of his being the only one to see the lady's temper.

He also wanted to keep her there as long as possible. "One other thing. What is it with that bird out there? It acts like it's the boss here or something. If I even look at it, it tells me to 'fud up.'"

Elise smiled. "If I were you, I wouldn't refer to Baby as an 'it' or as a bird, because *she* doesn't think she is one."

"Excuse me?"

"She was a wedding gift from my husband. We raised her from infancy. And now she believes she's human and that all the animals are under her jurisdiction. We have no idea where 'fud up' came from, but it's her favorite phrase when things don't go her way."

A bird that thinks it's a person? Dean couldn't comprehend the notion. But then again, until recently he hadn't known tortoises snored, either. "Sounds more like a spoiled brat."

"She's that, too, but she's also a sweetheart when she wants to be."

"And the tortoise that's disturbing my sleep?"

"That's Florence. Henry's in the coat closet."

"You have two?"

She nodded. "They're both land tortoises, about twenty years old and very intelligent. They both know what the refrigerator is for, and they love to have their heads rubbed. With the weather getting colder, they decided it was time to bed down for the winter, so we won't be seeing much of them until spring. The geese, Frances and Herman, were given to us by a neighbor when we moved in. As for the dogs, one was abandoned as a puppy at our gate, and the other two were dropped off at the clinic late one night. Most vets end up with a menagerie at home, and I'm no exception." Her lips curved. "But surely you grew up with *some* kind of pet? Something tells me you were the type to scare little girls with frogs.''

Dean shook his head. ''No, my mother wasn't into pets'' was all he said.

Elise's eyes softened, but she said nothing, having a pretty good idea Dean wouldn't appreciate sympathy. But her softening also had to do with the boneless grace he displayed, settled in her desk chair, and the way he looked at her as if something other than polite conversation were on his mind.

He leaned back in the chair. ''Nice quiet room.''

What made her think he was saying something sexy? ''It helps when I need to do paperwork.''

''Good place for privacy.''

Again she read something in his simple words, and her flesh tingled under his intense regard.

''With three girls in the house, privacy isn't the norm,'' she murmured.

''There are times when people need privacy. Desire it.'' His gaze dropped to her mouth.

For one improbable moment Elise thought about locking the door. The dark arousal in Dean's eyes told her he would recognize the gesture for what it was. Perhaps he was hypnotizing her to do just that! Her fingers hovered over the doorknob. Then the idea of three girls pounding on the door demanding to know why Mom had locked it burst into her mind.

''Do what you feel is right,'' Dean said quietly, as if reading her thoughts.

She flushed to realize he might know exactly where her thoughts were heading. Her usual acerbic response was stilled as she mentally groped for a reply. She was saved by the bell, literally. For a moment she stared stupidly at the phone until she roused herself sufficiently to walk toward the desk and place her hand on the receiver.

Dean's hand swiftly covered hers while the other gestured for her to walk around the desk to him. Not until her leg gently bumped his thigh did he release his grip so she could pick up the receiver.

"Hello?" Elise said quietly. Her body stiffened. "How did you get this number?"

The moment Dean realized it wasn't a run-of-the-mill call, he jerked her down into his lap so he could listen in.

"Hey, sweet baby." The taunting whisper slithered over the line. "We didn't get to finish our party five years ago—maybe we can this time."

She was stiff as a board, her eyes boring into Dean's as he carefully wedged the phone a little away from her ear so he could hear.

"If not," he went on, "there's always your cute little daughter. I bet we could have real fun," he went on. Elise felt sick and slammed the phone down in the cradle, narrowly missing cracking Dean's fingers in the process.

"That pig!" she choked. "That filthy pig!"

Elise watched Dean pick up the phone and punch out numbers. "What are you doing?"

"I'm calling Santee about having a tap put on your phone. Although it probably won't do any good." When his connection was made he spoke rapid-fire, detailing the call while casting quick glances at a white-faced Elise, who had gotten off his knee and stood away a short distance.

"Why do you think it won't do any good?" she asked when he finished his call.

"Because there's a good chance he won't call again. This time, he called to shake you up. He knows he's done that, so he'll probably hold off for a while. He's playing a sick game with you as the target," he explained. "Santee's going to arrange a tap as soon as possible. He's also having one put on your clinic phone."

Feeling the presence of others, Elise looked over at the now-open doorway to find Lisa and Keri standing there, wide-eyed and frightened. They were looking to their mother for protection, and she was finally realizing she couldn't provide it on her own. For the first time, she was grateful Dean was there to take charge.

"Girls, why don't you go on to bed," she suggested quietly with a facsimile of a smile. "Everything will be all right."

Lisa looked up at Dean. "If that slime comes to the house, you're going to blow him away with your gun, aren't you?"

"How about if I take him into custody and send him away to prison for a long time?" he suggested.

She shook her head. "That's what was supposed to happen before, and it didn't. And it won't this time, either." With bowed shoulders, Lisa trudged down the hallway on her sister's heels.

Dean left the office and headed for the kitchen. Mission accomplished, he went to find Elise. She was in the living room, looking dazed. He handed her a glass of wine and toasted her with a glass bearing an inch of amber liquid.

"I didn't think you looked like the Jack Daniel's type." He downed the whiskey, sighing happily when the liquor hit his stomach with a warm glow. "Perfect," he pronounced.

Elise settled herself on the couch, tucking her legs under her. "He's playing a game with me, you said?"

Dean took the chair beside the couch, stretching his legs out in front of him. He eyed her closely, noting her pale features and shadowed eyes, and wished he could give her more than a glass of liquid courage. "Yeah, I'm afraid so." He rolled his glass between his palms, staring down at the residue in the bottom. "It might be a good idea to send the girls somewhere else for the time being."

"No!" She downed the rest of her wine in one gulp and set the glass on the table in front of her. "No, they stay here. What if he decided to make them a target to get back at me? They're better of here, with you." Her voice came out muffled.

He glanced sharply at her. "Does this mean you're finally going to trust me? Go along with me? No matter how much you disagree with my methods?"

She met his gaze squarely. "I'll trust your methods as long as my daughters are kept safe. But if harm comes to any of them, I will go after that man and I will shoot him down like a mad dog."

"Elise, you'd only be stooping to his level," he reminded her. "Not to mention getting sent to jail."

Her smile held no warmth. "All I'll need is a police officer who can't spell, and I'll be out just the way he was."

Dean shook his head. "Revenge only makes things worse, Elise. It won't let you sleep at night, and it won't make life easier."

"If he was dead, I'd sleep just fine."

"That's what you think." He set his glass on the table with a thud, leaning forward to rest his elbows on his thighs, his laced fingers hanging loosely between his spread knees.

Elise's eyes lowered for a fraction of a second to notice the way the soft denim stretched in important places. She quickly raised her glance.

"Killing isn't like in the movies. There's real blood, real

gore, people screaming in pain. What you encountered in that bank is nothing compared to..." He trailed off, finally adding, "And a gunshot wound is usually pretty messy."

"I'm well aware of the consequences a bullet can have, Detective. Not only did I stop that bank guard from bleeding to death, but I saw my husband die from a gunshot wound to the head. Steve's death was brutal and senseless, and I will see it in my dreams for the rest of my life." She stood up. "As I said before, if you don't get Dietrich, I will."

Dean grabbed her hand to halt her leave-taking, holding it in a viselike grip. "You go after him and you'll be playing right into his hands," he warned. "You'll be doing just what he wants. And once he has you, he won't let you go until you're dead and no longer a threat to him." When she tried to jerk back her hand, he only tightened his hold. "Get smart, Elise. You might not like us cops, but we know how to handle types like him. You don't. Don't talk to me about senseless killings. In my line of work I've seen a hell of a lot more than I care to think about."

Her eyes flashed fire. "Then *you* bring me his head on a platter!"

His jaw tightened. "Let me do my job, Elise."

Elise looked down at his fingers encircling her wrist. The man was causing feelings long buried to surface, and the sensation was painful. She didn't want to feel again. Especially not with this man. She feared Dean could drag out emotions she'd never even experienced before.

"I don't want this," she said in a low voice, aware she was giving away her feelings but sensing this was a time to tell the truth. "If you don't mind, I'd like to go to bed. I have to get up earlier than usual tomorrow because it's my surgery day."

He didn't loosen his hold. On the contrary, he sat there as if they had all the time in the world. "On one condition."

She could feel the heat of his skin permeate hers and travel up her arm, providing a warmth the wine hadn't given her. "What?"

"Say my name from now on."

She refused to look at him. "I do use your name."

He shook his head. "No, you're real good at my title, but you don't say my name unless I force you to. You said it in the clinic this morning, and it sounded damn good. I want to hear it again."

Her voice had a slight tremble to it. "Dean."

He released her without hesitation. "I told you it wasn't so hard."

This time she did look at him, noting the shaggy black hair with a few streaks of silver running faintly through it. The heavy beard framed a well-shaped face. The deep brown eyes looked deep into her soul. He had a rugged face—not handsome but honest. Faint lines fanned out from his eyes, attesting to years of hard living. But it was those all-seeing eyes she feared the most. She feared that she wouldn't be able to hide anything from him if she didn't watch herself. And that, she knew, was dangerous.

"There's only one problem," she said. "If I stop using your title, I might forget your true reason for being here. I don't want to do that."

AFTER ELISE RETREATED to her bedroom, Dean returned to the kitchen for the Jack Daniel's bottle. As he sat sprawled in the chair, sipping the fiery liquid, he thought about the woman with the strawberry-blond hair and eyes the color of polished turquoise. It had been a long time since a woman had so completely snared his attention the way she had. He hadn't missed the fear in her eyes as Dietrich threatened her over the phone and he'd wanted nothing more than to take her in his arms and assure her no harm would come to her or her children. As a man, he wanted to make that promise. As a cop, he knew better than to make any kind of promise that couldn't be guaranteed. He stretched out an arm, snagging the telephone receiver. Setting the phone in his lap, he punched out a series of numbers.

"Yeah?" Mac's distinctive growl sounded in his ear.

"You a dad yet?"

"Not yet, and the waiting's driving me crazy. Stacy, on the other hand, looks so calm you'd think she was an old hand at this. I already told you you'd be the second to know, right after Amanda," he told him. "What's up?"

Dean filled Mac in on the day's happenings.

"What do you need from this end?" Mac asked.

"I wouldn't know where to begin." Dean took a hearty swallow from his drink. "Santee is going to put a tap on the home and office phones, but this guy isn't playing by the rules. He's going to make her life hell before he makes his major move."

"How about I talk to his accomplices?"

"They didn't make bail?"

"No way they could."

"You're on leave though," he warned. The meaning was clear. Mac wouldn't have any power to perform police activities.

"That hasn't stopped me before. I'll talk to them in the morning and get back to you if there's anything important to report," he promised.

"Thanks buddy."

"Dean?"

"Yeah?"

"Is she getting to you already?"

His laughter held no mirth. "My friend, the lady got to me the first moment I saw her."

BY HABIT, Dean did not awaken easily unless the phone was ringing, which usually meant a work call. Even an alarm clock couldn't galvanize him into action the way work could. Now he lay sprawled in bed, still foggy with sleep, as he dreamed of voices whispering near his ear and something cold circling his wrist. Then his nostrils twitched as he thought he smelled coffee. Yep, that was the smell, all right.

Ah, the smell of coffee brewing, mingled with the snores of the reptile hibernating under his bed. What more could a man want first thing in the morning?

Then something prompted him to finish waking up as he rolled over onto his side. *Tried* to roll over. He soon discovered he couldn't go far, and his eyes flew open. A quick scan of the area told him why. His handcuffs had been used to shackle his wrist to the brass headboard. He jerked up so violently he was almost thrown back to the mattress.

"Dammit!" he roared. "Elise, get the hell in here! Elise!"

Pounding feet sounded down the hallway before his bedroom door swung open, revealing Elise, the three girls and a fascinated Myrna. Dean closed his eyes. The last thing he wanted was an audience.

"I only recall asking for one particular person." His thunderous expression boded ill.

"You didn't ask. You shouted," Elise pointed out. "I guess the others were curious."

Her gaze took in the scene, and she had to bite down hard

on her lower lip to keep from bursting into laughter. Funny, she hadn't had much to laugh about lately, and the man sprawled before her wasn't exactly laughable even if the situation was. A magnificent specimen of masculinity lay handcuffed to the bed with the covers tossed every which way, allowing a view of a muscled chest coated with coarse dark hair and a pair of bright teal briefs that barely hid anything. She wished he wore boxer shorts. No, she wished she could stop looking at him so hungrily.

"Why Detective Cornell, I had no idea you went in for the kinky stuff," she drawled. "What kind of man did your department send to protect me?"

"Just get me out of this." He bit out each word as he scowled darkly at her—as if it were all her fault!

"You said he would laugh!" Becky attacked Lisa, pushing her sister away from her. "You said he'd know it was a joke!"

Elise grabbed her two younger daughters before they could escape and pasted on her tell-me-the-truth-or-else expression.

"We wanted to play a joke on him, that's all," Becky blurted out. "Lisa said he'd think it was funny if we handcuffed him to the bed. But he doesn't. He's really mad." She glared at her older sister before hitting her with a tiny fist.

"None of that!" Elise grabbed her hand. "Both of you go to the living room and wait for me."

"Hey, if you don't mind, I'd like to get out of here," Dean called out. Patience was not one of his virtues.

"Where's the key?"

"On the dresser next to my wallet."

Elise gave the two girls one more look. "Didn't I just tell you to go to the living room?"

"Yes."

"Yes," Becky's voice was more subdued than her sister's.

"Then I suggest you do as I say or you'll be without television for a month instead of a week."

"A week? *Mom!*"

"But she made me do it!"

"A week," she repeated. "Lisa, your idea of a joke isn't funny. And, Becky, no one can make you do anything you don't want to. Now go."

"Ladies, can't you continue your discussion later? I'd really like to get out of these handcuffs," Dean said plaintively.

"Now that's the way to keep a man around the house," Myrna chuckled, walking away.

"I think it's sick" was Keri's disgusted comment as she followed the housekeeper.

Elise found Dean's keys and selected the proper one. She unlocked the cuff around his wrist and dropped the keys onto the bed, all the while attempting not to look at his barely clad body. Lisa was right. He most definitely didn't have a beer belly. In fact, his abdomen looked so flat she could probably bounce a quarter off it. His body looked all too good to a woman who hadn't really given the opposite sex much thought over the past five years.

"Now that you've given us another show, I suggest you keep your door locked to discourage unwanted visitors," she said crisply, making sure to keep her gaze fastened firmly on his face. "Yesterday's explanation about your lumpy underwear was quite enough, thank you."

"I figured she'd forget all about it."

"Children never forget."

"So what did you tell her?" Dean's husky voice was music to a starving woman's ears.

She frowned. "Tell her?"

"About my lumpy underwear."

She looked everywhere but at him. "It was just a talk between mother and daughter."

"Come on, give me a hint," he coaxed. "I'm real curious."

"Detective, you're on duty," she hedged.

"I'm not on duty until my badge is pinned on, and as you can see, there aren't too many places to pin it right now." His eyes danced with wicked lights.

Elise walked to the dresser, picked up his leather badge case and tossed it onto the bed. "I'm sure I can find an appropriate place."

"What worries you more, Elise? That you looked at me more closely than you feel you should have, or that you liked what you saw?"

Elise knew when silence was golden, and this was definitely one of those times. She beat a hasty retreat without another word.

DEAN MADE ARRANGEMENTS to meet with Detective Santee again that morning. While he drove into town, he felt the tingling sensation that told him his prey was nearby. A careful scan of the traffic on the freeway revealed nothing. No motorcycle, anyway.

"He ditched it," Dean murmured, pulling into the sheriff's station parking lot. "He got rid of the bike and has a car now."

As he climbed out of his truck, he swept the area but saw nothing amiss. "Come on, you son of a bitch, show yourself." But he knew the challenge wouldn't be answered. Not this soon. He walked into the sheriff's station, furious with himself for being unable to do a damn thing.

HE SAT behind the wheel of the aging Chevy he'd picked up in a honky-tonk parking lot. A quick change of license plates and it was all his. He'd ditched the bike the morning after his raid on the bitch's property. He grinned. That, and his phone call had scared the hell out of her. And he wanted her that way, wanted her to know he'd get to her no matter how she tried to hide. Even that cop living there wouldn't be able to help her. Oh, yeah, he knew the guy was a cop. He remembered seeing him play hero at the bank. After all, he was the one who shot the bastard. Too bad he'd only winged him. No, not even Mr. Hero was going to be able to protect her.

Carl Dietrich rubbed the scar slashed across his arm. The dame had a debt to pay, and eventually he'd make sure she paid it in full. For now he would concentrate on the cop. He watched Dean across the street, visualizing a target painted on the man's forehead. He smiled, then pointed his forefinger at Dean, the thumb cocked.

"Bang, you're dead."

Chapter Seven

"If you barge into my clinic like the proverbial bull in a china shop one more time, I will sic Althea on you." Elise had to rise on tiptoe to do it, but standing nose to nose with the stubborn Detective Cornell was more than worth it. Her eyes spat fire while her mouth issued threats that would have made most men think twice about entering her inner sanctum.

Undeterred, Dean glared back. "Cheryl said you had three new patients today. I wanted to check them out for myself."

She nearly shrieked. "They were referrals from a colleague!"

"Oh, really? Who? The nimble-fingered idiot who drove you home that night?" he sneered. "Lady, you really should check out your colleagues more thoroughly."

Elise fleetingly considered what horrible torture would best suit this insufferable man.

"Detective Cornell, you are turning my clinic into a circus, and I don't appreciate it," she said, furious. "I run on a very tight schedule, and when you barge in here giving my clients that big-nasty-cop routine, as if they might be serial killers, you tend to scare them off. I would prefer they not know you're here, much less why. Your dentist must love you, considering how much you grind your teeth," she added sweetly.

"Only since I've had to deal with you," he growled. "In case you've forgotten, I'm here to save your butt. If you don't like it, you know what you can do." He turned to stalk out the rear door.

"I tried. Your captain refused to give me anyone else."

That stopped Dean in his tracks. He spun around. "You asked for a replacement?"

She wasn't about to tell him the reason behind her request—her growing attraction to him. "Yes, I did. But he told me you were the best. He also said he was glad to have you out of his hair—what's left of it. It wasn't difficult to figure out he doesn't like me any more than he likes you, so he devised the perfect punishment by putting us together. I wouldn't be surprised if he's hoping I'll go completely insane and murder you."

Dean looked at her, mouth open.

"My life has been turned upside down since the night you showed up," she went on. "I've already had my staff tell me we're better to watch than a sitcom."

He combed his fingers through his hair, sending the shaggy strands curving around his fingers. "I can't believe after only one week..."

"Nine days," she corrected. "Nine long, horrifying days."

Dean looked down at her, her turquoise eyes flashing with anger.

"You're beautiful when you're ticked off."

His husky voice caused her to falter. "Don't try to sweet-talk me, Detective Cornell."

He leaned closer until their mouths were a breath apart. "Doc, I can think of a hell of a lot more things I'd like to do with you than sweet talking. Wanna hear what they are?"

She'd never thought it physically possible for one's heart to jump into one's throat—until now. "Don't change the subject!" *Wimp!* she castigated herself. How come she couldn't come across as authoritative as she'd like?

"You were the one who started it." His warm breath fanned across her lips. "Shall we see what else we can start?"

She was tempted. Very tempted. But reason reared its cooler head. For a brief moment, she wasn't sure whether to be thankful or not. "Right now, I have to treat an iguana with an eye infection. Would you care to help?"

Dean backed off immediately. Now *he* was the one to call himself a wimp. He hated reptiles. "I think I'll look for someone to interrogate. But—" he visually sliced through her clothing "—once you rid this place of green, scaly things, I'll be back to continue our conversation."

For the next hour all Elise could think of was exactly what Dean's ideas beyond sweet talking would be.

"Come on, Elise, the guy is a hunk. Let loose," Donna told her boss as they grabbed cups of coffee during a blissful free five minutes.

Elise looked at her sharply. "Why are you suddenly trying to drum up a love life for me? Surely *you* don't need to live vicariously. Gary keeps you happy enough, doesn't he?"

Donna's lips thinned. "That jerk! That snake in the grass! That—"

"What did he do?"

"He decided one woman wasn't enough for him. He just didn't expect me to find out. I told him if he ever came near me again, I'd slice him into tiny pieces.'' Her dark eyes glittered with venom.

Elise chuckled at such a bloodthirsty description coming from her perky technician. ''And yet you're still in favor of men and romance?''

Donna's face turned dreamy. ''Only because I met Will. He's not as cute as Gary, but he has a way of making a woman feel special. Know what I mean?''

Not exactly, Elise wanted to say. Although, if she cared to admit it, Dean had a way of making her feel special—even if sometimes only a special case for the funny farm!

''Where did you meet Will?'' she asked idly as she poured herself a second cup of coffee.

''At Rick's Corral, that new country-western bar in Temecula. It was fate,'' she said with a sigh.

Elise smiled. If a night of twangy tunes at Rick's Corral qualified as kismet, surely a Pasadena bank robbery would fit the bill. ''Yes, it sounds like it.''

ELISE'S THOUGHTS about Dean hadn't dissipated as the day went on. How had she ended up with the sexiest man next to Mel Gibson in her house as her protector? And, she wryly wondered, who would protect *him!*

That evening, she ate her dinner quickly, ignoring her own rule of chewing each bite carefully before swallowing. All she knew was that she needed to spend as little time as possible around this man. The fact that Dean's eyes were on her every second didn't help her digestion one bit.

''I don't think any of this is fair,'' Keri announced as Lisa picked up the dirty dishes and carried them to the sink.

''What?'' Elise asked absently.

''Our having *him* take us to school every morning and pick

us up." She turned accusing eyes on Dean, who was finishing his third helping of beef stew. "It's bad enough Brian watches my every move. He acts as if he's been specially chosen to protect me."

"He was."

Keri looked horrified. "Do you realize how embarrassing that is to me and my friends? He hangs around me at lunch and during breaks. I swear he isn't more than three feet away from me at any time. He even follows me between classes!"

"He seems like a nice kid. You should give him a chance," Dean advised.

She rolled her eyes. "*Him?* Detective Cornell, Brian is a major geek."

"So was I at that age," he freely admitted. "I don't think I turned out so badly."

Four pairs of feminine eyes turned in his direction.

"You could never have been a geek," Lisa declared.

"Are geeks bad?" Becky asked, mulling over the word.

"No, Becky, they aren't. But for the detective, I imagine he might be telling us a tall tale. In reality, he was probably one of those rebels who wore black T-shirts and rode a motorcycle to school. The type of boy no self-respecting mother would allow near her darling daughter."

"Not me! I was one of those guys who made decent grades and pretty well kept to myself. I was the shy type." He tried for the demure look and failed miserably.

Elise shook her head. "That I can't believe. Who needs help with their homework?" Receiving blessed silence, she sighed with relief. "Then I'm off to catch up on some paperwork. Make sure the kitchen is straightened up for Myrna in the morning."

Dean watched her leave the kitchen. It was a good thing

she couldn't read his mind. If she knew what he was considering about her right now, she'd probably flee the house.

After studying the patient chart in front of her, Elise headed for her bookcase in search of a particular text. Somehow the lab results didn't check out. She grabbed a large volume and began leafing through the pages in search of an answer.

"You didn't ask me if I needed help with *my* homework."

She closed her eyes for a brief second, then opened them and turned around. Dean leaned against the doorjamb, waving several sheets of paper in front of him.

She gestured toward one corner of the room. "If you need to use the typewriter, you can take it into the living room or into your room. I won't need it this evening."

He straightened up and walked into the room. "That isn't what I need."

Elise silently vowed she'd bite her tongue off before she'd venture into that territory. "In case you didn't hear me at the table, I'm very busy catching up on my work. I have charts to review and reports to write. I don't have time to play games with egocentric rogue detectives."

His lips curved. "Egocentric rogue? I like the sound of that." He kept moving forward until he stood in front of her, one hand braced against the bookcase. Unless she ducked under the blocking forearm, Elise was effectively trapped. "You like me because I'm an egocentric rogue and not like all those other wimpy guys you feel safe with. You like me because I'm not in the least bit safe," he said huskily.

Her eyes snapped dazzling fires. "Let's get something straight, shall we? I'm not one of your little bimbo police groupies who would be only too happy to jump into bed with a cop. For one thing, my IQ is higher than my shoe size, I can form words of more than two syllables and I never drink anything that has a cute little umbrella in it. So of you're lonely for female company, why don't you try some of the bars in town? I'm sure there will be someone more than suitable for you there.''

Dean looked more amused than angry at her insulting remarks. ''Tell me something, Doc, what worries you more—the fact that you see my choice in women as brainless idiots, or that you're furious with yourself for actually being attracted to me?'' He dipped his head until their faces were mere inches apart.

She tipped her head back. Laughter bubbled up her throat. ''Egocentric? I understated the case, Detective. Actually, you're living in a fantasy world to think I would be interested in *you.*''

His teeth gleamed white against his dark beard. ''You can try pissing me off all you want, Ellie,'' he said with quiet intimacy, ''but it won't work. I can see past that touch-me-not act of yours. I've seen you watch me when you think I don't notice what you're doing. In fact, you tend to study my jeans just as much as you study my mouth. I'm wondering which interests you most.''

''Now I know you're suffering from delusions!'' She ordered herself not to blush. Did the man have eyes in the back of his head? Still, what could he expect, wearing jeans so tight she didn't understand how he could even breathe?

He leaned even closer, bringing the scent of coffee and warm male skin—suddenly a very erotic combination—to her nostrils. ''But I don't mind. You see, there's times when I watch you, too. Did you know your charming tush wiggles when you walk?'' His voice turned husky, flowing over her senses.

Now her face did flame with hectic color. "It does not!"

His wicked grin did strange things to her insides. "Does so."

Her eyes grew round as saucers. "I have never wiggled in my life!"

"Maybe I should take a video to prove it to you." He dipped his head, brushing his mouth against the sensitive skin behind her ear, causing her to jump in reaction. "Mmm, you smell really good."

Why had she taken the time to spritz on cologne before dinner? "It's hospital disinfectant," she lied.

"Must be a French manufacturer then." He nuzzled the graceful arc of her throat. "I never knew vets could smell so good."

Elise closed her eyes, vainly trying to recall the Latin names for every bone in a parrot's body. Instead, her mind catalogued other items. His lips were warm, his beard soft as it brushed against her skin, and his hands did marvelous things as they smoothed their way across her waist. She was sinking fast without any hope of rescue. Did she want to be rescued? She wasn't sure.

"This..." She cleared her throat; her voice sounded much too husky. "This isn't a good idea."

"Hmm?" His tongue lapped the area just behind her ear. He chuckled when she jumped. "I'm just doing my job, ma'am."

When the tip of his tongue dipped into the hollow of her throat, Elise doubted she could remember her own name. "Dean, please." She wasn't sure if she was pleading with him to stop or to continue. She was too busy concentrating on not melting to the floor. Slowly she lifted her arms. Her hands didn't need any direction as they tunneled through his thick dark hair, her fingers tangling among the silky strands that curled with a life of their own. His kiss came next, sending flashes of fire through her veins and leaving her short of breath. When his hand covered her breast, she trembled.

"Don't pull away, Elise," he muttered just before his mouth covered hers again.

Elise moaned at the intimate contact. Dean's tongue plunged between her parted lips, taking any remaining starch out of her knees. If he hadn't been holding her so tightly, she surely would have collapsed to the floor and pulled him down with her.

Her fingers tightened their grip in his hair, but Dean was feeling no pain. Not when he had the most delectable woman he'd ever known in his arms and she was kissing him back with more fire than he'd imagined. He closed his arms around her, bringing her up flush against his aroused body, cradling her hips against his. He rubbed his tongue against hers, twisting and turning in a fashion he wanted their bodies to follow as soon as possible. He pulled her shirt out of her jeans, moving his hand upward to the lace covering her breast. He slid his fingers under the lacy cup, unerringly finding the nipple, which grew taut under his caress. He swallowed her soft moan, then moaned deep in his own throat when he felt her fingers hovering over his zipper.

"Touch me, Ellie," he ordered in a raw voice. "Let me feel your hands on me."

She gingerly started to stroke the straining denim fabric, her fingers lingering at the zipper pull. One tug was all it would take.

"Mom, I can't find Billy Bear!"

Becky's wail was better than a cold shower in the middle

of a self-generated heat wave. Elise's eyes flew open. She braced her palms against Dean's chest and pushed him away.

"It's..." She breathed deeply, trying to regain her voice. Oh, Lord, if Becky walked in now, she'd have questions about Dean's lumpy jeans Elise wasn't ready to answer! "It's..."

"If it's that bear wearing the red-and-white sweater, it's by the bird cage," Dean called out.

Elise wanted to ask him how he could sound so normal, but her vocal chords still weren't working properly.

"Thank you," she whispered, stepping out of his embrace.

"My pleasure."

She shot him a suspicious glance, refusing to dignify his double entendre and unwilling to admit she had just acted like a hormone-crazed teenager. She vowed, then and there, if Keri ever tried anything like this before she was twenty-one, she would personally lock her in a convent until she was thirty.

"This..." She cleared her throat. She found she couldn't look at him, but looking down didn't help her peace of mind, either. "This was not a good idea. After all, you're here on police business, and as soon as it's settled, we won't be seeing each other again."

Dean didn't like the fact that she could so easily brush him off. "You didn't think about that a couple of minutes ago."

"You caught me at a weak moment."

"You weren't so weak when you dug your fingers into my hair. You wanted me just as much as I wanted you."

"Stop it!" she choked, furious at hearing the truth. "I'd like to be left alone now."

Dean frowned. What happened to the fiery woman he'd just held in his arms? "Elise?"

She held up a hand, palm out. "Dean, please."

He told himself it was a good sign that she used his first name. "We can't sweep this under the rug, Elise, as if it didn't happen."

She refused to look at him. "Do us both a favor and get out."

"We can't just ignore it. I'll let it slide for now, but we'll have to talk about this later," he promised as he walked out of the room. He made a point of closing the door after him.

Elise stumbled to her chair and collapsed in the leather seat. When she covered her face with her hands, she wasn't surprised to find her skin hot to the touch. Right now, she was nothing more than a mass of trembling nerves. A mass of trembling erotic nerves.

"Oh, no," she moaned, dropping her head to her crossed arms on her desktop.

DEAN WASN'T DOING much better. After lying in bed thinking about Elise just down the hall, he decided he wasn't going to get any sleep for a while. He pulled on a pair of jeans and crept out of his room, hoping there would be something boring on television to lull him to sleep.

He rummaged in the kitchen, fixing himself two thick sandwiches and pouring a glass of milk. He took his late-night snack into the living room and snapped on the television. Settled on the couch, his legs propped on the coffee table, he concentrated on classic reruns on the Nickelodeon channel.

"Ah, *Donna Reed*. Better than a sleeping pill." He bit into his sandwich and sipped his milk.

Except with each program, showing picture-perfect mothers of the fifties and sixties, Dean kept thinking about a mother of the nineties. By the time he switched to Bugs Bunny cartoons, he knew he was well on his way to being a lost cause. He may have kissed the woman first, but her hooks were already in him good and deep.

"Well, Carl Dietrich, you scuzzball, at least you did one thing right in your crummy life," he muttered. "You introduced me to Elise."

"Mom? Mom!"

Elise groaned and rolled over. "What are the rules in this household?"

"If your bedroom door is closed, we're not supposed to disturb you unless it's an emergency," Lisa recited.

The last thing she wanted to do was open her eyes. "Is this an emergency?"

"I'm not sure."

She opened one eye at that. It was still dark. "Explain."

Lisa stood at the side of the bed in her nightgown. "Dean's asleep on the couch, and the TV's on."

It took a moment for the statement to settle in Elise's sleep-fogged mind. "Is the house on fire?"

"No."

"Are any of you girls bleeding?"

"No."

"Is Detective Cornell bleeding?"

"No."

Now she opened the other eye. "Then I don't think we have an emergency, do we?"

"He looks awfully uncomfortable, and I thought you could wake him up so he could go to bed."

"I know I'm going to hate asking this, but what time is it?"

"Four-thirty."

"And why are you up?"

"I had to go to the bathroom. Are you gonna wake him up?"

It appeared she had no choice. After all, she couldn't allow the poor man to lie out there and freeze, could she? She flipped back her covers and groped for her robe. Shivering in the chilly predawn air, she wrapped the robe around her body. "Go back to bed. I'll take care of it."

She knew it was a mistake the minute she reached the living room. Only the glowing television screen highlighted Dean, who lay slumped on the couch. An empty plate and glass sat on the coffee table. She walked cautiously over to him. Was it safe to wake a police officer, or would he jump up and catch her in a hammerlock?

She stared at him for a long moment, noting his mouth was slightly open and a soft snore erupted from his chest. She couldn't hold back her smile at the big bad man looking like a harmless little boy with tousled hair and a boneless posture. That comparison ended rapidly, however, when her eyes lowered from his sleeping features to his bare chest. Dark hair blanketed his chest in a blatantly adult masculine way. Her fingers itched to discover if it was as soft as his beard. She shivered—and not from the cold.

"Dean," she whispered. She tried again, louder. "Dean."

"Fud up," a sleepy Baby grumbled from her covered cage in the corner.

"Dean." Elise touched his shoulder lightly, then snatched her fingers back.

"Hmm?" He blinked several times and looked up, slowly focusing. "Elise?"

She nodded. "Lisa found you out here and was afraid you'd get too cold or uncomfortable."

By now he noticed the late-night chill in the air and shivered. He stumbled to his feet and raised his arms over his head in a bone-cracking stretch. "Donna Reed didn't put me to sleep, but Bugs sure did," he mumbled, lazily scratching his chest as he picked up the remote control gadget and switched the television off.

Elise's mouth felt as dry as the desert as her eyes tracked every one of his movements. She knew not just any man could start this volcanic reaction in her the way Dean did. Desperate for distraction, she bent down and picked up the plate and glass.

"If I go to bed like a good little boy, will you tuck me in?"

She walked deliberately, putting one foot firmly in front of the other, toward the kitchen. "I think you're old enough to do that by yourself."

"Maybe so, but it's not as much fun." His husky tone cloaked her like a warm blanket. Not a description she wanted to consider. Blankets meant bed. Thinking about beds now was a very bad idea. "As they say, the night is still young, the moon is full..."

She turned around. "You seem to have a one-track mind, Detective." Her tone came out more amused than angry.

He grinned. "Yeah, well, there's something about you that just causes my mind to wander in that direction."

"Yes, I've noticed." And noticed that washboard belly and thick mat of chest hair swirling around copper-brown nipples rigid from the chilly night air.

"And you're not running off?"

She didn't look away. "Would it do me any good?"

He stared at her a long time. "No."

Silence surrounded them as they watched each other, as if looking for the right answer. Dean was the first to speak.

"Thanks for waking me up, Elise. I would have ended up with a horrendous crick in my neck if I'd stayed there much longer."

She nodded before finishing her walk into the kitchen. "You're welcome. Good night."

Elise took her time rinsing the plate and glass, setting them in the dishwasher and puttering around until she heard Dean's door close with a loud click she was certain was deliberate. Not until then did she walk softly down the hallway to her own room.

For the first time she didn't find it the relaxing retreat it used to be for her. It was too easy now to visualize Dean in her room, in her bed. Only knowing that he probably wasn't having an easy time of sleeping either, what with Florence's loud snores, finally allowed her to drop off into slumber.

"You don't get fed today."

Dean looked up at Myrna's unsmiling features. "Excuse me?" His mouth salivated at the sight of lightly browned French toast and crispy bacon slices placed on the plates.

She held his plate out of his reach. "I told you in the beginning, those who don't keep up their rooms don't eat. And I got a good look at your room this morning while you were showering. It looked like World War III had struck."

He winced. He couldn't believe one woman could make him feel ten years old again. "Myrna, I promise, right after breakfast, I'll pick everything up." He reached for his plate, but she didn't budge. "Honest."

She was unmoved. "Clean first, then eat."

Dean ignored the giggles revolving around the table.

"Give it up, Dean. Myrna's rules stand for all of us," Elise advised, smiling broadly.

He stood up, pushing his chair back. "This is not fair."

Myrna placed the plate in front of Elise, who promptly reached for the syrup bottle. "Anyone who has underwear hanging from the bedposts shouldn't talk about fair. The faster you straighten things up, the faster you'll get breakfast."

He glared at the housekeeper. "Just don't try driving in *my* part of town, lady." As he walked past Elise's chair, he leaned over and quickly snitched a slice of bacon.

"I'm quaking in my shoes," Myrna said dryly, reaching for the phone as it pealed its second ring. "Carpenter residence. Yes, he's here, but don't keep him long. He has to clean his room before he can eat his breakfast," she concluded.

Dean frantically grabbed for the receiver. "Cornell."

"You mean somebody finally got smart and is making you clean up your own messes?" Mac hooted. "This is one lady I'd like to meet."

"Yeah, you just wait until you have to change dirty diapers," he growled, scowling at the giggling females in his line of sight, none of whom seemed intimidated by his darkest glare. "So what's up old buddy?"

"Got a bit of info for you," Mac went on, now all business. "I talked to a few contacts who're familiar with Dietrich, and so far, news isn't good."

Why wasn't he surprised? Dean groped for a piece of paper and pencil, which Myrna dug out of a nearby drawer for him. "Okay, go ahead."

"Dietrich has an old buddy from San Quentin days who just got out of Chino about a week ago," he said, naming a minimum-security prison outside of Los Angeles. "According to parole records, the guy is living in Corona. He's got a job working as a mechanic in a car dealership there and is supposedly keeping his nose clean, but that's doubtful, considering his past record. The two go back a long way, so ten to one Dietrich's still around, hiding out with his pal's help, waiting for his next chance to get at the lady."

Dean hid his worry. Corona wasn't all that far from here. And things had been too quiet lately. Dietrich might strike at any time.

"Anything else?" he clipped.

"Yeah, one of his cronies still in the county jail has been talking a mile a minute. It appears Dietrich has a nasty temper and is pretty brutal with those he has a grudge against."

Dean casually turned away from the kitchen crowd. "I don't like this," he muttered into the receiver.

"You be careful, Dean. I don't think he'll stop to consider your badge if you get in his way with the doc. This guy has more than a few screws loose."

The idea of anything happening to Elise or the girls turned his earlier appetite to acid.

"He can try, but he'll end up the loser."

Chapter Eight

"You're going to *what?*" Dean roared.

Elise looked pained as she faced his incredulous features. "I'm sure you heard me correctly the first time."

He closed his eyes. He'd hoped his usually perfect hearing was wrong. "I don't think it would be a good idea."

"But Mom promised we could!" Lisa wailed. "She said there was no reason we couldn't still go." She glared daggers at the man she usually idolized.

Elise knew it was time to step in with the voice of reason. "It's only a trip to the Wild Animal Park, Dean," she soothed. "It's become something of an annual tradition with us. The girls each take a friend and we spend the day at a place of their choice. This year is the park. I doubt anything could happen there. Of course, knowing your feelings about animals, I would understand if you don't care to go."

Her smirk disappeared with his reply. "It appears I'll have to tag along."

"No!" Keri cried out. She turned on Dean. "What can happen to us there? It's not as if this man will even know where we'll be. If you're with us, you'll just ruin the entire day."

"Keri!" Elise admonished. "There's no reason to be rude. After all, Dean is here to protect us, even if nothing has happened for a while." She turned to Dean. "Actually, I'd say Dietrich has probably forgotten all about us by now, and it would be safe for you to return home."

He still hadn't told her about his talk with Mac a week ago regarding Dietrich's friend fresh out of Chino prison and living in Corona. And this wouldn't be the time to do so. While he didn't mind alarming Elise to keep her alert to danger, he didn't want to frighten the girls. He leaned back, tipping the chair onto its rear legs.

"I can't remember the last time I attended the Wild Animal Park," he said casually. "Sounds like a fun day."

Becky looked wary. "You're going to take your gun with you, aren't you?"

Dean paused. "Honey, I'm a policeman. I have to carry it, especially since my job is to keep you and your mom safe."

With the tip of her tongue sticking out, she pondered his explanation with all the seriousness of the young. "Okay," she said finally. "Just make sure you shoot the right person."

"Wonderful, now my youngest is getting bloodthirsty," Elise muttered into her salad. She wondered how much more she was going to have to take. Dean visited the sheriff's station a couple of times a week, continued driving the girls to school and kept a close eye on her clinic. She gleefully noticed he stayed out of there anytime she had reptile patients and made a mental note to schedule as many scaly creatures as she could find.

She tried to forget that night in her office, but she learned it wasn't easy to forget the kind of kiss that traveled down to one's toes and swept back up again. The man had kissing down to an erotic art, and if she didn't keep her wits about her, she would be happily seeking more of it. And she suspected she'd end up with a lot more than a few kisses! Fighting that now-familiar softening inside her, she fixed him with a warning glare. "Does this mean you have no more protests to our going this Sunday?"

His choirboy-innocent smile sent unholy tingles down her spine. "Nope."

"That's what I was afraid of."

Keri wasn't appeased. "If he's going, I'm *not*."

"Oh, yes, you will," Elise said grimly. "I'm not going to be the only one to suffer that day."

THE MINUTE DEAN WOKE UP the morning of the trip to the Wild Animal Park, he knew something was about to happen. And it wasn't going to be Dietrich's rearrest. The back of his neck started tingling when he woke up, continued while he showered and dressed and didn't abate during breakfast. He tried his best not to appear edgy, but, judging from the wary looks he received, he wasn't hiding it very well. Keri glared at him, Lisa looked disgruntled, Becky unhappy and Elise looked just plain grim.

"You can drive." She tossed him the keys to the Pathfinder. The girls climbed into the back, martyred expressions on their faces.

He spared a glance to the rear. "You're really letting Keri leave the house like that?"

Elise's back went up at anyone casting aspersions on her firstborn. "Like what?"

He jerked his thumb in Keri's direction. "She's wearing enough makeup for three people. Isn't that too much for a sixteen-year-old?"

Elise silently counted to ten, twice. "I don't think blush, lipstick and mascara is too much. And I don't believe it's your business how much or how little she wears."

"Okay, but if some sailor tries to pick her up, don't come running to me."

"So help me, if you ruin this day, I will draw and quarter you myself, and believe me, I have the instruments to do it," she threatened.

He held up his hands in surrender. "Hey, I'm only trying to help."

"No wonder your captain wanted you out of his hair for a while." She climbed into the passenger seat, pulling the belt across her chest. From then on, she only spoke to give directions to the girls' friends' houses. Pretty soon they were on the freeway heading for San Marcos.

During the drive, Dean heard bits and pieces of whispered conversations about policemen, guns and killers. He sighed. So much for keeping a low profile. Still, the cold shoulder Elise was giving him wouldn't easily lend itself to the charade of their being "close friends" either.

After he parked in one of the small lots alongside the main road leading to the park, Elise recited her usual set of rules. The older girls were on their own once inside, but they would have to check in at certain times, no eating too much junk food please, and they would set a time to meet back at the main gate at the end of the day.

Dean's nape tingled madly. "I don't think that's a good idea."

Elise looked as if she were spoiling for a battle. "Why not?"

His hands tightened on the steering wheel. "I think you know why."

She lowered her voice. "Dean, the girls need a simple good time for a change. Besides, the man is after me, not them. And how would he even know what they look like? It's not as if they won't be around a lot of people. They understand not to talk to strangers, and you've warned them so many times that they're almost afraid to talk to their own friends. What could possibly happen to them here?"

How could he explain that when the back of his neck tingled this way, it usually meant that trouble was close by? It wasn't something that could be documented, but he never ignored his internal warning device, since nine times out of ten it was accurate. Still, it wasn't something he could easily explain to the logical Dr. Carpenter, and he didn't feel right discussing the matter in front of the girls.

"They should stick with us," he stated.

"Oh, pu-leeze!" Keri wailed, looking as if he had just suggested they dance naked through the parking lot.

Elise sent her a warning look. She hadn't missed Dean's white-knuckled grip on the steering wheel. Finally she'd realized something was bothering him, and for some reason he wasn't going to go into it now.

"Maybe it *would* be a good idea to at least remain in sight of each other," she said quietly. "After all, Detective Cornell didn't think we should take this trip to begin with. He's been kind enough to travel with us, so the least we can do is go along with his suggestions."

Dean turned his head. She wasn't going to fight him on this! His expression was pure appreciation. They stared at each other, oblivious to the girls climbing out of the back of the truck.

"You know something, don't you?" she said quietly. "Something you can't, or won't, tell us."

He glanced at the girls milling around the truck, the back door now closed. "Word has it Dietrich has a friend in the area who was recently released from Chino. We'd hoped Dietrich might have left the state, but it looks like he's only gone underground. There's days when I feel as if someone is watching the property."

"And you think it's either Dietrich or his friend?" It was more a statement than a question.

His nod was firm.

Elise looked down at her hands, now laced tightly in her lap. "I don't care so much for myself," she murmured. "But if anything happened to my babies..."

He gripped her hands with one of his, feeling the chill of her fear invade his skin. "Nothing is going to happen to anyone as long as I'm around," he vowed fiercely. "He's not going to win this round."

"I can't let them know any of this," she said more to herself than to him. "They've looked forward to this day for a long time. My work keeps me so busy, we rarely have days out like this."

"Hey, are we going in or what?" Lisa knocked on Dean's window.

He opened the door. "Going in," he replied, tugging one of her short curls. He looked over her head at Keri. "You've got two choices. You stick with us, or you and Susan keep an eye on Lisa and Ginger."

"What?" Keri looked dismayed. "That's like glorified baby-sitting!"

"Those are your choices," he said firmly.

Keri nodded grudgingly. "I guess we should be grateful we don't have to have Becky and Kim tagging along, too," she grumbled.

Susan, a spritely brunette, looked up in awe, along with a bit of admiration, for the dark-haired man. "Wow, Keri, how many kids have their own bodyguard? And he's so cute for an older man" she could be heard to say as Keri dragged her up the road with Lisa and Ginger following at a slower pace.

Elise chuckled as she took Dean's arm. "Come on, old man," she crooned. "We'll take it easy up the hill."

"I'm hardly old enough to be that kid's father, and she just made me feel like her grandfather," he muttered, not lost far enough in self-pity to miss the advantage of grasping Elise's hand in a firm grip. Elise looked down at their clasped hands. "I'm old, not dead," he explained.

When they reached the ticket booth, Elise insisted on paying Dean's way.

"It could have gone on my expense report," he told her.

She shook her head. "Amazing what our taxes pay for. Besides, this is our treat. Just relax and enjoy." Before handing out the tickets, she led the girls to a secluded spot. "One last warning. I don't want any of you to say anything out loud as to why Detective Cornell is with us," she said in a low voice. "Call him Dean and leave it at that. Hear me?"

"So he's your boyfriend for the day?" Lisa asked.

Elise paused. She deliberately didn't look at Dean, although she couldn't miss him standing so close behind her. "Yes, I guess so."

"Sounds good to me," he murmured for her ears only.

She resisted giving him a good kick.

Lisa grinned broadly. Dean should have known that, if anyone would get into the act, Lisa would be the one to give it her all.

Once inside the enclosure, the small group headed for the

tram that would take them on a tour of the large safari park. Dean soon learned that going somewhere with teenagers meant you didn't sit just anywhere. You sat where you couldn't miss *anything,* which meant frequent sliding from one side of the tram benches to the other. Keri and Susan also insisted on sitting some distance from the others.

"They're afraid someone might automatically assume they're with us adults," Elise explained matter-of-factly.

Dean watched the three teenage boys eyeing the girls in a way he remembered from his younger days. He sent them a male glare that warned them to back off. The boys immediately wilted and rushed to take other seats before the tram left.

Keri turned around and caught Dean looking his fiercest. She immediately stared at her mother. "Mom, make him stop," she hissed, looking horrified.

Elise poked him none too gently in the side with her elbow. "Dean, behave yourself."

"I am. I'm acting like a man who knows exactly what those punks had on their minds," he groused, not in the least apologetic for his heavy-handed tactics.

"It's starting!" Becky squealed, looking out the window as the tram slowly left the station.

Dean wasn't as interested in viewing the wild animals as he was in Elise's sitting so close to him he could smell the light floral fragrance she wore. He also enjoyed the view of her faded jeans cupping her slender body and the oversize mint-green sweater skimming the curves his hands itched to explore. With her hair pulled up in a saucy ponytail and minimum makeup emphasizing her beautiful turquoise eyes, she looked as young as her oldest daughter. Gauging the admiring looks she received from some of the other men on the tram, he was glad he was with her to keep those jerks away from her. After all, he *was* there to protect her delectable rear, right? But deep down he knew it was more than that. He settled back in his seat, arms crossed over his chest, determined to enjoy this day to its fullest. If only his neck would stop its damn tingling!

Elise watched Dean under the cover of conveniently lowered lashes. She sensed something was bothering him and wished he would confide his worries to her. Not that she could do much, but sharing a problem generally helped.

Of course, she had only to look at him to know he wasn't the type to share worries or fears. If anything, he was the kind of man her mother would insist she stay away from. Scuffed boots, faded jeans and a black T-shirt that stretched lovingly across his chest. With the dark beard and shaggy hair, he needed only a motorcycle to complete the picture of the eternal rebel.

Hair that was thick and silky to the touch, she remembered. A beard that brushed tantalizingly across her tender skin...

"Watch it, Doc," Dean muttered out of the side of his mouth. "Your eyes are kinda glazed, and your face is a little too flushed for someone just watching the lions sprawl around out there."

Her gaze flew upward to catch a wicked sparkle in his brown eyes. She didn't even need to feel the heat in her cheeks to know he'd somehow read her thoughts. "You think you're hot stuff, don't you?"

He grinned. "You did, too, not all that long ago."

Aware she didn't have a prayer of having the last word in this conversation, she deliberately turned her back on him as she stared out the window. She could have been looking at a blank wall for all she cared; it was the message her position conveyed that was important to her.

Dean didn't mind looking at Elise's back. He'd already decided he liked all the parts that made up the woman she was. Wouldn't his buddies love to know he'd fallen for this frosty piece of womanhood? Dean, the eternal bachelor— probably because no sane woman would put up with him. At least, that was what one ex-girlfriend had told him. He hadn't minded playing the field in the past. Besides, in his line of business, he didn't know if it was a good idea to have someone else to worry about other than his own skin. And he'd seen the high divorce rate in his department, much less the entire L.A. County police force. It took a special woman to put up with his kind of life. Look how long it took Mac to find the right woman after one disastrous marriage. And now he was beginning a family.

Dean watched the three Carpenter girls. While they shared family similarities, each had her own personality. Keri, who tried to be so grown-up, was still a young girl dealing with a nasty problem she shouldn't even have to worry about. With her mother's composure and cool, touch-me-not manner, she must already drive the boys crazy. Lisa, who was just leaving her tomboy phase and preparing to enter that sacred teenage world, energetic and curious as hell. She'd make a great cop, he decided. And Becky, sweet little Becky, who entered true school life this year. Poor thing still allowed her older sister to drag her into trouble, but those big blue turquoise eyes could melt the coldest heart in no time.

He suddenly found himself wanting to be around when these girls grew up. To see what they would be like. Then there were Elise. In his eyes, she was the most important part of the package. Her potential wasn't too hard to visualize, either, since he'd already held her in his arms, kissed her and had the pleasure of her kissing him back.

He shifted uneasily in his seat. Good going, Cornell, he told himself. You're supposed to be thinking about catching bad guys, not about kissing Elise again.

Yeah, but kissing her was good, wasn't it? his libido asked in a taunting whisper. And you would like to kiss her again, wouldn't you? And touch her and find out about those interesting curves. Come on, Cornell, admit it, you're falling for the lady. And you're falling hard.

He glanced around, thinking about a cigarette for the first time in three years. It hadn't been easy to break his four-pack-a-day habit, but with his stubborn nature, he'd kicked it good. Now, all because of a sexy broad, he wanted to fill his lungs with nicotine again!

Hearing him shift around, Elise looked over her shoulder. "What's wrong? Do you want to trade seats?"

He shook his head. "Just got a cramp in my leg," he muttered, crossing his arms over his chest, then uncrossing them.

Elise frowned at him. "If you didn't want to take the tram, you could have waited for us at the station," she told him. "Unless you think the tram might be hijacked during the trip."

He half turned his body. "Look, I just want a smoke, okay?"

Her forehead creased in a puzzled frown. "I've never seen you smoke. And your clothing doesn't smell like a smoker's." Whoops! She'd just given away the fact that she noticed such things. Such as he always smelled of soap instead of stale smoke.

"I quit a few years go, but right now, I would kill for a cigarette," he bit out.

Elise knew better than to ask what had brought on the attack. Instead, she rummaged in her leather shoulder bag and tossed him a stick of gum. "Try that. I've heard it helps."

He unwrapped the foil and popped the rectangle into his mouth. "Mmm, spearmint." He chewed reflectively. "Thanks."

Now Elise had another sensory memory to battle—clean male skin with a hint of spearmint. Her sister and close friends had battled with her for years about getting out and dating; now she almost wished she had. Then she might not be well on her way to having a nervous breakdown right now just because a man's scent did incredible things to her.

"All right, girls, what next?" Elise made a show of studying the pamphlet detailing the special events for the day.

"Petting zoo!"

"Animal nursery."

"Watching the gorillas."

Elise held up her hand, forestalling the inevitable arguments. "You four older girls fight it out among yourselves. We'll meet at the snack bar in two hours for lunch, all right? Dean and I will take Becky and Kim to the petting zoo."

Dean looked undecided. "Maybe we should tag along with them."

"Mom, he's going to ruin our day," Keri insisted.

"Dean, they'll be fine," Elise assured him. "They'll be fine."

She nodded at Keri, silently telling her to escape while the getting was good. She took Dean's arm and steered him in the opposite direction, Becky and Kim racing ahead of them.

"Slow down, girls!" she called out. "We oldsters can't keep up with you. And you, stop acting so heavy-handed." She looped her arm through his. "Come on, relax and have fun. After all, how often do you get a cushy assignment like this?"

"Robbery doesn't give us too many. My last one was while I worked vice. I had a prostitution ring convinced I was a well-connected pimp from Chicago." Getting caught up in the game, he draped an arm around her shoulders in a possessive manner. "My partner, who played the part of my main lady, complained she'd never be able to walk again after wearing spike heels for six weeks."

Elise had an idea it wasn't at all like it was portrayed on television. "What was your complaint?"

His voice hardened. "Having to act like the slime I dealt with."

Elise was glad they'd reached the petting zoo. This wasn't the time to talk about Dean's work. She laughed as Becky and Kim ran around petting the goats and llamas wandering the enclosed area looking for cupped palms filled with grain. She laughed even harder when a daring young goat caught hold of the back of Dean's shirt and started chewing on it.

"Hey, this isn't edible," he informed the goat, trying to free his shirt from the stubborn animal who bleated his refusal to relinquish his prize. "Elise, help!"

"Big brave man afraid of a little goat," she chided, finally pushing the horned animal to one side.

"I told you, I never had pets." He sidestepped a llama hanging its head over his shoulder.

"Maybe not, but they sure seem to like you. Come on, girls, let's find Dean a safer place." She herded Becky and

Kim out of the enclosure and guided them to the elephant show.

Elise shared Dean's worries about the other four girls being out of their sight, but she didn't want to ruin their day, and she knew she had to trust them to have the sense to stay out of trouble. She had to think that way or go crazy. While Keri and Lisa's friends didn't understand the need for caution, Keri and Lisa did. She was just glad the two youngest were happy wandering around, watching the gorillas and walking to the lookout points to see the animals scattered in the park closest to the main area. Still, no matter how much she smiled, she couldn't keep from feeling relieved when the time came to meet the others at the snack bar. She only began to panic when the girls were five minutes late and she couldn't ignore Dean glancing at his watch every fifteen seconds.

"Sorry," Lisa panted when they ran up to the waiting adults. "Keri and Susan saw a boy they knew from school and had to stop to talk." She rolled her eyes.

Dean opened his mouth to remind Keri she wasn't to talk to *anyone*, then quickly snapped it shut.

"Let's get something to eat," he said abruptly.

After ordering hamburgers, fries and Cokes, they found two tables off in a corner where the four older girls could sit by themselves with the adults at an adjoining table.

"How do you handle this on a daily basis?" Dean asked, admiration for Elise's calm manner etched on his features. "I mean, all of this would drive a normally sane person to the funny farm in no time."

Elise shrugged. "You just try not to let the little things get on your nerves." She swirled a French fry in catsup and popped it into her mouth. "That way you're not a nervous wreck when the big stuff comes up. I won't get upset over Keri not keeping her room immaculate, but I will have a fit if she doesn't keep up her grades because she's decided the opposite sex or making junior varsity cheerleader is more important."

"You should be proud of yourself. You've done a great job with them."

"Mom, can we go through the gift shops?" Lisa stood by her mother's chair.

She looked around. "Where's Keri and Susan?"

She wrinkled her nose. "In the bathroom, where else? I think they're afraid someone might not think they have enough mascara on or something."

Elise sighed. "All right, but stay there until we show up, all right?"

Lisa and Ginger nodded, clearly eager to be off. "We will."

"Between your practice and the girls, you really don't have a lot of free time," Dean commented, gathering up empty food containers and dropping them onto the plastic tray.

Elise tipped her head to the side. "Oh, please, Cornell, you've never been coy before. Spit it out."

He stared her straight in the eye. "Men."

She stared right back. "Are you asking about my sex life, Detective?"

"Yeah."

"Fine, I'll tell you if you'll tell me."

Dean winced. "All right, let's try something else."

Elise flashed him a smug smile. "Chicken."

"No, just smart. A man in my position doesn't have a lot

of chances to meet appropriate members of the opposite sex."

"You mean the ones you can take home to meet mother."

"Right. We mostly meet the ones you take home when mother isn't home."

She nodded. She silently admitted she was very curious about the women Dean had seen in the past. The only thing she felt certain of was that he hadn't dated a woman with children before. "We're thrown together under special circumstances, Dean," she said softly. "Did you ever stop to think that, otherwise, you probably wouldn't have given me a second glance?"

He reached across the table and grasped her chin with his fingers, lifting her face. "Believe me, no matter what, I would have given you a hell of a lot more than a second glance." The rough timbre in his voice sent shivers running across her spine and heat coiling deep in her stomach.

"Careful, Detective," she whispered. "This park is family oriented, and you're straying a bit beyond the boundaries."

He smiled. "Then it will just give you something to think about, won't it?"

Determined to return her pulse rate to normal, Elise kept one eye on Becky and Susan, who were busy chattering as they dawdled over the last of their hamburgers, and the other on the ladies' room door where people streamed in and out. But two familiar figures hadn't come out yet. Each time the wrong people left the ladies' room, her irritation rose.

"What's taking them so long?" Becky moaned, fidgeting in her seat.

"Good question." Elise frowned at the door. "In about two seconds I'm going in there and dragging those girls out by their immaculately combed hair."

The tingling along the back of Dean's neck suddenly intensified. *The son of a bitch was here! Close. So close Dean could almost smell him!* He pushed back his chair so violently it fell over as he stood up. "We're going now." he headed for the restrooms.

"What are you doing? Oh, no!" A horrified Elise sensed his intent and dreaded the consequences. "Dean, you can't."

He ignored her as he walked over to the ladies' room door and pounded on it. "Keri, Susan, out now! Your hair must have been brushed at least five hundred times by now, and if you put any more of that eye stuff on, you'll look like damn raccoons!"

"Oh, no!" Elise moaned, covering her face with her hands. Maybe if she stayed in that position, no one would associate her with this madman.

Keri and Susan scuttled out of the restroom looking at Dean as if he were demented.

"I have never been so embarrassed in my life!" Keri yelped.

"Sure wish I had the nerve to do that to my daughter, buddy," one man told Dean as he passed them.

"I can't believe you did that." Elise pushed them all in the direction of the gift shops. She shot Dean a look fit to kill. "There was no call for that."

He clenched his jaw tightly. "It got them out, didn't it?" During the time he ushered them toward the gift shops to pick up the other girls, he kept scanning the area, looking for anything out of place. He silently cursed himself for allowing this trip at all. He should have guessed! His warning signal had gone off loud and clear when they arrived. Why hadn't he listened to it?

Elise was so angry with him, she didn't dare look at him,

because if she did she knew she would hit him. Her fury blinded her to his agitation and to the idea that there might have been an excellent reason for his hurrying the girls out of there. "No wonder you're not a father. No woman in her right mind would dare mix her genes with yours." She already dreaded the drive home, with Keri and Susan acting like typical teen martyrs convinced their lives were over. She knew she would see humor in the situation later on, but right now she preferred to remain angry with Dean.

"Dean!" Becky and Kim ran up to him with anxious expression marring their tiny faces.

He crouched down, balancing himself on his toes. "What's up, cherubs?"

Kim giggled at the nickname. "Becky said we should tell you about the strange man that talked to us."

His interest sharpened. "What man?"

Becky held out a folded piece of paper. "He gave us this for you and a candy bar for each of us." She also held out the candy, which Elise snatched from her hand and Kim's.

"What did the man look like?" Dean asked, masking his rage. He couldn't believe he hadn't seen the two girls lag behind for a minute!

"He had black hair, all kind of spiky, and really weird eyes," Becky replied. She wrinkled her nose in disgust. "And a picture on his arm of a skull with a snake coming out of its mouth. And a scar like the one on my knee from when I cut it on that fence last year. He said Mom operated on him once, but I told him she only operates on animals. But he said she operated on him once." Her eyes dimmed with worry. "I wanted to get away from him, but he held my hand real tight, and I was afraid to call out to you."

Elise's hand covered her mouth, muffling a cry of alarm.

Dean slowly opened the piece of paper and scanned the one word scrawled across it. He clamped down on the pithy curse rolling around in his head. The two small girls were nervous enough without his adding to their worry. Not to mention the shock darkening Elise's eyes.

"Is it...?" She couldn't say the name.

He held up the paper so she could read the single word.

A tiny moan escaped her lips as it penetrated her brain.

Gotcha.

Chapter Nine

"The bastard was right there in the park. He was so close to us I should have been able to catch him!" Dean paced back and forth in front of Detective Santee's desk, one fist clenched tightly, the other holding a lit cigarette. He'd lost his battle with nicotine that morning when he stopped at a convenience store for a carton of cigarettes after driving the girls to school. "Instead of doing my job, I was rousting two teenage nymphets from the bathroom." He dropped into a chair. He rubbed his forehead with the hand holding the cigarette. "Damn."

"Why should I sit there and tell you what an idiot you are when you're doing such a great job of it yourself?" Santee said amiably. He settled back in his chair and propped his feet up on his desk. "Frankly, you've called yourself pretty much any name I might think up and a few I haven't."

Dean scowled at him. "You want to leave here in one piece?"

"Detective Cornell, what you're thinking of is illegal. Not to mention you're on my turf here."

"You never can tell. Your colleagues might thank me for it." Dean stubbed out his half-smoked cigarette in the ashtray

Santee had set before him when he first entered. Within ten minutes it was filled with half-smoked cigarettes. "I hate eternally calm men," he muttered darkly.

"We're still checking out his old buddy, Bartlett. Maybe we'll get a lead there."

Dean glumly studied the toe of his boot. "Anderson isn't happy over Dietrich's not being caught yet." He winced, recalling his superior's screams of outrage earlier that morning when he talked to him on the phone. "He said if there isn't a viable lead within the next week, he wants me back. Although he didn't sound too eager about that, either."

The sheriff's detective shook his head. "What happened last week wasn't a viable lead to him?"

"Not if I didn't see the guy with my own baby-blues," he grumbled.

Santee chuckled. "Your eyes aren't blue."

"He doesn't care." Dean narrowed his eyes in thought as he stared at the other man. "I want to see this through."

"And you've got a week to do it."

He spoke slowly. "Unless I take my vacation." All along, Dean had feared time would run out before Dietrich was caught. And he knew, no matter what, he wasn't going to leave Elise and the girls alone on the property, no matter how many security alarms were activated, guard dogs on duty and loaded rifles in easy reach. The feminine foursome had come to mean a great deal to him, and he would do whatever was necessary to keep them safe from harm.

For a guy who'd always visualized himself as the perfect bachelor, he found himself settling into a homey routine all too easily. He knew it had something to do with Elise. Settling into any kind of routine would be easy where she was concerned. As it was, he discovered it was difficult to think about the time when he would have to return to L.A. Wouldn't the guys at the station have a good laugh over this. Dean Cornell, admirer of all women, was finally well on his way to falling really big for just one lady. Ah, but what a lady!

Santee shook his head. "Off duty means just that. You wouldn't have any authority."

Dean pounded his fist on the desk in frustration. "Yeah, but you can't have someone out there all the time. We both know if I leave, Dietrich will strike and disappear into some hole where we'll ever find him."

Santee settled back in his chair. "It would be a good setup. A way to bring him out of hiding," he mused.

Dean shook his head. "No, that kind of trap is too dangerous."

Santee easily read his mind. "We could put her daughters in protective custody."

"Even with them gone it's dangerous, and you know it. By just talking to Dietrich's scum friends, we've learned he's a pretty sick guy. Right now he's fixated on Elise Carpenter, and he isn't going to stop until he gets her." He glanced at his watch and pushed himself out of his chair. "I've got to go. The doc is taking Keri and Becky to the dentist and shopping, and I'm looking after Lisa, who's in bed sick. I figured it would be a good time to wash and wax my truck."

Santee glanced out the window that overlooked the parking lot. A dusty blue pickup sat in solitary splendor near the building's entrance. "I don't think it'll help."

Dean laughed. "Probably not, but I do my best thinking when I'm scrubbing down that monster."

He nodded. "I'll call when I hear anything."

"Thanks."

Dean drove along the freeway, keeping an eye out for anything unusual but knowing it would be a miracle if he lucked out. At the same time, his brain reminded him, catching Dietrich meant his time in the Carpenter household would come to an end, and he wasn't ready for that. No, he wanted him and Elise to have a chance together. To really get to know each other and see where it would lead.

Right about now, if there was one thing he truly knew about the lady, it was that she was one of the most stubborn women he'd ever come across. Her agenda for that day was proof. He still wasn't comfortable with the idea of Elise going out by herself and voiced that concern at breakfast. But she'd had the perfect argument ready for him. If he tagged along with her, what about Lisa? It already appeared the dogs and watch geese were no match for a man like Dietrich. He had to admit that watching an abnormally quiet Lisa refuse breakfast and say she preferred to remain in bed, especially on a weekend, was unusual. So Dean was elected to baby-sit.

When he arrived back at the house, he watched a stone-faced Keri march past him, a wary Becky follow and an amused Elise on their heels as they prepared to leave.

"Keri has decided she will never talk to you again," Elise informed him as she opened the car door.

"Tell me about it. She's been so quiet around me all week, I began to wonder if she'd lost her voice. Okay, so I handled that scene at the park badly," he admitted, curling his hands over the top of the car door. "I'm not used to females."

With solemn eyes she studied him. "Considering your age and obvious experience, I'd think you've lived with your share of females." It was a question as much as a statement. Her low voice didn't carry farther than his ears.

He shook his head. "Not exactly. Probably something to do with my less than meticulous habits at home," he said honestly. "And boys like me didn't have a chance to learn much about teenage girls like Keri."

"I still can't picture you as the geek you claim to have been." She eyed the ratty T-shirt he now wore.

He looked down at his shirt. "Yeah, well, maybe I went too far overboard in changing my image. I never was one for the suit-and-tie routine."

Elise couldn't picture Dean in a suit. He was too comfortable and sexy in faded jeans and that torn navy T-shirt that proclaimed Cops Make Better Lovers. Hmm, that idea merited thought. But not right now. Not if she wanted to have a fairly sane day.

She'd finally come to realize it wasn't what a man wore that made him capable in his work, but what was inside. Her antagonism toward the police force had softened a great deal when she saw how hard Dean worked at keeping her and the girls safe.

"I didn't date very much myself," she admitted, "because I wanted to keep a 4.0 grade-point average and get into veterinary school. As women in veterinary schools are still somewhat rare, I had to work even harder there. Sometimes I think the main reason I dated Steve was because he was always there. He shared my passion for veterinary medicine, and he understood the pressure I was under. Not that we didn't share other things as well. But that was what I considered most important at that time." She looked off toward the hills, her gaze tracking the clouds obscuring the mountaintops.

"Don't get too maudlin, Doc, or I'll have to do something

about it. Like throw you over my shoulder and carry you off to some romantic hideaway.''

She arched an eyebrow. ''And have your wicked way with me?''

''Naturally. Having my wicked way with beautiful women is what I do best.'' He lowered his voice to a husky purr. ''As much as I admire your mind, Doc, I'd like to have a chance to admire your body, too.''

How tempting he made it sound! ''Careful, Detective, you'd probably run for the hills if I threw myself into your arms and begged you to take me away from all this.''

''Try me.''

Elise decided this was the right time to back down—before things got too heated up. She already sensed Dean would be an excellent lover. He'd certainly pushed all the right buttons with her that night in her office. The memory had given her plenty of sleepless nights since. Yet in so many ways he was ignorant about women. Not that he was callous; he simply didn't always know how to act around them. Although, she was the first to admit, when it came to teenage girls, it wasn't easy.

''We'll take this under consideration later. As for now, Keri wants to do some shopping afterward,'' she told him. ''So don't worry if we're not back for a few hours.''

He nodded, suddenly edgy for a brand-new reason as he realized Elise would be out of touch for a while. ''What if— ah—Lisa starts feeling worse?''

''She's sleeping right now and may just do that for the rest of the afternoon. She'll call out if she needs anything.''

Dean shifted uneasily from one foot to the other. ''Are you sure it's safe?'' he asked.

She immediately guessed the reason for his hesitation.

"Safe for me to go or safe for you to handle Lisa? Dean, if I'm not worried, you shouldn't be either. I promise I'll watch for anyone showing too much interest in us. I just don't want to leave Lisa alone when she isn't feeling well."

"I guess if you feel comfortable about it, I should, too. Have fun." He tried to look as cheerful as possible.

She arched an eyebrow. "Fun at the dentist? Fun walking through who knows how many stores until my eldest finds exactly what she's looking for? If you'd prefer, we can change places."

"Mom!" Keri's wail of dismay was loud and clear.

"I'll stay home with Lisa," he said promptly.

Elise smiled. "I thought you would."

The moment Dean watched the Pathfinder roll down the driveway, he felt uneasy. He slowly turned and stared down the white goose watching him with what he was certain was malice in its beady eyes.

"I bet you'd taste great with orange sauce ladled over you," he told her.

Frances honked and ran toward him, wings flapping. Dean stood his ground for all of ten seconds before he jumped onto the porch.

"Why didn't you do this the night Dietrich showed up?" he muttered, entering the house.

He quickly changed into shorts and a fresh T-shirt and stopped by Lisa's room. The girl was wide-awake, huddled under the covers with her knees drawn up to her chin.

"You okay, kiddo?" he asked softly.

"Uh-huh," she mumbled.

"Would you like something to drink or eat?"

She shook her head.

He glanced at the small portable television Elise had evidently left on the dresser before she left. "Maybe the remote control for the TV?"

She didn't look at him. "Mom put it on my nightstand for me."

He couldn't remember ever feeling so helpless. "I'm going to wash my truck. If you need anything, you give a holler, okay? I'll be where I can hear you."

Still not looking at him, Lisa nodded.

Dean walked outside. He positioned his truck near Lisa's window before he went in search of a bucket and sponges. He also kept a sharp eye on Frances, who watched him from a short distance, her beak snapping open and closed as she muttered short, vicious honks.

"You are something else," he told the goose as he turned the faucet on and picked up the hose.

As he ran water over the truck, he could hear the dogs snuffling around the yard, the two geese playing their own games and Baby telling the world to "fud up." He laughed aloud.

"Quiet, dammit!" the macaw finally screamed, by now frustrated that no one was listening to her orders.

"Bet I know where you heard that," he murmured, running a soapy rag over the hood. He was just finishing rinsing it off when the ringing phone caught his attention. He quickly turned off the water and ran for the back door.

"Yeah?"

"Hey, buddy, Stacy gave me a beautiful daughter at 4:02 yesterday morning," Mac said without preamble. "Jennifer Anne McConnell."

Dean whooped. "That's great! You must be on top of the world!"

"Yeah, especially since she looks just like her mother. In

fact, everything went so well that we all just got home. It appears hospitals don't keep new mothers any longer than necessary.'' He sounded as if he strongly disagreed with that idea.

Dean tightened his grip on the receiver. He couldn't explain the jolt to his gut at this announcement. He always thought Mac was going to be the last holdout in the marriage market. Then Stacy came along and swept the gruff detective off his feet, even resorting to kidnapping him in the end! And in the two years they'd been together, Mac had looked happier than Dan had ever thought he could be. Dean found himself jealous of his friend's luck and, for the first time, hungered for that same kind of future.

"I'm really glad for you, Mac," he said quietly, sincerity ringing in his voice. "If anyone deserves it, you do. How's Stacy doing?"

"Said she's happy she doesn't look like she's swallowed a basketball any longer." His voice sobered. "How's it going there? Found out anything new?"

Dean had already filled him in on the scare at the Wild Animal Park.

"Not one damn thing," he said, disgusted. "It's as if Dietrich disappeared into thin air. I questioned people there, but no one remembered seeing him. All we have to go on is Becky and her friend. Now Becky looks at me as if I was the bad guy, Keri considers me an embarrassment to the human race and Lisa's been moping around the house all week. My luck with the opposite sex has been absolute zero."

"You didn't say what the lovely doc thinks of you."

Dean hadn't told Mac about the kiss in Elise's home office, but his friend knew well enough that something must have happened—just by how much Dean *hadn't* told him about Elise.

"She just wants Dietrich caught," he said finally.

After Mac rang off, Dean stared at the receiver for a moment before finally settling it in the cradle. He frowned when he heard faint whimpering sounds from the rear of the house. He headed down the hallway.

"Lisa?" He stood in the open doorway of her room. "Are you all right?"

She lay in a fetal position, her back to the door. "Fine."

He walked slowly into the room and sat gingerly on the side of the bed. His hand hovered over her huddled body. "Can I get you something?"

She shook her head. "When's Mom going to be back?" Her voice was scratchy with unshed tears.

"She wasn't sure. Is it something I can help you with?"

She shook her head again. "Can you call Myrna for me? Please?" She buried her face in her pillow.

"Okay. I'll call her right now."

Dean called Myrna's house. No answer. He looked through Elise's address book and even tried Donna and Cheryl. As he heard Donna's answering machine click on, he suddenly remembered her talking eagerly the day before about a date with the new man in her life. And Cheryl's line just continued ringing. He even tried the dentist's office, just in case Elise was still there, only to be told Dr. Carpenter and her daughters had left there more than an hour ago.

"I'm sorry, sweetheart, I guess it's just you and me," he told her when he returned to the bedroom.

Lisa's now-choking sobs left him feeling helpless as he stood there fervently wishing he knew what to do to make her feel better.

"You can't help me. You're a man!" she cried. "You don't understand anything about this. I just want do die!"

Dean then remembered someone he could call. He quickly left the room and headed for Elise's bedroom, snatching up the phone and punching out the numbers. He sighed with relief when Stacy answered, sounding somewhat groggy.

"Hi, there, little mother," he greeted her, hoping he sounded calmer than he felt.

"Hi, yourself."

"How are you and the newest McConnell doing?"

"Just fine, but something tells me you didn't call to ask about us," she told him with her usual insight.

"Okay, you caught me. And believe me, I wouldn't disturb you if it wasn't important. I've got a huge problem that I don't feel qualified to solve," he announced before plunging in with the few details he could give her. Stacy's gurgle of soft laughter didn't leave him feeling reassured.

"You're right. You would have trouble solving it, because you're a man," she told him.

"Funny, that's just what Lisa said," he said sarcastically. "Come on, Stacy, give me a hint!"

"Without talking to Lisa, whom I'm sure would not be happy talking to a strange woman, I can't be sure, but I'd say she's just entered womanhood."

Dean frowned. "Give it to me in English."

"Dean, it sounds as if she's having her first period," she said gently.

"Oh, boy," he muttered. Now he was lost. "Should I take her to a doctor? I mean, is she all right, or should she have medical attention?" He'd never felt so far out of his depth as now.

"No, but fixing her a cup of hot tea and finding a heating

pad to help her with her cramps wouldn't hurt. I'm sure she's taken care of the necessities herself, since girls are usually prepared for this in advance, but what she needs now is lots of TLC."

"Elise is going to blame me for this," he muttered.

"I don't think so. Look, if there's any more problems, call me, and if she's willing, I'll talk to her, okay?"

"Okay." He felt lost the moment he hung up the phone. "I can handle this," he told himself. "I can handle this." His chant didn't make him feel the least bit secure.

Taking Stacy's advice to heart, he searched through the linen closet and bathrooms until he found a heating pad. A hunt through the medicine chest provided him with a bottle of Midol, and he headed for the kitchen to heat a cup of tea in the microwave.

"Lisa, maybe this will make you feel better," he said softly, returning to her room. He plugged in the heating pad and placed it over her covered body. "I also brought you some tea."

She looked up, startled at the array of items before her. She could read in his face that he knew what was wrong with her, and her face turned bright red.

"I'm the first to admit I know more about being a boy than being a girl, but there is one thing I can tell you. I think girls are a lot more special than boys," he said conversationally, placing the mug of tea on the nightstand next to the bottle of Midol. "And more complicated. We guys only grow up worrying if we'll make the football team or if we'll be able to grow a decent mustache or beard, while you girls have to worry about makeup, hairstyles, prom gowns, jerky guys—you name it. Although, come to think of it, I wasn't too sure whether the girl I wanted to ask to my senior prom would say yes or just break down in laughter.''

She scooted backward until she rested her shoulders against her bunched-up pillows. "It's not fair," she mumbled, deliberately ignoring the pill bottle. "They don't tell you the truth about all this. The school shows you this dumb cartoon about how your body is changing, and they hand out booklets and say all the same dumb stuff about how wonderful it is. But they never tell you how you're really going to feel."

"Like what?"

She squirmed, clearly uncomfortable discussing this with a man. "Just that you feel sick and you hurt. They never talk about that. What's so good about hurting?" She stared down at her fingers plucking at the edge of her comforter. "All Keri could talk about was buying a dumb bra. She even bragged about it to her friends! She never talked about how it aches and feels funny."

Dean knew right away he was out of his depth. He sensed if he said one wrong word, he could create one very large emotional mess that Elise would not appreciate having to clean up. He felt as if he were tiptoeing through a mine field that could blow up in his face at any moment if he wasn't careful.

"Yeah, well, it means you're growing up," he said slowly. "You'll be viewing the world a little differently from now on."

"You mean I'll start acting stuck-up like Keri?" Lisa unconsciously snuggled closer to him.

"Not necessarily." He slid an arm around her shoulders. "Keri's her own person, just as you are your own. You don't have to follow any special rules. Just continue to be yourself.

This is all new to you, and because your body is changing, you do have aches now and then." He frantically searched his brain for the right words. "Look at it this way. You can do something we guys can't."

"What's that?"

"Have babies. Not that you should consider that right now," he hastily added. "That's something to think about a long time from now. A *long* time," he stressed. "But Lisa, just remember this, even with all these new and wonderful things going on inside of your body, you're still the same Lisa. And that won't change."

Lisa smiled wanly. "It really does make me special, doesn't it?"

He nodded. "You got it, sweetheart."

When Dean finally left her watching television, he felt as if he could handle the toughest problem that came along. After all, he'd helped Lisa realize that her feminine turning point wasn't so bad after all. Still, it didn't stop him from looking out the windows for the next two hours until the Pathfinder appeared at the end of the driveway.

"At last," he breathed in relief, hurrying outside.

Elise looked surprised at Dean practically running to the truck. "Was it that bad a day?" she teased. Then she noted the concern etched on his face. "Is it Lisa? Is she all right?"

"Yeah, but…" He paused, staring up at the sky as if he'd find the answer there. "How do I say this? Lisa's stomachache is because she…" He frowned. Exactly how could he word this?

"Because she what?" Elise demanded, now fearing the worst. "Dean, is she all right or not?" She moved to rush past him.

"She's fine," he assured her, grabbing her arm. "Elise,

Lisa feels kind of emotional right now. I may only be a guy who doesn't have a great sense of tact where your girls are concerned, but I'd say she just entered a new phase in her life, and she's not entirely sure how to handle it."

Elise's eyes widened as the pieces fell into place. "You mean...?"

He nodded. "I got out the heating pad, gave her some Midol and fixed her some tea."

"I have to see her." This time she did escape his grasp and ran inside the house.

"I had no cavities," Becky proudly informed Dean.

He crouched down. "Hey, that's great, sprite."

"Keri didn't, either," she confided. "But all she cared about was finding a new sweater."

Dean looked up at the teenager carrying bags into the house. After his successful mission with Lisa, he felt on top of the world. As if he could handle any obstacles that came his way. Including repairing things with Keri. "Keri, I know I handled things wrong last week. I'd like to try again," he said softly.

She paused and turned around. "You don't understand, do you? We don't need you here. We were fine before you showed up, and we'll be fine when you leave. *You're* the one making Mom afraid of that man. Besides, you haven't exactly done anything while you've been here except act like some macho cop. Why can't you just go back to where you belong and let us get on with our lives!"

"Keri!"

At her mother's sharp voice, the girl turned around. "I won't apologize for speaking the truth." She displayed her mother's stubbornness. "They say we need protection, but protection from what? A man giving Becky a note and a candy bar? A few phone calls? There's no proof that it's even the same man doing all this!''

Elise's face tightened with anger. ''That man killed your father and your baby brother,'' she said tautly. ''Nothing goes smoothly, and we're all feeling the stress of waiting, but if Detective Cornell is willing to wait this man out, the least we can do is be patient, too.''

Tears sparkled in Keri's eyes. Without saying another word, she ran into the house.

''It's always hard on people who feel they've lost control of their lives,'' Dean said quietly. ''It's even harder on kids.''

''She still didn't have the right to say that to you after all you've done for us. I can't imagine any of this is easy on you either, even if it is what you do for a living. Don't worry about Keri. She'll come around. After all, that lethal Cornell charm hasn't failed yet,'' she teased lightly, placing her hand on his arm. ''I want to thank you for helping Lisa. She was feeling frightened because there wasn't a woman around to help her through this, and from what little she'd said, you handled it beautifully. I thank you for that.'' Her eyes were warm sincerity.

He grinned. ''I'll be honest with you. I was scared to death I'd blow it. Something like that is more than a little out of my league. That kind of problem was never handled at the police academy or in the Boy Scout handbook.''

''Then you showed remarkable common sense for a usually less than tactful cop.''

Looking away, Elise chewed on her lower lip. ''I meant what I said, though, Dean. I want Dietrich brought out in the open. We can't remain in this limbo much longer.''

Now he knew he had to tell her. ''My captain is only

allowing me to stay another week. If nothing happens by then, I have to return to L.A.''

Fear flashed briefly through her eyes. Just as quickly, she masked all emotion. After all, she was used to having to handle things on her own. Having Dean there to count on was new to her. Still, in such a short time, Dean had become an integral part of the family, and Elise found herself unable to imagine what it would be like without him around. And, no matter what she said, she did fear the day Carl Dietrich might display his ultimate revenge.

"I guess you didn't think you'd ever hear this from me, but I'll miss you."

An admission of that kind from Elise *was* surprising. Dean couldn't imagine hearing better words from the lady. Except maybe...

To cover his sudden upsurge of emotion, he opted for humor. He ducked his head until his chin grazed her ear. "Will you miss me 'cause I'm such a great kisser?"

She bit her lip to halt her smile. "Myrna will miss cooking for you."

"She won't miss yelling at me to pick up my stuff. And I have to admit, I won't miss that tortoise snoring under my bed." His breath warmed her skin. "So tell me, does anyone snore under your bed? Or *in* your bed?"

She knew if she turned her head the slightest bit his mouth would be very close to hers. As it was, his beard brushed her skin. Tempting as it was, she continued concentrating on staring at the front of the house, idly wondering if it was time to paint the exterior again. It was definitely safer than thinking about the intense male standing next to her.

"Perhaps I should take the Fifth," she murmured demurely. "So I won't have to lie."

"Hey, you can lie all you want. I am one of the most comfortable people in the world to lie on," he told her.

"You paint an interesting picture, Detective," she drawled. "But all you've done so far is talk."

He leaned even closer over her. "Lady, you want action, you've got action." His eyes glittered.

"If I catch you in my room one more time, I will make you sorry you're alive!" Keri's scream was loud enough to shatter eardrums.

Dean stilled. "Back to reality," he said with a sigh.

Elise's smile drooped a bit at the edges. "In many ways."

He dipped his head, dropping a kiss that was definitely a promise of more to come. "We'll take up this discussion later—when reality is sound asleep." He walked off with that loose-hipped gait that sent Elise's imagination soaring with possibilities.

"Yes, we shall."

Chapter Ten

Feeling as if she'd scream if she stayed inside a moment longer, Elise sought the privacy of the front porch. She knew Dean wouldn't be happy to find her out here, but she was temporarily safe from his wrath since he was busy on the phone. She settled herself on the top step, greeting Bailey and Duke and Kola as each of the dogs came up for a hug and a pat on the head.

She looked off into the darkness, seeing the dim outline of the clinic. Memories swamped her mind. The busy hours involved in setting up a new practice, getting the girls settled in a new home and schools. Dealing with a grief that visited her at odd times, usually late at night when there was nothing else to occupy her mind. She was grateful those days and nights were over and she had gone on with her life.

Even though that same life had taken an abrupt turn lately, Dean's unusual entrance into her life wasn't something she'd care to change. She found herself unable to stop smiling. Dean had made a lot of changes in the way she viewed things. And he had given her a new outlook on men.

Thinking about Dean forced her to think about Carl Dietrich and the changes that man had made in her life. She couldn't help wondering if things would ever be the same again. To be honest, she wasn't sure if she wanted them to be. She did know one thing: she didn't want to hide anymore and felt there were few options open to her.

"Are you hiding?" Dean hunkered down next to her and passed her one of the coffee mugs he held.

She accepted the mug and sipped the rich brew. "Thanks. In a way, I guess I am. I looked around and felt as if the walls were closing in on me. During the summer, I come out here a lot after the girls are asleep. It's always peaceful and gives me a chance to think things over."

He sat next to her, their thighs brushing. "So what are you thinking about tonight?"

She took a deep breath. "I've been thinking about our situation."

"Good. Tell me more."

Elise looked away. She already knew what his reaction would be. "I think I should set myself up as bait to bring Dietrich out into the open."

"No." His reply was swift and emphatic. "It's too dangerous, Elise."

"It's already been established that he's watching us. All we'd have to do is get the girls off the property and let him think I'm here alone."

Dean swore under his breath. "He's not dumb, Elise. He'd smell a trap, which could set him off. And if he got past us, he'd take it out on you. There's other ways."

"Tell me one," she demanded. "Tell me one idea that you feel is foolproof that wouldn't require my participation. The girls are starting to grow afraid of their own shadows, and there's even nights when I'm tempted to look under the bed to see if he could be hiding there. This can't go on!"

She also knew she couldn't go on with the knowledge that Dean would be gone in a short time and that if she doesn't watch herself, she'd be nursing a broken heart long after he left.

Dean sighed. "Let me talk to Santee first. See what alternatives there are."

"All right." She bit her bottom lip. "I was so smug five years ago. I thought we would be safe here, that the girls would grow up happy and have normal lives. Yet, tonight, for all we know a madman could be watching us through binoculars, watching and waiting for the right time. He's hurt this family enough. I don't intend to see him hurt us anymore."

He slipped his arms around her shoulders and pulled her against his side. "Neither do I, love. No matter what, I don't intend to leave you here alone. We're in this together."

She rested her cheek against his shoulder, enjoying the warmth of his sweatshirt, the musky scent of his skin and the comfort of knowing he was there for her.

"Mind answering a personal question?"

He dropped a kiss on her forehead. "Go for it. My life is an open book."

She shot him a wry look. "And if I ask about women?"

He winced. "I'll take the Fifth."

"I thought so. Then I'll ask something a great deal safer for both of us. Do you have any brothers or sisters?"

He shook his head. "Just me. My mom said I was more than enough to handle." He easily read her inquiring expression. "She wasn't too certain who my dad was. He was either an aluminum-siding salesman or the guy who used to work on her car. She said it didn't matter because I was so much like her she felt as if she'd conceived me without anyone else's help. Still, I can't complain. She didn't drop me off on church steps or something equally depressing. She worked in a bar whose owner let me use the office for my homework or sleep on the couch until it was time to go home.''

"She was a cocktail waitress?" she asked softly.

He smiled and shook his head. "No, she was a stripper. And a pretty good one, according to the customers. Her stage name was Mona the Minx. She said it sounded classier than Phoebe. I used to wonder if Cornell was our real last name or if she picked it out of a phone book. But that didn't matter much, either. Mom was hot for me to get an education. The first time she found out I ditched school she whipped my butt good, then she sat down and put her arms around me and cried.'' He stared pensively into his mug. "She said she didn't want me to grow up to be a numbers runner or bagman. She felt I was smart enough to do better than that. She said if she had anything to do about it, she wasn't going to spend her last days visiting me in prison. You know, I never skipped another day of school after that,'' he murmured. "It wasn't the whipping as much as never wanting to see her cry again that made me stay in school.''

Elise tried to imagine Dean's childhood but couldn't. A childhood of strippers, bartenders and small-time hoods. Hers had been filled with loving parents, her sister, friends and a lot of pets.

"What does she think of your being a detective?"

"She hoped I'd become a lawyer, but she said if I ever took a bribe or turned the other way, she'd whip my butt again, and this time she wouldn't cry about it. She owns a tavern up in Lake Arrowhead now. She still has her figure and the best legs in town,'' he reflected. "She even has a couple of guys vying for her hand, but she thinks she's too old to get married. I hope one of them can change her mind."

"My dad was a purchasing manager for a medical manufacturing firm until he retired," Elise said quietly. "And my mom was the local Tupperware dealer. Very successful at it, too. Right now they're doing what they've wanted to do for years. They're taking a cruise around the world and having the time of their lives."

"So you grew up in a two-story house with a white picket fence, a collie, roses in the backyard, and your dad home by five-thirty and your mother baking brownies in the kitchen."

Elise chuckled. "Our house was one-story, my mother is allergic to roses, my dad never made it home before six and my sister and I did all the baking. But we did have two dogs, four cats and six hamsters. When my mother gave us each a hamster for Easter, she had no idea mine was pregnant. Kris eloped with her high school boyfriend when she turned eighteen and later divorced him. And while Mom and Dad hoped I'd become a doctor, I surprised them by going to veterinary school instead. So you see, there's no such thing as a perfect family. To me, what matters is having parents who love you no matter what."

Dean sipped his whiskey-laced coffee. "Mom would like you."

She smiled, warmed by his words. "Because I can keep you in line?"

"Because with all that's happened in your life, you never forgot your sense of family. You didn't crawl into a hole and wallow in self-pity. You went on with your life."

"I wanted to crawl into that hole," she murmured. "I wanted to go off somewhere and scream out my anger at the world, but I realized I couldn't. Not when I had three children who didn't understand why their daddy wasn't coming home anymore or why they weren't going to have a baby brother after all. They were my link to sanity."

Dean turned his head in her direction, looking at her with those dark eyes that could either say so much or nothing at all. This time they were speaking loud and clear.

Elise kept her eyes on his face as she slowly leaned forward, setting her mug on the coffee table. She opened her mouth to speak when the shrill ring of the phone broke the silence. For a moment she hesitated.

"Go ahead," he told her. "I'll listen in, just in case."

She didn't release her breath until the quavering elderly voice apologized for interrupting her evening.

"That's quite all right, Miss Turner," Elise soothed. "How can I help you?" She grabbed a notepad and scribbled across the surface. "Miss Turner, could you bring Tweetie in tonight? No, I'm sure it's nothing serious. But let's not take any chances, shall we? Yes, I'll meet you at the clinic in fifteen minutes." She hung up.

"Do you usually meet patients after hours?" Dean asked.

She shook her head. "Only Miss Turner. Tweetie is a budgie and her pride and joy." She grabbed a sweatshirt and pulled it on over her plaid cotton shirt. "I shouldn't be gone long."

"I don't like this. I'll come with you."

"No, Dean, you stay here with the girls." She flipped on the floodlights that illuminated the yard all the way down to the clinic's back door. "See? You can watch me." She grimaced when she saw his look of exasperation. "Look, I'll call as soon as I know something, okay?"

He knew he had to settle for that. "Every half hour."

Elise rolled her eyes. "I'll try" was all she could promise.

Dean remained in the doorway, watching Elise walk down to the clinic. He saw her unlock the door and close it behind her.

"You'd better have locked it," he muttered. He snagged the receiver the moment the phone rang.

"Just so you don't worry, I locked the back door," Elise informed him just before she disconnected the line.

He grinned. "She's improving."

Dean continued his vigil at the door until headlights swept across the end of the driveway and stopped in front of the building. Since Elise had floodlights around the clinic, he could see a tiny woman climb out of a car straight out of a fifties movie and walk slowly around the car to the passenger door. After retrieving a small cage from the front seat, she walked to the front door.

Dean didn't relax the first half hour until Elise called and tersely explained it would take a while. Before he could question her further, she ended the call.

"Damn fool woman," he muttered, glaring at the clinic.

Another half hour passed before he watched the woman leave, this time without the cage, and slowly drive away. By the time another hour passed, he was ready to chew nails. When an additional half hour ticked away, he considered dragging Elise out of there by her hair. With his limited patience now dissipated, he checked the sleeping girls and stalked out of the house, making sure he had a key before locking the door behind him. During the short walk to the clinic he issued dire threats on an unsuspecting Elise's head.

"All right, Elise, time to go home!" He pounded on the back door. "Dammit, Elise, let me in before I break the door down!"

He heard the snick of the dead bolt, but the door didn't

open. He tried the knob and found it turning easily under his hand. He entered the storage area and headed for the only lit room. When he entered he found Elise sitting beside a glass cage where a tiny blue-and-white budgie lay on a thick towel. She leaned over, adjusting the thermostat to her satisfaction, then continued her vigil over the small bird.

"He has cancer," she said abruptly. "It will be a miracle if he's still alive in the morning."

Dean crouched down beside her. He stared into the heated cage, watching the bird's chest rise and fall in labored breaths.

"I didn't realize birds could get cancer."

"Oh, yes, they can get many human diseases." She pressed her fingertips against her forehead and rubbed them in a circular motion. She suddenly looked very tired.

He touched the glass with his fingertips, not surprised to find it warm to the touch. "What can you do for him?"

She shook her head. "Not as much as I'd like. Basically, all I can do is make him as comfortable as possible and let him know he isn't alone."

Dean turned his head, not missing the sorrow darkening her eyes. "Didn't the owner want to stay?"

Elise shook her head. "I sent her away. I didn't want her to see this," she said softly. "Miss Turner is eighty-three, and Tweetie is all the family she has. It would kill her if she watched him die."

They remained together in silence, watching the small bird struggle for each breath it took. When the end grew close, Elise gently took him out of the cage and kept him cupped in her palm as she crooned to him and stroked his feathers. Dean watched her comfort the dying bird to its last breath.

"This is always the hardest," she whispered, placing the lifeless bird on a towel.

Dean stroked his beard in thought. "Is there a way to replace the bird without her knowing it's not the same one?" he asked finally. "I mean, I know the idea is crazy...." He could feel the tips of his ears turning red. "I'll pay for the bird."

Elise's head snapped up. "No, it's not crazy," she murmured. "In fact, I think it would work." She turned around and reached for the phone. She punched out a number and waited a few minutes. "Hi, Marilyn, it's Elise. Yes, I know what time it is. No, I won't apologize for waking you up because I have an excellent reason. Do you have a pale blue-and-white male budgie? No, not a baby, an older one, about two or three years old. Miss Turner's Tweetie just died." Her face lit up. "You do? Wonderful. Could we get it in the morning? Great. I'll see you then."

Dean watched her replace the phone. "Success?"

"Yes, and it's all due to you." Elise bustled around, cleaning up her supplies.

"And she'll never be able to tell the difference?"

She shook her head. "I don't think so. Miss Turner's eyesight isn't what it used to be. I think she'll be so happy her bird is healthy, she won't think to question it." She closed and locked cabinet doors. "Miss Turner is one of the kindest, most generous people I know. I'm glad you thought of this."

Dean smiled. "I bet you don't charge her your regular fees either, do you?"

She flushed. "She's on a fixed income."

Dean draped his arms over her shoulders. "Doc, you're a regular softie."

"Look who's talking about having a soft heart. Just don't

let it get out. I have enough problem keeping the girls in line as it is.''

"Come on. It's after two, and I need my beauty sleep." Keeping one arm around her shoulders, he guided her toward the back door. He took her keys out of her hand and secured the dead bolt, shaking the knob to make sure before they walked up the driveway to the house.

Elise curled an arm around his waist. "You're a very nice man, Detective Cornell."

"Does that mean you'll jump on my bones and have your wicked way with me?"

"I just might," she said archly.

Dean halted and turned her around to face him. "Don't tease me about this, Elise," he said seriously. "Anything else, fine, but not this. You know how badly I want you. I've sure shown you enough times how I feel."

She tipped her head back, her features backlit by the flood-lights. "I'm not teasing, Dean. I admit I was happy in my insulated world. I had my work and my girls, and I didn't think I needed anything else," she said softly. "Then this cop crashed into my life and turned it upside down. Nothing's been the same for me since. You've made me come alive again. I see life a whole new way, and what I've seen about the new me, I like."

His fingers stroked circles against her nape. "Since meeting you, mine hasn't been so calm either. In fact, you're the best thing to come along for me in a very long time."

"I'll be honest. Your being a cop still makes me a bit nervous."

"And I don't like having a tortoise snoring under my bed. The thing is, that's not what's been interfering with my sleep since I came here."

She didn't have to ask the question, but she wanted to. She wanted to hear him say the words. "What is?"

"You. Wondering whether you sleep on the right side of the bed or the left, what you sleep in, if you put goo on your face before you go to bed." His lips curved slightly. "If you snore."

"The left side, shortie pajamas, I only use a lightweight moisturizer and no."

"I also sleep on the left, I sleep raw, I don't put anything on my face and I don't snore."

Her faint smile mirrored his. "Yes, you do."

His eyes twinkled, but instead of looking amused he looked positively wicked. "You been spying on me, Doc?"

"I was the one to rescue you from the couch, remember?" Her fingers curled upward, halting his from another sweeping caress of her arm.

"You gonna rescue me again?"

"You're not asleep."

"I could arrange to be."

"I think I prefer you awake."

"And?" he prompted.

"I think I could arrange to find you a bed that doesn't have a snoring tortoise under it."

"Where?"

Her eyes didn't waver from his intent gaze. "In my room."

Dean drew back, his arms at his side as he allowed Elise to precede him into the house. Once inside, he kept one hand against the small of her back as she walked down the hallway.

When they reached her bedroom, she paused long enough to close and lock her door. She remained still, her hand on the doorknob. "You have to understand this is somewhat new to me," she said in a low voice. "There's only been one other man in my bed, Dean, and he was my husband."

He knew better than to touch her at that moment. It was still up to her how far they would go. "Elise, if you want to change your mind, it's all right. I'm not going to force you into something you're not ready for."

Her head shot up. "You wouldn't get angry?"

"Frustrated as hell, yes," he said ruefully. "Angry, no. This has to be your decision. I want to make love with you, but I don't want it to be just for me. I want you to want me as badly as I want you."

She turned around, leaning back against the door. "I do want you. I wanted you that first night you kissed me, but I didn't know if I was ready then. Oh, I've gotten over Steve's death, and I want you to know I don't see you as a substitute for him," she hastily explained.

His smile warmed her all the way through. Not the kind of heat that leaves one wanting, but the kind of slow warmth one seeks on a cold winter morning.

"I had hoped so, but hearing you say it makes it even better." Dean exhaled a rough breath. Could he honestly give this woman all that she deserved? He was sure going to give it his best try. He moved forward until she was trapped between the door and his body. He rested his forearms against the wood.

"Oh, lady, I want you so badly, but I want to make it as special for you," he groaned.

She toyed with his shirt. "I already feel special. Just seeing the way you look at me lets me know how wonderful we'll be together." One hand ventured southward until it rested against his jeans zipper.

He drew in a sharp breath. "Damn." He found it harder to speak as he heard the hiss of the zipper being lowered and several daring fingers dipping past the metal teeth. "You're making me crazy, Elise."

Her fingers found their way past the cotton briefs. She idly wondered what color he wore as she encountered smooth hot skin that pulsed under her touch. "Please, let me have my way."

"Elise, if you keep that up, I won't last more than ten seconds," Dean said in a rough voice.

She trailed her mouth across the taut skin covering his collarbone, hearing his sharp breaths as he held on to what little control he had left. "You taste so good," she murmured.

He hissed between his teeth. "More than one can play this game." Deciding turnabout was fair play, he slipped one hand under her sweatshirt until he could find bare skin. He was grateful to find her bra had a front closure and easily released the tiny catch. Her nipples hardened instantly under his touch. He caught her gasp with his open mouth as it covered her parted lips.

After being married for close to twelve years, Elise thought she understood lovemaking, but she quickly learned that there were many aspects she wasn't aware of. Dean's caressing hand on her breast alternately kneaded and teased. His lips and tongue first swept through her mouth, then darted along her lower lip in feather-light touches. She released him long enough to raise her arms and allow him to pull her sweatshirt over her head, then helped him dispense with his. She fumbled with his belt buckle until he took pity on her and quickly released it, leaving it hanging as she flipped open his jeans. During this time, their mouths continued to seek out each other, hungry for yet another taste, then another, then another.

"As much as I'd like to just make love to you right here, I'm afraid I might be a little too old for these crazy positions," he said hoarsely.

By then Elise didn't care where they were. They fell onto the bed and quickly pulled off the rest of their clothing. Dean admired her ecru lace bikini panties, while Elise discovered Dean wore purple briefs.

"I would look at you in the morning and wonder what color you were wearing," she murmured, smoothing them down his hips and pushing them off the bed.

"I would look at you in the morning and wonder if you were wearing a bra." He inspected the scant piece of lace that matched her panties and tossed it over his shoulder. "You know, for a prissy doc, you wear some pretty sexy underwear."

She delighted in the fur covering his chest and arrowing down past his waist to surround his pulsing erection. "I bet you were the kind of kid who peeked in the girls' locker room." She tongued his nipple, pleased when he moaned under the feathery touches.

"Not only peeked but got caught for it, too. I got a month's detention." Dean wasn't sure how much he could take before he would explode, so he decided it was time to take matters into his own hands.

Elise laughed when he flipped her onto her back and moved over her, cradling his hips against hers. Her laughter quickly turned into a moan when he found the nub that sent shock waves racing throughout her body.

"Dean!" she keened, throwing her head back, her neck

arched in a graceful curve. Her eyes were closed and her lips parted as she panted short breaths.

"Just keep saying my name, sweetheart." He found it harder to breathe as he realized just how ready she was for him. He parted her legs with his knee and moved down and in, entering her slowly as he felt her soft walls grip him tightly. No matter how aroused he was, he wasn't going to allow her one second of discomfort. Even if moving so slowly *was* driving him out of his mind.

Elise's eyes opened. Dean felt as if he were drowning in the brilliant turquoise depths with no chance of being saved. By the time he felt he was going down for the third time, he knew he was surely lost, because he knew he had fallen in love with her. He groaned and captured her mouth with his as their bodies moved into a rhythm that could have only one ending.

Elise couldn't believe the feelings coursing through her veins, the sensations washing over her body as Dean would shift his position just a bit and send himself deeper into her. Not content to simply hang on, she moved with him, faster and faster, until they both exploded. Her tiny scream of joy was swallowed by his mouth upon hers as they soared to completion.

Dean moved slightly to relieve her of his weight but kept his arms around her, reluctant to be parted from her.

"I had no idea," Elise whispered. "I never..." Her eyes clouded.

He understood immediately. She felt guilty because she'd felt more with him this first time than she obviously had all the years of her marriage.

"Don't forget that we've been engaging in foreplay for quite a few days," he whispered, rolling onto his back and pulling her against him, cradling her head in the crook of his shoulder. "In another minute I would have taken you against that door no matter how precarious our position might have been."

She turned her head and pressed a kiss against his damp skin. A thank-you kiss for understanding her feelings.

"I wish we could stay locked up in here forever," she murmured. "I don't want to return to the real world."

He turned, sweeping her under him. His thumbs caressed her cheeks as his fingers combed back her damp hair. "Then I suggest we make the most of it."

She smiled and shook her head at his knowing expression. "My darling, my medical specialty might be animals, but even I know that recovery time is—" Her eyes widened in surprise at the insistent bulge resting against her thigh. She laughed throatily as she linked her arms around his neck and pulled his face down to hers. "But then, medical science has been known to experience a miracle now and then."

MORE THAN ANYTHING, Elise wanted to ignore her insistent alarm beeping away and disturbing much-needed sleep. She heard a muttered curse, then a slapping sound before the alarm was abruptly silenced. Her next observation was that she was cold. It only took one open eye to realize why. She was minus her electric blanket. Turning over showed her that Dean was warmly covered from chin to toe under *her* blanket!

"Give that back!" she muttered, pulling on the blanket. She ignored his muttered protests and continued savagely tugging on the covers.

"It's cold!" he argued, gripping the sheet and blanket.

"No kidding, you hog." Elise dipped one cold foot under the blankets until she found a hair-roughened thigh.

"Aagh!" Dean almost shot out of bed. "Do you realize how close you were to freezing a certain part of my anatomy near and dear to me?"

"Not close enough." She pulled the loosened covers around her shoulders. "You took the whole blanket."

He leaned over her, planting one hand on either side of her head. "Then why didn't you ask for it nicely?"

"Because that never seems to work with you."

He dipped his head, brushing his nose across hers before covering her mouth with his for a good-morning kiss that rapidly escalated into something more intimate.

She sighed regretfully. "Dean, we can't."

He drew back. "Why not?" His expression turned instantly to concern. "I'm sorry, are you sore? I knew we were pretty active last night."

His regard for her was something Elise knew she wouldn't forget for a long time to come. Not to mention the night they'd just experienced. Medical science would have been very surprised indeed.

"You have to be out of here before the girls are up and around. It has nothing to do with you personally. I just don't want them to see you coming from my room, because they'll naturally assume one thing, and right now they're very fragile. Besides, I don't want there to be any awkward explanations." Her eyes silently pleaded for his understanding.

His immediate smile reassured her. "Think we'd have time for a shower together?"

She glanced at the clock and grimaced as she realized what time it was. "Not if we want to get clean, too. And I have to get that budgie for Miss Turner before she shows up at the clinic.''

Dean kissed her slowly, but avoiding too much passion that might overwhelm them. ''Okay, Myrna can take the girls to school, and I'll go with you to get the bird,'' he breathed against her mouth.

She was stunned by his easy capitulation. ''You're not angry that...''

Dean wondered if there might have been times Steve Carpenter hadn't appreciated having to put off some loving because the hour might not have been convenient. While he wasn't familiar with having an intimate relationship with a woman with children, he knew well enough that what happened between him and Elise was private. At least, for the time being. ''Not when you explain it so logically.'' After one last kiss, he rolled out of bed and hunted for his briefs.

Elise remained under the covers, enjoying the sight of a naked man walking around her room, picking up briefs here, socks there and jeans that had been flung in a corner. She didn't have to guess the origin of the round, puckered scar on his shoulder or several white lines across one thigh. The idea of his being wounded cut through her. But she had already come to terms with one thing. He was a cop. And danger was part of the job description.

''Dean,'' she said softly.

His head whipped up, his expression wary, as if he feared hearing something he didn't want to.

She sat up in bed, allowing the covers to drop to her waist. Longtime experience told her the girls weren't early risers and would sleep past the alarm unless someone routed them out of bed. Maybe they had enough time after all. ''I've come to the conclusion that cops aren't so bad if you put them in their proper place."

His teeth gleamed in a broad grin. It wasn't difficult to read her intent. "And I suppose you know that proper place for guys like me?"

"Intimately."

"And you're willing to share it with me?"

"Absolutely."

"Right now?"

"Most definitely."

Chapter Eleven

"Come on, Dean, just try it. This won't hurt a bit," Elise crooned.

The mutinous expression on his face reminded her of a little boy. A little boy who could grow up within a heartbeat into a devastating man.

"Yes, it will."

"Just grasp her behind her head and stroke downward slowly. She loves it when people do that." Her voice lowered to a sexy purr. "Just the way I do."

He didn't look convinced. "Yeah, but you don't bite."

"I don't? Where's that big macho cop who made love to me all last night?"

"You turned him into a shadow of his former self." Dean grinned as he watched the wash of color creep up Elise's throat. "You started it, sweetheart."

She held the python up in front of her. "And you promised you would meet Althea. She's a sweet little snake."

He eyed the eight-foot reptile with a cautious eye. "You call that little?"

Elise shook her head, amused by the brawny man in front of her so unsettled by a snake most boys would kill to own.

The same man who had wooed her into bed after the three girls were sound asleep and proceeded to show her an interesting version of a strip search.

In the past four days he'd turned her life even more upside down. By day he was the professional cop, talking to his partner, driving in to the sheriff's station and consulting with officers there, tracking down the slimmest lead in hopes it would take him to Carl Dietrich. By late afternoon, he turned into a playmate for the girls, urging them into a Frisbee match one day, snagging Elise into playing on the other team. She even thought he might be making a bit of headway with Keri, who still remained aloof in his presence. At least the girl didn't seem to snarl at him so much.

And late at night, he turned into *her* playmate, indulging in delicious necking on the living room couch before leading her down the hallway to her room, where the door was closed and locked against the outside world until dawn. He conquered her complaints about hogging all the covers by pulling her up against his heated body before they slept, and he even told her that, on her, flannel nightgowns were as sexy as silk and lace. That was when she knew the man was first-class trouble for her, because it was getting too easy to fall in love with him.

He even worked harder at keeping his room neater, much to Myrna's surprise, although the housekeeper's sly comments prompted Elise to think the older woman guessed his bed was only mussed in the morning for propriety's sake. The topper was when Dean made friends with Baby and Frances. Frances still chased him around the yard, but it wasn't with the malicious glee the goose usually displayed toward him. Now it was more an act of playfulness, as if the goose finally accepted him as part of the family.

She looked at him, admiring his forthright nature, desiring the man and finding herself falling in love. The idea that these beautiful moments could come to an end was something she preferred not to think about.

"Dean, are you afraid of Althea?" she asked gently, easily reading the expression on his face. If he thought he could hide behind his beard, he soon learned it didn't work with her. Already she knew him so well. But that didn't stop her from feeling eager to learn even more. "Wary of snakes in general?"

"Of course not," he said huffily, backing off another few steps.

"She's very affectionate," she assured him.

"Yeah, I saw that the first day when she tried to turn you into a human hot dog." He looked around the room, where a land tortoise dozed inside one hospital cage, and a cockatoo minus chest feathers watched him with suspicious dark eyes and frantically hopped back and forth on the perch while sending ear-splitting screeches into the air. He decided the only animal he felt comfortable with was the lop-eared rabbit chomping on his food while ensconced in a large animal carrier.

Elise watched him somberly. "Didn't you *ever* have any kind of pet, Dean?"

"Our apartment was barely big enough for the two of us," he admitted, wishing he hadn't given in that night and talked about his past. It wasn't something he did easily. Hell, even Mac didn't know all that Elise did. "There wouldn't have been room for a gerbil."

"Gerbils are illegal in California," she pointed out with a smile. "They're considered a harmful rodent to farmers." She shrugged. "Sorry, I tend to lecture at times."

Elise placed Althea back in her carrier, making sure the top was closed securely. Past experience had taught the clinic staff that the python loved to escape and roam the halls, much to the other clients' dismay when they encountered the friendly reptile slithering along the tile floor, eager to make new friends along the way.

"Are you ready to go now?" Dean asked, edging toward the back door.

"Not just yet, boss lady," Donna said airily, entering the room. "You lost the coin toss, remember?"

Elise groaned. "I was hoping you'd forget."

"Fat chance." Donna pulled her purse out of a locked cabinet and slung the strap over her shoulder.

Elise looked at Dean expectantly. "Dean," she cooed, "would you like to do a favor for me?"

He was instantly suspicious. "What?"

"Just like a cop," she tsked. "Always expecting the worst."

Donna burst into laughter. "Come on, Elise, he can't even look at Althea without turning green. How do you expect him to feed her?"

Dean could feel the green wash over his face. "Feed?"

"Just mice," Donna explained. "No biggie. It's just that none of us are really all that happy doing it, so we take turns feeding Althea when she boards here. Cheryl and I were very relieved it wasn't our turn."

He swallowed as he watched Elise pick up a mouse. "You're kidding, aren't you?"

She shook her head.

Dean suddenly found the ceiling very interesting. "Snakes that squeeze people and eat mice. Lizards bigger than your arm. Hell, the rabbits probably have teeth bigger than a cougar's. I'll go out and secure the front gate after Donna leaves. Another hot date?'' He knew he couldn't bear to watch Elise's grisly task.

"You got it. It's refreshing to date a guy who doesn't talk about himself all the time. He's interested in me, too,'' Donna told him as they walked outside.

"Coward!'' Elise called after him.

"With a capital *C*, sweetheart!'' he called back.

"You know, you're good for her,'' Donna commented as they walked outside. "Elise tends to forget that she's supposed to have a life of her own.''

"Yeah, well, I think she's pretty special, too,'' he admitted.

Donna opened her car door and slid into the driver's seat. "Catch this creep, Dean,'' she insisted. "I'm so afraid he's really going to hurt her. She's been through enough without all this happening to her, too.''

"That's what I intend to do.''

She managed a smile. "I know. It's just that it's left all of us on edge. You don't know who to trust anymore. Well, I'd better get going. See you tomorrow.'' With a wave of the hand, she was off.

By the time Dean swung the front gate closed and secured it with a lock, Elise was walking outside. He stopped for a second, enjoying the sight of her with wisps of hair springing free from her braid, her clothes rumpled from her work and several suspicious green stains on her jeans. The same kind of stains he encountered on his own clothing after handling Baby. What really punched him in the stomach was her smile as she walked toward him.

For too many years women had enjoyed being with him because he was a cop; therefore, he must be dangerously hot in bed. He was grateful Elise didn't see him that way. She'd probably be happier if he did something safe, like selling cars or insurance. So when she smiled at him or touched him with those delicate fingers, it was because of him—Dean, the man, not Detective Cornell, who had to wear a gun. He liked that. He liked it a lot.

"Think the girls will go to bed right after dinner?" He leered at her as he looped an arm around her waist and brought her up against his hip.

"Not without a major argument." She brushed her cheek against his shoulder. Her voice softened. "You're going to have to return to L.A. this weekend, aren't you?"

His jaw tightened. "Not if I can help it."

"But your boss will demand it, and you can't ignore orders."

"I have plenty of vacation time due me, Elise. I'm not leaving you until this is settled."

"What if it's never settled?" Her soft voice washed over him. "What if he's gone far away?"

"Do you believe he has?"

"No, but I hope he has. Then we could have a normal life again."

Yeah, with me in L.A. and you here. That doesn't sound all that normal to me. His gut wrenched at the thought of leaving Elise. For many years all that had mattered was his work. For the first time, he found himself willing to toss it down the tubes if it meant he didn't have to leave this woman, if he could persuade her to let him into her life.

"We'll talk about it when the time comes, okay?" His voice sounded hoarse.

She opened her mouth as if to say something more, then changed her mind. "Okay."

At the same time they saw the package lying innocently on the front porch. As Elise reached out to pick it up, Dean gripped her hand and roughly pulled her back.

"Don't touch it," he ordered.

She looked up, startled by his vehemence. "But, Dean..."

"No." He pushed her up the stairs, away from the package. "Go in and call Santee. Tell him to get some men out here, pronto. Tell him what we've found."

Elise looked at the package, then at Dean's stone-carved features. "Do you think...?" she whispered, horror washing over her face.

"Just go now, and keep the kids inside."

She fled.

Dean could hear the girls chattering their questions and Elise's voice trying to calm them. He wasn't about to leave the porch with its supposedly innocuous package lying there. He knew it hadn't been there when he walked down to the clinic fifteen minutes ago to get Elise for dinner. And he hadn't heard anyone come through the front gate.

"Dammit, what is it with those dogs and geese?" he muttered darkly. "Frances, you're not worth anything more than acting as the main course for Sunday dinner."

For the next few hours, Elise watched the commotion in her front yard from her front window. Dean had insisted she remain inside and keep up a semblance of normalcy by feeding the girls dinner. As if she could act normal with what looked like half the sheriff's department in her front yard. She had tried to eat, even forcing several bites of dinner down her throat until her stomach started to rebel. Now she just stood there, watching them, wondering when it would all be over. Wondering if her life would ever be her own again. It didn't take an expert to guess that a bomb squad had been brought out to inspect the package.

"What are they doing?" Becky demanded.

"Mom, why can't we go out and watch?" Lisa whined. "This is just like on *Police Story!*"

"Mom, what is going on?" Keri asked, her face taut with fear.

"All of you be quiet," Elise insisted, rubbing her fingertips against her forehead. Their constant questions didn't help her throbbing headaches one bit. "Keri, would you get me some aspirin please?" The girl nodded and disappeared into the bathroom. "Lisa, you and Becky load the dishwasher," Elise went on. "then go to your rooms and finish your homework."

"I finished mine already," Lisa argued. "Can't we watch TV?"

Elise's lips tightened. "You'll have to watch it in my room. And get that damn bird to shut up!" she practically shouted.

Baby's most recent "fud up" halted in midsyllable.

Keri handed her mother two aspirin and a glass of water.

"They think it's a bomb, don't they?" Keri whispered, although the other two girls had disappeared into the kitchen and only their squabbling could be heard.

"I don't know what they think." Elise swallowed the tablets and wrapped her arms around her body. She couldn't remember the last time she'd felt so cold. Had she felt this chilled and alone when she knew Steve was truly dead?

"Mom, Dean isn't going to let anything happen to us," Keri assured her.

Elise looked down at her oldest with surprise. "I thought he was your least favorite person."

She flushed. "Well, he is a bit obnoxious at times." Elise swallowed her chuckle at that. "But, as you said, he's only doing his job. And in his own weird way, he does care for us. I know I've been a beast to him, but it's because I was so scared. I didn't want to lose you, either."

Elise wrapped her daughter in a strong hug. "You aren't going to lose me that easily," she whispered, dropping a kiss onto her brow. "Now, would you mind making sure they don't break anything and herd them into the other room?"

Keri hugged her tightly for a second, then nodded.

Elise was left alone to watch. Officers dressed in special protective suits, inspecting the package before they gingerly picked it up. Dean and Detective Santee standing off to one side, both looking grim as death. She swallowed a sob as the description hit her mind. It was something she didn't want to speculate on.

She had no idea how much time passed before a member of the bomb squad nodded and handed the package to another man, who appeared to be dusting the package for fingerprints. When he finished his part of the job, he handed it to Detective Santee. He and Dean turned their backs to the house as they inspected it. Within a few minutes, they came inside.

"We want to borrow the VCR for a minute, Elise." The grim expression on Dean's face hadn't disappeared as he looked at the videotape case Detective Santee held.

She nodded and gestured toward the television set.

"Why don't you go back with the girls." It was an order, not a suggestion.

There would have been a time when Elise's ruffled feathers would have sent her stomping down the hallway. This time she nodded and escaped, but only as far as the doorway.

She knew Dean was trying to protect her from whatever was on the video cassette, but she had to know its contents.

"Maybe we should play this at the station." Santee's murmur barely reached her straining ears.

"Maybe you can wait, but I can't." Dean inserted the tape into the machine and pushed the play button.

Air hissed between his teeth when the picture first rolled, then settled into a close-up of a decidedly homey scene. Laughter was heard as Keri flipped the bright red Frisbee into the air and jumped up squealing when it sailed over Dean's head. For long seconds, the two men viewed the game as the camera panned on each participant in the game until it zeroed back in on a laughing Keri.

"Cute kid, lady doc," a low voice intruded on the scene. "A lot like you, but I bet she'd be easier to control. Maybe I'll save her for last. As for the cop boyfriend..." The camera swung past the others until it centered on Dean, who was involved in a tug-of-war with one of the dogs who'd decided the Frisbee was his. A crude target was drawn over his face. "Well, I'm sure you can guess what I intend to do to him."

Elise's hands flew to her mouth, muffling her cry, but Dean heard it anyway. He turned his head. The dark expression on his face frightened her nearly as much as the video had.

"Get out of here, Elise," he growled.

Eyes wide with fear, vocal chords paralyzed, she could only shake her head.

"Dammit, Elise, get out now!"

The picture crackled and darkened, turning their attention back to the screen. At first, only shadowy shapes were discernible, then soft sounds, muffled moans and whispers.

"Hey, cop, you really know how to protect a lady," the

voice on the tape cackled. "I just bet your buddies would love a copy of this. If I'd known being a cop came with fringe benefits like this, I might have switched over to the other side."

Dean looked as if he wanted to kick the television screen in. A string of curses fell from his lips as he quickly switched off the tape and ejected it from the machine.

"How?" Elise cried out, walking into the room with jerky steps. "How could anyone do such a terrible thing!"

Detective Santee stood off to one side. It hadn't been difficult for him to guess the last images were of Elise and Dean making love. The shock on her face and the murder written on his said it all. He plucked the cassette from the machine and pushed it back into the case before slipping it into his jacket pocket.

"What are you doing?" Elise asked, watching his every move.

"It's evidence, Dr. Carpenter." Seeing the stunned hurt in her eyes, he wanted nothing more than to apologize for putting her through this. No wonder Cornell had fallen for the lady, even if both men knew it was most unprofessional. That was a piece of information he'd keep to himself. What Cornell did could lose him his badge. But, hell, who could predict when you'd fall in love? She was just what the doctor ordered for a battered cop who needed love. He felt the need to tack on, "Although we couldn't find any prints on the case or tape, we have his voice to go on. There's no guarantee that will be enough, but it's something."

"But..." She dipped her head, searching for words. "It shows..." She sounded close to tears.

Dean ground his teeth. He didn't want that tape passed around the sheriff's station any more than she did, but he was aware of procedure. Right now, that procedure sucked. The fact that it showed him in a very compromising position wasn't what worried him. What bothered him was the raw pain on Elise's face. She didn't deserve this.

"I'm going to keep this locked up in my files," Santee said quietly, easily reading Dean's mind.

Dean breathed deeply several times, struggling to contain his anger. The bastard had been close enough to peer into Elise's bedroom! How often had he stood there watching them? Damn! Why hadn't Dean thought to close the drapes no matter how much Elise enjoyed having them open to catch the morning sun!

"Thanks."

"You want to call Anderson or shall I?"

Dean read his meaning loud and clear. This was the best reason for him to remain here. "I'll do it, but I wouldn't mind if you backed it up with an additional call tomorrow."

"My pleasure." Santee looked at Elise with compassion. She hadn't moved, still too stunned to comprehend what she'd seen. "Dr. Carpenter." He left the house.

Elise could only stand there staring at Dean. She tried to swallow the bile rising in her throat but found her muscles frozen. With a muffled cry, she spun around and ran down the hall.

Her frenzied retreat galvanized him to action. "Elise!" He took off after her.

Dean entered Elise's bedroom to find the bathroom door closed and three frightened girls huddled on the bed. The comedy playing on the television was incongruous with the scene playing out before him.

"What's wrong?" Becky cried, tears streaming down her face.

He picked her up and carried her into her room, all the while assuring her everything would be all right. After suggesting she put on her nightgown and he'd be in later, and ensuring the other girls were in their rooms, he returned to Elise's room. He found her crouched in the bathroom, her head hanging over the porcelain bowl.

"Oh, baby," he murmured, wetting a washcloth and filling a glass with water and mouthwash. He squatted down next to her, wiping her forehead with the cloth and letting her know he was there for her. Afterward, he helped her to her feet and urged her to rinse her mouth.

"He made it seem so dirty." Her voice trembled as she allowed him to strip her clothes off and drop a nightgown over her head. "He took something beautiful and made it cheap and filthy."

"No, he didn't, sweetheart. He just wanted you to feel that way," he told her, steering her toward the bed. He pulled the covers around her and turned on the electric blanket before settling on the edge of the bed. "Listen, I'm going to check on the girls. You really scared the hell out of them. Then I'm coming back here. You'll be okay for a few minutes?" His voice sharpened when she didn't reply. "Elise!"

She nodded jerkily. "Yes." Her voice was dull and lifeless.

Dean checked on Becky first. He was relieved to find her in bed with all her favorite stuffed animals arranged around her.

"Is that man going to hurt Mommy the way he hurt Daddy?" the little girl asked.

"Not if I can help it," he vowed, giving her a quick hug.

Her chin wobbled. "Can I have my night-light on, please? And the door open?"

"Sure." Dean stopped in the doorway. "Becky, if you wake up scared, you just holler and I'll come running, okay?"

She nodded, watching him with the same wide eyes as her mother.

Lisa was just as frightened, although she tried not to show it. "You gonna start sleeping with your gun?" she asked, sitting cross-legged on top of her bed. "You'll shoot the guy if he shows up, won't you?"

"Only if I have to. I like to talk first and shoot second," he told her.

"Yeah, but he's making Mom scared, and she never gets scared," she explained. "When Dad died, she used to stay up a lot of nights, walking around the house and coming into our rooms as if making sure we were still here, but she wasn't scared, just sad."

Dean rested a hand on her head strawberry-blond curls. "Lisa, my love, you're growing up too fast," he said gruffly.

"Yeah, but I still like softball more than I like boys."

"Thank God for small favors," he intoned, walking out of the room and starting to pull the door closed after him.

"Can you leave it open please?"

If he didn't feel so much like crying, he would have laughed. Lisa hadn't grown up so much after all.

Dean found Elise's sixteen-year-old replica sitting up in bed, a textbook propped against her knees. When she looked up, he saw Elise's eyes looking at him gravely.

"There was something bad on that tape, wasn't there?" she asked. "Something about us kids."

How could he lie to this child-woman? "He videotaped us during a Frisbee game," he said baldly.

Keri's swift indrawn breath gave away her reaction. "Then he's in the hills behind us."

"He could be anywhere. A zoom lens can eat up a lot of distance."

She shook her head. "The closest house to us is that horse ranch, but there's guard dogs patrolling the area, and they're really mean, so he couldn't sneak in that way. And old Mr. Myer lives on the other side, and he hates people so much he'll go after someone with a shotgun if they stand too close to his fence. It has to be the hills. Especially if the house was in the background."

Dean considered this. "That's very good deductive reasoning, Keri. I'll pass it on to Detective Santee."

She watched him closely. "If you'd like, I'll check on Lisa and Becky for you, so you can keep the bedroom door locked like you always do."

Dean, who'd never thought he had an embarrassed bone in his body before he came to the Carpenter household, found himself blushing in front of this girl who apparently knew a great deal too much.

"Oh, it's all right," she rushed to reassure him. "I don't feel traumatized or anything. I mean, it's not as if I think that because Mom is sleeping with a man I have to run out and do the same thing. It's just that for a while after Dad's death, Becky used to have nightmares and would crawl into bed with Mom. If she calls out, I'll bring her in here." She grimaced. "Although she kicks in her sleep and takes all the covers."

For a minute, Dean looked at her, unsure whether to laugh or cry. He opted for leaning over and pressing a kiss to her forehead. "If I wasn't in love with your mother, I'd wait for you to grow up."

She wrinkled her nose. "No offense, but you're more than a little too old for me."

Dean grinned. "Thanks for the kick in the ego. Don't stay up too late studying," he cautioned as he left. "And if you hear anything, yell."

"Did you mean it, Dean?" Her question stopped him. "That you love Mom?"

He nodded. "Does that bother you?"

She considered his reply. "Not as much as I thought it would. But can I make one request for the future?"

"What?"

"When I start dating, please don't see if my dates have a police record or act like a cop around them. That kind of thing could kill my social life before it even got started."

The future. That was something Dean hadn't dared to think about. He had a hunch that a future with Elise and the girls would rapidly turn his hair gray. But, yeah, he could live with that.

"Honey, if you grow up to be a fraction of your mother, I'll lock you in your room until you're thirty," he gravely promised.

Keri's smile was enough to warm Dean's heart.

He made a detour to the kitchen before returning to Elise's bedroom. He wasn't surprised to find her with the covers pulled up to her chin. Nor to find the drapes pulled tightly across the window. He felt saddened at the thought of not seeing the morning sun spill across the bed to highlight her hair and face. At the same time, he felt anger that Elise had to fear having the drapes open.

"Here." He held a filled wineglass out to her.

"I don't want any."

"Yes, you do."

Recognizing his do-as-I-say look, she grabbed the glass and downed the wine like water. She coughed when she finished and defiantly handed the empty glass back.

"Well, that was a waste of a good vintage," Dean said dryly, pulling his sweatshirt over his head and tossing it onto a chair. His jeans, socks and briefs soon followed.

Elise watched his movements with suspicion. "What do you think you're doing?"

"Getting ready for bed." He padded into the bathroom, where Elise could hear water running while he brushed his teeth. When he walked back into the bedroom, she could see a fleck of toothpaste on a corner of his mouth. The last time she'd found one she'd licked it off.

She licked her lips. "I think you should sleep in your own room tonight." She didn't flinch under his glower. "Tonight frightened the girls. Becky might have a nightmare and need me."

"Keri already said she'd take care of Becky if she woke up." He pulled up the covers on the left side of the bed and climbed in, nudging her with his hip. "Move over, Doc."

Having no choice, she moved a few inches. "Keri? You mean, she knows about...?" Hadn't she had enough shocks for one night?

"About her mother having a sex life? Yes." He picked up his wineglass and sipped it. "I'll share if you won't chug-a-lug it." He held out the glass.

She grabbed it and swallowed a mouthful. "I can't handle this."

Dean retrieved the glass and set it back on the nightstand.

"No kidding." He pulled her into his arms and held on tightly as she struggled. "Ellie."

"I can't!" she cried. "Not after that bastard..." She couldn't bear to finish her tortured thought.

"Yes, you can," he said firmly, rolling over onto his side, keeping her close to him. "Don't let him win this round. What we have is beautiful and very special. No one can ruin it as long as we don't allow him to."

"Maybe you're used to this kind of filth, but I'm not!"

His eyes darkened. "And neither am I. Elise, you are the best thing that's happened to me, and I'm not going to let that creep influence what we have. Dammit, woman, I love you!" he roared.

Elise's eyes turned into saucers. "You do?" she breathed. It was amazing: it only took three words to break through her shock.

He looked as if he was afraid Althea might be hiding under the covers. "Yes," he admitted grudgingly. "And since Keri already gave us her blessing, you can't back away from allowing us to find out just what we could have together."

Disjointed thoughts ran through Elise's mind. She tentatively lifted her hands and traced the muscular arm draped across her waist. "Maybe it's just sex," she whispered, more than a little fearfully.

He muttered a pithy curse. "Trust me, it's more than sex if I can look at you wearing that truly ugly nightgown and still want to make love with you."

"You do?"

He nodded.

Elise suddenly knew that was what she needed, too. She needed Dean's possession to cleanse her of the night's memories, to make what they had pure again. She stared into his eyes, watching the dark irises widen with his arousal. The same arousal she felt brushing her belly.

"I don't need a gentle lover tonight," she whispered. "I need to forget, to be swept away until I can't think."

He raised himself up over her. "Then I suggest we get rid of something first." He gripped the neckline of her nightgown and easily ripped it down to the hem.

His kiss threatened to devour her, his lips nipping and biting her, silently urging her to follow his lead. Elise didn't need a second invitation. She turned into a streak of fire in his arms as she returned every rough caress with one of her own. She nipped his ear until he growled, and invited his thrusting entrances with her hips arching upward.

Time stood still for the lovers. Elise lost track of the world around her as Dean swept her away into a climax so shattering that she was positive the world exploded around her. She fell into a sleep so deep she didn't move a muscle all night. But Dean remained awake until dawn, listening to every sound in the house. When Becky's tiny cry intruded on the charged silence, he started to get up, until he heard soft noises from Keri's room and her whispers assuring her younger sister that everything was all right. Then it was quiet again. Which was fine with him, as long as he could hold Elise in his arms and consider her all his.

Chapter Twelve

Elise understood the expression "easier said than done" when she tried to wake up. She found herself much too comfortable under the warm covers to want to wake up and face the world. If she did that, she'd have to remember last night. Last night. Well, not all of it was bad.

"You're smiling, so I know you're awake."

"No, I'm not."

"I've got coffee."

The heavenly scent reached her nostrils. She opened one eye. "You know all my weak spots, don't you?"

Dean grinned the grin of a wolf holding on to its favorite sheep. "I sure do. But I noticed you found a few of mine along the way, so I guess we're even."

She sat up, accepting the coffee cup he held out. She drank the dark brew, savoring the caffeine racing through her veins.

Dean leaned forward and brushed his lips against hers. "I'm afraid it's later than usual, though, and we're going to have to face the real world."

Elise looked at the clock and grimaced. "You're right." She cradled the coffee cup between her palms. "You're going to have to call your captain about last night, aren't you?"

He nodded.

She appeared to pick and choose her words. "Are you going to tell him about the tape?"

He didn't want to answer that. "I have to."

Her expressive eyes seared his soul. "Everything?"

"It's procedure, Elise," he said reluctantly.

She slowly nodded. She slipped out of bed and headed for the bathroom. "I'd better shower and dress. Would you please tell Myrna I won't have time for breakfast." The door closed after her with a decided click.

Dean swore under his breath and pounded the bedclothes. Did she think he liked this any better than she did? In a mood to commit murder, he stomped out of the room and quickly showered and dressed, reaching the kitchen before Elise. The girls were grouped around the table, finishing their breakfast, and Myrna stood at the stove.

"That Detective Santee called," the housekeeper announced, setting a plate in front of him. "Said you weren't to bother calling your captain until you came down to see him, and you should make it a conference call."

For once Dean felt no appetite when he looked at the food. "Thanks," he muttered. "Elise said she won't have time for any breakfast." He drank his coffee but couldn't bring himself to touch the golden-brown waffles.

Myrna looked at him with shock. "You're not eating?"

"I'm not hungry."

"Now I've seen everything," she clucked, taking the plate away.

Dean ignored her. "You girls almost ready?" he asked in a subdued voice.

The three nodded in tandem.

He pushed his chair back and stood up. "Okay, let's roll."

The ride to the schools was made in silence. When Dean stopped the truck in front of Becky's school, she started to climb out, then turned and threw her arms around his neck.

"I love you, Dean," she told him, kissing him on the cheek before climbing out.

He sat there, watching her race for the front door, where she stopped to talk to friends.

"Oh, boy," he said, sighing. "I'm caught, hook, line and sinker."

When he reached the sheriff's station, he found Detective Santee sitting at his desk, looking as if he'd had little sleep.

"Considering your superior's attitude, I figured a little backup wouldn't hurt," the man greeted him after handing him a mug of coffee that looked like black ink.

"Yeah, he's a real charmer," Dean said ruefully, grimacing after his first sip of the coffee. "Used a new brand of battery acid this morning, didn't you? This is almost drinkable."

Detective Santee punched out a phone number and tapped on the speaker phone. Within seconds, he was connected with Captain Anderson. Using as few words as possible, the sheriff's detective related the previous night's events.

"What's on the videotape?" the police captain demanded before Santee finished speaking.

Santee didn't even look at Dean. "He filmed a Frisbee game going on between your detective and Dr. Carpenter's daughters," he said crisply. Dean shot him a look filled with surprise.

The other man sputtered out curses on Dean's head. "What does that idiot think he's down there for? He's supposed to catch an escaped criminal, not run around playing kids' games!"

"Captain Anderson, there was a threat made on the older Carpenter girl, and a target drawn on the tape over Detective Cornell's face." His voice hardened. "If I were you, I'd worry more about this man taking potshots at an innocent girl or one of your men than what they happen to be doing. The way I understood it, Detective Cornell was sent down here to work with us, and that means protecting Dr. Carpenter and her daughters. He can't keep them inside all the time, and if that means he has to participate in one of their games, I'm all for it."

The silence on the phone spoke loud and clear. "I want a copy of the tape."

"It's already made and on its way to you. Do you care to say anything to Detective Cornell? He's right here."

"Only that he'd better get on the ball and do his job before he finds himself pounding a beat," the man snarled.

"Since you obviously sent your man, I don't know why you're so worried. Unless your head is also on the line regarding this case," Santee said mildly.

"Who the hell do you think you are to talk to me that way?" the man roared.

"Easy. I'm the man in charge of this station. If you have any complaints about me, I suggest you—" His reply was the buzz of a disconnected line. Santee gave Dean a rueful look. "Your captain is very impolite."

"I told you he was a charmer." Dean shifted in his chair. "You already sent a copy of the tape?"

Santee nodded. "Sure. It's only a Frisbee game, right?"

Dean carefully set his coffee cup on the desktop. "I realize what happened was unprofessional and can cost me my badge but..." How could he explain something to someone else when he couldn't truly understand it himself?

"I'd say Anderson would like nothing better than to get something on you that would throw you out of your butt," Santee said. "I've had to deal with his kind for more years than I like to remember. Dr. Carpenter is a nice lady, and she doesn't deserve having him use that small piece of tape as ammunition just because he seems to carry a personal grudge against you."

Dean heard Santee's implicit message. *That small piece of tape*—which could be easily edited out. He was grateful to the man.

"You're dead right. Anderson would have spouted regulations loud and clear right before he kicked me out," Dean replied. "Especially since my partner married a woman who was once a suspect in a series of robberies. She proved to be innocent of all charges, but she had a fairly long juvenile record, and Anderson still feels she wriggled out of something she was guilty of. There's no shades of gray in his world.

Santee shook his head. "I don't think I'd care to meet the man."

"There's days when I wish I hadn't wanted out of vice." Dean leaned back in his chair. "I'm forty-two years old, and some days I feel a hundred and forty-two. I quit smoking a few years ago, and I started up again."

"Why don't you take your pension and get out?"

"It's beginning to sound better all the time." He stretched his arms over his head. "Just as soon as I figured out what else I can do with my life."

"You thinking of relocating out of L.A.? Maybe somewhere hereabouts?"

"Could be."

"I wouldn't blame you. It's a nice area, fairly smog-free. Nice people." Santee stressed the last word.

"If I did, would you be willing to tell me your first name?"

He smiled. "I doubt it."

Dean sobered. "I have a hunch Dietrich is stepping up his campaign, and the videotape is just the beginning."

Santee nodded his agreement. "I just wish we had more information on the man."

"Yeah." Dean sighed. "All we know is he likes his drugs and he puts the fear of God into his so-called friends so they're afraid to talk about him too much. What little Mac learned was only because he was able to put more fear into the guy than he felt for Dietrich. This guy is one mean individual. Right now, he's using scare tactics against the doc, making her afraid for her kids more than for her own life. I don't want to think of the day he makes his move."

Fear for Elise cut through his body like a knife. What if he wasn't able to protect her? It wasn't his job he was worried about. That didn't matter one bit. What mattered was Elise. How could he put into words how he worried when he was away from the house? Even if a patrol car drove by more often than usual. It wasn't enough. He knew it. Santee knew it. But they were all powerless in one way or another, and Dietrich seemed to know that. The man was playing a dangerous game, and Dean could only hope to remain one step ahead of him.

"Time's running out." Santee spoke Dean's thoughts out loud.

"Yeah, but what will be his plan? What move will he make next? Will it be against one of us personally or another mind game?" Dean muttered curses under his breath. "The bastard doesn't have a pattern. That's why he's eluding us so easily."

"Maybe there is a pattern and we just haven't figured it out yet."

Dean considered his suggestion. "Maybe," he mused. "Okay, let's look over what's happened so far."

More than three hours later, Dean's stomach burned from too much coffee and no food and from frustration at not finding anything revealing a pattern. Even looking into Carl Dietrich's past didn't give them any ideas.

"If nothing else, he's an equal-opportunity criminal," Dean concluded. "Robbery, murder, rape, drug possession. This guy has his fingers in a lot of pies." He snapped his fingers. "That's it!"

Santee looked up. "What?"

"He deliberately doesn't have a pattern."

"Tell me something we don't already know."

"No, this is how he plays his games. By not finding a pattern in any past crime, we can't figure him out, and he knows it. This way he figures we'll be running all over the place. So we don't," Dean said softly. "We just sit back and wait for him."

Santee's interest sharpened. "Set a trap?"

Dean shook his head. "Not exactly. He'll expect a trap."

"Now you've lost me."

"If my ears weren't deceiving me, he was sounding a little strung out on that videotape. If he's getting low on his favorite good grub, he'll be looking to make a drug buy soon. If you keep your ears open, maybe you'll hear about it. And we can pick him up then."

Santee slowly nodded. "It might work."

Dean looked grim. "We can hope so."

He kept that thought for the rest of the day. Dinner that evening was more subdued than usual, and he noticed Elise didn't have to voice her suggestion about homework more than once to the girls. Even she looked weary, as if it were all finally getting to her. She had demanded the not-very-hopeful truth about his meeting with Santee, and he'd given it to her. Now she looked as if she regretted asking.

While he sat in a chair with a bottle of beer in one hand, she curled up in a corner of the couch, not even pretending to watch the blaring television.

"I keep wondering what he's going to do next," she said quietly.

He didn't bother to ask who she meant. "Worrying will only give you ulcers."

She studied her hands lying clenched in her lap. "What did your captain say about the tape?"

Now he understood part of the reason behind her tension. "Santee talked to him this morning about Dietrich catching the Frisbee game on tape and told him he'd sent a copy."

Elise's head snapped up. "That was all?"

Dean nodded. "Yeah."

"If—" She swallowed. "If he knew about the other, you could lose your job, couldn't you?"

"They'd consider my behavior on the case unprofessional" was all he said.

She appeared vastly interested in her fingers, which now plucked at a loose thread in her sweater. "I won't have you get in trouble because of me."

"Hey, where's that fire-eater I first met?" Dean demanded. "The one who looked down her nose at me that day in the bank."

A smile reluctantly tugged at the corners of her mouth.

"Your watch is still forty-five seconds slow," she murmured. "You still dress deplorably, and you desperately need a haircut."

He felt relieved to see her smile. "I wouldn't know how to act if I had an accurate watch, dressed decently more than twice a year and had my hair cut on a regular basis. Ellie, you can't worry about everything," he said quietly. "What's between us is nobody else's business, and Santee was nice enough to keep it that way. The fact that he doesn't like Anderson any better than I do helped a lot."

"What if Dietrich tries to hurt me through you? If he can catch you on videotape, he can catch you just as easily with a rifle, can't he?" Her eyes pleaded with him for the truth. "He could hide out there and pick us off one by one. What's stopping him from doing that?"

"Nothing, except he's still having his fun playing mind games."

"But it could end at any time," she pressed.

He saw no reason to lie. "Yeah, it could."

She drew in a deep breath. "Then we're all powerless. We're just pawns waiting for his next move!" Frustration laced her voice. She pounded her fist against the arm of the couch.

"Elise, you can't lose it now!" He spoke sharply. "You have to remain strong."

Her eyes blazed with more fire than he'd seen in the past few days. "I want the man dead, Dean. I want to know he'll never bother us again." With that, she stood up and left the living room. A moment later, Dean heard her bedroom door close.

He took his time making sure all the doors were locked and windows secured. Baby glared at him and squawked when he pulled the covers over her cage, but a walnut seemed to soothe her irritation.

When Dean settled on his bed in the guest room, he wearily listened to the soft snores coming from under the bed.

"I didn't miss you one bit," he informed the sleeping tortoise. "But something tells me she would not welcome my company tonight, and I don't deal real well with rejection."

AFTER A SLEEPLESS NIGHT, Elise didn't look forward to a full day at the clinic. She left the house early, intent on looking over her schedule before her staff arrived. Not to mention she didn't want to see Dean just yet. She'd spent most of the night thinking about him. About what would happen when the case was finally over and he was back in L.A. Would that be the end of it? Would he dismiss her as a fond memory and return to his former life?

One part of her argued that Dean wasn't the kind of man to tell a woman he was in love with her, then just take off. But this wasn't a normal courtship, and she was feeling unsettled about so many things that she was afraid to believe in anything just now. Afraid she might be wrong. Afraid she might lose Dean before she truly had him.

She unlocked the back door and walked inside, stopping a few paces inside the door. Something was wrong. For a moment, she wasn't sure whether to continue into the building or run back to the house yelling at the top of her lungs for Dean. She opted for the former, all the while telling herself the door had been locked and everything appeared to be in its place. Except the animals were agitated, which fed her unease.

"Hey, guys." She comforted a screaming cockatoo, who

hopped around his cage, before moving on to check an African Gray, who looked wild-eyed. "Everything's fine. Honest."

But it wasn't, some sixth sense insisted loud and clear. Something was very wrong. Pulling her sleeve down over her hand, she carefully opened cabinets and eyed the rows of medicines, then checked the refrigerator, where other medications were kept. Nothing, looked out of place, but something still didn't feel right to her. Keeping her sleeve over her hand, she gingerly picked up the phone and dialed the house.

"Myrna, please have Dean come down here right away," she said without preamble.

While Elise waited, she walked through the rest of the clinic, looking at supplies and office equipment in hopes she would find something, anything, that didn't look right, but still she couldn't find anything amiss. She knew her calm exterior hid a very frightened woman when Dean tore through the back door, the expression on his face unnerving her even more. He looked like a man ready to do battle.

"What's wrong?" he demanded.

She shook her head. "I don't know, but something is."

Dean's intuition had saved his life too many times to question hers. "You'll have to close the clinic for the day."

"I assumed you'd say that. I got the names and numbers of today's appointments, so they can be contacted," she replied.

Dean looked around. "Let's lock up until a lab team can come out. You can call everyone from the house. I knew I shouldn't have let you talk me out of a security system for this place."

"There's no guarantee someone was here," she argued.

"What makes you think someone broke in?"

"The animals are upset, and I just feel it."

"That's good enough for me." He dragged her outside and locked the door.

During the short walk back to the house, Dean quizzed Elise on her every move from the time she entered the clinic until she called him. The fact that she could only give him a bad feeling for a reason didn't bother him one whit, and he sensed it wouldn't faze Santee, either. After he called the sheriff's detective, he left Elise to phone her staff and give them the day off, then contact her patients, using the excuse that there was an electrical malfunction in the building, causing it to be closed until further notice. She didn't promise to be open the next day, just in case.

"How up-to-date is your inventory?" Dean asked her when she finished her calls.

"Every day we track everything used on an inventory sheet to make sure we never run short of anything important," she explained.

"Where is it kept?"

"On the inside of the cabinet doors, and that's updated in our computer on a weekly basis. I'm a real stickler for accurate records." Elise ruefully noted the arrival of the crime-scene van. "I guess by now they can find their way here with their eyes closed." She watched Dean head for the door. "I know, stay inside."

"Just until we make sure there's nothing wrong," he told her. "I'd still like to know how he's getting past the dogs and geese."

"Maybe because they're not true guard dogs," she admitted. "Their size puts off most people, but they'd rather lick strangers to death than attack them."

"Oh, that's great!" he exploded. "Why didn't you say anything sooner?"

"Because I knew you'd react just the way you are right now." Elise didn't bat an eyelash under his fury. "They often bark at strangers, but if someone tells them to be quiet, they'll usually settle down without too much argument. Besides, the first time he drugged them. I didn't think he'd try to enter the property again."

Dean rolled his eyes. He strode to the door and suddenly spun around, pointing his finger at her. "You need a full-time keeper." With that pronouncement, he walked out, slamming the door behind him so hard the windows rattled.

"I wonder if he's volunteering for the job," Myrna commented.

"I don't think he meant it as a compliment," Elise countered, watching him cross the yard in ground-eating strides.

"Do you want him to stay?" she persisted.

Elise's quiet reply floated through the air. "Yes, but what matters most is whether he wants to stay."

DEAN STOOD inside the clinic, watching the lab technicians dust for fingerprints, take a random sampling of medications and anything else in boxes or bottles and even leaf through the shelves of file folders for anything that looked out of place.

"How does she work with all this?" Santee asked, wincing as an Amazon parrot kept asking everyone if they wanted a cup of tea.

"Meow, I'm a cat, I'm a cat," an African Gray parrot insisted.

"Hey, buddy, you're a bird," one of the police technicians informed the parrot.

The African Gray snapped his beak at the man. "I'm a cat!" he shrieked. "Meow."

"Okay, you're a catbird." The man shrugged his shoulders at one of his colleagues, who chuckled at the scene.

The bird dipped his head, looking coy. "I'm a bird," he cooed.

"That's Oscar," Dean explained. "He did that to me, too. He's boarding here while his owners are on vacation."

Santee looked around. "My idea of an exotic pet was a lizard or a king snake, but now it seems like anything goes. At least snakes don't talk back to you."

"If you catch this guy, he'll probably get put away in the state hospital." The head technician approached Santee.

"Does this mean I'm not going to like what I'm about to hear?"

The lab man nodded. "I won't be able to tell you more until I can run some full tests, but what I've been able to check out here isn't good."

Dean didn't need to see his grim expression to guess that. "Meaning?" he asked.

"Meaning this guy has a very nasty sense of humor. So far, we've found traces of hydrochloric acid in the soap dispenser in the bathroom, a hallucinogen in the drinking water dispenser and we even found ground glass in the Kleenex box."

He paused, then continued carefully. "Not all of the medication bottles were touched, just enough to make trouble. They were played with by an expert. If you weren't looking for something out of the ordinary, you wouldn't find anything wrong with them. He seemed to pick them at random. Something was put in them, we're not sure what, but I won't be surprised to find some kind of poison. According to the inventory records, a box of latex examination gloves was taken, along with about fifty hypodermic syringes. He probably used a pair of the gloves but didn't leave them behind. Everything's clean as a whistle. We couldn't even find prints of the regular staff on anything, much less anyone else's. The guy is thorough.''

Dean and Santee shared a long look.

"She's not going to be happy about this," Dean said finally. "She could go over the edge."

"Which he'd enjoy," Santee finished.

"That's not all." The technician spoke again up. "There's no sign of forced entry. One of the men is checking this out further."

Dean looked ready to explode. "I don't like any of this."

"Tell me about it." The young man sounded reluctant. "This guy had a lot of fun while he was here. He even changed the message on the answering machine. I think you'll want to hear this for yourself."

He led the way to the front of the office, where another technician had just finished dusting the desk and files for prints. Dean and Santee stood behind the reception desk, watching the man depress the announcement button on the answering machine.

"I'm sorry, but Dr. Carpenter's clinic is closed indefinitely due to a death in the family." Dietrich's voice was unmistakable.

Dean spun around. He felt so furious that he doubted even putting a fist through the wall would dissipate his rage. He'd never *wanted* to kill before, but he wanted to see Dietrich dead, and he'd be more than happy to do the honors.

"How?" he roared. "How is he doing all this without leaving one damned clue?"

Santee looked grim. "I don't know, but more than ever I want this guy caught. He's getting way too brazen. I don't want to think what he'll try next."

Dean breathed deeply to contain his fury. "Elise has already called her clients and explained the clinic was closed until further notice. He's going to know this and realize he has one less place to hit again. If nothing else, we're narrowing his playground for him. If necessary, we'll send the girls off somewhere and narrow it even more. I want to piss him off enough that he'll realize I'm the one behind it, and he'll start coming after me. I want this fight."

"Just remember one thing." Santee stepped in as the sensible one here.

Dean was past thinking sensibly. "What?"

"He might decide to piss you off more by going after her."

Dean found it painful to draw air into his lungs. "Yeah, I know. That's another thing I'm afraid of."

The technician was called away by one of the other workers, and the two conferred in low tones. He returned to Dean and Santee with an unhappy look on his face. "One of the guys just discovered something that's not going to make you two happy."

Dean closed his eyes. What could possibly make this situation any worse? "What?"

"There's no sign of a break-in for an excellent reason."

Dean and Santee looked at each other. They knew the answer before they heard it.

"It looks like he used a key."

Chapter Thirteen

"How comforting to know he used a key instead of breaking a window or smashing in a door to enter my clinic." Elise's eyes spat out turquoise fire as she paced the length of the kitchen. "I'm sure the insurance company will be so happy to know they won't have that additional cost."

Dean didn't say a word. He just straddled a chair, resting his arms across the back. He looked over at Santee, who sat in another chair, his own expression shuttered. "I've discovered it's safer to remain out of the line of fire," he muttered to the sheriff's detective.

Elise rounded on him. "You—you cop you!"

Undaunted by her temper, he grinned up at her. "I love it when you talk macho to me."

Incredibly, her face turned a bright rose color, but she visibly tamped down that emotion and worked on bringing back her anger. "That man invaded my clinic. He tampered with my equipment, poisoned the drinking water and left a disgusting message on my answering machine. I'm only grateful he didn't harm any of the animals! And now you're telling me he barely left any trace of a physical presence other than his sick idea of a practical joke!'' She looked at them as if they were complete idiots.

''Dr. Carpenter, my boys combed that place for clues, but this man is very clever,'' Santee told her in his low voice. ''He's a world-class games player.''

She stood there, her arms crossed over her chest, her very posture indicating she wasn't buying any excuses, no matter how logically the detective presented his case.

Dean simply remained in his seat, admiring the picture before him. In deference to the warm day, Elise had changed into yellow shorts and a yellow-and-white-striped tailored shirt. Her outfit, coupled with yellow socks and white running shoes, left her looking as young as one of her daughters.

His stomach tightened as he watched her. He'd never felt such an intense need for a woman. But the more he was with Elise, the more he wanted of her. There was only one problem. No matter how much he wanted to think about the future, he couldn't as long as he had a job to do. He was only here as long as Santee deemed him necessary.

Dietrich should have been caught long ago. He looked up at the one thing that made this whole miserable scenario bearable. At least it kept him close to Elise. But he could see the strain she was under. Shadows under her eyes, testifying to the nightmares that didn't fully awaken her but left her listless and out of sorts most mornings. And now one of the few places she thought safe had been invaded.

He couldn't blame her for being angry. He could only blame himself for not having seen this coming. He rested his chin against the wood, only half listening to Elise rant and rave to Santee. She was usually so cool and controlled that most people would assume she was ice clear through. He knew better, and he'd liked being the only one to see both sides of Elise Carpenter. Santee, he knew, would probably steer clear of Elise after this.

"Maybe there is a pattern after all," he mused.

Elise stopped her tirade in midstream and turned toward him at the same time Santee did. Dean shifted his gaze in their direction.

"He has to know how important her home is, so the first step he took was to invade her property with the kind of tactics a bunch of kids would use. You have to admit, it's a great way to throw off the police—make them think it was a bunch of kids pulling a sick joke. Except you didn't believe it. And I came down, so Dietrich knew *we knew* he was around.

"Then there was the episode with Becky at the Wild Animal Park. Still keeping a little distance, so to speak, but getting more personal. Then came the videotape—up close and personal and meant to show us that he was very close and in control, that he could take any of us out any time he wanted to.

"The clinic would be his next step, because he knew that invading it and polluting it the ways he did would be almost like violating her." Dean had stated his thoughts as reasonably as he could. Now he waited for feedback.

Santee closed his eyes, obviously mulling over Dean's words. "You could be right. He's slowly invading her territory by first showing he could get on her property without any problem, approach her kids in public without anyone noticing anything wrong, spy on the household and now invading her workplace. He's working on her bit by bit, each time coming just a little bit closer, trying to break her down."

Dean smiled at Elise. "Trouble is, he doesn't know the

doc has a spine made out of tempered steel. She doesn't break easily."

She bowed her head. "If necessary, I'll pull the girls out of school and send them away," she murmured. "I can't take the chance of something happening to them."

"If you'd like, I can arrange for an officer to drive them to school and pick them up," Santee offered. "I'll be honest with you, Dr. Carpenter, I don't think you should be left without protection from now on. He's getting too close."

Elise sighed. She knew she looked as defeated as she felt. Her earlier fury had left her drained of any more emotion. "Yes, whatever," she murmured, turning away. She walked out of the kitchen without another word.

"What can I do to help?" Myrna spoke up. She had refused Elise's suggestion to go on home, instead saying she intended to remain close by.

Dean stood up and pushed the chair under the table. "Just be here," he told the housekeeper.

Santee also got up and headed for the door. "I'll call you later if we find out anything else," he told Dean as he left.

"I only hope we do," he murmured, intent now on finding Elise.

He didn't have much trouble. He found her curled up on her bed, the pillows propped up behind her as she stared at something braced against her knees. Dean sat down by her feet. He picked up the picture frame she held and studied the family photograph. Elise, smiling at the camera with a tall man standing beside her: a younger Keri, with braces glinting on her teeth; Lisa, her face a bit plumper than now; and a tiny Becky perched in her mother's lap, a broad grin on her face. For a brief second, Dean hated the man in the picture. Hated him because he feared that when he made love to

Elise, she might be thinking of her dead husband, comparing them.

"He's in my heart because we had twelve good years and he gave me three beautiful children, and he's gone, Dean," Elise said softly, reading the thoughts etched on his grim features. "I've never needed to pretend you were Steve."

She reached forward, plucked the frame out of his hands and laid it to one side. She grasped his hands between hers, rubbing them in a circular motion. "Steven and I had a good marriage, but I suspect he put the clinic even before me. His work was his life, and his greatest joy was in coming up with new surgical techniques and writing papers about them. By all rights, we shouldn't even have been in the clinic that night, but Steve took the call and assured the owner we would take care of his bird right away."

She stared down at their hands, absently noticing how callused his finger pads and palms were. "I was tired. That pregnancy was more difficult than the others, and I wanted nothing more than to go home and put up my feet, but I let Steven talk me into staying to help him."

Her brow creased in thought. "There are so many things I don't remember about that night, and so many things I wish I could forget. The sound of the bullet hitting Steve, that maniac's laughter, then his curses as he realized we didn't have the kind of drugs he wanted. I don't really remember any pain when he beat me, probably because I was in so much shock over Steven being shot. I have no memory of picking up the scalpel and cutting him."

She trailed off for a few moments, then continued with quiet vehemence. "I just wish I had connected with his throat instead of his arm. Do you know I even welcomed the pain from my miscarriage because it told me I was still alive? In the space of a few hours I lost my husband and my baby, but I couldn't cry over either of them," she whispered, lifting her head. She looked at Dean with eyes filled with such agony it hurt him to look at her. "The doctor said it was shock, but I knew what it was. I couldn't cry because, to me, it wasn't over. It can't be over until that man is tried and convicted for his crimes. And even that didn't happen." Her voice choked. "Dean, I feel as if something is eating away at me inside, and I can't stop it."

He reached for her, pulling her onto his lap and cradling her against his chest. "I wish I had a ready answer for you, Elise, but I don't think there is one. It was left unresolved five years ago because Dietrich had to be freed. You saw your chance when he was arrested again, only to have it snatched away when he escaped. Now you have to sit and wait, again a victim. And due to what's been going on, you're more the prisoner than he was when he was in jail. It's all built up inside you, and you haven't been able to let it out."

"I hate smart men," she muttered against his chest.

He grinned. This was the women he knew best. "No, you don't."

"Yes I do."

He pulled her shirttail out of her shorts and ran his hands over her back. "Hmm, I thought you weren't wearing a bra." He nipped her earlobe. "Lady, you should be ashamed of yourself for going around half-naked in front of Santee."

"He didn't notice."

"The hell he didn't. I saw the way he looked at you."

"And I noticed the way *you* looked at me. Those kind of looks are almost as obscene as those shirts you wear." She plucked at the soft cotton of his navy T-shirt. "I hate to think what kind of influence you've been on the girls."

"I haven't seen any signs of trauma."

Elise's chest rose and fell with a heavy sigh. "You've stopped rubbing my back."

"I'm still rubbing."

"Yes, but that isn't my back." She tipped her head in order to look at him. "Sex can't settle everything, Dean."

He laid her down and leaned over her, his hands braced by her shoulders. "No, it doesn't, but I feel the need to touch and love you," he said seriously.

Elise studied his face and saw something new there. No hint of his usual teasing manner, no light quips, just a man who needed her as much as she knew she needed him.

"It's the middle of the day." It was more a statement than a protest.

"I can close the drapes."

"Myrna might need one of us."

"We both know she's happier when we stay out of her way. If you're worried, I can lock the door." He didn't move a muscle as he waited for her decision.

She moved her hands upward until she could lace her fingers through his. "When this is all over I want you to take me out on a real date," she murmured. "I'm talking calling and asking me out, flowers and candy, you wearing a suit with a shirt and tie, dinner reservations at a nice restaurant, then dancing." With each word she spoke, Dean's head lowered until his mouth hovered just above hers.

"Shouldn't that be my idea?"

"Considering the way you dress, I thought you might need some assistance in that area. I have a feeling your idea of a fancy restaurant is the kind with a drive-through window."

"What happens after the dancing?" he breathed.

The corners of her lips tipped upward. "I'm sure you can think of something."

He released one of her hands and began unbuttoning her blouse. "Yes, I'm sure I'll have no problem there."

"I FEEL AS IF I could sleep for days," Elise murmured, burrowing in closer against Dean's side. She felt boneless and thoroughly loved.

"Considering all the nights you haven't been sleeping well, I'm not surprised." He yawned.

She rolled over until she could prop herself on his chest. "I have something to say, and I don't want to hear a word from you until I finish," she said quietly.

"Okay."

She chewed on her lower lip. "Carl Dietrich is either remarkably clever or totally insane, and if he decides to truly come after me, I might not survive. I need to know that the girls will be taken care of. I realize what I'm saying might be presumptuous, but if something does happen to me, I want you to have guardianship of the girls."

Dean wasn't sure whether to feel horrified or awed by her trust in him. "Ellie, I'm not going to allow anything to happen to you."

"What we want might not come into it in the long run," she argued. "We've both already seen that by what's happened so far. He seems to appear out of thin air, then vanish just as easily. How can we stop someone who doesn't seem to exist? I need to know the girls will be taken care of. There's more than enough insurance for their material needs, but I need to know their emotional needs will be taken care of as well."

He still couldn't take it all in. "What about your sister, or your parents, or even your in-laws?"

"I love my sister dearly, but her patience with children is next to nonexistent. She's best as the aunt they see on special occasions. And my parents are getting older, and they've earned some time for themselves. As for the in-laws..." Long-buried pain surfaced in her gaze. "Steven was an only child, and the only way his parents could deal with his death was to blame me. They felt that I was the one who forced him to work in the clinic that night, and I somehow enraged Dietrich into shooting him. They haven't had anything to do with any of us since the funeral."

Dean could only wrap his arms around her and hold on tight. "They gave up so much," he murmured. "And here my mom would be ecstatic to have grandkids to spoil."

"Then you won't argue with my idea, because I want to make it legal and binding." She rubbed her cheek against the coarse hair on his chest.

"There's no reason to, Ellie."

"For my peace of mind?"

With her cheek resting on his chest, she could hear his chuckle rumble under her ear. "Are you sure you want this tactless guy who's a slob at heart, wears obscene T-shirts, not to mention is a cop, to be a role model for your daughters?"

She turned her face enough to kiss a dark brown nipple embedded among the coarse curls. "With luck, *they'll* influence *you* and turn you into a model citizen."

Dean grasped her arms and pulled her upright. "When this is all over, we're going to have a long talk." he said hoarsely. "And I do mean *we*, because I don't intend for anything to happen to you. Do you understand me, Doc?"

She rubbed her thigh against his. "Before, during or after that dinner date you'll take me on?"

He was past teasing. "I'm not going to lose you, Ellie." He couldn't remember feeling as serious about any subject as he felt right then. "I'll fight the very devil to keep you."

She didn't smile. "I think you're already fighting the devil."

DEAN DIDN'T HAVE much of an appetite. Myrna puttered around the kitchen, muttering about how a person's chicken and dumplings weren't appreciated anymore and she might as well throw out that blueberry cobbler she'd slaved over. Even the girls were quieter than usual, without the usual dinnertime squabbles over whose turn it was to clear the table or who had the best or worst day at school.

While Dean had roamed the house, furious with his inability to nail down one man, and spent time on the phone arranging for a security system to be installed, Elise had spent the afternoon on the telephone arranging for a colleague to take over her patients until further notice. Since she hadn't wanted too many people to know her troubles, she merely said that her clinic had to be reoutfitted before she could reopen for business. A sheriff's deputy had picked up the girls and deposited them at the front door with a few words to Dean and a brief smile at Elise. Elise sat them down and explained the situation and then quickly left the room before she broke down in the tears she had repressed for so long.

"How about a game of Frisbee?" Dean had asked, hoping to divert the girl's attention. "I bet Kola and Bailey and Duke would be happy to join in."

"Maybe we should try something else so Dietrich doesn't

get bored taping us doing the same thing." Keri spoke up, her delicate face furrowed with worry.

Daunted by the grim reminder, they had all chosen to remain inside.

"Dean, will you watch movies with us after dinner?" Becky asked now, touching his hand as the group sat around the table, picking at their food.

He managed a smile. It wasn't difficult to guess they needed reassurance. "Sure. I'll even help with the dishes."

"Wait a minute—*I* want to get a picture of that," Myrna jibed.

Dean shot her a dirty look. "Hey, you have to admit the guest bedroom is a lot neater these days."

She looked down her nose. "Yes, and we know why, don't we?"

"You'd better behave or you'll find a snoring tortoise under *your* bed," he threatened.

"I'm worried, I'm worried."

ELISE SAT behind her desk, lost in stormy thoughts over the invasion of her clinic. Dean had arranged for someone to come out that very afternoon to install a security system.

As she sat there, she stared at the floor-to-ceiling bookshelves filled with veterinary medicine textbooks and journals Steven and she had accumulated over the years.

She had already given up one practice because of Carl Dietrich, and she refused to lose another. And there was another consideration in her life now: Dean. How ironic that the man she'd fall in love with would be a police officer. A cop.

Not to mention that his job was seventy miles away, and her work was here. She couldn't ask him to give his up, but could she really think of starting over again? She laughed without humor. As if Dean had even brought it up. All he mentioned was having a long talk when this was over. That could mean any number of things. She was finding it difficult to think positively after everything that had happened lately.

She had no idea how long she sat there, reliving the past few weeks that she doubted she would ever recover from.

"You going to stay in here all night?" Dean stuck his head around the door.

She turned. "I thought you were watching TV with the girls."

He groaned. "I have been. We had a *Star Wars* marathon. Becky fell asleep halfway through the second movie, and Lisa barely made it through the third. I just carried Becky into her room, and Keri's getting her into a nightgown." He flexed his shoulder muscles. "Either I'm getting old or your youngest isn't as lightweight as she looks. I'm just glad I was able to prod Lisa to her feet. Carrying her might have given me a hernia."

She smiled. "You didn't know? A sleeping child automatically gains twenty pounds." She was shocked when she glanced at her small desk clock. "I must have lost track of the time. How could you let them stay up so late?" She shot out of her chair and headed for the door.

He grasped her by the shoulders. "One, there's no school tomorrow, so I figured you wouldn't mind. Two, it helped get their minds off things." He didn't need to elaborate on what things they might be worried about.

"Even considering what happened to their father, I hoped they'd never have to deal with the darker side of life." Elise sighed. "I should have known it wouldn't be possible. How can Keri indulge in worrying about whether the boy she has a crush on will invite her to the winter dance when she has to think about a madman out there stalking her mother? Or Lisa—how can she think about all the changes going on in her body and the new emotions she's feeling? And Becky, who's entering the mainstream of school and friends. It isn't right," she bit out. "It isn't right that they can't laugh and not worry about anything more pressing than what to wear to school the next day or how they'll spend their weekend. It just isn't right!"

His hands dug into her shoulders. "Elise, you're letting it affect you more than it's affecting them."

She raised her chin in that obstinate gesture he already knew so well. "Really? Do you know Becky used to sing to herself almost all the time? Keri and Lisa complained constantly because they said she sang tunes that stuck in their minds whether they wanted them to or not. I can't remember the last time I heard her even hum a tune, much less sing. Have you heard her sing?" She barely waited for him to shake his head. "And Lisa never stayed in the house if she could be outdoors, even if it was to just play ball with the dogs. Keri thought the only decent television channel was MTV and danced around the living room. They had friends running in and out of the house at all times, and either Keri or Lisa tied up the phone constantly with their friends. Have you seen them doing that or heard me yelling at them to get off the phone?" she demanded.

"No," he had to ruefully admit. "No, I haven't seen or heard any of that." He shifted uncomfortably under her direct gaze. "Dammit, Elise, you're making *me* feel guilty," he grumbled. "What is it with you women? Is this some trait that comes out at puberty, or what?"

She bit down on her lower lip. "Dean Cornell, no man

has ever made me as angry as you have. But what I hate the most is when I get mad at you, you have a talent for making me want to laugh at the same time." She covered his hands on her shoulders with hers, squeezing them gently. "Now that I see what time it is, I think I'd better check on the girls and make sure they're in bed and not reading or listening to the radio."

"I'm going down to the clinic to check out the security system," he told her. "I'll be back in a few minutes."

Elise dropped her hands until they rested lightly on his waist. She frowned, sensing something wasn't quite right. Before Dean could guess her intent and move away, her hand slipped around to his back and encountered a lump under his sweater. She quickly slid her fingers under the hem and found smooth leather and hard steel. She snatched her hand away as if it had been burned.

"You're wearing your gun," she said woodenly.

"You know I've been wearing it when I go outside the house," he reminded her.

"Yes, but..." How could she explain that it had finally sunk in *why* he had to wear it.

"I've kept it out of the girls' reach when it's not on me," Dean sought to assure her.

She shook her head. "Funny, it took until now for me to finally see why you wear your gun and why it's so necessary. As if it's been nothing more than a bad dream I'll wake up from soon." She stepped to one side. "I'm sorry, Dean, I'm probably not making much sense. You go on and check the clinic. I think I'll take a shower before bed."

Sensing she needed some distance, he merely nodded and walked away.

Elise checked the bedrooms and found Becky sound asleep

under the covers with her favorite stuffed bear, Lisa sleeping with her pillow partially covering her head, and Keri reading a teen magazine. As Elise moved through the house, she could hear the dogs' joyful yips diminish. She guessed they'd probably followed Dean down the driveway.

Before she headed for her bathroom, she stopped at the locked cabinet that held her rifle and a handgun. She quickly unlocked it, took out the gun and loaded it.

"If Carl Dietrich dares to enter this house and Dean doesn't get him, I will," she vowed under her breath as she slid the gun under her mattress.

Instead of a shower, Elise opted for a bath, scenting the hot water with her favorite bath oil. She stretched out in the tub with the water covering her to her chin. By closing her eyes, she could almost forget about the real world and transport herself back to simpler times. The tension in her muscles slowly eased.

"Now there's decadence for you."

She opened her eyes. Dean stood in that doorway, holding a glass filled with Baileys Irish Cream and an open beer bottle. He sat down on the commode and held out the glass.

"Thank you. I decided a shower wouldn't relax me as much as a bath would." She sipped the drink.

Dean lifted his head and sniffed the air. "Smells real sexy in here."

Elise arched an eyebrow. "Do you equate everything with sex?"

"Only where you're concerned." He rolled the bottle between his palms.

Elise set her glass on the side of the tub. "So much has happened, Dean, that I wonder if what's gone on between us is because of the situation and, therefore, not real."

"No!" He shot to his feet, towering over her and looking more angry than she'd ever seen him. "What we have is about as real as you can get, and don't you dare try to deny it!"

"But how do we know?" Elise persisted, a part of her knowing she was pushing even when she shouldn't.

He put the bottle to one side and hauled her up out of the water.

"Dean!" She struggled to keep her balance.

His dark visage should have frightened her, but it didn't. She knew she was the reason for his anger. She'd tried to dismiss what they had, tried to say it wasn't real, when all she wanted was to hold what they shared close to her.

"Elise Carpenter, you're the best thing that's ever happened to me," Dean said, his voice raw with emotion. "And I'm not giving you up for anything or anyone. Understand?"

She stared deep into his dark eyes. "Yes," she whispered.

They remained in their precarious position, Dean uncaring that suds smeared his clothes and Elise not feeling the chill.

"Everything will work out just fine," he told her. "Everything." He hooked an arm under her knees and picked her up. "Just remember that."

She slid an arm around his neck. "I don't think you're going to let me forget."

HE REMAINED in his crouched position among the rocks overlooking the darkened house. The small lit window—the bathroom, no doubt—went out, and no light went on in the bedroom.

Damn. No lights, and the drapes remained closed. He knew he shouldn't have sent that tape of them rolling around in bed. Now the drapes were closed all the time, taking away his fun.

He ran his fingers down his arm, feeling the scar tissue marring the tattoo he'd gotten when he was stationed in the Philippines. He'd never hated anyone as much as he hated that bitch when she cut him up with that scalpel. She'd 'bout near took his damn arm off! His lean features tightened.

He'd sat up there that morning watching the fool cops run all over the place. He wondered if they found all his little clues. They didn't worry him. Only that bastard who was there all the time was trouble. But Carl Dietrich had known trouble before, and he wasn't afraid of it.

"Soon, lady vet," he murmured. "Soon it will be just you and me. And payback time."

Chapter Fourteen

"What were you trying to prove with this dumb stunt?"

Elise didn't falter under Dean's low-voiced rage, nor did she look at the gun he held in his hand. "I'd be careful with that if if I were you. It's loaded."

He took several deep breaths to contain his anger. "Naturally, that was the first thing I checked, and now it's unloaded. What were you thinking, putting it under your mattress?"

"You must be like the princess and the pea."

"A pea this size would hard to miss," he informed her. "That was a crazy stunt, Elise. Or didn't you think I could protect you properly?"

She lifted her chin. "I thought it best to hedge all my bets."

With an expression of distaste, Dean tossed the gun onto the bed. "Do you realize how many people are killed by their own guns?"

"That lecture won't work. It used to be my own argument against having a gun in the house." She poked her forefinger gainst his chest. "And I hate that damn shirt!"

Puzzled, he looked downward. "What's wrong with it?"

"Feel Safe Tonight—Sleep With A Cop," she snapped. "Why can't you wear plain shirts like most adults?"

He didn't seem angry with her insult, but he didn't appear happy with her, either. "I'll wear what I please. But what you're trying to do here is change the subject, and I'm not going to allow that."

She dropped onto the bed and buried her face in her hands. "I'm tired, Dean." Her voice was muffled. "I'm tired of hiding out, of not even being able to go into work, of having to allow my answering service to pick up my calls and know anything suspicious is being traced. And I'm so afraid that our next step will be to take the girls out of school and send them away."

"Those five cups of coffee you've already had this morning haven't helped either," he said dryly.

Elise held out a hand, palm down. He was right: she had the jitters,. "Good thing I'm not performing any surgery," she said sardonically.

"Right about now I wouldn't even ask you to remove a splinter."

She looked up. "How do you handle this? This constant waiting for something to happen. How can you do this every day without going insane?"

He crouched down in front of her, placing his hands on her knees. "For one thing, it doesn't happen every day. Some days we sit in the station and do nothing but type up reports."

She allowed herself the briefest of smiles. "It only takes you that long because you're such a rotten typist."

"That, too," he agreed, relieved to see a bit of her spirit returning.

Elise stared over Dean's shoulder, lost in thought. "He's

narrowing the battlefield. He doesn't want anyone to escape the trap when he finally springs it. I know someone who trains guard dogs. I should have asked him if I could borrow a few for the yard. There's nothing like a Doberman going for a man's throat to make him think twice.''

Dean shook his head. ''This guy wouldn't think twice about shooting a dog. That tranquilizer-dart business the last time was just part of his game.''

''Dobies don't give up easily.'' She needed to keep talking, just to know she was looking at every angle, if nothing else. ''Dean, I am so frightened,'' she whispered. ''Not for myself, but about what could happen if he decided to go after one of the girls to get back at me.''

''I won't let him,'' he insisted fiercely. ''You know that.''

She covered his hands with hers, pressing down tightly. ''But you can't watch all of us twenty-four hours a day! I'm not immune to the tension building up every day. You and I are snapping at each other like junkyard dogs!''

He allowed himself a grin. ''Pretty good description, Doc, although I would think you'd describe us more as mauling macaws or leaping lop-ears or—''

''Enough!'' She held up a hand. ''I hate it when you make me laugh!''

''It's better to laugh than to cry. And in this business, we learn early to indulge in gallows humor. Now, come on.'' He jumped to his feet and pulled her. ''We're going to coax the girls into going to the movies, where I can hold your hand in the dark and steal your popcorn.''

She shot him a dry look. ''Dean, girls of certain ages refuse to be caught dead going to the movies with a parent.''

''Keri?''

''Keri *and* Lisa. They would insist on walking in a different door, pretending they don't even know us and, if possible, even sitting in a different theater. In fact, Keri would probably refuse to sit in the same theater as Lisa. Not exactly what you want us to do, is it? Since you prefer to keep an eye on all of us and can't manage to be in more than one place at a time.''

Dean grimaced. "Teen years are hell."

"And they won't get any better in a hurry." A part of her wanted to warn him now. After all, if there was a way for them to make it together, Dean had to learn just how difficult the next few years would be. By the time Lisa left her teen years, Becky would be in the midst of hers. The idea was daunting even to Elise. She hugged him briefly, savoring the clean, soapy smell of his skin. "You never wear any kind of after-shave or cologne."

"When I'm crawling around on bank floors, I don't want anyone to smell me first," he explained.

"And you say the robbery detail is easy?"

"Easier than vice or narcotics," he told her. "Come on, let's find something to get our minds off what's going on."

"You said I could wear it!" Lisa shrieked.

"I never said any such thing! And now you've ruined it, you little idiot!" Keri's voice was shrill with anger.

Elise and Dean barely stepped out into the hall before they heard the sounds of war coming from the family room.

"Fud up! Fud up!" Baby screamed, joining in.

Elise sighed. "When I was seventeen I thought it would be wonderful to have eight children. I'm so glad I wised up in time." She hurried down the hall. "All right, what's going on here?" She had to shout to be heard above the girls' screams of outrage.

Dean stood on the outskirts, watching Elise deal with both

sides of the heated argument. "I wonder what Robert Young would do here," he murmured, crossing his arms over his chest and leaning against the doorjamb. He decided it was much safer to remain a spectator. He wanted to tell Elise the girls' fighting was an outlet for the tension permeating the house but sensed this wasn't a good time to offer any such *Father Knows Best* opinion.

"She took my new sweater, and look what she's done!" Keri glared at her younger sister. "It's ruined, Mom, and I never even had a chance to wear it."

"She said I could wear it!" Lisa argued. "I wouldn't have spilled anything on it if she hadn't grabbed my arm."

The two began speaking so rapidly that Elise just stood there for a moment, taking in the verbal volleyball as Keri, Lisa *and* Baby kept on screaming.

"Enough!" She breathed deeply, grateful for the brief spate of silence. She looked at the once pale green crewneck sweater Lisa wore. The sweater Keri had begged Elise for for more than two weeks. The sweater that hung on Lisa's bony shoulders and now sported a large ink stain in front.

"I'm not saying you're lying, Lisa, but I do know that Keri would never have allowed you to borrow this particular sweater," she said slowly.

"She said I could borrow some of her clothes!"

Elise placed her hand over her middle daughter's mouth. "Don't dig your hole any deeper, Lisa. You will not receive any allowance until the sweater is paid for." She held up her hand to forestall further arguments. "You will have kitchen duty for the next month, and no television for two weeks."

Lisa opened her mouth, then quickly closed it, recognizing the look on her mother's face. If she voiced a protest, the punishment would only harder.

"You wanted the sweater, Lisa. It is now yours."

Lisa looked down. "But it's dirty."

"You know where the washer and the stain remover is. I suggest you try it." Elise turned to Keri. "Why don't you call the store and see if they have another sweater you liked," she suggested, easily reading her daughter's expression. "Don't worry, I realize you won't necessarily want the same one."

By the time Elise left the family room, she felt as if she'd lived five lifetimes.

"Very good," Dean applauded. "But how did you know Keri wouldn't want the same sweater she loved so much?"

"I have a sister, too," she replied. "Our bloodiest battle dealt with a favorite blouse of mine she wore on a date and spilled pizza sauce on." She paused. "The scary part is, Dean, this is only the beginning. It has to get worse before it gets better."

"I guess the idea of going to the movies is out, huh?"

Elise nodded. "You got it. Unfortunately, we'll all have to suffer right along with Lisa." She looked him square in the eye. "I told you the tension was getting to all of us."

He nodded. "One time I was lucky enough to baby-sit an important witness to a gangland killing. This guy thought room service was designed just for him, he cheated at poker and he snored worse than your tortoise."

"You snore almost as bad."

"No, I don't."

"Yes, you do. I'll tape-record you just to prove it."

"Mom! The washer is making funny noises!"

Elise closed her eyes and swore under her breath. She quickly opened them and glared at Dean when he chuckled.

"This is not going to be a fun day," she predicted.

DEAN QUICKLY REALIZED Elise's prediction was on the mark. The girls didn't want to do anything or go anywhere. Elise refereed arguments all day and finally sent all of them to their rooms until they reached the age of twenty-one. By bedtime, Elise fought a raging headache that even aspirin and a neck rub from Dean didn't help.

"Wave the white flag," she murmured. "Tell him we give up."

"No, you don't. Everything will be fine in the morning," he assured her, digging his thumbs into her tense neck muscles. "Sunday will be great. You'll see."

"Ha! You weren't the one to hear the washer repairman say he can't come out for two weeks, nor were you the one to listen to Becky scream bloody murder because she couldn't find her pink sweat shirt. Or Keri realizing she'd left her French notebook in her locker at school, or Lisa suddenly remembering she has a science project due on Monday. Tomorrow will be even worse."

"Only if you let it."

Elise knew better but didn't try to persuade Dean differently. Once they were under the covers and he wrapped his arms around her, she should have been ready to succumb to blessed sleep. Instead, she lay wide-awake.

"Not sleepy?" Dean rumbled in her ear.

"Just thinking."

"About what?"

"Wishing things were different. Wishing we'd met under other circumstances."

"If I'd hit on you and asked you for a date, would you have said yes after you learned I was a cop?"

She hated his logic. "Maybe," she opted.

"Maybe no. You don't like cops, remember?"

She lazily traced a finger around his beard. She'd never thought of beards as being soft and sexy until she knew Dean's. "You're beginning to change my mind."

"Yeah, I figured I did that once I didn't have to sleep with that tortoise anymore." He yawned broadly. "Now, be a good girl and go to sleep. I need my beauty rest."

As Elise listened to Dean's deep-breathing slumber, she only wished she could find the same.

THE NEXT DAY was a repeat of the one before, with tempers rising steadily until Elise threatened corporal punishment, not one of her usual choices, and banished everyone—including Dean, for trying to calm her down—to their rooms. Dean was smart enough to hide out in the guest room until things cooled down.

He wished he could break the thick cloud of tension hovering over the house. He wanted nothing more than to let the Carpenter women return to life as usual, but he knew better. He knew time was running out and Dietrich could strike at any moment. He wanted it over just as much as Elise did, because then he could talk to her about a subject that was growing more important every day. He figured his best argument would be that Elise wouldn't have to change her initials.

Elise spent Sunday night and the early hours into Monday walking the floors, looking in on her girls and staring at the drawn curtains. She jumped each time she heard the dogs moving about, and she peered out through the curtains but saw nothing other than the yellow floodlights illuminating the yard. As far as she was concerned, it was much too quiet. She had no idea as she wandered through the house that Dean lay awake listening to her footsteps, wishing he could make things all better, and knowing, as she did, that time was running out.

SIGHING IN RELIEF, Elise watched the sheriff's deputy drive off with the girls. She enjoyed the idea of savoring a leisurely breakfast with Dean as they talked about anything that came to mind except for the problem that refused to go away. She had just finished loading the dishwasher when she turned around to find Dean shrug on a denim jacket.

"I'm going in to see Santee so we can make our usual idiotic call to Anderson," he told her. "Want to come with me?"

She shook her head. "I think I'll take advantage of the peace and quiet and read one of the books I've been meaning to read for the past year. And, no offense, but police stations aren't my idea of fun."

"Mine either. Okay, then do me a favor and stick close to the house." He looked around. "I won't be gone long."

"Dean?" She waited until he looked at her. "No offense, but I'll be very happy to have some time to myself. That's why I told Myrna not to bother coming in today."

He hesitated. "There's a patrol car parked near the front gate."

Elise smiled. "Stop fussing like a mother hen, Dean. I know the routine. If I even hear a leaf rattling, I'll holler good and loud. I promise." She kissed him for effect.

"As much as I'd like to pursue that kiss, duty rears its head." He sighed with regret. "I'll be back as soon as I can."

"I know."

She watched the blue truck rattle down the driveway and make its way out of sight.

"Enjoy the quiet, Elise, it won't be for long," she murmured, turning away.

It took her less than a half hour to realize none of her books looked interesting, and even the idea of cleaning out her closet wasn't appealing. She ended up in the kitchen, thinking about baking brownies, when the phone rang, making her jump.

"Dr. Carpenter, this is the answering service," a cheerful voice trilled in her ear. "I'm sorry to disturb you, but the gentleman insists it's an emergency with his bird."

"That's all right, I'll take the call." She waited for the telltale clicks indicating the call was being put through.

"Hey, lady doctor."

Elise felt the hairs on the back of her neck stand on end. "What do you want?"

"No, I think it's more what *you* want, and that would be your littlest bird," he jeered. "A great touch with your answering service, don't you agree? Your big bad cop lover is gone, so it's between you and me now. And I'm going to talk fast just in case this call is being traced."

She looked down and quickly pushed a button on the answering machine.

"I got your kid, lady, and if you don't want anything to happen to her, you'll get out of there without that cop near your house following you."

"I don't believe you." Except she did.

"Mom?" Becky's tearful voice tore through her bluff.

"Is that enough?" Dietrich jeered. "You meet with me, and the kid stays in one piece. And don't try any tricks, or she'll be the loser. I want this to be strictly between us. The kid is my insurance that you'll behave yourself."

Elise blanked her mind to all but the instructions given to

her. By the time she hung up the phone, she felt ice-cold. All thought processes were on automatic as she headed for the locked cabinet. She knew exactly what she wanted and wasted no time getting it.

"*WHAT?*" Dean exploded the minute the news was relayed to him.

Santee looked grim. "Rebecca Carpenter's school just called us to say that she didn't return to her classroom after morning recess. The principal was under orders to contact us immediately if something like this happened."

"It's Elise he wants, and he's using Becky to get her." He grabbed the phone and dialed Elise's number. After dealing with the answering service and listening to the distant ringing, he slammed down the phone. "I'm heading back to see what's happened. And when I find that son of a bitch, I'm killing him," he vowed.

"You call in!" Santee yelled after him.

"Go to hell! I promised Elise we wouldn't screw up this time, and I mean to keep that promise." He stormed out of the station,.

ELISE HAD NO TROUBLE leaving the property after summoning a cheerful smile and informing the officer outside that she was only heading for the nearby grocery store for some brownie ingredients. He hesitated, suggesting it might be better if she waited for Detective Cornell to return, but she overrode his objections by insisting she was only traveling a mile and wouldn't be gone for more than ten minutes. She wasn't surprised when the young man finally backed down. She purposely kept her speed level until she was out of sight. Then she floored the accelerator.

As she drove, she only hoped Dean picked up the message she'd left behind. She wouldn't be surprised if Dietrich was somehow watching her leave, and she intended to make sure Becky wouldn't be harmed. As she drove up the winding road into the hills, her expression grew more grim. She was glad she remembered Dean's habit of snuggling a gun against his spine and only hoped her jacket would hide the bulge that dug painfully into her back.

"This time, you bastard, you won't get away," she vowed, pressing down on the accelerator and sending the Pathfinder racing at a death-defying speed. "I'll make sure of that."

ELISE PULLED her truck off the road and slowly climbed out, swiveling her neck from left to right as she scanned the area. Nothing looked out of the ordinary, but she had learned the hard way that that didn't mean danger might not be right around the corner. She took several deep breaths as she headed for the footpath that led to the outlook point Dietrich had told her about. As she walked up the steep path, her ears strained for any sound from Becky.

With each step her rage grew, until it turned dark and cold and endlessly bitter. She was determined that not one ounce of emotion would hinder her intention of destroying the man who had made her family's life such hell. She had just stepped over the rise when she found Carl Dietrich standing a short distance away, holding a sobbing Becky against him.

"All right, I'm here. Now let her go," Elise called out. She drew deeply upon that cold, dark part of herself, the part that wouldn't allow emotions to confuse her. She already knew any sign of fear would automatically sign her and Becky's death warrants.

He laughed and shook his head. "Not so fast, baby. How do I know you didn't call the cops?"

"Mom!" Becky shrieked, starting forward, only to be jerked back by Dietrich's arm wrapped painfully around her throat.

Elise wanted nothing more than to claw the man's eyes out. Instead, she forced herself to remain calm. If she showed the least bit of weakness, she would lose. "You know I didn't call the cops because you have my daughter. Now let her go. I'm the one you want, not her. Although I have no idea why you're going to all this trouble. You'd be a lot better off if you'd just leave the state."

"Lady, no bitch cuts me up and gets away with it," he snarled, ignoring Becky's distress.

Elise looked into his wild eyes and saw his jerky movements and knew it would take all her wits to get her and Becky away alive. Carl Dietrich's heavy drug use had finally caught up with him, and there would be no reasoning with him; he was caught up in some bizarre world of his own making.

"That happened five years ago," she said carefully. "Why are you coming after me now? Because I recognized you at the bank?"

But he wasn't listening as he ranted about past sins that had nothing to do with Elise.

"I want all of you dead!" he screamed, waving a knife close to Becky's terror-stricken face. "I'm going to start with this kid and work my way through the family and your cop lover. You're never going to bother me again!"

"*No!*" Elise screamed, reaching behind her at the same time Dietrich's knife hovered too closely to Becky's face. She didn't have to think about what she was going to do.

All she knew was that her baby was going to be killed if she didn't do something first. She swept the gun out and fired with deadly accuracy.

"No!" Dean also screamed, running up the path as fast as he could, his gun drawn. He skidded to a stop, finding Becky in Elise's arms as Dietrich lay on the ground, screaming curses at the world. It only took a glance to see blood streaming down Dietrich's arm and a quick kick to knock the knife out his reach. After making sure the man had no other weapons on him, he grasped Dietrich's shirtfront in both hands and pulled him partially upright.

"You slimy son of a bitch, I ought to finish the job here and now!" Dean snarled, savagely twisting the fabric between his fingers.

"Hey, man, I didn't hurt them!" Dietrich blubbered, recognizing the murderous glint in the detective's eyes.

"Dean, let him go," Elise called, also aware of what might happen. "He's not worth it."

Dean stared down at the wounded man for another minute, breathing heavily, concentrating on regaining his sanity.

"If you'd harmed one hair on either one of their heads, you would have been dead meat, Dietrich," he said tightly. "And I would have made it the most painful way to die I could find." He let go of him as if he were the vilest creature he'd ever encountered.

Dean turned and headed for Elise and Becky, wrapping his arms around both of them. "I was so scared," he muttered, raining kisses on them.

"I wanted to kill him for all he'd done to us. But I was also afraid I might hit Becky, so I aimed for a shoulder,"

Elise babbled, holding Dean tightly with one arm while keeping the other wrapped around Becky.

Dean scrambled to pick up Becky in one arm and wrap the other around Elise's shoulders. "I know, honey, I know. You did great." He laughed shakily when he heard sirens. "Sounds like the cavalry's a bit late in arriving again."

She wiped her tearful face against his T-shirt. "You guys better do it right this time, Cornell, because next time I promise I won't just wing him."

"Hey, you know the old saying, 'third time's the charm.'" He stood there feeling more than a little tearful himself, wondering how a seasoned cop like himself could even think about crying. Then he looked down at the woman he'd almost lost and the little girl talking a mile a minute about how Mom had rescued her. No wonder there was moisture in his eyes.

"SHE OUGHT TO BE in here begging me not to go," Dean grumbled, gathering neatly folded T-shirts and underwear out of a dresser drawer and tossing them onto the bed. "Can't she see I'm exactly what she needs? I can't imagine anyone else putting up with that temper of hers." He kept on mumbling to himself as he stuffed his duffel bag, heedless of whatever mess he was making.

In the past twenty-four hours he'd been busy writing up reports and giving statements. The best part was seeing Carl Dietrich kept under close guard. This time, there would be no escape for the man.

Except now, Dean had no further reason to remain. Oh, he had plenty of personal reasons, but he wasn't sure Elise was ready to hear them yet. While he was good with flippant retorts, something from the heart was a lot more difficult to phrase.

"Can't she see how much I love her and don't want to leave her? Damn woman, we're good together! She can't be so blind she can't see it," he groused, closing the zipper so savagely he almost took off a finger. He grabbed the bag by the handle and turned around, stopping short when he found Elise standing in the open doorway. Her face was paper white, her lips trembling.

"All packed?" she asked quietly.

He nodded jerkily. If he could say all the right words a couple of minutes ago, why the hell wouldn't they come out now?

Elise opened her mouth as if to say something but quickly closed it again. Dean hoped she was going to ask him to stay. At the same time, why should he expect *her* to say the words? Why couldn't he? Why couldn't they say them at the same time?

"Well, I guess this is it." Dean shifted from one foot to the other as he looked at Elise.

She kept her eyes downcast as she stepped back to allow him to leave the room. Was he so eager to leave that he barely finished writing all his reports and he was off? Tears pricked at her eyelids, but she exerted all her willpower to keep them at bay. After all, she still had her pride. If Dean wanted to leave so badly, she wasn't about to ask him to stay. Although the idea of placing Althea in the doorway to keep him from leaving the house *did* cross her mind.

Say something! her brain screamed. *Tell him how much you need him. Take a chance for once!*

Dean walked outside, telling himself to give her a little space, let her settle down a bit before he started honest-to-

God courting procedures, beginning with that dinner and dancing she'd teased him about. Still, he couldn't believe she could stoically watch him pack up and could stand there and say nothing about their future! Hell, even the girls looked a little sad at his leaving! Why couldn't she?

Elise looked up at him with those brilliant eyes that could look, oh, so cool or oh, so warm. Now there was no expression. But she blinked a lot—as if she were trying to hold back tears?

"Thank you for all your help," she said in a low voice.

Dean bit down on a curse. He hated himself for not having the nerve to say the right words and hated her for not saying them, either. "Well, if you need anything, you know where I am," he said in a rough voice. "Bye, girls." He looked beyond Elise, who stood as still as statue.

"Bye, Dean." Becky's lower lip trembled.

"I'll miss you," Lisa mumbled.

Keri managed a small smile. "Me, too."

Dean started to turn away, then shook his head and muttered the curse he'd wanted to say a second ago. He grabbed Elise by the shoulders and hauled her into his arms. He kissed her so deeply he could feel her start to sag in his arms. Then he stepped back.

"See if you can forget that," he bit out, and he headed for his truck without a backward glance. "See you at the trial, Doc," he threw over his shoulder.

Elise stood there, stunned. How dare he leave after kissing her senseless? Only pride kept her from running after the truck that now roared down the driveway with the dogs barking after it. Pride kept her standing there, watching the man she loved drive out of her life as if she'd been nothing more than a job he'd finished successfully. Pride... She was about to say to hell with her pride and run after Dean when another idea came to mind.

"There is no way I'm going to allow him to leave this county, dammit," she vowed, running into the house.

Keri's head swiveled as she watched her mother streak past. "What's wrong, Mom?"

"Mom, you're swearing!" Lisa sounded delighted that her mother had indulged in a vice she wholeheartedly discouraged in her daughters.

"If this doesn't work, I'll be doing a lot more than that in a few minutes." Elise picked up the phone and quickly punched out the numbers printed on a card she held in one hand.

"DAMN CRAZY WOMAN," Dean muttered, shifting gears with a heavier hand than usual. "She could have told me she wanted me to stay. It wouldn't have hurt her to admit she needs and loves me. I made all the other moves first. It's her turn to get off that high horse of hers and admit the truth about us." He switched the radio on, listened to a song about hard-hearted women and quickly turned it off. "I'll show her. I won't call her for a month." He bobbed his head, pleased with his description, even though he was dying inside. "I'm not going to be the only one to suffer here."

Dean glanced over his shoulder and into the side-view mirror before changing lanes.

"Okay, maybe I'll only give her two weeks. And she'd better be grateful I'm going to call her at all. Not many men would put up with a snoring tortoise and a prissy woman like her." He swore loudly and slapped the steering wheel with his palm. "Damn her! Why couldn't she give me one little sign that she wanted me to stay?" He looked up to see a patrol car with its red-and-blue lights flashing. "Now what?" He swore several more times just because it made him feel better, and he quickly pulled over to the side. He opened his door and hopped out of his truck. "Santee? Hey, you didn't have to come out here to say goodbye." He grinned. "I was going to stop off at the station and see you on my way out."

The man's face remained impassive as he stood a short distance away, his hand resting lightly on his gun. "I've got orders to bring you in, Cornell."

Dean was incredulous. "What? Okay, so maybe I was going sixty-eight in a sixty-five mile zone. What can I say?" He chuckled, thinking this was all a joke. "Last I heard, it wasn't a felony."

"No, but the crime you're accused of is." The handcuffs he dangled from one hand didn't look like a joke. "Turn around and spread 'em," he ordered.

"Wait a minute!" Dean found himself spinning against his truck and frisked before the handcuffs found their way around his wrists pulled behind his back. "What's this all about? What are the charges?"

"Grand theft." Santee pushed him toward the patrol car. "Don't worry about your truck. I'll arrange for someone to pick it up."

"Grand theft!" Dean yelped just before his head was pushed down as he was guided into the back seat of the patrol car. "Hey, watch it!"

By now Dean didn't see any humor in the situation, but none of his questions were answered other than by Santee quietly saying, "You'll find out soon enough."

Dean sputtered and cursed the entire drive, but the sheriff's detective ignored him. By the time he realized they were pulling in behind the Carpenter Avian and Exotic Animal Clinic to the house in the rear, he was hopping mad. He glared at Elise, who stood at the foot of the steps, while the three girls stood on the porch just outside the front door.

"What is this?" he demanded once he was taken out of the car.

"Grand theft," Santee repeated.

"Get these things off me so I can commit some bodily harm," he growled, vainly trying to wiggle his bound wrists as he advanced on Elise. "I didn't steal anything!" he yelled at her.

"You stole my heart, you jerk!" she yelled back. "And if you think you're going to get away with it, you've got another thing coming, mister!"

"You had me arrested!" Dean bellowed.

"You were going to leave me!" she shrieked, once and for all dashing the image of the cool, collected doctor.

"Only because you were so damn stubborn you didn't ask me to stay!"

"I didn't think I had to. I figured you had brains enough to figure out on your own that I wanted you to stay! Besides, you could have told me you didn't want to go! There's no reason you couldn't say the words! I should have known better! Cops only have brains enough to write a lousy parking ticket!" She stood toe to toe with him.

"It would have been nice to be asked. For all I knew, if I said I was staying, you might have decided to kick me out. I'm not real good with rejection."

Elise almost crumpled at his reluctant admission.

"I think it's time we went inside so they can talk privately," Keri murmured, herding the girls toward the door.

"Are you kidding?" Lisa argued, twisting her head one

way, then the other. "Things are just starting to get good! This is even better than the movies!"

"In, Lisa."

"I think you two can handle it from here on," Santee said quietly, unlocking the handcuffs from Dean's wrists before heading back to his car.

Dean didn't move one inch from his position of towering over Elise, who didn't look one bit daunted. With her eyes blazing and her cheeks flushed, he decided she'd never looked more beautiful. "Okay, lady, you want it, you got it. But with a few revisions in your rules. I don't intend to be threatened with no meals if I don't pick my clothes up twenty-four hours a day. I like my beer, and I don't intend to apologize if I cuss a blue streak once in a blue moon. I can't cook worth a damn, I have a horrible temper, I hate reptiles of all kinds, especially snoring tortoises, and I don't remember my own birthday, much less anyone else's," he ground out. "As for you, you wear the ugliest nightgowns known to man, you're a bit prissy, though I intend to change that real quick, and you need to learn when not to argue with me about my choice in clothing or hairstyle, but, dammit, woman, you're never going to find another man who loves you and your girls as much as I do, and whether you like it or not, we're getting married as soon as possible!"

She smiled at his expression. "Anything you say, Detective."

He stopped and blinked. He looked a little wary, as if waiting for the other shoe to drop. "No arguments?"

Elise shook her head.

Dean took several deep breaths. "Then why did you stand there like an idiot and watch me pack? Why did you watch me drive out of here? And why did you have to drag Santee into this?"

"I hoped you'd change your mind," she said softly. "And since you didn't, I called Santee, who was only too happy to arrest you for the first charge that came to my mind."

For a moment, Dean felt as if he'd been outmaneuvered somehow. "I'll screen Keri's dates and do the same when it's Lisa and Becky's turns, and they'll hate me for it," he muttered.

"For a while, but they'll eventually learn you only do it because you love them." Elise's eyes warmed. "Besides, the time might come when you'll have more to worry about than their dates, when you're walking the floor with a colicky baby and learning to change messy diapers."

Hope slammed into his chest. "You mean you wouldn't mind having another baby?"

"Not as long as it's yours." Elise combed her fingers through the dark hair curling wildly around his ears. She knew nagging wouldn't prompt him to get regular haircuts, but that was all right. She decided she liked this man who dressed and acted like a thug most of the time, because he was *her* thug. And no matter how rough and gruff he got at times, she knew she'd be able to handle him. "But I don't want you to give up your work, Dean. It's too important to you."

Something else he didn't expect. "Santee said we might be able to work something out. Either way, I have other options. I just want you and the girls, Ellie. Nothing else matters."

She couldn't stop smiling. "Then I only have one request."

By then he was ready to give her the world. "Ask and it's yours."

She braced her hands on her hips in her old fighting manner. "No more crawling through bank windows to rescue hostages. I won't have you meeting other women that way!"

Dean drew her into his arms and picked her up. "Doc, you're more than enough woman for me." He glanced over her shoulder at the three hopeful faces peering out the window. "All right, give us some privacy here!" he yelled. "As your stepfather-to-be, I command you to go to your rooms and stay there until further notice!"

Three "Yeas!" sounded from inside as the faces disappeared.

"Why don't I ask Myrna to take them out to lunch and shopping. Then *we* would be the ones to go to our room and stay there until further notice," Elise murmured, linking her arms around his neck and nuzzling his chin with her lips.

Dean bumped the door open with his hip and carried her inside. "Doc, I do like the way you think."

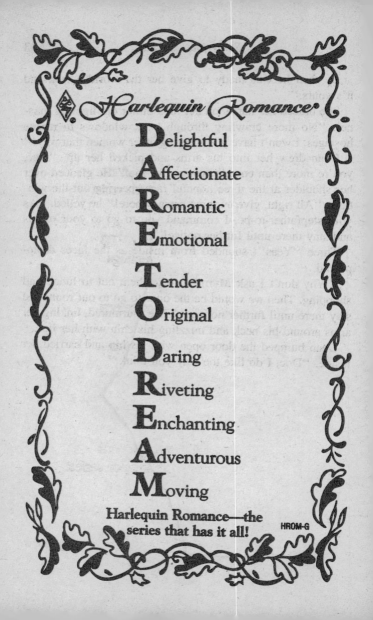

Harlequin Romance®

Delightful

Affectionate

Romantic

Emotional

Tender

Original

Daring

Riveting

Enchanting

Adventurous

Moving

Harlequin Romance—the
series that has it all!

HROM-G

HARLEQUIN PRESENTS®

HARLEQUIN PRESENTS
men you won't be able to resist
falling in love with...

HARLEQUIN PRESENTS
women who have feelings
just like your own...

HARLEQUIN PRESENTS
powerful passion in
exotic international settings...

HARLEQUIN PRESENTS
intense, dramatic stories that will keep you
turning to the very last page...

HARLEQUIN PRESENTS
The world's bestselling romance series!

Harlequin® Historical

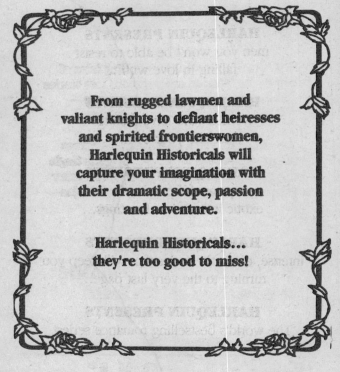

From rugged lawmen and
valiant knights to defiant heiresses
and spirited frontierswomen,
Harlequin Historicals will
capture your imagination with
their dramatic scope, passion
and adventure.

Harlequin Historicals…
they're too good to miss!

HARLEQUIN®

AMERICAN ◆ ROMANCE®

LOOK FOR OUR FOUR FABULOUS MEN!

Each month some of today's bestselling authors bring
four new fabulous men to Harlequin American Romance.
Whether they're rebel ranchers, millionaire power brokers
or sexy single dads, they're all gallant princes—and
they're all ready to sweep you into lighthearted fantasies
and contemporary fairy tales where anything is possible
and where all your dreams come true!

You don't even have to make a wish...
Harlequin American Romance will grant your every desire!

Look for Harlequin American Romance
wherever Harlequin books are sold!

⌇ HARLEQUIN SUPERROMANCE®

...there's more to the story!

Superromance. A *big* satisfying read about unforget-
table characters. Each month we offer
four very different stories that range from family
drama to adventure and mystery, from highly emotional stories to romantic comedies—and
much more! Stories about people you'll
believe in and care about. Stories too
compelling to put down....

Our authors are among today's *best* romance writers. You'll find familiar names and
talented newcomers. Many of them are
award winners—and you'll see why!

If you want the biggest and best
in romance fiction, you'll get it
from Superromance!

Available wherever Harlequin books are sold.

LOVE & LAUGHTER™

Humorous love stories by favorite authors and brand-new stars!

These books are delightful romantic
comedies featuring the lighter side
of love. Whenever you want to
escape and enjoy a few chuckles
and a wonderful love story,
choose Love & Laughter.

Love & Laughter—always
romantic...always entertaining.

Available at your favorite retail outlet.

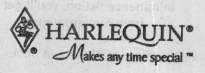

HARLEQUIN®
Makes any time special ™